"I Don't Want You to Leave."

"I must!" she said, her heart beat increasing in quite a startling fashion.

He seemed astonished by his own behavior. "I want to protect you," he said with awe. "I want you here with me. And I have not felt such things in a world of time!"

Her cheeks burned. "Mr. Brummell!"

"I have fallen most hopelessly in love with you, my darling child!"

He drew her to him and his lips caressed hers. And he held her close and sighed. . . .

And He Left Her with the Knowledge
That What They Wanted Most
They Might Never Have. . . .

FAN THE WANTON FLAME

CLARISSA ROSS

A Historical Romance
by Clarissa Ross

PUBLISHED BY POCKET BOOKS NEW YORK

A POCKET BOOKS/RICHARD GALLEN Original publication

**POCKET BOOKS, a Simon & Schuster division of
GULF & WESTERN CORPORATION**
1230 Avenue of the Americas, New York, N.Y. 10020

ISBN: 0-671-83446-0

First Pocket Books printing February, 1980

10 9 8 7 6 5 4 3 2 1

Printed in the U.S.A.

I dedicate this book to JOLLY, my West Highland Terrier, a friend and long time companion, who died when I was mid-way through this novel.

FAN THE WANTON FLAME

Chapter One

Julia Crawford paced back and forth restlessly in her tiny bedroom on the third floor of Dornford Parsonage. Her lovely, oval face was clouded with despair as many troubling thoughts raced through her young mind. She was eighteen years old and no longer a child. She would not be treated as a child!

She ceased her pacing for a moment to cross to the small window overlooking the garden and saw that dusk was settling. She brushed back a lock of the soft, black hair which fell onto her shoulders, and tears brimmed in her hazel-gray eyes. John Lane was leaving with the other village lads who had signed up with the enlisting officer. They were due to go the following morning and she would not be able to say goodbye to him.

It had all come about so stupidly. She had pleaded with John to remain in the village and work with his prosperous farmer father, but he'd been impatient. Anxious to improve his lot in life and so he had chosen the army. In this year of 1805 with the threat of Napoleon very real, many lads were doing the same thing.

She and John had met at classes taught by her guardian the Reverend Edward Weir. The youth had been sent to further his studies with the fine, old clergyman because he had shown an unusual brilliance

1

at the village school. So he enjoyed the same private tuition which she had. It was inevitable that they become childhood friends, playmates, and now sweethearts.

Happy memories of sailing on the river, romantic trysts in hay mows, and journeys together to the county fair filled her mind. She felt lost and terribly lonely at the thought of his going away. She had always feared it might happen one day but had tried to dismiss the idea whenever it had occurred to her.

Now the moment was at hand and she wasn't even to be allowed to bid John goodbye. She had promised to meet him in the garden below and go for a stroll along the nearby lane as they discussed their parting. She had put on her good, blue frilled dress and carefully arranged a bow in her hair. Then, when she went downstairs all her plans for the evening had crumbled.

Waiting for her at the bottom of the stairway was her guardian, the Reverend Edward Weir, a troubled look on his thin, white face. She had come to love the old scholar with his shabby black suits and gaiters and his saintly character. But now she saw a firm look in his sharp, blue eyes.

"Where are you proposing to go, my dear?" he asked.

Her hand on the railing, she stood on the second step and said, "To say goodbye to John Lane. You know he is leaving with the other lads tomorrow morning. They are due at army training camp."

The old man nodded his bald head with its edge of white hair. "I do know about that," he agreed. "A sad business. A lad like John is capable of more than being a mere soldier."

"He hopes to do better. Perhaps earn a commission."

"Commissions are bought, not earned," the old man said bitterly. "And he will be subjected to the roughest companions."

Julia ventured, "Perhaps when I see him tonight

there will still be time to dissuade him. He might somehow escape the recruiting sergeant."

"That is most unlikely," the old clergyman had told her. "In the first place you'll not be seeing him."

Her lovely eyes widened and she could scarcely believe what she had heard. "Not be seeing him?"

"No," the Reverend Edward Weir explained. "He and some of the other lads who enlisted caused an upset in the tavern last night. The Sheriff had to be called and if the boys were not on their way to the army they would all now be in the local jail."

"I don't believe John would do such a thing!"

"He was one of the group," the clergyman assured her. "They were all drunken beyond reason. Most distressing. And in the circumstances I cannot allow you to see this young man."

She came down a step. "But I must see him!" she cried plaintively.

Her guardian eyed her stonily. "I have never denied you anything which I believed was for your good. But in this matter, dear girl, I have no choice!"

She could not think this was his last word. "But Reverend Weir you know how much I care for John. He is as dear to me as any brother I might have."

The thin face of her guardian betrayed no change of expression. "I'm truly sorry, Julia but I cannot allow this roisterer to come here. Nor you to be in his company!"

Sensations of panic and pain surged through her. She begged the old man, "Do overlook what he did for this once. Please, Reverend!"

The old man's thin face had become fretful. "Do not plead with me child. I cannot in good faith give way after hearing the Constable's story. So you had best go up to your room at once."

"I cannot allow him to leave without talking with him," she cried.

The clergyman blocked her way and left her staring at him, "Let us argue no more, my dear," he replied and there was no hint of his changing his attitude on this night in the early summer.

She turned and raced upstairs and closed the door of her room. She first wept copiously and now was pacing back and forth in an effort to determine what she would do. Since she was three she had been the ward of the old man and his housekeeper. Her mother had died of fever that year and having no near relatives, had left Julia to be brought up by the Reverend Weir.

Julia had enjoyed a happy childhood in the small Surrey village. The Reverend Weir was not wealthy but he had the house and a good living. And he had given her an excellent education. One which John Lane had also shared.

Until now she had always thought of herself as the most blessed of creatures. But the old man's unbending attitude towards the youth she cared for so much was hard for her to accept.

After the first overwhelming feeling of pain and despair she had returned to her room to pace. Just as she was doing now when her attention was distracted by the sound of a pebble bouncing off the glass of her window. Since she was far above the level where a stone might come from the wheels of a passing carriage she could only assume that it had been directed up there.

She hurried to the window, opened it and stuck her pretty head out. To her amazement she confirmed that the pebble had not reached her window by accident. For as she looked out she saw far below the strained face of young John Lane as he made his way up the side of the building by using the ancient vines which grew there.

Stifling a cry of alarm she watched his progress as he slowly made his way up to her window. He tested the strength of the green vines every so often and sought out footholds with caution. By now he was a frightening distance above the ground. If he fell it could go hard for him. She was so terrified she was scarcely able to breathe.

She waited until he could stretch out his hand and touch hers. Then she gripped him fiercely and helped him up and over the sill of the small window. He tumbled safely into the room. Rising from the hardwood floor he was like the materialization of an enchanted prince in his breeches and open-necked white shirt. He had a bronzed, good-looking face and curled corn-silk hair with the bluest of eyes.

All pretence of calm left her as he stood before her in the candle lit bedroom. The lovely, lithe body under her nightgown was trembling and a tremor showed in her voice as she advanced to him and whispered, "John, my love."

"Julia!" he said with deep emotion and took her in his arms so that their bodies were tightly pressed together and he was aware of her trembling. He kissed her gently and told her, "You must not be afraid."

"My guardian refused to let me meet you!" she said.

"I know," John said. "The brawl wasn't of my making, but no matter now. What is important is that I'm here."

Her eyes met his. "I feared I would never see you again. Never be in your arms another time."

His smile was boyish. "No fear of that."

She had ceased her trembling and now a calm and a great hunger had taken her over. She touched her lips to his ear and in a tense whisper, said, "John, before you go you must take me properly. I must be yours."

Still holding her, he hesitated, "It would not be right, lass. Not fair to you!"

"John!" She insisted and guided one of his hands beneath her nightgown to her breast.

"Julia, love!" he whispered hoarsely. "Julia, who will be my wife!" And with that he lifted her tenderly and took her over to the bed and set her down on it.

Her deep emotion was apparent in her labored

breathing and she herself hastily doffed the nightgown so that her lovely body was exposed and waiting for him.

John had as quickly made himself ready and she saw his erect manhood as he lowered his sturdy, tanned body over her. "It will be all right, lass," he whispered in her ear.

His hands were on her naked breasts and his mouth greedily on hers. Their kisses were rapid and passionate and suddenly began the experience for which she had longed, his penetration of her. She felt pain and ecstacy within seconds. But the pain was of relatively short endurance and the ecstacy filled her with a bliss of the like she had never known before.

Julia moaned happily, lost to all around her, except for the careening mad beauty of it. John's thrusting became more rapid, as did his breathing. Then the supreme moment of their joining came in a throbbing climax! She felt fulfilled and rested as never before as John rolled over and lay beside her. Their two perspiring bodies close, as he held her in his arms.

"Never forget tonight," he whispered. "I will return an officer and we will marry with the Reverend's permission."

"I shall hunger for you," she lamented. "Always!"

"My memory of you will bring me back safely," the lad assured her. "You will keep house for the Reverend and grow more beautiful."

"You will forget me," she worried.

"Never fear," he said. "Now we must dress quickly." And he rose to do so.

Tearfully she donned her nightgown again. Later she stood to embrace him, now that he was fully dressed. "So wonderful!"

"There will be more when I return in the King's uniform with the money to set us up in a home of our own," he told her.

"I care not for the money," Julia told him. "Only for you." And she made sure that he knew she meant this by seeking out his lips and making union with them again.

So they were there on the bed in the darkness when the door of the room was hurled open and a shocked Reverend Edward Weir stood staring at them from the doorway with a candle held high in one hand. There was a moment of silence.

Then the thin-faced old man burst out, "A fine situation I find here! How in the name of all that is evil did you make your way to this room, young man?"

They had both jumped up and were ashamedly facing the old clergyman. John blurted out, "Climbed up the vine, Reverend, but I mean no harm."

"Climbed up the vine!" The old man exclaimed, blinking with disbelief. Then his eyes caught the open window and he gasped, "So you did!"

Julia now stepped forward to her guardian and told him, "We had to see each other. We love each other."

"It appears there is more lust than love in this," the old man said grimly. "The two of you in each other's arms here in the dark."

"I love Julia, sir, and it is my intention to return and marry her," John said bravely.

"Indeed!" the Reverend Edward Weir sniffed. "Well, I now ask you to take your leave. And be lucky I don't report you for breaking into my house!"

"Yes sir," the boy said nervously. And he turned to Julia once again and told her, "I love you, Julia. And I shall always be true to you!"

"And I to you," she said piteously.

"I must go. You will hear from me," the young man promised. And then he made for the window.

"Halt you there!" The old clergyman said sharply. "What sort of madness has overtaken you? Do you think I want your poor silly head on my conscience? Do not try to leave by the window. Go down the stairs properly in a Christian manner!"

John smiled in gratitude at the old man. "Yes, sir. And thank you Reverend for all you did for me. I shall remember it." And he dashed out of the room and hurriedly made his way down the black stairway.

"And I shall remember you," the old man said grimly. Then he turned and holding the candle close surveyed Julia in its glow. "You have behaved like a silly, stubborn child."

She raised her pert chin defiantly. "I am eighteen, sir!"

His rheumy, old eyes opened wide at this and he showed a slight surprise. Then he recovered himself and said, "I know full well your age. But eighteen or not you have a duty to obey me! You were placed in my care by your dear, departed mother. Do not ever forget that!"

"I have not, dear father," she said, using the term he liked best. "But in this I had to disobey you. For I have come to love John Lane."

"Don't be a fool, lass," the old clergyman said. "He is off to another world. You must live your own life."

"We shall be together again," she said with a firm, childish confidence which she would remember later and wonder at.

The old man's thin face showed a slight hint of tenderness. In a voice with some emotion in it, he said, "Perhaps, for it is truly a strange world. But just now I want you to erase these wild thoughts from your mind and go to bed."

"Yes, dear father," she said. And she went over and kissed the old clergyman on the cheek.

"Goodnight, my child," he said with a sigh. "I pray for your protection in this harsh world. I have tried but it is not easy."

She smiled at him sweetly. "I love you, dear father. You have always been too good to me."

The thin old face regarded her with a gentle look and he nodded somewhat dolefully. Then he went out and closed the door after him and she heard him slowly making his way down the stairs.

She at once went to the window and looked out

hoping to see John somewhere below. But there was no one. He had gone. She reluctantly closed the window and then found a match and lit a candle. She sat for a while in the spot where she had been with John. A sad smile crossed her young face and then she rose and began to undress for bed.

It had turned out not too badly though John had been forced to risk his neck to get to her. But they had known the sweetness of each other's arms and even though her guardian had discovered them, he had not been too angry. All in all, the evening had ended better than it had begun.

She was too excited to sleep. And after she put out the candle and went to bed her active mind kept turning on things past and present as well as anticipating the future. She first thought of her own circumstances. Her mother, Ann, had been the daughter of a grocer in the village. The shop had been prosperous enough and Ann as the only daughter had excellent prospects.

Her widowed father doted on her and while not in the best of health was able to carry on the business with his daughter's assistance and that of a lad. All went well until a dandy named James Crawford came to the village to recover from a riding accident.

Almost every day the handsome city man limped on his cane from his lodgings above the tavern to make some purchase at the grocery shop. Ann's father welcomed him and enjoyed his talk of London and the great people there. Ann kept shyly in the background and listened with awe.

Then one day when she was alone in the store the dandy confessed that his daily visits were on her account. That he had fallen in love with her and wanted to marry her. Ann was literally swept off her feet by the charming stranger from the great world beyond.

Her father worried a little but consented to the marriage. Not knowing that the wedding would mark the beginning of tragedy for his daughter. Shortly after the wedding, his health became worse and he died.

Ann attempted to carry on the shop with the aid of help. She was encouraged in this by her new husband.

At the same time, the dandy, James Crawford, took all the ready cash he could from her poor mother. He spoke of gambling debts in London and the need to return and look after certain affairs. Ann gave him more of her capital than she ought to have but she was much in love with the dark, charming man.

Then she discovered she was to have a child. James made an occasional visit back to the village but showed less interest in the fact that he was soon to be a father than he did in extracting more money from her. Ann now found herself so hard up for cash she could not pay her debts nor get new stock for the shop.

The business began to fail when a rival store opened. In this sad state of affairs Julie knew she had been born. But her mother had loved her dearly. James Crawford returned only once more and not being able to get any money from the unhappy Ann left in a rage. Her mother later told her that he had not even wished to see his new daughter.

Ann accepted a position as housekeeper to the Reverend Edward Weir' a kindly old clergyman and a bachelor. The old man further agreed to tutor Julia as part of the bargain. When Julia was six her mother received word that James Crawford had been killed in a gambling dispute. The letter came from a woman friend of Julia's late father, who made it a point to let her widowed mother know she and James Crawford had been closer than mere friends.

From that day on Ann rarely mentioned the man who had so upset her life. She dedicated herself to her new duties and had seemed happy enough in seeing Julia grow to a lovely young woman. Then twelve months ago in a bitter winter snowstorm her mother had been trapped in a sleigh on a snow-blocked road. She was returning from a visit to an elderly woman friend in a neighboring village who was ill. By the time she was rescued and brought to the parsonage she had the beginnings of a bad cold. A condition which soon changed to pneumonia.

Julia and the old minister had stood by in her mother's bedroom down the hall while the local doctor stayed by her bedside until the stricken woman's last breath. Death, when it came, had been swift and peaceful. Ann died in more tranquility than she had lived.

Julia was devastated and so the companionship of John Lane came to mean more than ever to her. The youth had been a genuine comfort to her in the worst days of her sorrow. Now she was just beginning to have the wound of her mother's loss heal when she suddenly was faced with losing John.

It was little wonder that in spite of being a docile, studious, young woman she had become frustrated and impatient with the elderly Reverend Edward Weir's pronouncement that she could not say goodbye to John. And so she had been glad when John had found a way to outsmart the old man. She went to sleep finally with the warm feeling that the blond, young man did love her and would fulfill his ambitions and one day return for her.

But it took no longer than the following morning for her to learn that she was about to experience a vast change in her life style. She went down to breakfast feeling somewhat shy after the events of the previous night. It was a bright, sunny morning but she wore a rather heavy dark brown dress in an effort to look somber and suitably repentant. She looked rather pale in it and she hoped this might impress the old clergyman.

At the breakfast table she found herself alone. And Matilda, the overweight housekeeper, glared at her as she served her and said, "The Reverend Weir is in his study. He wishes you to go there when you have had your breakfast."

"Yes, Matilda," she said meekly.

Matilda apparently could not resist adding, "The

early stagecoach went by this morning a full two hours
ago. That recruiting sergeant and all those rascals he
enlisted were in it." And with a haughty sniff the big
woman went on out to the kitchen.

Julia lingered over her breakfast. The news that John
had already gone left her with little appetite. She felt
very alone now, she had almost no other friends of her
own age in the village. The days would go by heavily
despite the kindness of the old clergyman.

When she finished at the table she made her way
along the dark little hall which led to the old man's
study at the rear of the house. The door was open and
she saw him seated at his desk with his reading
spectacles on as he studied the Bible and some other
books and made notes in preparation for his coming
Sunday sermons.

She stepped inside the musty, book-lined room and
clearing her throat to let him know she was there said,
"Reverend Weir."

He glanced up at her and his manner was not at all
angry. He indicated a chair and told her, "Do sit down,
my child."

She took a plain chair across from him and eyed him
earnestly. "I'm sorry about last night."

His swivel chair creaked as he turned to stare at her
above his spectacles. His thin, scholar's face showed a
sad smile. "I have no intention of condemning you," he
said. "On consideration I realize I was to blame. My
dictum about your not seeing John was much too
harsh."

Her face lit up. "Oh, thank you, dear foster-father."

He waved this aside with a thin hand. "I should have
known how much you two meant to each other. And
for that matter, the business of the fracas at the tavern
was little more than a youthful outburst to mark the
leaving of the lads. A sad time for them and no wonder
they drank too much and fought."

"John assured me he was not a part of it aside from
being there."

"That pleases me," the Reverend Edward Weir said. "And perhaps in a way, last night's happening was a good thing. Apart from the fact you and the lad were able to say your goodbyes it has given me much to think about. You are no longer a child, my dear. And there is little more I can do for you."

She felt a small panic. She guessed that his purpose behind all this was to send her on her way. Out into the world for which she was so truly unprepared. She said swiftly, "Please do not make a sudden judgement. I'm aware that I'm a young woman and should earn my keep. There is little that would be open to me anywhere except perhaps the position of governness and I have small patience with children. Could I not remain here and take on Matilda's duties as housekeeper? The work my mother did until her death."

The old clergyman showed surprise. "My dear girl I have not intention of forcing you out into the great world. You may remain here as my ward as long as you wish. Your presence and the small chores you do would repay me in full. But I'm now thinking of you and the small future which you have here."

"It is enough," she said bravely. "I shall be lonely without John. But I will learn to live quietly and one day he will return to me."

The old man stared at her sadly. "I understand your feelings but I do not think that sort of future is enough for you. First, you must remember that John has left to become a soldier. And soldiers are often killed in the line of duty."

"John will not be! I shall pray nightly for his safety."

"And that may do much to protect him," the old man agreed. "But there is another possibility. He may change and may not ever come back here."

"He will! He promised!"

"The promises of youth are good but sometimes unable to be kept," the Reverend Edward Weir told her. "You ought not to remain here meekly awaiting his letters and his return. You ought to live a fuller life of your own. Develop your own person, so that whoever comes to marry you, be it John or someone else, they will be proud of you as an assured young lady."

"Those are fine words," Julia said. "But I'm not sure I can live up to them."

"That is why I have called you here."

"I do not understand," she said.

He folded his hands on the threadbare black vest of his clerical garb. "I have not travelled far in life. I'm only a humble clergyman in this small Surrey village."

"You are much loved here and you do good work."

The old man smiled. "Thank you, my dear. The satisfaction that I have in my calling is all I require. But had I wished I might have gone further. My family is a good one and although I have never mentioned it, I have a sister well-married in London."

"In London?" she echoed. London was truly the great world and a long way off. Out of her reach entirely. She'd read many articles about the great city in the newspapers and magazines which came to the parsonage but she had regarded it as a distant land beyond her horizon.

"Yes," the old man said. "My youngest sister, Jane, is married to a titled man of wealth and family, Sir Orville Hewitt."

"A man of title!" Julia said in awe.

"Yes. My sister is now fortyish and her husband only a year or two older. They are much occupied with London society but they have no family. And it is unlikely she will have children now."

"What ill-fortune for them," Julia commiserated.

"My sister feels badly on that score," the Reverend Edward Weir said. "And that brings me to my reason for calling you here to talk with me. I'm sure, if I wrote her, and told her of your attractiveness and great promise, she would accept you in her fine home as a ward and companion."

Julia was stunned by the disclosure of what the long conversation had been leading up to. She gasped, "You are saying you might send me to your sister's in London?"

"Only if you wish to go."

"But what about John? He expects me to wait for him here."

"I could send on any letters he wrote and you could give him your new address. Indeed, you might have a much better hope of seeing him again there. Most troops spend some time in London, either before shipment to the Continent or when home on leave."

She listened and slowly it came to her that all the old man was saying was true. This could be a real opportunity for her to grow in experience. She would see the fabled city of London, and live in a house of the gentry. And she might even have a better chance of seeing John soon again. It was little wonder that the exciting prospect dazzled her.

"Do you think it possible?" she asked eagerly.

"If I have your approval I shall write my sister this very day," the old man promised.

"I think I should like it," she said.

And so the old man sent the letter to his sister in London. For several weeks Julia waited nervously, hoping for a letter from John, and some word from the clergyman's sister in London. But nothing came. She became depressed, but tried to buoy up her courage by telling herself that probably John was too busy to write. It would be a while before he'd complete his training. She must not expect too much of him.

As for Lady Jane Hewitt it seemed clear the clergyman's sister was not interested in her. She could not blame the great lady, to accept the duty of looking after an awkward country girl could have not seemed attractive to her.

But on at least this score Julia was proven wrong. The elderly Reverend Weir came rushing out to her where she was working at a rose bed in the gardens and flourished a letter aloft in his thin hand.

"It has come!" he said triumphantly. "The reply from my sister."

She rose from her knees and cleaned her hands on her apron. Smiling, she said, "I declare I had quite given her up."

"Not I," the old man said happily. "It appears that when I wrote, my sister and her husband were in Brighton in company of other London socialites including the Prince Regent, no less."

Julia's eyes widened. "She does move in high circles."

"The highest," the old man agreed with pride. "And she is most interested in my offer. She shows that in her letter. She apologizes for the delay and says she will come for you within the week."

"Within the week!" Julia said incredulously.

The old man nodded. "Yes, dear child. My sister is coming to fetch you personally. It will also be a chance for her to see me. We have been apart for some years."

She stared at the old man with a rush of emotion changing her elation to a feeling of regret. "I do not know," she said. "I will miss you and living here in this quiet old house."

"Far too quiet for a girl of eighteen as lovely as you," Reverend Edward Weir said. "I predict you will be a sensation in London!"

She eyed him fondly. "And if I'm not happy there, may I return to you?"

"My door is always open to you," he said, and leaning close he gave her a paternal kiss on the temple to bind the bargain. "But now we must make haste and pack your clothes and other things. Everything must be cleaned and pressed in readiness for your journey to London."

The elaborate carriage with a crest on it arrived one afternoon two weeks later. In addition to Lady Jane

Hewitt and her maid, Lena, there was the coachman, all to be put up at the parsonage overnight. Matilda was in a state and with her employer's permission had hired a man and his wife, familiar with service in one of the neighboring big houses, to help with the guests. The Reverend Edward Weir insisted that Julia should do no more than play the young lady for the occasion.

Julia did not immediately see the coachman. He was a gaunt, aging man who at once busied himself looking after the horses in the stables while Lena, the maid, plump and red-faced, bustled about making the room assigned to her mistress comfortable. Julia's meeting came over tea in the living room perhaps an hour after the arrival of the company.

The Reverend Edward Weir met her at the bottom of the steps and gave her an encouraging smile, "My sister is most anxious to meet you."

Julia had worn one of her most fetching dresses, a pale green crinoline, with lace trim. Her cheeks were burning with excitement and she whispered, "I hope she'll like me."

"Have no fear." The old man assured her and led her into the parlor where Lady Jane Hewitt was seated at the tea table. She was younger than her clergyman brother but had the same thin, intellectual type of face. Only a hint of youthfulness remained and her hair even had a look of faded yellow. But she was carefully made up and wore the latest type of dress in a rich silk. A string of diamonds at her throat matched the sparkling stones on her hands.

"So this is your charmer," Lady Jane said with a thin smile and invited Julia to come closer to her. "You are very lovely," she said. "Though I must say that dress does not do you justice. Not in the proper fashion of today at all."

"We have little guidance in such matters here in this small village," the Reverend Edward Weir apologized.

"That is to be expected and can easily be corrected,"

his sister said grandly. She had the air of one much
accustomed to authority. "Do sit here by me, Julia, and
have some tea and cakes."

"Thank you, ma'am," Julia said blushing fiercely
now and feeling more awkward than ever in her dress.
To make it worse she had set such store on it. She took
a place on the love seat beside the titled lady and was
aware of the delicate air of expensive perfume which
emanated from her.

"You must not talk like a servant, Julia," the older
woman reprimanded her. "You must begin at once to
call me Aunt Jane since my brother has long been your
foster father." And she handed her a filled teacup.

"You are too kind, Aunt Jane," she said, with some
difficulty, aware that her words had come out in stiff
fashion. She also saw that the woman's thin face was
traced with tiny worry lines about the eyes and mouth.
Indeed, there was a suggestion of continual anxiety
about her expression, even when she smiled.

Reverend Edward Weir stood hovering above them
and said, "I feel Julia can be a true decoration to your
home, sister."

"She is a lovely child," Lady Jane agreed. "And
when she gets over her shyness I'm sure she will fit in
very well."

"Your husband approves?" her brother asked.

She frowned slightly for a moment, then said, "In
these matters he lets me have my way. I'm certain he
will voice no objections."

The old man said, "I have explained to Jane that
your world is much different from mine. That she will
gain a great deal in living with you."

The thin woman looked pleased. "I may say with
modesty that we entertain everyone. The Prince Regent often attends our balls as do many of his friends.
During the season we entertain frequently and are
much entertained by others."

"What is Sir Orville's business, Aunt Jane?" Julia
made so bold to ask.

The thin woman exchanged an amused glance with her clergyman brother. "My dear child, gentlemen of my husband's position in life do not engage in business. They have interests, hobbies and the like, and they play their role in society."

"I see," she said, chastened. "I did not understand."

"London is a city of such wealth you cannot believe," Lady Jane said. "Oh, we have the poor as well but that must be expected since they breed like animals and have no thought to making a place in life. But London is a city of manners and money and great opportunity. A pretty girl like you, my dear, should be able to marry into a fortune."

Julia was startled at this frank comment and said in a quiet voice, "I have already promised myself to a young man."

The older woman's reaction to this even more amazed her. Lady Jane laughed rather shrilly and said, "Do not be silly, my child. Becoming engaged to some village lad is not to be taken seriously. Not at all."

Reverend Edward Weir gave Julia a warning glance and then told his sister, "My foster daughter hopes that the young man in question will one day have suitable prospects!"

"Is that so?" Lady Jane said with amusement still in her tone. "We'll say no more about it. I'm sure Julia will meet many interesting young gentlemen in London and soon will be having a difficult time to choose among them." The older woman rose. "And now I must rest before dinner. The journey here was tiring and we must leave again in the morning."

The Reverend Edward Weir worried, "I wish your stay might be longer."

"Quite impossible," his sister said. "I have certain social engagements awaiting me in London." She smiled at Julia and took her by the arm, saying, "You may see me up to my room, dear child."

"Of course," she said, pleased to be of some use to the worldly woman.

As they crossed the room to the stairs Lady Hewitt said, "I'm sure Sir Orville will like you. And that you will find him pleasant enough."

"I'm sure I will," she said as they started up the stairway.

"Though I must warn you not to try to impress yourself on him," the woman continued carefully. "He is best managed with a certain aloofness. He will come to you on his own soon enough."

"Yes, Aunt Jane," she said, although she did not quite understand what the woman meant.

At the door to her room Lady Jane halted and offered her a thin smile, saying, "I'm sure we'll get along well, child. And I need someone. I'm subject to severe headaches and I have a secret sorrow which I cannot speak of, but which all too often troubles me."

Julia nodded and waited until the great lady moved on into the room in her dignified manner. Then she continued on to her own room thinking of what the woman had just said and remembering those many worry lines about her eyes. Was it possible that the gilded life of London also knew tragedy?

Chapter Two

Dinner at the parsonage that night was truly a magnificent affair. Matilda, with the aid of her helpers, prepared and served such a meal as Julia had never before known in the simple parsonage. The candle lit table was decorated with the old man's best linen tablecloth, silverware and fine china. The male servant moved about the table attending to their needs as if it were his nightly duty in the old house.

Lady Jane, seated at the opposite end of the table from her brother commented on the service, saying, "You have an excellent man, Edward."

The old clergyman smiled apologetically. "I must confess, dear sister, that he has been merely hired for this important occasion."

"Oh!" The elegantly clad woman looked slightly surprised. "In any event he has had excellent training."

"He and his wife were formerly employed at the manor house. They are accustomed to catering large dinners," the Reverend Edward Weir said.

"Well, the fare may be modest but it is well cooked and most enjoyable," Lady Jane said. "Don't you agree, Julia?"

Julia had been sitting silently listening to the other two. She quickly forced herself to reply, "Yes, Aunt Jane." In fact she was thinking that the society woman must be used to veritable banquets if she accepted this as a modest fare.

The meal had begun with tureen of turtle, progressed through crimped salmon, turkey a la perigeum, cutlets of mutton in sauce, along with baked woodcock and a rich trifle for dessert. Not to mention the selection of wines to wash the food down.

"What are the feelings in London about the political situation?" the old clergyman asked his sister.

She paused regally over her trifle and with authority said, "England will never be safe until Napoleon is defeated."

He said, "Surely as an island we are protected. And especially with a fleet with such leaders as Nelson."

"We have a good navy. That is agreed," his sister said. "But Napoleon is a master strategist. When he feels the time has come to conquer England he will have a plan."

"What sort of plan, do you think?" the old man wondered.

"I cannot say," Lady Jane replied. "But I have heard stories of giant rafts to bring his army across the channel. And also that he is attempting to join the navies of the Continent against us."

"The English Channel is the important barrier at the moment then?" Reverend Edward Weir suggested.

"All the informed in London say that," his sister replied. "Our set take little interest in the wars. The Prince Regent has his own regiment but his attention is mostly given to enjoying himself."

The old clergyman nodded. "I have been told the main purpose in life of your Regency gentlemen is the pursuit of enjoyment. They dedicate their careers to this!"

Lady Jane Hewitt smiled. "There is much truth in it. My own husband is a hunting man. He rides with the hounds when he can. And he always has a race horse or two."

Wishing to contribute something to the conversation, Julia made herself say, "I have read in the London papers that many of the men set more store on dress than do the ladies. That these men are called dandies."

The older woman eyed her tolerantly. "That is true, my dear. Perhaps the outstanding leader of style is Beau Brummell. You must have read of him."

Julia smiled. "Yes. I hear he changes his dress many times during a day. And that he has individual tailors do his jackets, waistcoats and trousers. Can it be really true?"

"That and more," the older woman said. "You will find out when you reach London. You will meet Beau Brummell and many of his cronies when he comes to one of our parties."

Reverend Edward Weir glanced at her with a twinkle in his rheumy, blue eyes and said, "I'm sure this girl has great ability. All she needs is moulding."

"She shall have that," the matron declared all too emphatically.

Julia was so nerved about leaving the parsonage that she spend a virtually sleepless seven hours the night before they were to leave. Aunt Jane sat up later than usual talking to her brother and Jane thought it polite to leave them to their private conversation. So she retired. She was certain they would include her in their discussions but she did not mind since she also knew the old clergyman and his sister wanted to only do good for her.

Still, leaving the house and village which had been her own for so long, was difficult. She almost burst into tears when the old clergyman kissed her goodbye and whispered in her ear, "Remember, my door will always be open to you."

Tears brimmed in her hazel-gray eyes as she told him tremulously, "Thank you for everything, dear father."

Then she was seated in the elegant carriage next to the perfumed Lady Hewitt with the maid seated silently across from them, a needed extension of her ladyship when the time came, but in the meanwhile expected to remain there as if she were not present at all.

The wagon began its journey over the rough, dusty road with the village soon left behind. Lady Jane glanced out the nearest carriage window and commented, "Dear me. It is so dark a day. Surely a great promise of rain. And I had hoped we might get to London before nightfall."

Julia asked, "Will the rain make that much difference?"

The older woman stared at her in surprise. "It is evident you have done no travelling. These roads become most abominable when it rains. In places they become foul swamps into which the wheels of a carriage can sink so deeply that the vehicle needs assistance to be hauled out!"

"I hadn't realized," she said. "I've not been that far away from the village."

The rain came and soon it was a veritable downpour.

The progress of the carriage was slowed and Julia felt sorry for the driver perched up on his outside seat with only a raincape and hat to protect him from the storm.

At last the coachman halted the vehicle and came around to open the door of the carriage and thrust his wet, bewhiskered face inside and say, "I think we must stay over at the nearest inn, my lady."

"What a bother." Lady Jane sighed. "Very well, you know what is best."

"Yes, my lady," the coachman said respectfully. "We'll not make London this night. Glenford is just ahead and the Bull and Ram is a respected inn."

"Very well," Lady Jane said impatiently. "Let us get there before all the available rooms are taken."

A short run in the gathering darkness brought them to the "Bull and Ram". Julia thought she had never witnessed such noise and confusion as in the courtyard of the inn. They drove in followed by a smart mail-coach which splashed a goodly amount of mud over their coachman as he opened the door to let them out onto the wet ground. At the same time several stable workers were shouting as they hurried to change horses for the mail-coach which would continue on.

The coarse shouts and banter of these men filled the air as she and Lady Jane moved past the plush waistcoats and cordury breeches of the ostlers. To the left a farmer and a wagon carrier were having an angry argument over a load of pigs still oinking memorably in the wagon. Coach-lanterns cast wavering, dancing lights over this animated scene.

Lady Jane was met at the door by a bowing landlord who came to them. The reception room of the inn also served as eating place and tap room at the other end and so the place was filled with people and noise.

Lady Jane shouted, "I shall require rooms for two and accomodation in the servant's area for my coachman and maid!"

The moon-faced innkeeper remained half-bowing and spread his hands in despair. "Alas, my lady, I can only provide you with one room and that with a narrow bed. Though I can supply quarters for your servants!"

"But what of my ward?" Lady Jane asked, still dignified in spite of her sodden clothing.

"I'm very sorry!" the innkeeper said.

"We cannot both fit into a bed as narrow as you describe and neither of us wish to sit up all night," Lady Jane said.

Julia quickly put in, "I do not mind. I can sit by the fireplace and dry myself."

"I won't hear of it!" Lady Jane complained. "There must be something!"

The innkeeper continued to scrape and bow. "I would wish to take care of your Ladyship's needs but just before you arrived I rented a sitting room and adjoining bedroom to a young man."

"Indeed!" Lady Jane said, glancing about the noisy room. "And may I enquire where he is now?"

The innkeeper pointed and said, "He's standing there with a whiskey in his hand at the far end of the bar."

Lady Jane stared at the figure of a young man in brown jacket and fawn breeches standing languidly by the bar and exclaimed, "Why, I know him! It is Jimmy Fitzroy! Bring him over to me, innkeeper."

"At once, your ladyship," the moon-faced man said and hurried off to deliver the message.

The young man at the bar stared at the innkeeper with some surprise on his pale, thin face and then glancing over saw Lady Jane. He at once put down his glass and came towards them. As he approached Julia saw that he was elegant of manner and dress, and had aquiline features topped by brownish hair. His smile was friendly as he joined them.

"My dear Lady Jane," he said, bowing. "What a delightful surprise."

The older woman accepted his greeting and quickly told him, "There is a problem. My ward and I require rooms and there is only room for me. I understand you rented the last two rooms. Would you be so good as to share one of them with the young lady?"

James Fitzroy laughed. And giving Julia an admiring look, he said, "It is the best offer I have had made me in a long time."

Lady Jane at once was all dignity. "You know well what I meant, Jimmy. Let the girl have one of your rooms while you sleep in the other!"

"Ah!" James Fitzroy said, regarding Julia with twinkling eyes. "That requires a sacrifice on my part but I shall make it, providing you and the young lady join me in my living room for a light supper before retiring."

Lady Jane looked mollified. "That is a fair enough bargain. As soon as we have dried ourselves a little we shall be happy to join you."

He said, "And I shall have the innkeeper make me a bed of some sort on the cot in my living room." He bowed and left them.

Julia had not actually said a word during all this. But she had admired the young man's stylish dress and manners and felt reasonably certain that he considered her attractive. He had not seemed able to take his eyes off her.

"Show us upstairs," Lady Jane demanded of the innkeeper. And to Jane she ordered, "Do come along, my dear. Don't stand there dumb and motionless."

Julia was destined to become used to the occasionally tart comments of the older woman. But she put it down to nerves and age rather than a bad disposition. For the most part Lady Jane Hewitt was kind to her.

The room to which Julia was shown was small and adjoined the living room rented by James Fitzroy. The innkeeper brought up a large key and conspicuously turned it in the lock of the door joining the two rooms.

Then he turned to her and said, "For your protection, miss."

"Thank you," she said.

The moon-faced innkeeper offered her an unexpected wink, confiding, "Mr. Fitzroy is a proper gent, but he could be given to a bit of sleepwalking, if you understand." And then laughing at his own joke he left.

Julia dried herself before the blazing fire in the small fireplace. Then she made her way to the room which Lady Jane was in. She knocked at the door.

Lady Jane's maid opened it and said, "Her Ladyship will be ready in a minute. You can wait out there."

So she waited in the dark upper hallway for Lady Jane to complete her toilet. As she stood there two waiters brought up covered trays of food and took them to the room occupied by James Fitzroy. She had only a whiff of the roast beef but it made her realize that she was truly hungry. She hoped Lady Jane would not be long.

The older woman presented herself within a few minutes, complained of being wet and the inadequacy of her room and enquired of Julia whether she had dried herself or not. "I do not want you ill when we arrive in London," the woman said.

"I'm really quite dry now," Julia told her.

"Very well, then, we shall join Jimmy," the older woman said and they moved on down the dark hallway.

James Fitzroy greeted them warmly and ushered them into his large room. A temporary bed had already been made up on a cot in one corner of it and there was a table with two candles on it placed close by the fireplace with three chairs around it. The table was generously laden with the roast beef and other good things.

He saw the two ladies seated and then took his place between them. He asked Lady Jane, "Where have you been hiding this lovely girl? I have never seen her at your place."

Lady Jane said, "She has been living in the house of my parson brother and has only lately become my ward."

James Fitzroy gave her another of his knowing smiles. "May I say, Miss Crawford, you will be an ornament to our London social scene."

"Do not try to turn this village girl's head with your flattery, Jimmy," Lady Jane reprimanded him. "Give her time to accustom herself to London and its ways."

The young man laughed. "It's wicked, wicked ways if I may so state. Now do let me help you to some food and drink."

The cosy supper went well and Julia found herself liking the thin, young dandy although there was somehow a hint of the unhealthy about him. She put it down to his pale face and felt she ought not to judge his character by the color of his skin. Perhaps she was wary of him because he was so glib, having an answer for every question, and a tart comment on every subject.

"We were in Brighton," Lady Jane told him. "I made this journey on our return from a holiday there."

Fitzroy said, "Then you saw the Prince and his cronies. Was Beau there?"

"Beau Brummell was very prominent," Lady Jane agreed. "He and the Prince Regent are still boon companions."

The thin-face of the young man showed a hint of what might be jealousy. He said, "Indeed? How fortunate for George Bryan Brummell! It will keep his creditors at bay as long as it is known he is close to fat George."

Lady Jane raised her eyebrows. "Fat George, you say! Be careful young man, you speak of our Prince Regent. And as for Mr. Brummell, I have always understood him to be a man of some wealth."

"His father was little more than a clerk who married a wealthy woman," Fitzroy said with disdain. "And I hear that Brummell for all his airs, lives largely on gifts from his friends and the good will of his creditors!"

"I cannot believe it," Lady Jane exclaimed. "There is too much gossip!"

Julia felt she must join in the conversation and so she said, "I have been told that in addition to being the best dressed man in England he is especially witty."

"The best dressed man in the world!" Lady Jane Hewitt observed.

"He may well be," James Fitzroy said. "But I tell you this, Julia. He pays for only a little of what he wears and as to wit, he has a sharp tongue."

Lady Jane looked amused and said, "Is it true, Fitzroy, that he said you are a bore who insists on telling everything, but depend on your imagination for your facts?"

Fitzroy looked displeased. "I have heard he made such a comment. A rather long-winded way of saying I'm tiresome and a liar."

"How typical of Beau!" Lady Jane laughed.

"He likes hurting people," Fitzroy said, "I predict that will one day be his ruination. You know what he said of dear Lady Mary to whom he was betrothed, 'I could not marry her, dear boy, not when I actually saw her eat a cabbage.' And one day when at a fine house for dinner he found the chicken tough and passed it down to his dog, saying, 'Here, Atons, try if you can get your teeth into that, for I'm damned if I can!' That is typical of his small talk."

Julia said, "Since he has a pet dog he must be fond of animals."

"Very much so!" Lady Jane said. "The dog is rather a nuisance! But he and the Duchess of York share in common a love of dogs!"

"I have heard they share a good deal more than that," Fitzroy said slyly.

Lady Jane ignored this and continued, "Beau visits the Duchess at her country home. They are good friends. I understand she has more than a hundred dogs on the place and she keeps several large, unkempt animals in the house with her."

"It is difficult to picture our dandy in such surroundings," Fitzroy said. "But then he has a liking to attach himself to royalty."

Lady Jane rose from the table. "You are altogether too critical of Mr. Brummell, Jimmy. He gives a great deal of color to London society. It would be a dull place without him. Thank you for the food, now my ward and I must retire."

He saw them to the door and smiling at Julia said, "I trust you sleep well. You will be near to me in more than my kindly thoughts since you occupy the next room."

"Yes," she said. "The landlord provided me with a key to lock the door between our rooms."

"Did he, now?" Fitzroy said looking a little bleak. "I must say that it wasn't necessary. But these fellows seem to get all manner of stupid notions. I wish you a sound sleep."

Lady Jane nodded. "We much need it and then on to London!"

Julia saw the older woman escorted to her room door by the young dandy, and then she hurried on to her own small room and bolted the door. She smiled to herself as she glanced at the door to the room adjoining and occupied by James Fitzroy. Removing the key to it from her pocket she pursed her lips prettily and placed it on a nearby table.

She could imagine what the young London man thought! She was an innocent country girl ripe for the taking. And so he'd gone about his preposterous plotting to have a rendezvous in her room. What he didn't know was that she was herself in a sensual mood. Since her mating with John she'd been subjects to fits of arousal which had stunned her!

Tonight she was aflame with what the Reverend would surely call lustful desire. With a sudden impulse and another smile, she picked up the key and went to the door to Fitzroy's room and gently turned it in the lock. Then she went back to the blazing log fire in the fireplace and slowly disrobed.

She was standing naked with the flames playing on her neat young breasts and the occasional gusts of the chimney draft wafting her striking black pubic hair as she wryly considered what James Fitzroy might do next.

Julia did not have long to wait. After a little there was a gentle knocking on the door, a pause, then more insistent knocking, followed by a pause and a plaintive voice from the other side, begging, "Dear girl, why do you not let me in?"

She laughed lightly and turning towards the door asked, "Why do you not let yourself in?"

The door opened and he came in wearing only his nightshift and when he saw her lovely body he showed shock. It took him a full few seconds to recover. Then he stammered, "Gad! You made a fool of me! You are lovelier than any London wench, I vow!"

Julia pressed her fingers to her lips and told him, "Do be more quiet!"

"In the face of such beauty!" And he seized her in his arms and greedily kissed her, first on the mouth and then over the rest of her body.

She finally pushed him away and whispered, "You thought to take me against my will. Let me warn you, no man does that. I have given my promise to marry to a good lad. But I have my hungers, as every woman must, deny it or not, and if I wish I may dispense my favors."

Fitzroy chuckled with delight. "Vixen! And I thought you an innocent!" And he lifted her up and took her to the bed. After which he quickly doffed his nightshirt and lay on her.

Her first reaction was that while his body was adequate he was not the match in manly equipment of her dear John. But once he was upon her he managed well with what he had. His prodding of her was more expert and prolonged, so that her passion welled to the point where her excited and delighted cries mixed with his panting exultation. Again she knew fulfillment and again she realized that her passionate nature would sometimes rule her mind.

As he drew near a climax his mouth ravished her, his tongue thrusting like a brand, burning into her, making her his! The almost cruel crush of his lips and his strong arms clasping her added to her enjoyment of the rapturous interlocking.

Fitzroy groaned and his member throbbed wildly within her as she allowed herself a rewarding climax. It was over and he lay beside her gasping and admiring.

It was then she told him, "You must forget this. And you must know it will never happen between us again."

He propped his perspiring self up on an elbow. "But why?"

"Because I wished it tonight and I do not wish to enter into an affair with you or anyone else," she said almost primly.

"Gad!" he said. "You talk like a man about bed play!"

"I think a woman should have a perogative," she told him. And she rose and slipped into her nightgown. "Now you will return to bed and I will lock the door."

He stood naked and smiling before her. "We could do it again."

"No!" she said. "And if you ever mention this I will deny it."

He sulkily picked up his nightshift. "So you will now rest comfortably with dreams of the man you truly love."

"That may well be," she said, turning from him. "Goodnight."

"I shall send you roses for remembrance," he told her and left.

The journey to London was somewhat uneventful on the pleasant day which followed the rain. Julia was filled with anticipation of seeing the great city of which she had read and heard so much. Lady Jane seemed weary and her head drooped in sleep soon after the trip began. The little maid sat silent and wide-eyed on the opposite seat.

Julia was not prepared for the first views she had of London. She had envisaged it as a city of stately buildings, churches and great glamor. The kind of squalor among the run down streets through which they entered the city dismayed her. The streets were swarming with people and vehicles and all was dirty and noisy.

Lady Jane came awake with a start to peer out and say, "So we are in London!"

"It seems very noisy!" Julia said.

The older woman gave her a grim glance. "You'll become used to it. But this is a slum section. Shortly we'll be moving into the better sections of the city. And in Ward Square, where our family house is, you will find it much more sedate."

And so it turned out to be true. As they moved along to the wealthy areas of the city the houses were as palatial as she'd expected, even more so. The streets were not nearly so crowded. And the few carriages which passed were driven at a pleasant pace and filled with fashionable people.

They drove in between stone gate posts and she noted the Hewitt crest was affixed to one of the gate posts, worked in iron it made an impressive decoration. They went by gardens and finally halted before the entrance of a great town house. The door was at once opened and an elderly man in butler's livery ordered several servants scurrying out to help them.

Julia followed Lady Jane out of the carriage and to the front door where the gray-haired butler stood stiffly. The older woman greeted him with a weary smile and said, "This is Miss Julia Crawford, Bates. She will be living here as a member of the household."

The old man bowed. "Very good, madam."

"Give her the blue room, Bates," Lady Jane said. "See that her things are taken up there at once."

"Yes, madam," the gray head bowed again.

"Is my husband at home?"

"Sir Orville was in the library," the butler said.

But he had no sooner uttered the words than there appeared a tall, rather handsome, middle-aged man with thinning black hair and a prominent nose which was the only thing marring his otherwise pleasing face. He was dressed in a blue jacket, white cravat and gray breeches. He came straight to Lady Jane and embraced her.

"My dear! I was alarmed when you did not return last night," he said.

"The bad weather! We stayed at an inn for the night."

"Of course!" he said. And turning to Julia with a pleased smile, he asked, "And who, may I ask, is this? Surely not the country maid your brother was so anxious for you to take on."

"Yes," Lady Jane said, "This is Julia Crawford. Julia this is my husband, Sir Orville Hewitt!"

"Welcome to Hewitt Hall, my dear girl," Sir Orville said embracing her warmly and kissing her on the cheek.

"You are too kind, sir," Julia said somewhat overwhelmed.

"Don't fuss so over the girl!" Lady Jane said in a sharp, petulant tone.

Her husband at once turned to her with a surprised smile on his almost handsome face and said, "Is it not my duty to make her welcome?"

"You have done well enough for the moment," his wife told him. And to Julia, she said, "Come along, I will let you see your room."

Sir Orville remained by the door beaming at them as they made their way to the stairs. As they mounted the stairway Julia could not but help wonder about Sir Orville. He looked years younger than the weary-faced Lady Jane, and he had been more than warm in his embrace. She began to understand why his wife had warned her to treat him with coolness.

They made their way along a wide hall and finally to the doorway of a room delicately furnished in blue tones. The wall paper, the paint and the draperies as well as the bed coverings were all in white and blue. It was a lovely room with two large windows to offer a view of the gardens and the trees beyond.

"I think you should be happy here," Lady Jane said.

"It is more lavish than I could have hoped," Julia told her. "You are very kind."

"I want to help you, my dear," the older woman said, her eyes fixed on her. "And you can help me. I'm often lonely here. I would enjoy your reading to me as my eyes tire quickly."

"At any time, Aunt Jane," she said.

The woman sighed, then said abruptly, "Don't mind my husband. We mustn't let him spoil things."

Having delivered herself of this somewhat remarkable statement the thin woman abruptly left the room. Julia now was certain she knew what she meant and also what Lady Jane's secret sorrow might be. It seemed that her husband was a womanizer, with a weakness for any pretty face or sharply turned ankle. She would have to be wary!

She spent the rest of the day unpacking and making herself familiar with the house. She had a personal maid assigned to her, a small girl whose name was Sarah. The girl was talkative and anxious to make Julia feel at home.

"You'll like it here," the maid promised her. "They have a lot of parties. All the toffs of London come here including his nibs, the Prince Regent hisself!"

Julia had smiled, "I'm sure it must be exciting."

At dinner that evening Sir Orville was again in an expansive mood. He paid particular attention to Julia at the table and hastened at every opportunity to help her with her chair. When dinner was over he strolled at her side as they moved into the drawing room for sherry and brandy.

Lady Jane in black looked especially pale and fragile. She said little but it was evident she felt her husband was making a fool of himself.

In the drawing room he said, "Julia must see the city. I know how you dislike sight-seeing, my dear. I feel I should appoint myself to be her guide."

"No!" Lady Jane said emphatically.

Her husband looked hurt. "But surely it is a good idea?"

"I agree Julia ought to see London," his wife replied.

"But it would be much more enjoyable if she were shown the sights by someone her own age."

"Come now! I'm not all that old!" Sir Orville protested.

"I think I know the exact person," Lady Jane said with a thin smile for Julia. "I shall get Elizabeth to take you around. She is about your age and the daughter of my oldest woman friend."

"Elizabeth!" Sir Orville said disdainfully. "That young woman doesn't properly know the city herself."

"She knows it well enough," his wife said firmly. "I shall send a message to her house tomorrow morning."

Julia pleaded, "Please don't go to a lot of bother on my account!"

"It won't be a bother. I want you to meet Elizabeth in any event," Lady Jane said.

Sir Orville's face had become crimson and he silently accepted the brandy which Bates had quietly poured out for him. It was clear that he was angry. Julia hoped he wouldn't go on behaving in such an adolescent manner and ruin everything for her.

Elizabeth Lang came the following afternoon. She wore a pretty white muslin dress and a straw bonnet with gay little flowers around it. She was auburn-haired with a sprite's merry face and a jolly disposition. She was a little taller than Julia though not really tall. Lady Jane introduced them and then had Julia take the other girl up to her room so they could quietly become acquainted.

"You have the Wedgewood Room!" Elizabeth exclaimed as she gazed around Julia's room. "I slept here overnight once after a very late party."

"Then you are familiar with it."

"Yes." The other girl turned to stare at her frankly. "I like your dress," she said.

"It's only an old dress," she said. "Lady Jane plans to buy me an entire wardrobe."

Elizabeth laughed. "She's doing that for her own

enjoyment. That linen you have on is just fine. And I love your raven, black hair!"

Julia blushed. "I haven't done it up yet."

"Don't!" Elizabeth said, swinging her own long auburn curls with a toss of her head. "My mother says that putting up one's hair adds years to your age."

"Really?"

"Yes," Elizabeth said. "And I think she's right. I intend to let my hair fall on my shoulders as long as I can."

"So do I," Julia said.

Elizabeth smiled at her happily. "I know we're going to be the best of friends. And I will show you London."

"When do we start?"

"Why not now?" the other girl said. "I have a carriage waiting and I don't want to lose time."

"Very well," Julia said. "I'll put on my bonnet and take a wrap in case it gets cooler."

"Very wise," Elizabeth agreed. "I have one in the carriage."

Thus began one of the most exciting afternoons of Julia's young life. She was taken to see St. Paul's and visit it for a little, she also saw the Houses of Parliament, several of the palaces including that of the Duke of Buckingham. Then Elizabeth took her to the theatre district and pointed out the various showplaces to her. They kept on until they were too weary for anything but return home.

"I expect I shall be late for dinner," Julia worried as the single horse carriage took them back along the busy London streets.

"Don't worry about a small thing like that!" Elizabeth said with disgust.

"But my position is different," she pointed out. "These are not my real parents. They expect very careful deportment of me."

"I know they do," her friend said. "But you have to also let them know you're human."

"I promised to be home before six!"

"It's only half past the hour," Elizabeth told her. "And Sir Orville won't be angry with you!"

She gave the girl a surprised look. "How do you know?"

"I know!"

"Tell me!"

"Very well," Elizabeth said with a wise smile. "He won't be angry with you because he hopes to make love to you!"

She turned to her friend and gasped, "You can't mean it!"

"I do!"

"How do you know?"

Elizabeth was smirking. "Because he tried to make love to me. He does it with every woman he meets. That is why Lady Jane is always so unhappy. At least, that's what my mother says."

Now it was out in the open and Julia found it disgusting. "What an awful old man he is!"

"He's not all that old. Younger than his wife."

"No matter. He shouldn't behave in such a way. Cheapening himself and her!"

Elizabeth warned, "You must learn to be stern with him."

"I'll surely try."

"You must or you won't last at Hewitt House," Elizabeth warned. "And you're never liable to get a better home."

She was upset. "I don't like this at all!"

"Don't worry about it," her friend advised. "But be ready to deal with it if it happens."

"I'm not sure I can," she worried.

"You can and you will," Elizabeth said. "I laughed in his face and that finished it. He can't bear to be laughed at."

Julia said, "He was much too warm towards me in his welcome. And he didn't want you to show me the city. It was his idea to take me out on a tour of the town."

"Count yourself lucky," her friend said.

"I knew something was wrong because of the reaction of Lady Jane," she said worriedly.

"Well, now you have been properly warned," Elizabeth said in her pert manner.

Elizabeth dropped her off at the door of Hewitt Hall and she rushed upstairs and washed and changed for dinner. Lady Jane was in a pleasant mood and at dinner asked her about her reaction to the great city. Julia was still filled with excitement from the experience.

"It is a most marvelous place!" she summed it up.

From his place at the table Sir Orville offered her a sullen look. "You ought to have had a proper guide," he said. "That child doesn't really know the city herself."

His wife reproved him with, "That is most unfair, Orville. From all that Julia has told us I'd say Elizabeth was a most excellent guide."

Julia, as usual, found herself caught between the two. She knew that as long as this situation existed she would never be truly comfortable in the house. In spite of her interest in the city she began to wonder if she might not be wise to return to her country village and the parsonage.

The next morning an event happened which caused her some wonder. She was in her room when a knock came on the door. She went to answer it and found the butler standing there in his reserved fashion with a vase of red roses in his hands.

He said, "Flowers for you, Miss Crawford."

She stared at them. "You must be mistaken?"

"No, miss. There's a card with them," Bates told her. "It is clearly addressed to you."

"Thank you," she said, taking them.

She placed them on a table in her room and tore open the envelope with the card. In a neat hand was written: "To one more lovely than any of these roses, James Fitzroy."

Her cheeks burned as she read the message and

realized it and the flowers had come from the young dandy whom she'd met at the inn on her way to London. He had left early in the morning and so she hadn't seen him again but it appeared that he hadn't forgotten her!

She went downstairs and sought out Lady Jane in the drawing room. She asked her, "Would you like me to read to you this morning?"

Comfortably seated in an easy chair by an open window the older woman offered her one of her familiar, weary smiles and said, "That would be nice. Perhaps some of Mr. Coleredge's poetry. There is a volume over on the table which he left when he was last here."

Julia was impressed. "He is a friend?"

"Yes. Since he came to live in London with Dr. Gilman."

Because she felt she should inform the older woman, she went on to say, "I received a bouquet of roses this morning from Mr. James Fitzroy."

Lady Jane's thin face showed surprise. "Did you? That is most interesting. That young man is usually too involved with his gambling and race horses to think of anything else. So he remembered you?"

"Yes," she said, blushing. "He sent this with the flowers." And she let the older woman have the card to read.

Lady Jane scanned the card and gave it back to her with a wise look. "You'll hear from him again before long, I'm sure. Perhaps he will call. He is well born, you know."

"I judged that," she said.

"You might do worse than Jimmy Fitzroy," Lady Jane said. "If he should propose marriage to you I would strongly advise you accept."

Julia was confused. "I really don't know him that well," she said. "And I'm not all that interested in marriage. I'm sure he only sent the letter as a polite gesture."

"We shall see," the older woman said quietly. "Now get the book and read to me."

The day went by quickly enough. After dinner Julia had to hurry out alone into the garden to escape the unpleasant pawing of Sir Orville. On the pretence of showing her the art hanging on the walls of the old mansion he escorted her around with a continually more brash hand loosely around her. At last she complained of a headache and left him to hurry outside.

She waited until she was sure he'd have returned to his study where he usually loaded himself with brandy until it was time for him to retire. In her room she decided she would use the latter part of the evening to enjoy a leisurely, warm bath. She rang for the maid and when Sarah appeared, told her of her wish.

Shortly afterwards Sarah and another girl lugged in a large tin tub shaped somewhat like a sauce bowl. Then they returned with large earthenware containers of hot and cold water and towels. She had the girls mix the water until it was a pleasant temperature for a bath.

Julia undressed and now gently slid down in the warm, soothing water. It at once made her feel better. The tub had been set out near the foot of her bed and the towels were on the bed.

Sarah, the little maid, said, "I'll go now, miss, and come back after a while with more hot water."

"Plenty here for the time being," she told the girl.

Sarah nodded and went on out. Julia luxuriated in the tub and scrubbed herself. She thought about the events of the day and wondered if she would really hear from James Fitzroy again. Her Aunt Jane had seemed to approve of him despite the fact she'd noted he was a gambler. Julia had found him both pleasant and alarming. She felt that he was much more complex than he seemed.

She was considering all these things when she heard the door open. Thinking it was Sarah back with the hot water, she rose naked and dripping from the tin tub, and said, "I won't need any more hot water, Sarah. Just get me a towel!"

Turning, she was shocked to see that she'd made an error. It wasn't Sarah standing there gazing at her with eyes bright with admiration!

"Dashed lovely body!" he said.

Chapter Three

Before a shocked and angered Julia could make a reply the titled man made a smirking exit, closing the door after him most carefully. She remained standing erect in the tub, trembling now. Sir Orville had played a wicked trick on her. No doubt he'd seen the comings and goings of Sarah in preparing her bath and had carefully chosen this moment to slyly open the door and spy upon her.

She had no doubt that he'd apologize profusely and claim it had all been an accident. But at the same time she was grimly convinced that the promiscuous Sir Orville had done exactly as he intended.

Reaching for a towel, she began briskly drying her lithe, dripping body as the door opened again and this time it was an anxious Sarah with some extra towels.

"Sorry to keep you waiting, miss," the maid said.

"It's all right," Julia replied, taking a towel from her to finish her task. "In the future when I'm bathing I think we should lock the door to the hall."

The surprised look on the maid's face indicated that she had no knowledge of what had taken place. "Really, miss?"

"Yes. Someone almost came in here and caught me as I was stepping out of the tub."

The maid looked upset. "In that case you are right, miss. I never thought of it. I should have remained with you and had the towels here."

"There's no harm done," Julia said slipping into her nightgown.

From then on she knew that Sir Orville was not to be trusted and that she would be wise not to let herself be found alone with him. She made no mention of the event the next morning nor did he. But when he glanced at her she thought there was a mocking gleam in his eyes.

She did not have to wait long for James Fitzroy to pay his respects and bring more roses. She came in from the garden to take them and give them to the housekeeper. She reproved the young dandy, saying, "We have a garden here with more flowers than we know what to do with. It is nonsense bringing these here."

Fitzroy, splendid in purple jacket, pale yellow breeches slotted under brown shoes and wearing an enormous white neckcloth merely smiled at this.

"I wished to show my appreciation of your beauty which I may say is fresher than any bloom!"

"Do be seated, Mr. Fitzroy," she said, taking a chair for herself. She was glad she had chosen a yellow muslin dress to wear that morning. Their clothes were pleasantly matched.

"Let us settle something at once," he insisted. "You must call me Jimmy and I shall call you Julia."

"On such short acquaintance?"

His thin face showed a wise smile, "We did spend a night together in my suite at the "Bull and Ram". Have you forgotten?"

Blushing, she said, "I have not forgotten nor were the events as you make them sound. I was very much alone in my room!"

"More's the pity for that!" He drawled his hand

languidly placed on the back of a chair as he stood gazing down at her.

"You mustn't say such things, Jimmy!" she responded.

"Ah!" he said, satisfied. "Now we have established a fine beginning."

At this point a pleased-looking Lady Jane joined them. The young buck at once saw her securely in a chair and hovered over her with several compliments.

The older woman tapped his hand playfully with her fan and said, "Now you mustn't waste your blandishments on me, my dear boy. I know perfectly well you have come to see my ward, Julia."

"I will not lie, madam," Jimmy Fitzroy said. "I have come to request that tomorrow afternoon, if it be fair, I shall be allowed to invite Miss Crawford for a ride in the park in my carriage."

"I admire your frankness," Lady Jane said with one of her sad smiles. And turning to Julia, she asked, "Would you like to go?"

Feeling that frankness should be met with frankness, she nodded, "Yes. I think I would truly enjoy it."

Lady Jane waved her hand. "There, you have your answer."

Jimmy looked pleased. "You are sure that Sir Orville will have no objections?"

"Why should he?" the older woman asked.

The young dandy hesitated, then seemed to change his mind about what he was going to say and declared, "Why should he, indeed!"

Jimmy left a short time after the afternoon meeting had been arranged. Lady Jane indicated that she thought the young man was much taken with Julia and that if she played her cards right she might well win him for a husband.

But when Sir Orville heard the news at dinner his almost handsome face became purple with annoyance. "You must be mad!" he accused his wife. "To allow this naive child to go out alone with that roue?"

"Only for a carriage ride in the public park, my dear," his wife replied.

"I do not care. You are encouraging him and you shouldn't!" Sir Orville went on angrily. "Not only has he been a boon companion of that infamous Beau Brummell, but the word about now is that the two have quarreled over some gaming debt and no longer speak to each other!"

"We have had them both to our parties and they always seemed to be on the best of terms," Lady Jane said with a frown. "This must have come about lately."

"It has!" Sir Orville declared. "You do not hear the gossip of the town as I do! I may have these fashionable gents under my roof at large gatherings but they are never to be counted among our friends."

"I'm sorry," Julia spoke up. "I do not wish to be the cause of controversy. I can always plead a headache when the young man calls."

"Very wise," Sir Orville growled in approval.

"No. We shall not begin Julia's stay in London with such deviousness," Lady Jane replied firmly. "She will keep her date with the young man."

At this Sir Orville snatched his napkin from his neck and stood up from the table. "I will not remain here and listen to your plans to place this young woman in moral jeopardy. We both know Jimmy Fitzroy to be a rake and a gambler!"

"All young men are a little wild and gamble," his wife said. "I'm sure you, of all people, know that!"

He stood there near to apoplexy. "Very well, madam," he said stiffly. "Put the girl in his way. Bait him with her! But do not blame me for what transpires!" And with that he marched from the table.

Julia was aghast. "We have ruined his dinner!"

"He eats far too much in any case," Lady Jane said with an annoyed sniff. "You must not listen to him! He is far too prejudiced against poor Jimmy!"

Julia accepted this as truth knowing of the titled man's unhealthy interest in her. The tension of living at

Hewitt Hall had not eased at all. Next morning when her friend, Elizabeth, came to spend an hour with her, she took her up to her room and told her of the incident of Sir Orville bursting in on her when she was naked in her bath.

Elizabeth was not surprised. As the two sat, on the edge of the bed she warned Julia, "I told you what he is like!"

"He's worse than I expected," Julia admitted. "And it is so painful for Lady Jane."

"I know," the other girl agreed.

"I'm sure that is why she gave her permission for me to take a carriage ride with Jimmy Fitzroy this afternoon!" Julia confided in her friend.

The auburn-haired girl's mouth gaped open. "Did you say Jimmy Fitzroy?"

"Yes. Do you know him?"

"I've met him at parties," Elizabeth said. "I dare say he's known in every fashionable set in London!"

"What about him?"

"He's awfully wild!"

Julia smiled. "Some think that a sign of spirit in a young man."

Elizabeth looked amused at this. "If that is so, then he is a most desirable person. He's paid court to many young women but the story goes that he offered marriage to none of them. He is rich and spoiled and one of Brummell's dandies."

"I hear he and Brummell quarreled."

"It could be," the other girl said. "There are almost daily changes among that high living set. The friends of one day are the enemies of the next. Their petty quarrels are about everything from who owes the most money to whom on to who has the best wardrobe!"

Julia found virtuous indignation stirring in her. She said, "These young men should have more important things on their minds. Such as the threat of Napoleon. England may need them in the army."

"La!" Elizabeth laughed. "More than half of them

have army commissions of some sort which they have bought or been given. The Prince Regent, they say, gave Beau Brummell a high commission in his regiment. And the Beau is not apt to battle with anything more dangerous than his tight-fitting waistcoat!"

Julia was shocked. "I consider this all stupidly degenerate. You say these people consider themselves army officers but have no intention of ever rightly serving?"

"I do."

"It is a shame. A while ago, when I was still in the country, I gave my pledge to marry a young man whose only ambition was to be a soldier. A fine young man! The son of a prosperous farmer!"

Elizabeth stared at her in silent consternation for a moment. "You cannot mean it? The son of a farmer, with plans to be a common soldier! And you said you'd marry him?"

"I still will if he returns safely!"

Her new friend shook her head in dismay. "You mustn't think of such a thing! You are far above a marriage like that! It would be disastrous!"

"To marry the young man I love?"

"My mother says love has nothing to do with marriage," her friend told her. "And I'm sure she is wiser about it than we are. Oh, one should like a fellow! But love is another matter! I'm shortly to be married to Sir Gerald Giles. I'm fond of him but certainly not madly in love!"

Julia was surprised. "You didn't tell me you were soon to marry!"

Elizabeth blushed happily. "Yes. I must admit my mother and father had a good deal to do with the arranging of it. But I'm sure Gerry and I shall be happy. The only thing I dislike about him is his restless nature. He has companions interested in racing. And he continually goes to races all over England."

"You could always travel with him," she suggested.

"No. I should hate it," the other girl said. "I'll let

him attend his races and I shall remain at home. We are going to have a house on St. James Street!"

"I wish you every happiness," Julia said, taking her friend's hands in hers. "I hope I do not lose you as a friend. I have no other in London."

"I shall continue to be your friend," the auburn-haired girl promised. "And you'll like Gerry. And with some luck maybe he can find someone suitable for you to marry. Someone better than your young soldier friend!"

"I'm not sure I want anyone else."

"You don't want Jimmy Fitzroy, do you?" Her friend sounded worried.

She laughed. "No. But I shall see him if only because he amuses me. And because it is a good move to play him against Sir Orville. If Sir Orville thinks I have interest in a younger man he may not bother me so much!"

"Or bother you more!"

"I surely hope not!" Julia said with mock dismay. "Anything but that!"

Julia was beginning to think that life was filled with the unexpected in London. Jimmy came to call for her in his handsome open carriage and they were driven through the streets of affluence to Regents Park where the titled and the wealthy paraded their horses, carriages, wives and mistresses in that order of importance. Or so Jimmy Fitzroy warned her.

The lanes of the great park were much unlike the quiet, country lanes she had known at home. But it was pleasant to ride along the busy ways and have Jimmy nod to various people in the passing carriages and tell her afterward whom it was. He appeared to know almost everyone and to be in turn known by all the fashionable owners of carriages.

The common folk strolled outside the fenced lane and gawked and pointed at their betters. Jimmy and Julia were engaged in a discussion of the importance of proper dress in which she was taking the position that

Brummell had started a fad which was altogether unimportant.

"I cannot agree," young Fitzroy told her. "You do not know how sloppy some of the gentry were until Beau came along. He has, at least, set standards."

"You approve of him?"

"To a degree," Jimmy said with shrug. "I follow his fashion in dress. We used to be friends. Unhappily that is no longer the case."

"Why?"

Jimmy gave her one of his languid glances and said, "I pray you not ask tiresome questions, dear Julia."

So the subject was changed to the breeding of fine horses in which Jimmy considered himself an expert. She mentioned that her friend, Elizabeth, was soon to marry Sir Gerald Giles who was interested in racing.

Fitzroy frowned. "I can't believe that," he said. "To the best of my knowledge we've never met at the races."

At that moment their talk was interrupted by the sound of cheers from the railing ahead. The crowds of common folk had seen some favorite and were cheering them. A carriage crested with crimson and gold trim and with liveries seated up front and two on a perch at the back, rode by. Inside, facing them sat two men. One stout and almost stupid-looking with a face crimson enough to match his uniform jacket with its gold epaulets. Next to him sat a handsome man in a white cravat which ran high up his neck, a black coat of stylish cut and a black tophat.

As their carriages passed, the coachman slowed the carriage she and Fitzroy were in, almost to a halt. Cheers continued to fill the air and some of the common folk were running along to get a better view of the two men in the colorful carriage.

The stout man stared grimly ahead, looking neither to right nor left. The man in the high white cravat and black tophat stared directly at them without revealing any expression. Julia was struck by the Grecian beauty of the even-featured face and piercing dark eyes. She had never before seen a man of such commanding presence.

Then the carriage moved on and Jimmy turned to her with a wry smile and said, "Talk of the Devil! That was Beau Brummell and the Prince Regent!"

"I guessed it had to be," she said, in an awed tone.

"Beau chose not to speak to me," the young man at her side said bitterly. "But I could tell that he was impressed by you."

Julia protested, "I'm no stylish town beauty but a simple, country girl in plain white muslin and straw bonnet. Don't tell me the great fashion plate of the town even noticed me. I saw no hint that he did."

"I happen to know him better than you," Fitzroy told her. "He saw you!"

This proved to be the high spot of the afternoon. None of the other carriages or their passengers matched the royal one in interest. Fitzroy directed his coachman to take them from the main lane to a winding road that led to a small lake. When they reached the lakeside he helped her down from the carriage and they strolled to the bank of the lake.

"How lovely to have all this in London!" she enthused.

Fitzroy smiled at the water-lilies in the greenish-tinged water and said, "Didn't Johnson say that any man who didn't appreciate London was a fool?"

She laughed. "I don't know. But I thoroughly agree."

The thin faced young dandy had removed his tophat and now he was staring at her in a special way. "I say anyone who doesn't appreciate you is a fool!"

"Please, Jimmy!" she said. "You embarrass me. Let us be more casual in our friendship."

He shook his head. "It is not in my nature."

"Surely you can manage that!"

He came a little closer to her and said earnestly, "I

know exactly what will happen when you're seen at one of Lady Jane's parties. The dandies of the town will be scrapping over you and the most aggressive one will snatch you away for his own!"

"That is nonsense talk!"

"It is the truth," he said firmly.

"Then let us wait and see it happen."

He shook his head. "I cannot do that. I don't want to risk losing you. And that is why I ask you now to be my wife!"

"Jimmy!" she said, staring up at his intense face in bewilderment.

"I love you, Julia. I swear it," he said. And he took her in his arms and pressed his lips hard on hers. The kiss lasted for what seemed an unending time.

She pushed him away. "Jimmy! What will the coachman think?"

He smiled and glanced back to where the coach with the coachman sitting on it, waited and said, "He is paid to drive not to think. Well, what is your answer?"

"I have no answer, Jimmy," she said softly. "I'm terribly flattered. But I have been in London only a short time. I'm not in any mood to make such decisions. Nor would Lady Jane allow it."

"Would you object to my asking her and Sir Orville?"

"Yes," she said quickly. For she feared that Lady Jane in her urgent need to prevent Sir Orville from carrying on his mad behavior, would quickly reach out for any offer which would remove her from the scene. In fact, Lady Jane had already hinted that Jimmy would not be a bad choice for her.

"Why would you object?"

"They would be sure to refuse at this point," she improvised quickly. "Allow us to be friends a little longer and perhaps then."

So she managed to placate him for a little. The days and weeks passed and she met many other friends of the Hewitts. Also, Lady Jane had her make the rounds of her favorite seamstresses with the result that Julia soon had a new, chic wardrobe. As yet, there had been no large parties held at the house, but she knew one was being planned.

She tried to make herself as useful as possible as she dearly wanted to earn her way. One worry of this period was the fact she received no mail from John Lane. She had heard with regularity from the old Reverend Weir. But the kindly minister informed her that no letters had arrived from John. She began to feel sadness about their affair and think that perhaps in his new life he had forgotten her.

Elizabeth was to be married the following month and was already busy with preparations. Julia and she met whenever they could and the auburn-haired girl was still doubtful that Jimmy Fitzroy was an ideal person for her to spend so much time with. But whenever Jimmy took Julia out she found it fun and she was reluctant to believe that he was an undesirable person.

Sir Orville continued to complain about her friendship with the young dandy. He also continued trying to press himself on her. Julia spent as much time with Lady Jane as she could and tried to avoid being alone with the amorous older man.

One morning after breakfast he sent a maid to fetch her to his study. She went there feeling uneasy but not daring to refuse. And she found him waiting there with a small, wrinkled-faced man.

Sir Orville was in an expansive mood on this bright morning. As she entered he turned to the little man and told him, "This is our Julia!"

The little man peered at her through slits of eyes in his smiling, wrinkled face and then studied her through a quizzing glass. "She is a true beauty!" was his final decision.

Julia was unaware of what it all meant. She said, "I'm afraid I do not understand."

"I will explain," Sir Orville said, chummily placing an unwanted hand about her waist. "This is Christopher Pratt, noted fellow of the Royal Academy of Artists. He wishes to do a portrait of me. But I told him that first he must do one of you."

"But I'm a person of no importance!" she protested.

"You have a rare beauty," the artist said. "That is all important!"

"I couldn't have stated it better," Sir Orville said, his eyes gleaming, his face alight with the idea. "And I shall hang your portrait in here."

Julia protested, "I have no wish for it. I cannot take the time for sittings."

"I need only a few," the little artist assured her. "And I beg you to allow me to put down on canvas such perfection."

So Julia was cajoled into having her portrait painted. And at every sitting Sir Orville came to sit and watch her. The presence of the debauched peer and the way his eyes fixed greedily on her at these sessions, made them more difficult.

Lady Jane cautioned her, "Don't try to oppose him in this. If it gives him temporary satisfaction, you may as well humor him. Meanwhile, you and I, shall be busy making up and sending out invitations for our next large party here."

The party took place two weeks later. Workmen busily decorated the great ball room and made the gardens a fairyland of small lanterns. They were hung from the trees all over the gardens and great swaths of colored cloth was also hung in decoration between some of the trees. Lady Jane had a new gown for the ball in rich Venetian silk and Sir Orville had several sessions of fittings for his black silken jacket with matching trousers.

"Bound to be the talk of London," the older man boomed in his arrogant fashion.

Little Christopher Pratt came faithfully every second

day and the portrait was in the progress of completion.
Sit Orville insisted that it be left out and there was no
arguing with him. So it remained in an ante-room
adjacent to the ballroom. Julia hoped that in the
excitement of the evening Sir Orville would forget
about it.

She wore a pale blue gown with a low cut bosom and
back. She had at first thought it too daring but Lady
Jane insisted it was quite proper. Telling her, "I assure
you there will be many ladies present less modestly
dressed."

As it turned out she was right. When the ladies and
gentlemen of this fashionable London set arrived many
of them wore daringly cut gowns. Sir Orville stood at the
entrance to the great town house and greeted his guests
as they arrived. The carriages were driven off to return
when the ball ended. Torches were set out to light the
entrance way when darkness had fallen.

Sir Orville turned his guests over to Lady Jane, who
in turn, introduced Julia. It was the most exciting
experience of Julia's young life. As the leaders of
Regency society were presented she recognized some
of the names, but found the personages in flesh quite
different from what she had expected. James Fitzroy
arrived with his usual charm and as he kissed her hand
murmured that he would insist on the first dance with
her.

Then Elizabeth arrived with her betrothed, Sir
Gerald Giles, and Julia had her first meeting with him.
He was a rather short man with a squarish, good-
looking face and eyes which twinkled with good humor.
His hair was as black as Elizabeth's was auburn and his
skin swarthy in contrast to Elizabeth's pale white skin
texture.

The parade went on with literally several hundred
arriving. Julia wondered if it would ever end. She heard
the music in the ballroom and knew that some dancing
had already begun. Then suddenly Lady Jane said very

clearly to her, "And this, my dear, is Mr. George Bryan Brummell!"

She felt herself freeze with nerves and with a ghastly smile she looked up into the cool, serene face of the famous dandy. His cravat and white tie were even more spectacularly high than usual so that his chin was upturned. His black silk suit of stylish cut made him stand out from the other males in their jackets and breeches of varied hues.

The handsome Brummell smiled and at once she felt less afraid of him. Gazing down at her, he said, "Miss Crawford, I never forget a truly lovely face. Surely we have met before?"

She managed a real smile in return and said, "I believe our carriages passed once in Regent's Park. You were with the Prince Regent."

"I'm often with his Royal Highness," Brummell said airily. And then his expression changed to almost a frown. "Of course, I do remember. You were with Fitzroy!" His tone indicated that he was not entirely approving of her companion.

"Yes," she said. "That is right. I recognized you because he pointed you out to me."

"We were once friends," the elegant Beau said with a coldness again in his voice. Then he turned to Lady Jane and said, "Is this poor girl to be chained to the reception line for the entire night? I insist that you allow me to escort her to the ballroom and be her partner for her first dance!"

Lady Jane cast a nervous eye on Sir Orville who was at the moment occupied with a late comer. After what seemed a long moment of hesitation, she said, "I agree with you, Mr. Brummell. Do rescue the child!"

Brummell gave Julia one of his winning smiles. "You see, aggression pays!" And he led her off to join the other dancers in the brilliant atmosphere of the great ballroom.

She whispered to him as he led her on the floor, "I'm

but an indifferent dancer. I have lived most of my life in a small village."

"You have but to follow my lead," the famous dandy told her. And with complete assurance he led her out to join the others.

She kept one eye on the movements of the girl next to her and heroically attempted the same steps. It was not as difficult as she'd expected. The steps were fairly simple and the debonair Brummell led her well. After her initial nervousness she experienced a second bout of panic as she realized most of the other dancers were watching them out of the corners of their eyes. And the onlookers in the room were unabashedly giving them their full attention.

The dance ended and Beau Brummell bowed to her. "I thank you, dear Miss Crawford. I trust that we may dance again later." He led her over to the area where the onlookers were standing and after a moment politely excused himself and moved on to talk with a white-haired man.

Sir Orville appeared in a bad temper. He came straight to Julia and said, "Not only did that idiot dandy not bring the Prince Regent with him as he promised, but he stole you off for the first dance. I looked for that honor myself!"

She tried to placate him by saying, "We can always dance later."

"Now," the weakly handsome Sir Orville said. "We shall dance together now!"

"Shouldn't you dance with your wife first?" she worried.

"The devil take my wife!" Sir Orville said angrily and he waved to the orchestra to strike up again. It did and he at once led her out onto the floor.

As they danced she wondered where Lady Jane was and what she would think. Sir Orville, now all smiles, was dancing in a rather antic fashion. She could only think that he was deliberately trying to attract attention to them.

Breathing heavily, he told her, "Let the young bucks see that an older man can capture beauty in spite of them!"

She suffered through the dance and when it was over and he led her off the floor Lady Jane was waiting for him with an impatient expression on her thin face.

Lady Jane warned her husband, "There are many ladies here expecting you to dance with them, Orville. You must not spend all your time with Julia."

He scowled and said, "My dance with her will be the only part of the evening that I have enjoyed!"

Julia was relieved to have Jummy Fitzroy push his way through the crowded room and rescue her. He took her by the arm and led her off a few steps.

"Instead of the first dance it seems I shall have the last!" he said.

"I'm sorry, Jimmy," she apologized. "Mr. Brummell swept me onto the floor and before I could recover Sir Orville had me out there again!"

"I saw his shameless capering," Jimmy said fiercely. "He made it plain to everyone he is drooling over you!"

"Jimmy!" she reproved him.

"You shall pay penance by dancing with me alone for the rest of the evening," the young dandy told her.

"I'm not used to such excitement and exertion. I shall probably faint in your arms!" she warned him.

He led her out onto the floor again, saying, "In that case I shall carry you off to a secret place!"

"You wouldn't dare!"

"Try me!" he begged her with a smile.

Happily Jimmy was a less energetic dancer than Sir Orville and so she did not tire as she had feared. They had several dances in succession. Then he took her aside and they went to the adjoining room where servants behind a long table were serving punch. He went and got a glass for her and himself.

He said, "Dancing is good exercise. Almost as good as fencing."

She asked, "Are you a swordsman?"

"I fear not," Fitzroy said. "I have little interest in it. Though a gentleman must know how to handle a blade. I learned enough to use one properly. But I'm by no means an expert."

"Does Mr. Brummell fence?"

"He can. He's very good as a matter of fact," Fitzroy said. "But he never touches a sword. He is continually having quarrels with people and insulting or making fun of them. If he indulged in fencing he would be challenged to a duel every second day."

Julia sipped her wine. "He is prudent then. The last thing I would expect of him."

"Much more prudent than someone like myself," Jimmy said. "Yet when it comes to speech he is the most imprudent man I know."

"Perhaps that is a pose," she said. "He keeps insulting people because he thinks he is expected to do it."

"He enjoys it in any case," Jimmy said finishing his drink.

She gave him a knowing look. "Mr. Brummell didn't sound too happy about you. He said you two were once friends."

"That describes it," Jimmy said. "And don't ask me for any more details."

Julia had wanted to ask but now knew that it would do no good. There had been something magical for her in the company of the famous dandy. Just being with him for that short time had excited her and made her feel that she would very much like to know him better. But she could not see herself having any luck with him when he had the pick of London's society ladies at his feet.

Elizabeth came up rather breathlessly, hand in hand with her husband-to-be. She said, "You're the belle of the ball, Julia. Everyone is talking about you. And of Beau bringing you in to dance."

Julia laughed, "That was mostly by chance. He took pity on me."

"From what I saw he showed a good deal more

interest than that," Elizabeth told her. And then, "Gerry wants to dance with you!"

The bronzed young man showed a good-natured smile on his squarish face and said, "I can ask for myself. May I have this dance, Miss Crawford?"

"Julia, please," she begged him. "I'm to be a bridesmaid at your wedding."

"Of course. Elizabeth says you're her best friend," the young man agreed as they walked out to the dance floor.

"I hear you travel a lot. That you are an avid racing fan."

He glanced at her. "I suppose Elizabeth told you that."

"Yes."

Gerry shrugged at the entrance to the ballroom. "You know she doesn't approve. She has no interest in horses or racing. I fear it means that after we are married I shall have to often leave her alone."

"You place your racing before your marriage?"

"It isn't a question of that," the young man explained. "I have large investments in my stables. I need to watch over them."

"You must make that clear to her," she advised. "And don't leave her alone too often!"

The pleasant Gerry laughed easily, "You are giving me advice. I like that from one so young and lovely."

"I'm thinking how I might feel in the same position," she said. "I'm anxious not to see Elizabeth hurt."

"Thank you," the young man said sincerely. "I admire your frank style, Julia. Elizabeth is lucky to have such a friend."

Their dance over they returned to Elizabeth and Jimmy. They were in earnest conversation about the situation on the Continent. There had been new rumors that Napoleon was plotting an invasion of England.

Jimmy smiled at Gerry and asked, "What about you, Gerry? Going to join your old regiment?"

The sturdily built Gerry shook his head. "No. I resigned my commission some time ago."

"And so did I," Jimmy laughed. "We may not have the best of sense but we know better than stay in the army at a time like this."

Elizabeth turned to Gerry and said, "I agree with Jimmy. Why should the best of London's fashionable young men go off to die miserably somewhere on the Continent?"

Julia was shocked by the path the conversation had taken. She stared at the elegantly clad trio and said, "If all our Englishmen felt as you do we would not be so freely enjoying ourselves here tonight."

"I dare say we should do as well under old Boney," Jimmy said lightly. "In spite of his difficult habit of conquering everyone he has an eye for pretty women and a taste for good wine."

"No one can accuse you of being patriotic," Julia said with some scorn.

Jimmy teased her, "I know what Julia is thinking. She is mooning about a village lad who was so reckless as to enlist in the army to win his fortune! Can you imagine anything so idiotic?"

Julia was angry. She said, "I cannot forgive that!" And she turned and moved away.

The first to follow after her and apologize was young Sir Gerald Giles. He touched her arm and with a serious look on his face, he said, "You were quite right. We were talking in a disgraceful fashion. You did well to reprimand us!"

Elizabeth next joined her and said, "I'm sorry. I'm sure none of us meant anything."

A shame-faced Jimmy Fitzroy was the last to come up to her and say, "My apologies! I had little right to criticize someone I've never met to cover my own cowardice."

Julia gave him a meaningful look. "As long as you really believe that!"

"Of course I do!" he said with another of his fetching smiles. "And now it is back to the dance!"

She allowed him to lead her out to the dance floor

and danced with him. But as she danced she began to question all that was going on around her. Wonder about these people and this glittering party? It struck her that they were involved in a decadent kind of make-believe. Living in a world of their own creation. And that she was really an alien in this world.

As Jimmy led her off the floor she was bothered by the sight of Sir Orville coming towards them. But he was not in an ugly-looking mood. For once the long-nosed man seemed in good humor.

Coming up to her, he said, "My dear, Christopher Pratt and I are showing his painting of you to a friend of my old friends. They have asked to see you close by your likeness. Will you be so good as to join me?"

She protested but Sir Orville insisted. With a wry smile of parting, she left Jimmy and let the excited Sir Orville almost drag her across the ballroom to the small adjoining room where the partially completed painting was on an easel.

She said, "Really, this is embarrassing for me."

Sir Orville held on to her and said, "Never be ashamed of your beauty."

Christopher Pratt and several elderly men were standing before the easel. When Sir Orville brought her in, the little artist came to her smiling and said, "This is the young lady! And you must admit I have a most unusual model!"

The others murmured approvingly and Sir Orville then introduced her to each of them. Sir Orville was touching his hand on her back when it wasn't necessary and generally making her uneasy. He told the assembly, "When this painting is completed it will hang in my study where I can constantly see it!"

He had no sooner finished speaking than a cool voice from behind said, "The painting should be auctioned and sold to the highest bidder! And I warn you gentlemen, I will outbid what ever offer is made!" Julia turned in surprise to see Beau Brummell who had come in unobserved and now dominated the room.

Chapter Four

The unexpected appearance of the elegant Beau Brummell and his startling announcement caught everyone by surprise. Sir Orville stood with his silver-haired friends and gazed in outraged silence at the famous dandy. Little Christopher Pratt offered an uncomfortable smile. Julia turned to Brummell with an amused expression on her pretty face. She had not wanted this business of showing her painting in the first place. It was Sir Orville who'd insisted on it for his own devious satisfaction and now he was himself being made uncomfortable. She didn't mind at all!

The middle-aged host finally found his voice and in an angry tone, declared, "Let me inform you, Mr. Brummell, I have commissioned this portrait. It will not be put up for auction and it is not for sale!"

Brummell eyed Sir Orville with a kind of contempt, saying "You are going to keep it for yourself?"

"That is correct, sir," Sir Orville snapped.

"What a waste of beauty," Brummell said and then turning to her, he continued, "If I'm to be deprived of the likeness at least let me enjoy the original. May I escort you to the buffet table, my dear?"

Glad of an excuse to escape, she said, "Thank you, Mr. Brummell!" And she told Sir Orville and his elderly friends, "Please excuse us!"

With that Brummell led her out of the room and across the ballroom to another area where a sumptuous buffet table had been set out and the guests were already lining up.

The tall, handsome man gazed down at her and said, "I have a confession to make. I never eat at these affairs."

"But you said?" she replied in a puzzled tone.

"I wished to rescue you from that scoundrel Sir Orville and his slobbering companions," he said airily.

She laughed. "I did truly wish to be rescued."

"You are a beauty," he told her. "And of spotless reputation. London will be difficult for you. Our dandies can not believe that a female might prefer a good reputation to a good time!"

"You are making fun of me," she protested.

"I'm perfectly serious," he insisted. "Look about you, this is a hateful society. A moral swamp in which one man's pleasure is too often another man's wife."

Julia admitted, "After hearing some of the conversations I have been concerned about the values of many of these people."

"You are caught between two threats," he told her. "Sir Orville is one and James Fitzroy the other. I warn you there is much gossip about him."

She gave him a challenging look. "There is also a lot of gossip about you!"

"Indeed?"

"It is said you take hours to dress and change your clothing at least three times a day. And that you employ at least a dozen tailors!"

He sighed. "That is nonsense! One dislikes gossip when it is about one's self."

Julia said, "I see you as a brilliant man as well as a handsome one. And I think it worthwhile that you do set standards of proper dress. Your good example may live long beyond you."

Beau Brummell looked pleased. "You have intelligence to match your beauty. That is rare. I should like to talk with you further but I must be going. I have another urgent appointment."

"You really must leave?"

"Yes," he said. "I shall say goodnight to Lady Jane and go. But I would like to continue our conversation.

I'm having some friends to tea tomorrow afternoon at four in my lodgings. I would like to introduce you to them. Would you be so kind as to favor me with your presence?"

She smiled. "I think I should like that. I'm sure your friends must be interesting."

"A few are perfect dolts, but their lack of brains is balanced by the size of their fortunes," Brummell said. "I will be expecting you, my dear." He bent low and kissed her hand and then left to seek out Lady Jane.

Julia watched after him with a strange mixture of feelings. Somehow he was closer to her than anyone else at the party. She could not quite understand the empathy between them. But she saw that beneath the veneer of coldness and dandyism, there was warmth, shrewdness and kindness. All qualities which she appreciated. She knew Sir Orville would rage and Jimmy Fitzroy would complain but she was determined to accept the famous man's invitation and attend his tea party.

Her thoughts were interrupted by the arrival of Jimmy Fitzroy. He said, "I've been looking for you."

She turned to him with a small smile. "I was saying goodnight to Mr. Brummell. He's leaving early."

Jimmy eyed her with suspicion. "It seems to me you're disappointed about his going."

"I do wish he'd been able to stay. I find him brilliant."

The young dandy frowned. "It is a charade he performs for every pretty girl he meets. He'll shower you with flattery but it ends there. Beau has no place in his life for a woman, he is too much in love with himself."

"I can't believe that!"

"It is true," Fitzroy said bitterly. "I have known him to use women to further his plans but never to care for them."

Her eyes met his. "What spoiled your friendship with Mr. Brummell?"

He looked away. "Our quarrel was silly. I told you it is nothing I wish to discuss. Let me take you to the buffet table."

The rest of the evening was routine. It was long after midnight when the last of the party guests left. The great house was littered with the debris of the exciting event and both Lady Jane and Sir Orville were weary enough to hurry off to bed. Julia found herself surprisingly fresh after the long evening and looking forward to her visit to Beau Brummell the following afternoon.

Lady Jane slept late the next morning and had breakfast served in her bedroom. Julia arrived just as the older woman was having tea. Lady Jane waved her to sit down in a chair by the bed.

The older woman said, "I feel the party was a great success and that everyone was charmed by you."

"Thank you," she said.

Lady Jane gazed at her from the bed, where she'd stacked pillows to allow her to sit up comfortably. She said, "Your blue dress was just right. And you seemed to make a really strong impression on Mr. Brummell."

Seated there in her dressing gown, she blushed and confided, "I much enjoyed him. And he has asked me to call on him today at four. He is giving a tea party. May I have the use of the carriage?"

Lady Jane showed concern. "You know Sir Orville will not approve."

"That is why I have first spoken to you," she said.

The older woman sighed. "My husband can be ridiculous in his dislikes. I cannot think why he hates Mr. Brummell. But he does."

"Perhaps because Mr. Brummell is young, popular with the ladies and has a biting tongue."

"I expect that is probably true," Lady Jane said. "Do you truly wish to attend this party?"

"I think I might gain by it. Mr. Brummell seems a very wise man."

"I know him in a most casual way," Lady Jane said. "My knowledge of him is mostly through gossip."

"And they can be so unfair!"

"I realize that," the woman in the bed said. Then she smiled one of her rare smiles and told her, "I'm sure we can arrange for a carriage to take you there and back."

"You are too kind to me!"

"Nonsense! You have brought youth and lightness to this rather gloomy, old house. Just don't mention it to Sir Orville. There are some things it is best not to tell him."

She rose to leave. "I understand."

"And I need not remind you to always be careful about finding yourself alone in his company. He is a strange person. Sometimes he allows his emotions to undo him."

"I know," she said quietly.

Tiny spots of crimson showed on the thin cheeks of the mistress of the house. "I'm sure Elizabeth has confided to you of her difficulties with him in the past."

By careful planning Julia was able to avoid Sir Orville in the hours which followed. She was anxious to get away from the house without his being aware of it. In the early afternoon Elizabeth arrived for a short visit and they both went up to Julia's room where they could talk freely.

"What a wonderful party!" Elizabeth said standing by the window in her wide-brimmed straw hat and brown linen dress. She slipped her white gloves from her hands and smiled. "Weren't you exhausted this morning?"

"I didn't feel too badly," she said. "I've even accepted an invitation to a gathering at Mr. Brummell's this afternoon."

Her friend's pretty mouth gaped open. "Brummell has actually invited you to his place?"

"Yes."

"You know he might try to seduce you?"

Her eyes twinkled. "After enduring Sir Orville I can risk that."

"I mean it," her friend insisted. "You may find him there alone with evil intentions. He is a bachelor with the name of being a womanizer."

"My invitation is for a tea party not a seduction," Julia told her.

"I hope it turns out that way."

"I'm sure it will. I have every respect for Mr. Brummell."

Her auburn-haired friend came over to where she was seated and with a wise look said, "Why don't you ask Jimmy Fitzroy what he and Brummell quarreled about? Fitzroy was one of the Beau's cronies and now he can't say anything bad enough about him."

"I've asked," she said. "He won't tell me anything."

"Gentlemen's agreement," her friend said bitterly. "These men protect the reputations of their male friends but when it comes to women they tattle every time."

"I've no intention of telling Jimmy Fitzroy about the visit and I'm also keeping it a secret from Sir Orville. I told Lady Jane and she is arranging the carriage for me."

Elizabeth said, "I'd like to see Sir Orville's face when he finds out."

"I expect he shall," Julia admitted. "But that will come later."

"Jimmy Fitzroy won't be happy if he hears. Especially since you are trying to keep it from him," her friend ventured.

"I'll deal with that when the times comes," Julia said firmly.

"So you intend to go?"

"Yes."

Elizabeth leaned close and kissed her. "Then I won't stay and keep you from dressing. Good luck and promise to tell me all about it."

Julia rose to see her friend on her way. "I don't think it will be anything eventful."

Elizabeth put on her gloves. "Gerry likes you. You ought to be flattered. He thinks most of my friends vapid and silly."

"I'm glad," she said. "I also like him."

"He can be difficult," Elizabeth sighed. "But perhaps he will improve with marriage."

"I'm sure he will," Julia said. Though privately she knew she had rarely seen this happen.

Left alone she selected a favorite gown of purple and a golden bonnet with long strings of the same color. She also was careful to choose a delicate, almost odorless perfume and made up very little. She did not feel the need at her age.

Lady Jane arranged for the carriage to be brought quietly around to the side entrance of Hewitt House. It happened that Sir Orville was out somewhere so there was no danger of his causing any problem. The older woman checked on Julia's dress and approved. She wished her well and waited to wave the carriage on its way.

Julia felt terribly important. A few months ago she had been an unknown country girl in a Surrey parsonage. Now she was on her way to visit one of the most famous men in London in her own carriage. She sat up proudly as the vehicle rolled through the cobblestoned streets. All the houses of the gentry were in the same section of the great city between Regent's Park and St. James Street and so they could visit and carry on with living without seeing any of the hideous slums she had witnessed on her first entry to the metropolis.

Here in this area of the homes of the elite it was all order with many of the streets tree-lined and some green grass to be seen almost everywhere. The few work wagons that went by invaded the district for a short time only. This was a special contained world. And much of it revolved around the figure of Prince George.

Brummell's house turned out to be quite ordinary

with a red brick front and gray stone steps. Its windows
were tall and regularly set out. Other fine carriages
waited in the street before the house. The coachman
helped her down onto the cobblestoned street. She
asked him to wait for her and rather nervously made
her way to the sidewalk and the entrance to the house.

An elderly manservant in livery answered the door
and ushered her in. Beau Brummell came rushing down
the dark, wood-panelled hallway to meet her. He was
wearing a blue coat and fawn trousers and a distinctive
checkered waistcoat. At his neck was the usual elon-
gated white cravat which looked well on him.

He took her hand and gazed at her fondly. "My dear
Miss Crawford! You did decide to come! I was afraid
you wouldn't."

She smiled at him. "I wanted to come."

"Delighted to have you!" the dandy said. "Our party
is mostly male and a pretty female will brighten it a
good deal. You may find some of these people rather
tiresome but for one reason or another they are my
friends!"

He escorted her into the drawing room where at least
a dozen or so men and women were standing around or
seated. They were in several small groups and Brummell moved from one to the other introducing her.

The names were familiar to her. There was Lady
Holland, a pleasant woman of dubious age, said to be
the most famous hostess in all London. Lady Copland,
a blond beauty not much older than herself. Lord
Alvaney, a genial old man whose passion was pretending to be a coachman, and who often paid to take the
place of the regular drivers on regular coach runs.

As Brummell led her away from the old man, the
dandy murmured, "It is a cult! Fellows like Alvaney try
to imitate coachmen in dress, speech and manner. A
case of too much wealth and idle time along with a taste
for the vulgar!"

"This is Skiffy," he said introducing her to a foppish

fellow exuding a smell of perfume and wearing a purple jacket and white breeches of satin. "He hopes to write better plays than Sheridan but I feel the odds are all with Richard."

"Fie on you, Beau!" The satin clad man giggled. "You must not pay too much attention to this cynic!"

"I shall try not to," she said.

The man standing with the would be playwright bowed and with a smile on his lean, lined face said, "I shall introduce myself. I am Lord Petersham."

Beau Brummell chuckled, "My one rival when it comes to collecting snuff boxes. Would you believe it this fellow has a different snuff box for every day of the year!"

Lord Petersham said seriously, "It is most practical! One should select a snuffbox to suit the weather. I'd never risk a cold by using a light snuffbox in an East wind!"

Brummell moved her on across the room to where a man clad all in green and a stout, elegantly-dressed gentleman stood talking seriously before the fireplace.

Brummell told her in a low aside, "The fellow in green is Henry Cope of Brighton. He wears only green. His entire wardrobe is of green clothing. And the stout man with him is the Prince."

She gasped. "The Prince! Here as your guest?"

"Why not?" Brummell asked casually. "George and I are close friends. You must meet him."

So she found herself red-faced and tense being introduced to the paunchy Prince. George had a genial smile on his puffy, purple face. His hair was thick, parted on the left, and of a light brown shade. His eyes shrewd and friendly as she curtisied before him.

"No homage required here, my girl," he said smiling, his manner bluff and open, his voice loud. "I hear you were the most beautiful girl at the ball last night!"

She blushed. "Someone is given to flattery!"

"I take credit for the statement," Beau Brummell said airily. "As to flattery, I do not indulge in it. I'm forever critical! I distrust those who flatter, they resemble friends as wolves do dogs!"

"Gad, Beau, that is very good!" the Prince exclaimed, bursting into laughter. "He is sharp, Miss Crawford. I warn you of that!"

Brummell easily led her away from the royal personage and his friend dressed in green, saying, "George is well-meaning but he sometimes continues conversation when he no longer has anything to say!"

Julia laughed discreetly behind her fan. And in a low voice said, "You are a wicked man to talk so about your friend the Prince."

"I adore the fellow," the elegant Brummell said seriously. "But that does not mean I'm blind to his weaknesses. And he has many, including an amazingly quick temper."

She studied the Prince from their safe distance by the windows of the drawing room and said, "He is inclined to weight."

"Don't ever say that before him," her companion warned. "He is most concerned about his poundage. Yet he will indulge himself with food and drink."

Julia confessed, "I'm very tense in this company."

"No need to be," Brummell said. "I value your presence more than any of them. And I want you to remain for a little after they have left."

She lifted her eyebrows. "I would be scandalized if I remained!"

"Nonsense!" the tall, handsome man said with good humor. "Assembled here are the most liberal-minded group in all London, and the most tight-lipped. Their own lives are so scandalous they dare not think of discussing those of others."

The talk was mostly of parties, gambling and horses. She learned that Brummell's pet dog was temporarily in the country at the home of his good friend the Duchess of York. She found that Lady Holland and the Prince both enjoyed teasing Brummell about his insistence on perfection in clothing.

At one point a mocking Lady Holland asked him, "Is it true that the only person who can do your wash to your taste lives in distant Canterbury?"

"Wrong, madam," Brummell replied with pretended gravity. "The only washerwoman I fully trust lives in Liverpool. I send my things back and forth by coach!"

The Prince roared with laughter and pointing at Brummell continued to tease him, asking, "What about your cleaning your boots in champagne?"

"A silly rumor, Sire," Brummell said drolly. "I use nothing but the finest brandy!"

Lord Skeffington, the perfumed fop, she'd met as "Skiffy" tried, "Beau, I heard that you require three people to make your gloves!"

"Not so, Skiffy," Brummell replied with a smile. "The man who requires that is Squire Asquith of Dover. And only because the poor chap was born with three hands!"

This brought another burst of laughter and so the afternoon went on with banter, teasing and occasionally some frank expressions of wisdom. Julia was enchanted by it all. They did not expect her to be one of them and she was quite content to be an onlooker.

As the afternoon moved on the guests began to leave. The Prince was the first to go, then Skiffy, and after that Lady Holland and the others. Finally she and Brummell were alone. He brought her a glass of champagne and one for himself and indicating a nearby love seat, suggested, "Let us sit here and converse."

She smilingly accepted the champagne and sat down. "I should not have more. I've already had several. I'm not accustomed to champagne or to drinking in the afternoon."

He leaned back and studied her. "Not everyone is witty, nor are many as bright as you. You will learn that to make a success of little gatherings like this afternoon there must be a liberal offering of champagne."

"I have never had a more amusing time," she said. "At least, not at a party."

"Thank you," the elegant Brummell said. "I fear for

myself it has all become a repetition. That is why the youth and freshness of someone like you is so welcome."

She eyed him over her champagne glass. "You are not all that old!"

"You think not!"

"No. I'm sure it is a pose with you!"

"I'm a good deal older than you."

"It is fitting that a female seek out older male companions," she said seriously. "We have much to learn from you."

"Thank you," he said dryly. "But I do not presume to be your schoolmaster."

She blushed. "I did not mean that! I find you charming, handsome, intelligent! Everything I have imagined a fine man to be."

"I have deceived you with my talent for acting," he said quietly.

"I think not!" she said.

"If Sir Orville Hewitt were to describe me, he would say I am a witless, profligate dandy! A parasite of the prince!"

"Sir Orville is not a reliable authority."

Brummell smiled. "Except on tampering with under age females! You know his reputation?"

"I hide from him regularly."

He laughed at this. And then he said. "Let us talk of more serious things. What are your plans for the future?"

"I do not honestly know," she said. "I would like to wed one day, have a good husband and a home of my own."

"All commendable," he said.

"Why do you ask?"

The elegant Beau moved closer and placed an arm around her. "Because I must warn you that you'll find none of these things with Jimmy Fitzroy!"

"You hate him?" she said with awe. "And he was once your friend."

"That may be the reason I hate him more," he said.

"Tell me why?"

"I cannot," he said. "I ask only that you trust me. I'm giving you my best advice."

"Sir Orville dislikes him as well. But then he hates anyone who shows an interest in me," she said ruefully.

"He is right in this case," Brummell said. "Has Fitzroy ever made you any serious offer?"

She hesitated. Then, she said, "Yes. He has asked me to marry him."

"What was your reply?"

"That I was not ready to give him any answer. I was too new to London and this way of life."

Brummell nodded approvingly. "Keep to that!"

She looked at him with troubled eyes. "In Surrey I gave my word to marry a village lad who went off to join the army. I'm sure I loved him as much as anyone I will ever meet. But it seems he is lost to me. He has not tried to write me."

Sadly the man at her side told her, "Childhood romances seldom develop as one expects. I do not speak lightly of them, but it seems the way of the world that young lovers drift apart."

She rose quickly. "I must go! Lady Jane conspired to arrange this carriage for me. I will be truly scandalized if I'm late arriving home and Sir Orville raises a storm!"

He stood smiling down at her in gentle manner. And in a voice which contained a tone of mild surprise, he said, "I don't want you to leave."

"I must!" she said, her heart beat increasing in quite a startling fashion.

He seemed astonished by his own behavior. "I want to protect you," he said with awe. "I want you here with me. And I have not felt such things in a world of time!"

Her cheeks burned. "Mr. Brummell!"

"Beau," he said softly, his eyes fixed on her. "I hate myself for admitting this to you. I have fallen most hopelessly in love with you, my darling child!"

The champagne and the stunning surprise of his

words, made her unbelieveably frank as she gazed at him with happy tears in her eyes and whispered, "And, I with you, sir!"

He drew her to him and his lips carressed hers. And after their kisses he continued to hold her close and she heard him offer a great sigh. After that he let her go and touched his left hand to his temple and looked troubled.

"Forgive me," he begged her. "I have misbehaved."

"No! You have made me most happy!"

"I'm old enough to have fathered you! I have no right!"

"Age should not enter into love," she replied. "I'm grateful and proud of your words to me."

There was infinite sadness in his handsome face and he said, "I promise you I meant them all. But I did not mean to offer them so boorishly. We will meet soon again and talk of this more. Now let me see you to your carriage."

He escorted her to the street and her carriage. At its door he bowed with a meaningful look for her and pressed his lips to the back of her hand. Then he helped her into the carriage and stood there, looking lonely and troubled, waving as the carriage moved away.

Julia did not know quite what to make of her mood as the carriage took her back to Hewitt House. On the one hand she was proud and happy that a man so famous as Beau Brummell should have declared his love for her. At the same time she worried that the new relationship which this would mean could bring both of them sadness.

She had noted his almost instant regret after he had voiced his love for her. And she could only interpret this as meaning there was some barrier between them. In female fashion she wondered if the barrier might be another woman. Perhaps the Duchess of York whom he visited so often and who was openly rumored to be his mistress. Or was it something else, his profligate way of life which he had no intention of abandoning for any love?

He had become famous as a cynic and dandy. His role did not fit that of a dutiful husband. And so, though he might love her, it was extremely unlikely that she could truly hope to win him. Unless, and this was all important, she could make him come to value her above all else.

Sir Orville was waiting in the reception hall when she arrived. He was in one of his worst tempers and a nervous Lady Jane stood in the background. He asked Julia angrily, "Did you have to remain at Elizabeth's so late?"

Julia glanced quickly at Lady Jane, who nodded lightly so that she would understand.

Boldly, she said, "We were discussing the wedding plans. Time went quickly. All the bridesmaids were there and several of them asked about you and commented on your charm at the party last night!"

Sir Orville's weakly handsome face slowly lost its anger and he looked mollified. He said, "I'm happy to hear that I'm not seen by everyone as a dotard! I shall forgive you this time. But Lady Jane was most concerned about you. Up the stairs and change for dinner!"

"Thank you sir," Julia said with a small smile and hurried on upstairs.

Julia spent the evening in a kind of ecstatic rapture as she recalled the scene at Beau Brummell's. She could not doubt his love for her and she now realized that she had fallen in love with him. Jimmy Fitzroy's offer of marriage had not touched her to the same degree. And the warmth she'd felt for youthful John Lane had been a childish thing, and this romance was lost to her in any case.

She fell asleep warmed by the remembrance of the afternoon. And when she went downstairs the next morning she found that a messenger had come bringing her a gift box. She opened it and found inside a delightful bunch of delicately scented white violets. She did not need any enclosed card to know who had sent them.

Lady Jane joined her in time to see the violets and exclaimed, "How lovely! From an admirer?"

Julia smiled. "From someone."

"Jimmy Fitzroy, I vow," the older woman said at once. Her pale face showed excitement, "Perhaps you will be the next after Elizabeth to marry."

"I hardly think so," she said, not daring to say where she thought the violets had come from.

The same messenger brought the same bouquet to her for the next three mornings. And on the fourth morning the elderly manservant of Brummell came with a message for her. It suggested that she join him for a ride in the park that afternoon. She wrote her acceptance and sent it back to Brummell.

So at three o'clock on that sunny afternoon she found herself seated beside Beau in the same spot where the Prince usually sat. The carriage was well known to everyone and she was aware of the attention they were drawing from the other carriages and the common folk strolling alongside the carriage lane.

Brummell smiled at her and placed a hand on hers as he said, "You know what this means? You'll be put down as my latest conquest."

Deliciously happy, she eyed him with a merry twinkle and said pointedly, "And you as mine!"

"Excellent!" he exclaimed in delight. "You have the right sort of wit. You make an apt pupil!"

"And so handsome a teacher!"

He sighed. "I have thought much about the other afternoon."

"Yes."

"I meant all I said. I surely love you."

"Though you wish you didn't?" she prompted him.

The handsome Brummell showed a melancholy yet humorous look on his classic face. He said, "I fear I have met my match."

"You have!" she assured him. "And I do not mean to let you go lightly."

"So be it!" he said as they rode on, ignoring the crowds or the carriages as they passed. "We are in love!

I trust we always shall be! I shall see that you become the most popular young woman in all London."

"Not necessary," she shook her head. "I only wish to be first with you."

"You are!"

"And the Duchess of York?"

"An old friend," he said at once. "Our relationship has nothing to do with my feelings about you."

She looked directly into his eyes and said quietly, "I believe you."

"But you must not hope for more," he told her. "My life style does not leave room for a wife or marriage. I could not be fair to any wife."

She said, "Because of your dedication to fashion?"

"Partly that. I sometimes take several hours to dress. And I have need to change my costume three times in a day and night to match the social occasions on which I have to be present."

"Dandyism is your career."

"Grant me more than that," he pleaded. "Believe that I wish to set a certain life style which if given enough attention will be followed by others. I believe a value of proper style in living can only lead to an improvement in character."

She said, "That is most pompous, Mr. Brummell!"

"You mock me!"

She laughed. "Only to a point. All you say may be right. But why be a martyr to such a cause? You have a right to live a normal, happy life."

"I'm also Chief Jester to the Prince," he reminded her. "A role which takes more of my time than you might imagine."

"That could end one day."

He looked alarmed. "Say not so! If the Prince ever turns on me my creditors would move in swiftly. I would be ruined!"

"So we come to another thing," she said. "Your gambling, your reckless spending. You should show more judgement."

He chuckled. "You already sound like a wife."

"I hope to be one."

"You say that to make me jealous and miserable," he said. "But I shall keep you so busy with parties you will soon forget this painful ambition!"

It seemed that he appeared dedicated to doing just that. From that afternoon on he became her regular companion. She was his hostess at many of the small gatherings at his flat, and she decorated his arm on many public occasions. This had the result of making both Sir Orville and Jimmy Fitzroy terribly angry.

Lady Jane worried, "I do not think you ought to be seen so often in Mr. Brummell's company. It is causing a great deal of talk!"

"I do not wish to embarrass you," Julia replied. "But he and the Prince seem to have taken a liking to me. I expect that my naiveté amuses them."

Lady Jane worked her hands together nervously. "I'm quite content about it. And I shall stress to Sir Orville that the Prince has especially asked you to be present at the various parties."

She did this and so managed to hold an angry Sir Orville in rein. At the same time on several occasions he managed to get Julia alone and make nasty insinuations. By his reckoning she had long ago graced the beds of the Prince and Brummell and he could not understand why she wouldn't offer him her favors.

"Lady Jane need never know," he whispered to her urgently.

Pale and tense, she said, "I have no idea what you mean, sir."

His face turned purple angry. "It would seem I'm not regal enough for your tastes!" And he strode off in a rage.

James Fitzroy was not much easier to deal with. They both attended Elizabeth's wedding and the reception after it. During the reception he took Julia outside to the garden and began to talk of their seeing so little of each other.

She said, "I have been busy. I read a good deal to Lady Jane. And she has assigned me supervision of some of the household duties."

Young Fitzroy shook his head. "Don't lie to me!"

She halted and said, "Why do you speak to me like that?"

"I know what is going on!"

"I do not follow you," she told him. "And it is time we returned to the others."

"No," he said, an ugly light in his eyes as he seized her roughly by the arm. "You will stay here and listen!"

"You're hurting my arm!" she protested, trying to free herself of him.

"I mean to," was his grim reply as he kept the unrelenting grip on her.

"Please!"

"Listen to me," he said angrily. "You aren't deceiving me or anyone else. All London is talking! It is Brummell!"

"Beau and I are good friends! That is all!"

"I question that. Remember I know Beau well!"

She tried to pull away from him. "I will scream if you continue! I do not care whether the wedding party be spoiled or not."

He at once released her and showed himself penitent. Abjectly, he said, "Forgive me! It is only because I care so!"

She was now flushed with rage of her own. "You have a fine way of showing it!"

"I cannot help myself at times," he said, full of contrition. "I'm madly in love with you. I have asked you to marry me. Why will you not give me an answer?"

She did not wish to risk another scene so she said, "This is neither the time nor the place. We must go back inside!" And she hurried on ahead towards the stone mansion where the wedding party was still in progress.

Chapter Five

Elizabeth and her new husband Sir Gerald Giles had taken a house in Grosvenor Street. Unfortunately Sir Gerald continued his racing interests and so left his young bride at home alone a good deal. It was only natural that the auburn-haired girl should resent this and complain about her unhappiness to her friends.

Julia, as the young woman's closest friend, often called on her. But she worried that Elizabeth was becoming neurotic about her plight. It was on one of these typical afternoon visits that Elizabeth shocked her by tackling her about her friendship with Beau Brummell.

Seated in the sewing room behind closed doors, so that the servants would not overhear their conversation, the two young women talked frankly.

"Gerald is neglecting me!" Elizabeth said, sitting primly in a high-backed chair by the window. "I do not know whether it is for his racing or for some other female. But I cannot close my eyes to it any longer."

Seated across from her, Julia attempted to placate her by saying, "But you ought not to be surprised. He told you before you were married that he had this interest in racing and owned a great many stables. You cannot expect him to neglect them if only for financial reasons."

Looking hurt, Elizabeth pouted, "If he cares for his investments more than he does me, it is surely not comforting. Marriage is not what I expected at all. I must say I have found it most disappointing."

"I'm sure if you show patience it will work out," Julia said, in an attempt to make her friend feel better.

Instead of being appreciative Elizabeth turned on her and said sharply, "You mean as you have been toward Beau Brummell?"

Surprised, she said, "I do not follow you."

"Surely he is taking his time about deciding to marry you!" her friend said with sarcasm.

"He never made any promise to marry me," Julia replied quietly.

"But you expected he would! And now you've been seen in his company for more than a year! You must know that people are talking!"

"Let them talk!"

"Your behavior is the scandal of London," Elizabeth went on, seeming to enjoy condemning her. "You cannot expect to keep your reputation if your close friendship continues with him."

"I certainly hope it will!"

Elizabeth shrugged and smiled. "So you are willing to share him with the Duchess of York and Harriete Wilson!"

"Our friendship is a special thing," Julia said carefully. "I have never surrendered to him physically nor has he asked it. So in that sense I share him with no one!"

Her friend smiled grimly. "You may expect me to believe that, but not others. I assure you the majority view is that you and he are lovers. And it is with the Duchess and that courtesan that he usually is linked!"

"Courtesan?"

"Harriete Wilson who with her sisters Amy and Fanny run the most opulent bawdy house in all England. Not only the Prince, but Beau Brummell and most of the dandies spend many of their leisure hours in the arms of the prostitutes there. James Fitzroy's name has also been mentioned along with that of Harriete Wilson."

"I have not seen Jimmy for a long while," Julia said.

"I know," her friend said. "He has visited me and spoken angrily of your treatment of him."

"Beau does not like him. He has forbidden me to be seen with him."

"So Mr. Brummell wishes to have a husbandly authority over you without the problem of having to marry you!" Elizabeth said acidly.

Julia fought fo keep her temper. In a quiet voice, she said, "That is utter nonsense! He simply thinks that Jimmy is an unreliable person and might do a danger to me."

"A danger?"

"Yes. Jimmy has been described to me by Beau as having a cruel temper."

"He is enraged at your deserting him for Brummell. And he says Brummell will never marry."

"I do not mind," she said. "I have known that from the beginning. I find Beau the most interesting man in London. I have learned much from being with him."

"Most people think him an idiotic dandy! I have ruined my life in one way and you are doing it in another!"

"Do not say such things!" she admonished her friend. "I know you are still in love with Gerald and do not mean to leave him. And I, for my part, am enjoying myself thoroughly."

"I wonder that Sir Orville and Lady Hewitt encourage your being seen with Brummell," Elizabeth sniffed.

"Lady Hewitt realizes it is innocent enough and she loves to hear my stories about the Prince and Beau's other friends."

"No doubt she is satisfied to have you interested in a man and out of Sir Orville's reach. I imagine he still tries to make you his conquest!"

Julia said, "He is not likely to change. But I have learned to better manage him. So I do not feel so defenceless with him these days."

Elizabeth lifted her small chin pertly to observe, "I have heard he is trying hard to become one of the

Prince's inner group. No doubt he has heard tales of their gross orgies and wishes to be part of them."

Julia smiled. "Gossip exaggerates much that happens! I can promise you the Prince is more interested in gambling than in most anything else. So, unhappily, is Beau."

"You do not consider gambling a sin?"

"I cannot condone it," Julia admitted. "But there are surely many worse vices. Beau has promised that he will take me to White's tomorrow night."

"White's in St. James Street?" her friend exclaimed in amazement. "But that is a known gambling place and women are forbidden to enter there."

"Beau has been president of Witier's for years and has also frequented White's a good deal. The manager of White's is known to him and as a favor has given permission for me to visit the place."

"You cannot!"

"Why?"

"Your reputation will surely be in shreds if you do! They will think you a fast woman from the Wilsons' house!" Elizabeth warned her.

Julia laughed. "That is utterly ridiculous. Beau has made the arrangements and I mean to go with him. I think it stupid to miss such an experience because of convention."

"And you are the little country girl I befriended when you first appeared in London!"

"Years ago!"

"And years of change!" Elizabeth said. "In a little more than a short number of months you have become the protege of Brummell and the queen of his set! While I sit here and languish for my missing husband!"

"You may come with me if you like! As my chaperone!"

"Not likely!" Elizabeth declared. "I value my good name. Lady Castlereagh has asked me to join Almack's. It is the fine London ladies club. No person of commerce may join. And not only must male guests have skill in dancing they must wear knee breeches and white cravats. One night the Duke of Wellington was turned away because he happened to be wearing trousers. A ball and a supper are given each week during the season."

Julia rose. "It sounds most impressive but I prefer to settle for my one visit to White's!"

Elizabeth stood to see her out. "And the notoriety? Are you willing to bear that?"

She smiled. "I enjoy that already if what you say is true, my dear Elizabeth."

The auburn-haired young woman saw her to the door and Julia promised to come again soon, though privately she wondered if she should. She and Elizabeth were moving further and further apart. Since her marriage, Elizabeth had become prim and prudish, and Julia, traveling in the fast Regency set, had gained a much more liberal notion of how life should be lived. It was a pity! She disliked losing a friend, but she doubted that Elizabeth was truly her friend any longer.

She was walking along the narrow sidewalk on her way home when she saw a familiar figure turning the corner and coming her way. It was Sir Gerald Giles, walking swiftly, and looking handsome in a dark brown coat and hat and yellow checkered trousers. On seeing her, he halted and removed his hat.

"My dear Julia," he said, his bronzed, squarish face lighting up. "Have you been visiting with my wife?"

"I've only just left her," she said.

"And what, pray, is her present mood?"

"Not the happiest."

The young man looked dejected. "I was afraid of that. I have been away more than a week. She always is in a rage when I return."

Julia gazed at the young man from under the broad rim of her gray bonnet, saying, "Surely you must know your continued absences have to upset her."

"I know it only too well," he sighed. "But I warned her before we were married that for a period of at least a few years my stables would mean my being away from London a good deal. She agreed. Now she does nothing but complain."

"I'm sorry," Julia said. "Perhaps if you took her with you."

"It would not work out," he said firmly. "I shall have to hope that she sees things sensibly. But on to other matters, I hear you and Brummell are cutting a wide swath in our London town. Only the Prince has more gossip retailed about him."

"Most of it is just that! Gossip!" she said. "You may be safe if you believe at least a quarter of what you hear."

Sir Gerald studied her with his pleasant brown eyes and said, "You have grown more beautiful, I swear it!"

"Your imagination, I fear," she said with amusement.

"I mean it," he insisted. "And thank you for visiting Elizabeth. It generally puts her in a better humor."

She smiled. "I put in a good word for you."

"I fear I shall need several," he said ruefully. Then bowed again, and continued on toward his house.

Julia could not help but feel sorry for him. She believed that he had warned Elizabeth about his racing interests. And no doubt Elizabeth had agreed to let him continue. But now that the first excitement of the marriage had ended they were at odds.

Lady Jane and Sir Orville were waiting for her in the drawing room when she went down to dinner that evening. She could tell at once that something was in the air. Lady Jane was seated nervously by the fireplace and Sir Orville was standing behind her chair with a scowl on his face.

Sir Orville opened the first sally, saying, "What is this rumor about your going to White's?"

"Mr. Brummell is taking me there tomorrow night," she said.

Lady Jane's thin face showed distress. "But ladies are not allowed. No lady would ever go there!"

She explained, "It is a favor on the manager's part. I

shall only stay for a little. Beau and the Prince want to do it for a stunt."

"And devil care what happens to your reputation," Sir Orville complained. "Let me warn you that I have talked with the Prince myself and he is not as fond of Brummell as most people believe!"

Julia knew that Sir Orville was capable of trying to make trouble between the Prince and Beau because of his jealousy of her. She eyed him coldly, and said, "I do not think Mr. Brummell is worried."

The weakly handsome face of Sir Orville showed a sneer. "His luck can't always last. He'll be out of favor one day!"

Julia replied, "Until that happens you waste your time worrying about it."

Lady Jane gave her husband a look of reproach and said, "You ought not to go on so about Mr. Brummell. He has done you no harm. And he has introduced Julia to court circles. If the Prince approves of her venturing to White's tomorrow night, I expect no real harm will come of it."

So Julia barely had the consent of her protectors. The following evening she rode in a carriage to the St. James Street gaming house flanked on one side by Beau Brummell, elegant in a dark blue coat and gray trousers and the Prince wearing a black coat and blue trousers, both looking much pleased with themselves.

Beau, his white cravat as perfect as usual, gave her a smiling side glance and said, "What people see and hear tonight will not be all that startling, but what is repeated about it will grow with the telling!"

"Damned if you're not right, Beau!" The stout Prince said and his big body rippled with laughter.

"I'm all nerves, gentlemen," she said in a voice which did have a tremor in it.

"It will go well," Brummell assured her. "I would not expose you to anything which I felt might hurt you."

They reached the modest entrance of the ornate stone building with its fancy, iron railings at the second floor and the interesting carvings on the facade above. A stout man, all in dark brown, was about to enter the club when their coach drew up. He halted and stood there with his tophat in hand and his bulging, florid cheeks sunk in his collar, as he waited for the Prince and his party to alight.

The Prince gave the waiting man a friendly pat on the back and said, "Alvaney, you know our fair companion?"

Lord Alvaney bowed. "I have met Miss Crawford and am delighted to see her about to enter the club. I have a small wager placed with Skiffy, who insisted she would not arrive!"

"You'd wager on your mother's death date, I vow," the Prince told him.

"Indeed, I have, sire," the stout man assured him.

Beau Brummell extended his arm for Julia to take and said, "Come, gentlemen, we are delaying this unique moment too long!"

Julia was actually trembling as the club door was swung back and they were ushered inside. They passed through a reception hall and then were at once in a drawing room filled with a number of gaming tables with groups of men gathered around each. The room was as elegant as any in a fine London house and everything hinted of wealth and luxury.

A silence fell on the room as Beau and the Prince led Julia from one table to another explaining the different games to her. Not until she had completed her round of the rooms was there any reaction. Then someone offered polite applause and this was taken up gradually by everyone else. Julia in a ruffled, white gown stood there smiling and accepting this spontaneous tribute.

Beau eyed her triumphantly. The handsome dandy said, "I told you! You have won them completely over. Now let us settle at the roulette table. The Prince wishes to test his luck with you at his side."

She was given a chair at the table and an interested crowd gathered as the Prince began to play. It soon appeared that she was bringing him good fortune with every turn of the wheel. He accumulated several wins and insisted on turning over a fistful of bank notes to her.

"Take them, my dear," the Prince said. "Play them where you like. I'm off to have a brandy and celebrate my fortune."

Julia passed the notes to Beau and said, "You use them for your own benefit."

"But they are yours," Brummell protested.

"I want you to have them," she said. "The Prince told me I could do as I liked with them. This is what I like."

Brummell bowed. "As you say."

As the handsome dandy said this a newcomer joined them. A tall, dark clad man with a lean, shrewd face. He had thinning black hair and scars on one cheek as if from ancient fencing wounds. There was a kind of reckless air about him.

He bowed to Brummell and said, "I would like to meet our first female guest."

"Julia," Beau said, "This is the manager of the club. His name, like yours, is Crawford. So you have an immediate basis for friendship."

"How do you do, Mr. Crawford," she said, thinking he looked exactly as she would have pictured a professional gambler.

His smile was cold and his eyes were sharp as he bowed to her. He said, "Mr. Brummell did not exaggerate your beauty. I regret that your visit here is an isolated one and not likely to be repeated."

"Thank you," she said, thinking that he had a remarkable charm in spite of his rather plain, lean face and being older.

"If there is anything I can do to add to your enjoyment this evening, please ask me," the dark man said.

"I shall," she promised. And after he left them she told Brummell, "I find that man a most interesting type."

"He is," Beau agreed. "From what I have heard he

has been to almost every part of the world. And always as a gambler. He is known from Constantinople to Paris!"

Brummell escorted her around until she tired of the place. Then, leaving the Prince there, they summoned their carriage and returned to Brummell's flat for conversation and end of the evening drinks. Beau poured her a sherry and a brandy for himself.

The handsome Beau was in an elated mood. He stood facing her to say, "You came through just right! All London will be talking by tomorrow! You are the first woman ever to visit White's. And likely to be the last."

"I found it interesting, and my namesake has a mysterious charm. You must thank him on my part."

"I venture when the newspapers are finished retailing the escapade, both yourself and the club will be known from one end of the country to the other."

She frowned a little. "There, I knew something was most strange! Where were those lively fellows of the press?"

"At the back waiting to be let in when you went," Beau explained with a smile. "Crawford and I cooked it up between us. It also protected the Prince from unwanted contact with the press."

She laughed. "I wonder they kept their word. They so often don't!"

Beau chuckled. "They had to tonight. Crawford would have refused them an audience otherwise. And he is a man known for keeping to his promises."

Julia sipped her wine. "How silly to make so much of such a minor adventure!"

The dandy sat down by her. "You are thinking of our army on the Continent and what is happening there. And you think this of small import!"

"I confess I do find the life here somewhat decadent."

Brummell studied her fondly. "Still not afraid to voice your thoughts."

"Never," she said. "I wish things were different. You

dare to shock London by taking me to White's. But you will not risk offending your friends by turning your back on their life style to marry me!"

"We have been over this before!"

"And I must say it again," she insisted. "Yesterday a dear friend told me of the gossip about us and asked why you did not wed me."

"Matrimony is the one crime I refuse to commit, since my partner is always bound to pay the worst penalty."

"I'm willing to accept any punishment," she said.

He bent and kissed her lightly. "Your good, kind heart would allow you to commit any number of rash things. I, on the other hand, must use my judgment to protect you."

"You prefer the charms of the Duchess of York or maybe those of Harriete Wilson!" she exclaimed.

"Julia, my child," he said with a sigh. "You must never be jealous. No one can take your place in my heart."

"But I want to be with you all the time! Not a mere plaything to be at your side when you wish!"

"My life is complex," Brummell said. "And you know my fortunes are bound with those of the Prince. He would not think well of my marrying."

"I have heard the Prince has talked ill of you to some. That he may not be the firm friend, you think!"

The handsome Brummell stood up and moved a few steps away from her. "It is because I know that I must be extremely cautious." He turned to face her, the face she loved so well shadowed with concern. "Do you not think I want to marry you?"

"Darling!" she rose and went to his arms.

He held her close, saying, "I must somehow establish a reasonable fortune. Then I can turn my back on the Prince. To do it now would mean ruin. My creditors would swoop down on me like vultures."

"What can you do?"

"Continue the charade," he said wearily. "Remain the best of the best dressed men in London. Cater to the whims of the Prince. Trust that fortune will shine on me."

"It won't happen at the gaming tables," she warned him.

"There have been a few cases. I must hope," he replied.

Still clinging to him, she said, "People envy me being your close friend. And my access to the Prince. They cannot guess what sadness it all brings me."

"I know," he said. "And I must ask you to be more considerate. Tomorrow I leave with the Prince for an indefinite stay at Brighton!"

"May I go with you? Visit you?"

He shook his head sadly. "The Prince would not wish it. I dare not cross him!"

"So it will be the Wilsons and their brothel girls who will decorate the fine summer houses of Brighton," she said with anger.

He took her by the arms and showed annoyance as he told her, "You must not think such things let alone mention them. You must have faith in me and the purity of my love for you!"

She lowered her head. "I'm sorry, Beau. I feel it all to have become pointless."

"Do you love me?"

"Need you ask?"

He touched his hand under her chin and smiled at her gently. "True love conquers!" And he kissed her again. "Now, I must take you home."

Memory of that last evening together lingered with her in the days that followed. The newspapers made headlines of her presence at White's. It was given more prominence than the latest war news from the Continent. Her conquering White's seemed of more import to them than Napoleon conquering the Continent.

Julia found this notoriety distasteful and she was also saddened by the departure from London of Beau Brummell. She felt deserted and lonely without him. In the long months of their being together she had devoted herself almost entirely to him. And though she knew she would never feel the same sort of love for anyone else, she was forced to accept that Brummell would never be free to marry her.

It was while she was in this despondent mood that a much subdued Jimmy Fitzroy came to the gardens at Hewitt House to visit her one day. His top hat in hand he strolled with her and somewhat awkwardly apologized for their differences in the past and hoped that she would forgive him.

"I hold no grudges, Jimmy," she said.

"Then we can be friends again?" he asked.

"Why not?"

He gave her a grateful look. "I thought that since you had become so involved with Brummell he would not allow you to be friends with me."

"I do not see that," she said. "Since Brummell and I are no more friends. He cannot choose who I may wish to have near me."

Jimmy looked much happier. And it was inevitable that he should become a caller nearly every day. Julia accepted an occasional invitation to a ball or dinner with him, since she did not think Brummell would expect her to avoid all pleasures while he was absent. Jimmy seemed to enjoy her new notoriety, even though it had come from her friendship with Brummell, and they were often the focus of attention at London social affairs.

It was a little while before Jimmy ventured to talk to her of marriage again. And in her depressed mood she gave his offer more consideration than she ever had before. Her girlhood romance with John Lane had long ago been relegated to her past. No letters had ever reached her from the young soldier and she could only assume she had been forgotten by him.

But Jimmy was another matter. She did not truly love him as she did Beau. But he was an attractive young man if somewhat mercurial in temperament. As Lady Jane pointed out his prospects were excellent and he had a sound position in London society. Julia began to question whether it might be better to marry for a combination of these things and hope that love would follow.

The thing which deterred her most was the strong dislike Beau had shown for this former friend. He had been unrelenting in his attitude towards him and had warned her against having anything to do with the young man-about-town. But Beau was giving his first loyalty to the Prince, even if from necessity, and so she began to wonder whether he had any right to stop her from marrying Jimmy.

The matter came to a climax when Jimmy called on her one evening and told her that his invalid mother had returned from a stay in the country and was most anxious to meet her.

Jimmy offered her one of his boyish smiles and said, "I'm hoping when you two meet you'll decide my fate. I think mother may persuade you to be my wife."

She was touched by his suggestion. "Has your mother really asked to see me?"

He said, "Yes. My carriage is waiting out front. We can be there in twenty minutes. She does not remain up late."

Julia smiled indulgently at him. "You really want me to go meet her?"

"More than anything else."

"What have you told her about us?"

"That I love you. I have asked you to be my wife."

She reproached him gently. "Don't you think you should have waited? She might not like me at all when she sees me."

"I know she will," he said with assurance.

"And if we do not marry she will be disappointed," Julia warned him.

"She wants to try and persuade you it would be good for both of us," Jimmy said. "She is counting on your visit."

She worried about it a moment and then decided that no harm could really come from getting to know the older woman. And there was a strong chance that she might marry Jimmy. In this frame of mind she decided to accompany him to his London home.

Jimmy was nervous on the way across the city. He talked quickly and in a nervous fashion about his mother and what a fine marriage his parents had enjoyed. She was amused by his uneasiness and felt him to be boyishly appealing.

They arrived at the house and he dismissed the carriage, saying "I can call a public hackney cab when you are ready to leave. No point in keeping my man waiting."

"But I mustn't stay too long," she pointed out. "You say your mother isn't well."

"She isn't," Jimmy agreed. "But after you see her I'd like you to visit the rest of the house. A house which one day may be yours."

Julia smiled, "I haven't accepted yet."

"Mother will convince you," Jimmy repeated.

A doleful, old man in butler's livery let them in. And Jimmy at once led her up a wide, curving stairway to the second floor of the old mansion. She noted the expensive paintings and carpets and the marble steps. The Fitzroy fortune was much in evidence in the imposing house.

He led her along a dark hallway and in a low voice, said, "Sometimes she takes a short nap. We may have to wake her."

"Should we?" she worried.

"Of course," he said. "She would be angry if I brought you here and she didn't meet you."

"Very well," she said, sensing by his voice that he was still nervous.

He halted before a heavy oak door and gave her a nod, then opened it and allowed her to silently enter. The room was in shadow and she gazed toward the bed to see if his mother might be asleep. To her surprise the bed was empty. As this fact registered with her she heard the bolt slide in the door behind her.

She turned and said, "Your mother?"

Jimmy was standing smiling at her in what she felt to be an unpleasant way. Nervously, he said, "Did you really expect to find her here?"

"Certainly!" her reply was sharp.

He took a step toward her. "Let's not pretend!"

"I'm not pretending," she said, "Let me out of here!"

"Come now!" he continued with that forced smile. "You knew what I was up to and what I want!"

"You lied to me! Brought me here by deception!"

Jimmy shook his head and removed his jacket and tossed it on the chair by him. Then he made a rush at her to seize her in his arms. She screamed and backed away trying to dodge him. He sprang at her again and this time grasped her by the upper arms.

A savage look had come to his face now and he spoke rather breathlessly, "You'd be better off not to struggle! You should be willing to give me what you've been giving Brummell!"

"Let me go! You are disgusting!" she cried.

"And Brummell isn't?" he gloated.

"He's worth a thousand of you!"

He laughed and forced her struggling into his arms. He tried to kiss her but she somehow avoided his lips and pounded at him with her fists. He became increasingly angry and with a cry of fury hurled her down onto the floor.

"Now maybe you'll be reasonable!" he said, down on the floor with her.

She was stunned by the impact of her fall for a brief moment and in that short interval he was upon her tearing at her clothing. He literally ripped the front of her dress and her under clothing so that her bare breasts were exposed!

"No!" she screamed, trying to fight him off.

But this partial nudity seemed only to madden him further and he continued to tear at her clothes and try to reduce her to complete nakedness.

She managed by a lucky chance to plunge her finger in one of his eyes. This brought a shout of pain from him and he released his hold on her for just a second. It was enough for her to squirm out from under him and struggle to her feet.

He was holding onto his eye with one hand and coming at her like a madman! He swung out at her with his right fist and struck her in the mouth! She felt her lips break and the warm, salt blood spurt from them as she fell staggering back.

"No, please!" she sobbed.

He cursed her and came at her again. As he did so she fell back against a table and her hand came in contact with a heavy vase. She lifted it up and using both hands brought it crashing against his forehead as he moved close to her! The vase broke and she saw the line of cut flesh on his forehead as a wide wound began to bleed. His eyes were open but he toppled to the floor like a log and remained there.

Sobbing she backed away from him, horror filling her as she wondered if she had killed him. The room was reeling about her and she unsteadily groped her way across the big room to find the door and the bolt. She momentarily expected him to rise up and come after her but he remained there silent and motionless!

Fumbling with the bolt she finally slid it back and got the door open. Her mouth was paining terribly now and blood was trickling down her chin and onto her bare breasts.

She made a futile attempt to repair the damage done to her dress. And had to be satisfied to hold it up in place to cover her nudity. Now she slowly staggered along the dark hall, feeling nauseated as well as in pain. She reached the landing and clutched the stairway railing with one hand and step by step made her way down.

Below there was no sign of anyone. She expected the old butler was perhaps the only one in the house. The rest of the staff being out or away in the country with the rest of the family. Perhaps the butler was deaf and that was why Jimmy had assumed he could safely attack her without being heard.

Reaching the front door she let herself out and was grateful for the cool rush of evening air. It was now close to darkness. She was too desperate to think of anything but escape, knowing that the man who'd attacked her so cruelly might revive at any time and come after her again. She had no doubt he'd follow her into the street and try to capture her once more.

So she thought only of finding a hackney cab and hailing it and getting back to Hewitt House. She stood by the curbside swaying, her mouth growing more painful and the other injuries he'd inflicted on her beginning to nag. She thought she heard the sound of a carriage approaching and took a step out onto the cobblestones of the street. There she lifted a hand and waved frantically to attract attention.

The carriage came rolling up and she tried to shout something but found her lips too swollen for her to be able to properly make herself understood. The driver jumped down from the cab and came to her.

A startled look on his face, he asked, "What has happened to you, miss?"

"Take me home," she managed in a hoarse whisper.

"What is going on, Walker?" a boisterous, middle-aged, male voice demanded.

She realized that the carriage had a passenger and that he was also out in the street by her now. Staring at her with dismay.

"Hewitt House!" she whispered.

"My God!" The passenger said. "It is Julia Crawford. What have they done to you, my dear Julia?" He supported her with the aid of the driver.

"Fitzroy," she managed. "The house!"

The older man frowned. "So Jimmy Fitzroy has been up to his pranks again! And with you, this time. I'm Lord Alvaney, we met at White's and at Beau's!"

"Help me!" she said and then the world became black and she descended, descended into nothingness. No sound, no sight, no pain!

When she opened her eyes again she was in bed in a lamplit room. A grave, side-whiskered man was bending over her whom she recognized as the family physician, Dr. Stanley. Behind him stood a distraught Lady Jane, and with her an angry looking Sir Orville and Lord Alvaney.

Dr. Stanley said sympathetically, "You've suffered a severe attack, my poor girl. It will be better if you do not try to speak. I shall give you something to help you sleep until morning."

She stared up at him, tears forming in her eyes. Tears of pain and dismay. He moved away from her bed and was replaced by an anxious looking Lady Jane.

Her thin face was unusually pale as she said, "To think that I encouraged you to marry that dreadful, young man. I shall never forgive myself. I should have found out more about him."

Julia raised her right hand and clasped the older woman's hand in it. She wanted to speak and tell her that it wasn't her fault. But it was just too painful.

Lady Jane said, "The doctor thinks you will be all right. What you need now is rest. You must forget all about this."

Sir Orville came and stood by his wife and placed an arm around her. He said, "Come, my dear. You are not helping Julia any. The doctor wishes to give her a sedative." And they both moved away.

The doctor returned with a glass half-filled with a ruby liquid. He said, "This will ease your pain and make you sleep. We must try and get it down."

With that he eased her up and touched the rim of the glass to her swollen, broken lips. It's mere contact gave her searing pain but she attempted to get her mouth open. Some of the liquid managed to get down her throat while a little dribbled away.

"That will do," the doctor said and eased her back on the pillow and arranged the bed clothes about her.

Then, at last, Lord Alvaney came to her bedside and with anger showing on his large face, he leaned close and in a low voice said, "I shall notify Beau of this!"

She wanted to beg him not to, but she could not manage it before he turned and strode out of the room.

Chapter Six

It was forty-eight hours before Dr. Stanley allowed her to have visitors. Until then, only her maid came to the room, taking care of her and bringing her broth and other easily consumed foods. Julia lay in dull pain not knowing or caring what went on. But by the third day she felt better and left her bed to sit in a chair by the window in her dressing gown.

That afternoon a subdued Sir Orville came to see her and tell her, "I have called on James Fitzroy and advised him that he is no longer welcome here. And that only to avoid a scandal I would have him prosecuted."

Julia felt some relief. "He was so still when I ran away. I was afraid I'd killed him."

The weakly handsome face of Sir Orville showed a smile. "His head is still bandaged and he'll show a mark of where that vase hit him for the rest of his life."

She sighed. "It is all like a nightmare!"

"You should have realized," the older man said santimonious to the point where she had to find it amusing or revolting. "All that crowd are the same. Including his friend Brummell!"

Julia at once said, "He and Beau have not been on friendly terms for a long while. The group shouldn't be indicted because of one man."

Sir Orville rose saying, "Well, I thought I should let you know that I have given that cowardly scoundrel a stiff warning."

Fear showed in her eyes again as she recalled the

incident. "There is something of madness about him. After he began to beat me he couldn't seem to stop."

"You're looking very well," Sir Orville said. "As soon as your mouth heals and the bruises vanish you'll be as lovely as before."

"And ever so much wiser," was her grim reply.

"I would hope so," Sir Orville said self-righteously and left her.

But recovery was not as fast as he'd predicted. It was a full ten days before most signs of her injuries had vanished and she felt well enough to stroll in the garden. She was out there when a carriage arrived bearing the stout, old Lord Alvaney.

He came hurrying out to her, leaning on his walking stick, and breathing heavily. He halted and removing his top hat said, "I wanted to let you know that Beau has returned to London."

She could not help being excited by this news. She said, "When?"

"Yesterday."

"He has not come to see me or sent any message," Julia worried.

"He has probably been too busy," the old aristocrat said with a grave look on his florid face. "He left the Prince in Brighton as soon as he heard what had happened to you."

"I wish it could have been kept from him," she said.

"He had a right to know. He would have been angry if I had not informed him," Lord Alvaney said.

She gave Lord Alvaney an anxious glance. "I hope he does nothing rash!"

The florid face bulging over the hard collar showed a delighted smile as the old aristocrat announced, "He has already done it!"

Julia was at once concerned. "What are you saying?"

"Beau confronted Fitzroy at Witier's last night. They met by the blackjack table. Beau ordered him out and told him he was never to enter the place again. Beau is president of Witier's, so he had the right. Fitzroy snarled something at him and Beau slapped him!"

"And?"

"They are meeting at a secret place tomorrow morning for a duel. The weapons will be swords and I am to be one of Beau's seconds!"

"You mustn't allow it!" she protested.

Lord Alvaney raised a pudgy hand to placate her. "You must not interfere, you know."

"But he is doing this for me! He may be killed!"

"I don't think so," the old man said, shifting his weight on his walking stick. "It is liable to be the other way. Beau has resolutely avoided any quarrels which might end in a duel. But that does not mean he is an incompetent when it comes to fencing. I know better!"

"Fitzroy is disgraced because of what happened. That is all the satisfaction I need. There is no need for this duel!"

"Beau thinks differently," Lord Alvaney said. "It has gone too far now to withdraw."

Julia was in a state. "I must talk with him! Where can I find him?"

"I left him at his place a short time ago," the old man told her. "I rather think he may still be there."

"Please take me to him!" she begged.

He stared at her. "You want to go now?"

"Yes. I don't want to waste a moment. These two men must be dissuaded from their planned violence."

"I do not believe seeing Beau can possibly change the course of events," he warned her.

"Do take me!" she begged.

"Very well," the old man said at last.

She found a cloak and bonnet and told Lady Jane she would be out for a little, much to that good woman's upset. Lady Jane called after her, "But you are not yet well enough to go about."

"I shall be all right," she shouted over her shoulder as she hurried back out to join Lord Alvaney and be driven to Beau's house. The old man tried to make some sort of small talk along the way to distract her. But it did little good. She was in a distraught frame of mind.

On reaching Beau's house she did not wait for the old man but quickly emerged from the carriage and made for his front door. Beau's man answered and looked frightened at the sight of her.

She brushed past him, saying, "I must see Mr. Brummell at once!"

The butler attempted to block her way, explaining, "You must understand, miss. Mr. Brummell never sees anyone at this time of day. He is dressing!"

"What I have to say will not take long," she said. And she somehow managed to brush by him and hurry to Beau's bedroom at the rear of the house.

His door was open and he was seated in a plain chair, his booted feet propped up on a table. His head was back and a younger servant was meticulously at work winding a twelve inch roll of white cravat about the dandy's neck. On seeing her, Beau ordered the servant to halt and stood up with the cravat's end hanging down to his waist.

He came to her and said emotionally, "Dear Julia, you look so well! I had feared your beauty would be permanently harmed!"

"No!" she said and he took her in his arms and kissed her gently. As he released her, she said, "I have come to try and stop the madness you plan."

The handsome Beau stood gazing at her. "I do not know what you are talking about."

Old Lord Alvaney thrust his head in the door and in a tone of regret, told Beau, "I let the news drop, my dear fellow. I'm sorry! I shall see you early in the morning!" And with that he withdrew.

Beau looked down at her sadly. "I did not mean to see you until after tomorrow morning."

"You could be killed tomorrow morning!" she exclaimed in despair.

"Do not worry!" he said. "You have interfered with my dressing and I have an important appointment."

"I do not want you risking your life for me," was her tearful reply.

Careful not to let the hanging length of cravat touch

on anything he led her over to an easy chair. When she was seated he crossed to a sideboard and poured out sherries for them. Returning, he handed her a glass and then sat on the edge of the table facing her.

"Drink the sherry," he said. "I have something to tell you."

She did as she was ordered and then said, "You will not make me change my mind. Fitzroy is disgraced. The word has gotten around!"

"You think that punishment enough?" he asked gravely.

"Yes!"

"I cannot agree," the handsome Brummell said. "And I shall tell you why. You have heard the name of Harriete Wilson spoken by many."

She nodded. "Yes. I know her to be the proprietor of a high class brothel."

He nodded. "That is correct. She and her sisters are the owners and operators of London's finest house of ill-fame, if I may so designate it. They try to offer this service in the most dignified way possible. As a result, the elite of London society have at one time or another frequented the place. The Prince is no stranger there."

"Nor you."

"Nor I," he agreed.

"Why are you telling me this?" she asked.

He put aside his empty glass. "You have often asked me why Fitzroy and I ceased being friends."

"Yes. You would not tell me."

"I should have, I realized that as soon as I heard what had happened to you," he said gravely.

Her eyes widened. "Please go on."

"Fitzroy was a regular at the Wilson house. His main interest there was a girl called Betty. A pretty little blonde creature a favorite with all who knew her, including myself. He seemed to forget she was a paid prostitute and came to regard her as his own property."

"And?"

"Betty went to Harriete Wilson and told her Fitzroy had cruelly abused her. She showed the bruises and burn marks on her white young arms and legs. Harriete took Fitzroy aside the next time he came to her house and told him that if he ever did anything of the sort again he would be refused admittance.''

"A sort of madness seems to come over him," she said, remembering.

"So it would seem," Brummell said dryly. "Fitzroy's reaction was to lock himself in a room with Betty and pummel her with his fists. The sound of her shrieking for help and the furor of tumbling furniture could be heard clearly in many parts of the house. Harriete herself went to the door and demanded he open it and set the girl free. He cried out some oaths and came out with the inert body of Betty in his arms! Rushing by Harriete he lifted the girl up and literally hurled her down a flight of stairs."

"Was she killed?" Julia asked in awe.

"She died a few hours later."

"How awful!"

Beau sighed deeply. "Harriete could not bear a scandal. It would have ruined her. So the girl's fall was reported as accidental! A harlot drunkenly tripped on the stairs to her death. It was easy to hush up. Harriete had friends in high places. But Fitzroy was ordered never to return, and many of his friends, including myself, have cut him dead from that time."

Julia was shattered by this revelation. "He is a murderer! Nothing less! And he tried to give me the same sort of treatment!"

Brummell said wearily, "So he ensnared you by pretending you were to meet his mother. I could have warned you and I didn't. I should have been here at your side instead, as usual, I was having to curry favor with that fat oaf of a George in Brighton!"

"Do not blame yourself," she said. "It was my fault. I resented you leaving and staying so long in Brighton. I ought not to have resumed seeing him since it was evident that something was badly wrong! You had not turned from him without reason."

"When I face Fitzroy tomorrow it will be in an effort

to rid the town of a mad dog! He is not safe to be at large!"

"You have always avoided duels!" she pointed out.

He smiled grimly. "Not because of any lack of ability to wield a sword. I had expert training in fencing as a youth."

"And Fitzroy?"

"Considers himself a duellist. We shall see."

She stood up, "If anything happens to you I will know it's my fault. It is on my account you are doing this."

"No. I'm doing it to try and save Fitzroy from committing more of the same crimes. Neither of us need necessarily be killed. But I trust it will teach him a lesson."

"You are saying this to placate me," she worried.

"No. It is the truth," Brummell said. "Now I will have my carriage take you home while I continue dressing!"

They embraced and then he saw her out to the door. She left him filled with grim forebodings. She was sure she had not been told the full truth. That the younger James Fitzroy was probably a more competent swordsman. Brummell had told her nothing about where the duel was to be held and so she supposed it would remain a secret.

She slept little that night and when dawn came she rose and paced in her room. She had only a strong cup of tea for breakfast and continued her vigil of waiting. Surely someone would soon come to her, bring her news of what had taken place. It was close to noon before a carriage drew up before the door of Hewitt House and the stout Lord Alvaney descended from it.

As soon as he entered she ran to him and asked, "Is he safe?"

"Beau suffered no more than a scratch on his arm," the old man told her.

"Heaven be thanked!" she said with deep sincerity. "And Fitzroy?"

"Beau disabled him with a deep wound in the thigh. The attending doctor says he will recover but he received a sliced tendon. He will walk on crutches for the rest of his life."

"At least he is still alive. The same can't be said for that poor girl!" Julia said.

"I agree, the fellow was lucky," the old aristocrat said. "Beau could easily have finished him and I think perhaps he ought to have. Though I doubt Fitzroy will make any further trouble. His name is in disgrace and he will be humiliated by his condition. His family has interests in the colonies. I have an idea he will vanish from England."

"Where is Brummell now?" she asked.

The florid face of Lord Alvaney showed embarrassment. He coughed and said, "I suppose I cannot deny you the truth. The fact is, he is being toasted at Harriete Wilson's. The Prince arrived back from Brighton this morning and is there with Beau. Miss Wilson feels a blow was struck for justice."

"I quite see her point," she said dryly. "Did Beau offer you any message for me?"

The old man beamed. "Yes. He said to bring you the news and to tell you he is calling for you tonight to take you to the Cafe Royale for dinner. He wants all London to see you together, so there will be no ugly rumors."

She smiled. "Tell him I shall be ready at seven."

It was the most famous restaurant in London. Not only was the fare of special merit with oysters and roast beef the favorites with its patrons, but its decor was superb. The oak-panneled walls with crimson drapes and benches and chairs upholstered in the same material contrasted with the shining white cloths of the many tables. The lighting was always properly subdued and there were a multitude of waiters, captains and servers always hurrying back and forth.

Julia, in a demure white gown sat opposite Beau who had worn his black evening suit for the occasion. They had a prominent table atop a tier on the right side of the big dining hall. She was sure he had arranged this spot for them so that they would be seen by all the diners below. And she was also aware their presence was creating a good deal of interest.

Leaning forward across the table a trifle, she said, "We are being so stared at!"

"Consider it a compliment," the handsome Brummell said with a smile.

"I believe all London has heard about the duel."

"I rarely engage in such a violent and primitive means of settling a difference," he said. "But in this case my duty was plain."

"I hope that Fitzroy will accept his defeat like a gentleman."

"That is too much to ask. I only insist that he keep out of my sight," Brummell said with disgust.

"You have a bad enemy in him," she worried.

"My dear, if a man makes no enemies he is almost bound not to have any friends," Beau said in his languid way.

She smiled and said, "Sir Orville claims he was on the edge of challenging Fitzroy to a duel himself. But you managed it ahead of him."

"I fear if we waited for Sir Orville to be the challenger we would all be too old to take any interest in the event."

"I'm sure that is true," she said.

"How has he behaved lately?"

"Better than at the start," she said. "Yet I know he is constantly watching me. And I fear to be alone in the house with him."

"I do not think you should be there," Brummell said seriously.

She gave him a knowing smile. "My best hope to escape Hewitt House would be marriage."

The handsome Beau showed an amused smile. He touched his prominent white cravat with the fingertips of his left hand and murmured, "What a pity I'm wed to fashion!"

"Surely you could free yourself!"

"I wonder," he said. Then their dinner was served and the subject was dropped. But she hoped that he might discuss it again and that she would eventually persuade him that he could marry her and still maintain his position as the fashion leader of the Regency rakes.

"What are your plans for the next few months?" she asked.

"The Prince is doing some travelling about the country. He insists that I accompany him."

"Which means you will be absent from London again," she said, feeling desolate at the news.

"I regret it, my dear," he said. "And I'm coming to dislike my dependence on the fat fellow but what can I do?"

"You'd better not let him hear you calling him the fat fellow," she warned.

He laughed. "The temptation is daily becoming greater. I vow if he lives long enough he will be as mad as his poor father."

The dinner was an unqualified success and he held her close to him in the carriage. At her door he kissed her goodnight and promised to send her a message within a day or two when his plans were more settled.

The following evening Lady Jane was called to the house adjoining Hewitt House, because of the illness of the widow of Baron Drysdale, an old friend. She sent a maid back with a message that because of her friend's condition she felt she should spend the night with her.

Sir Orville grumbled that it was a nuisance and the woman should depend on her doctor and staff, not on his wife. Julia paid little attention to him since he was nearly always complaining about something.

She went up to bed early and as it was a pleasant night she opened the French doors to the balcony to get a taste of the fresh air before retiring. She had removed her clothing but had not yet put on her nightgown. She stood in the flood of moonlight, her

face upraised. A delicious sense of freedom surged
through her as the soft night air caressed her lithe,
naked body.

And then suddenly she heard a sound which sent a
chill of fear through her. The door of her room slowly
opening. She realized with dismay that she had forgotten to slip the bolt in place. And it had to be tonight
with Lady Jane out of the house! Worse! The lecherous
Sir Orville might think she had left it unbolted by
intent!

She hastily covered her breast with her hands and
turned hoping that it might be only her maid. But it was
Sir Orville who had entered. He came slowly toward
her like a man in a dream state.

"Get out!" she cried.

"You mustn't be afraid of me!" he said soothingly.
"Don't back away!"

"Please!" she begged him, moving a little onto the
balcony.

"You're so beautiful!" he gloated, reaching out for
her.

"No!" she cried and darted to the right.

He moved with surprising swiftness to block her from
reaching the door to the hall. "If you're a sensible girl
you'll stop all this nonsense! We can enjoy ourselves!"

She moved back slowly to the wall and he advanced
as she moved. Soon there would be no retreat. She
blamed herself for forgetting the bolt when she knew
him to be a constant threat.

"Don't touch me!" she cried as his hand groped for
her breast.

"Don't play games!" he said. "I know you've slept
with Brummell and who knows how many else! Don't
play the virgin with me!"

"You're mad!" she said, cowering tightly against the
wall.

"Orville!" The name came sharp and clear in the
high-pitched voice of Lady Jane.

He turned, and stood stupidly gazing at his wife who

had suddenly appeared in the doorway. "My dear!" he croaked.

A great relief surged through Julia and she ran to the bed and picked up a dressing gown and hurriedly covered her nakedness.

"What does this mean, Orville?" Lady Jane said coming further into the room and behaving as grimly as any Lady Macbeth.

"She invited me in here," Sir Orville said in a panic. He pointed a shaking forefinger at Julia, stammering, "the vixen tried to seduce me!"

"That is not true, Lady Jane," Julia said going to the older woman. "I neglected to bolt my door and he came in on me unannounced and unwanted!"

"I have no doubt of that," Lady Jane said grimly. "I began to worry. I came back to warn you to be doubly careful while I was out of the house. And I find this!"

Sir Orville made an attempt to bluster. "Will you take the word of a woman without virtue against that of your husband?"

"I could only wish you half as virtuous as Julia," his wife said bitingly. "I'm not surprised by your behavior. But I warn you, I will condone it no more."

The weakly handsome Sir Orville glared at them and said, "Damn all women!" And he stalked out.

Julia broke the silence which followed his departure by saying, "I'm so terribly sorry!"

Lady Jane suddenly looked very old and weary. "It is not your fault, my dear. He simply cannot be trusted. He knew I was out of the house."

"I forgot the bolt. I don't know why."

"You should be safe here without having to bolt yourself in," the older woman said. "We'll discuss it all in the morning. You needn't worry. I'll be here the rest of the night. Lady Drysdale is feeling better and needs me no longer."

Lady Jane then said goodnight and left. Julia had a sudden, unhappy reaction to the incident. She began to tremble and could not stop. Even after she was safely in

her warm bed she still had fits of trembling. She felt it
was because this incident had brought back the one
with Jimmy Fitzroy in which she had been so badly
beaten. She was still suffering mentally from that
vicious attack.

What was she to do? She could not remain in Hewitt
House after this ugly business. And Beau seemingly
was not ready to make her his wife, if he ever intended
to take that step. She was in love with a man whose life
was dedicated to a style of living. Whose financial
position was so desperate he depended on the goodwill
of the Prince to protect him from his creditors. He
might never be in a position to marry.

She must find other employment. It was a simple as
that. Return to Surrey was an impossibility. Her years
in London had given her a sophistication and a taste for
high living which would be lost to her in the country.

She fell into an uneasy sleep struggling with all these
problems. So it was natural that her dreams should be
haunted by ugly visions of Fitzroy and his attack on her.
She went all through that ordeal again and woke up
perspiring and crying out. Staring up into the darkness
and realizing it was a dream she began to sob.

If only she had someone! Most girls of her age had a
parent, often both parents, along with brothers and
sisters. On the death of her devoted mother she had
been left to depend on the kindness of strangers. First,
the Reverend Edward Weir and now Lady Jane and the
despicable Sir Orville!

She could not even look to a lover for solace. Beau
cared for her, she knew that, but he was unable to
marry her. At least he thought this to be the case. And
as long as he had this attitude there was no future for
them. So she was almost all alone. She thought of the
actor father who had so cruelly deserted her mother
and her. And she felt hatred in her heart for this man
she had no memory of. He had brought her into the
world and deserted her.

Morning came and she went downstairs in a depressed mood. She breakfasted alone and then Lady Jane summoned her to her sewing room. She bade her sit down and then sat with her, hands folded in her lap.

Sympathetically, the older woman said, "I'm sure you do not wish to remain here after last night."

"I think it impossible to remain, my lady," she said with sadness.

Lady Jane's thin face was understanding. She said, "I know that. And I have given it some thought."

"I have also been thinking," Julia said. "It is clear I must find employment."

Lady Jane brightened. "How fortunate! We have both been thinking along the same lines."

"Until I am employed I must find another place to stay."

The older woman raised a hand to calm any fears she might have and said, "I already have a plan."

"You do?"

"Yes. Old Lady Giles is in sore need of a companion. She lives quite alone in a large house in St. James Street. Apart from her household staff she has no one. Her only living relative is her grandson Sir Gerald Giles, whom you have met.

"Of course!" she exclaimed. "Do you think this elderly Lady Giles would wish a companion as young as myself?"

"She enjoys young people," Lady Jane said. "I told her about you and she expressed a desire to have someone of your type. Now, I, unhappily, must let you go. So it shall be her good fortune!"

Julia said, "I have come to respect and be fond of you, Lady Jane. I wish it could be otherwise."

"My husband is not responsible," the older woman sighed. "I realize now I must have an older woman as my companion."

"It might be better," she agreed.

"Pack your things and be ready to move," Lady Jane

said. "I shall send a message to Lady Giles this morning and it is most likely her carriage will come for you before the day is over."

Julia impulsively kissed the cool cheek of the older woman. "You are too kind to me!"

"Nonsense! You're still a child and London has not been all that kind to you," Lady Jane said with sadness. "I'm going to see you in a home where you'll be protected."

Julia went upstairs and slowly began packing her things. Thanks to the bounty of Lady Jane she had gained a number of possessions. She had many dresses and other items of clothing. They filled her valise to capacity. Several of the more fragile gowns she intended to carry draped over her arm.

It was a sunny day and after she'd packed she went down to bid farewell to some of the help and take a last look at the gardens. She had worked on the rose beds and felt the pleasant garden to be part of her own creation. It had also been her retreat. Often she had come to this quiet place to think when problems had arisen.

She was standing alone in the garden path thinking along these lines when she heard a footstep in the gravel and turned to see a flowering Sir Orville confronting her.

"So you would prefer to run away rather than be considerate of me!" he said angrily.

"Your idea of consideration is revolting to me," she replied.

"I revolt you, do I?" he fumed. "What about that fop, Brummell? I suppose you bed with him and enjoy it!"

"I have no wish to discuss my friendship with Mr. Brummell with you. Or to talk of anything else," she said.

His look was one of sheer hatred. "Do not think I will let this slight go by easily."

"I must return to the house," she said.

"Wait!" He stood in her way. "I'll pay my debt to you and Mr. Brummell in my own manner. I happen to have friends close to the Prince. Brummell's hold on him can be broken and I shall take pleasure in helping his destruction!"

"I'm not afraid of your threats. Nor is Mr. Brummell!"

"Wait and see!" Sir Orville said. "When the Prince turns his back on Brummell it will be the end. Brummell will be worse than impoverished, he will go to prison for his debts!"

"Is that all?" she asked, her trembling beginning once again.

"It is enough for now," the older man said. "You and Brummell will both pay for what you did to me!"

He stood aside and she hurried past him. She went into the house feeling ill. Lady Jane came to meet her and said, "You poor child! You're trembling!"

She tried to control herself and the urge to cry as well. In a flat voice, she said, "It is nothing."

"I saw him approach you out there, What did he say?"

Julia looked down. "He was abusive. He threatened to pay me by harming Mr. Brummell."

"Pay no attention to him, my dear," Lady Jane said, putting an arm around her. "He is sour now because of his injured pride. He will get over it!"

The return message from Lady Giles came at mid-afternoon. She would be delighted to have Julia accept the post of her companion. Better than that she had sent her fine carriage to move Julia and her belongings to the Giles mansion. There was a tearful parting between Lady Jane and Julia and then she was making the short journey to another fashionable part of London.

The Giles mansion had little grounds aside from a stable yard and stable buildings in the rear. Mrs.

Glenn, the housekeeper greeted Julia warmly. She was a tiny woman with graying red hair pulled straight back and tied in coils at the base of her neck.

Mrs. Glenn said, "I'm Scotch. I've been here five years and am used to running the household. I also know the old lady's ways."

"Is she very old?" Julia asked as they stood together in the reception hall.

"Seventy-odd and confined to her bed," Mrs. Glenn said. "She was once a beauty, though you wouldn't think it now. She likes the latest gossip and every scandal! She wants the details of every party and so her friends keep her up-to-date on the London goings-on even though she is not able to get out herself."

"I know her grandson," she said.

The woman nodded. "Giles. A nice, young man but I fear his marriage is not too happy. I have overheard him say as much when talking with his grandmother."

"Elizabeth, his wife, was my friend," she explained. "Does she come to see the old woman regularly?"

"Never!" Mrs. Glenn declared. "She came two or three times at the start then the old woman said something which made her angry. And Sir Giles can't get her to come back again."

"That is too bad."

"It is," the Scotch woman said. "Especially as the old woman likes youth and lively people around her."

"Elizabeth is somewhat quiet and repressed. She seems to have become more so since her marriage."

Mrs. Glenn made a face. "There are some gets fine ideas about themselves when they marry high and become Ladies. I say they're no better than the rest of us and needn't put on airs."

Julia smiled, "I'm sure you're right."

"Do come and see the poor old soul," Mrs. Glenn said. "She has been waiting for you."

They went upstairs and entered a wide door to a large bedroom which would surely overlook the street. It was lavishly furnished with fine paintings on the walls and in a great canopy bed an old woman sat propped up against pillows. She wore a cap with a ruffled edge and she had a round face which must have once been appealing but with age had become as wrinkled as a prune. But in the middle of this ruined face there were sharp eyes.

The old woman said in a loud, deep voice, "Is this the girl?"

"Yes," Mrs. Glenn said smiling. "This is Miss Julia Crawford."

Lady Giles studied her with grim interest. "You're pretty enough. I can see why Sir Orville tried to molest you!"

Julia blushed. "Please, Lady Giles!"

"No false modesty here, child," the old woman said. "We all know that Sir Orville has a difficult time keeping in his breeches when there's a female around. Lady Jane wrote me all the circumstances of your having to leave."

Her cheeks still burning, she stood by the bedside and said, "I see."

"My good fortune!" the old woman boomed. "I need a young and pretty face around me. Mrs. Glenn hires nothing but ugly Scotch harridans! She brings them down from the North! Her relatives, I imagine!"

"We'll have none of that saucy nonsense, my lady," Mrs. Glenn said firmly. "I hire Scots lasses because I know them to be honest and hardworking!"

"So you do," the big woman in the bed chuckled. "Go on with you! I want to get accquainted with this girl."

Mrs. Glenn smiled at Julia and said, "Your room is on the third floor, just to the right of the landing. Your things will be in there."

"Thank you," she said. Mrs. Glenn went out and Lady Giles instructed Julia to sit by her bed.

"I know your grandson," Julia told her. "And his wife."

"His wife, bah!" Lady Giles snorted. "But Gerald is

a good boy." She gave Julia another of her sharp looks. "I'm told you have been seen a lot in society with Beau Brummell."

"We are friends," Julia said rather shyly.

"You can be frank with me, my girl," Lady Giles said. A smile crossed her ruined face. "Not all that long ago I was a favorite of the London set. I never missed a party! And the parties I have given! Everyone wanted to attend my parties!"

"I'm sure of it," she said.

"This Beau Brummell is a most particular man about his dress, I understand. And Gerald tells me that before this dandy dresses he bathes for two hours in scented water."

"I believe that to be true."

"Times have changed," the old woman told her. "When I was young the Duke of Norfolk was the most sought after man. And the only time he could be washed and cleaned up was when he was too drunk to know what was happening!" Lady Giles shook the bed with her laughter at her story.

Julia joined in and said, "I have heard it was not long ago the style for men of distinction to be downright dirty about their persons. But Mr. Brummell has changed all that."

"You must bring him to see me," Lady Giles said. "I like to keep my finger on what is happening here in town."

"I'm sure he'd like to meet you," she said.

"He shows good taste in you," the old woman observed. "I like to be read to. Do you read well?"

' Lady Jane complimented me on my reading skill," she said.

"Hah!" Lady Giles said. "We shall see! You will read to me tonight. Mr. Sheridan's "School for Scandal". I no longer get out to plays but I enjoy having them read to me."

"I shall be glad to," she said.

"Go settle yourself in," the old woman said with a

regal wave of her hand. "And close the door when you go out. I wish to sleep for a little."

"Very well," Julia said. And she went quietly out and carefully closed the door.

She was about to start upstairs when she saw a head and shoulders of a young man coming up the lower stairway. It was Sir Gerald Giles, and judging by the expression on his face he was glad to see her.

Chapter Seven

"Julia Crawford!" Giles exclaimed.

She smiled as he joined her on the landing. "I've come to be with your Grandmother."

"Wonderful news!" he said. "Mrs. Glenn just told me. How is the old girl?"

Julia glanced toward the closed door. "Very well, I would say. But she asked me to leave her for a little so she might have a nap."

He nodded. "In that case I won't disturb her. I'll see her later. But I would like to talk to you."

"All right," she said, wondering what might be on his mind.

"Let us go down to the library," he suggested.

They went downstairs to the pleasant, book-lined room at the front of the house. He ushered her inside and then shut the door for privacy. He pulled out a chair for her and stood facing her.

"It is about my wife I wish to speak."

"I went to see Elizabeth a week ago," she said. "But she was not at home. I've seen little of her lately."

The good-looking Sir Giles eyed her directly. "Shall I tell you the truth?"

Startled, she said, "Of course!"

He sighed. "She was at home. She told her maid to put you off with a lie."

She stared at him. "But why?"

He shrugged. "You know how she has changed. She's decided that because of your friendship with Brummell you're not quite respectable."

She gasped. "In that case she must feel the same way about a number of people, including the Prince."

"She does."

"I cannot understand it," Julia worried. "She was so kind to me when I first came to London. Right up until her marriage. Then she began to show signs of prudery!"

Sir Gerald showed a grave look on his bronzed face. "You are right. One reason is that your lives have taken different directions. Another surely has to be that she is unhappy in her marriage to me."

Julia said, "She hinted that to me. I'm sure it hinges on your being absent so much. Must you continue to give such a lot of your time to your stables and racing interests?"

Gerald hesitated a moment and then reached for an armchair and drew it out near her and sat in it. He said, "If I confide in you will you swear to keep what I say secret."

She was amazed by the intensity of his manner. She said, "Yes, I expect so."

He sat back in the chair, his hands clasped across his fawn waistcoat, and very calmly told her, "The business about my owning stables and race horses is a cover up. I own a horse or two and have an interest in several stables. But that is not what keeps me away from London."

"Then what?"

"Long before my marriage I became a member of the

Foreign Service," the young baronet said. "I wished to serve my country during these years of struggle with Napoleon and was told I could best do it as a secret agent."

Astonished, she repeated, "A secret agent!"

"Yes," he said grimly. "I wanted to tell Elizabeth before I asked her to marry me. But I knew what her reaction would be. She would want me to give up the service. I could not do that. So I kept silent."

Julia was confused. "But you are at least risking your life and serving your country," she said. "That is very different from running about the race tracks. If Elizabeth is told the truth she will surely feel different about you."

He shook his head. "No. I understand her now. She would simply have tantrums and insist I retire from my spy work. I am not prepared to do that."

"You feel you cannot trust her with the information you have offered me?"

"I fear that is the truth, dear Julia," Gerald said in a weary tone. "I have made a marriage that is right neither for myself nor Elizabeth."

"You should not despair so easily."

"I have not come to this conclusion without pain," the young man said. "We are no longer living as man and wife. She has her own room and I have mine when I'm at home. It is all a charade. She is surrounding herself with a lot of narrow-minded prigs who sneer at the Prince and his friends. And that is why she has turned against you."

Julia said, "I shall try to see her again. Try to let her understand there is much good in what may seem only a corrupt court circle."

"She would not believe it and she will not see you."

She said, "How can she be so unfair?"

Gerald said, "I think the basic prudishness was always there. Now that she is a married lady she has allowed it to bloom. She came to see Grandmother several times and because the poor old woman enjoyed court gossip and used some racy language, Elizabeth has now refused to ever visit her again."

"That is cruel. I know your Grandmother needs company. And especially family."

"So I come alone as I have today," Gerald said with a sadness in his voice. "I have worried a great deal and not known what to do. I guess that is why I have decided to trust you with the truth."

She asked him, "Where does this spying take you?"

"The Continent mostly," he said. "You know that since Trafalgar direct naval action against us has been postponed. But by the Berlin decree of 1806, we are under blockade. Now, fifteen months later, we are cut off from our export markets and trade is being slowly throttled. Napoleon's plan is to cause a revolution in this country or at the least make us so impoverished that we will beg for peace!"

"And?"

"Meanwhile Napoleon is trying to build a new navy using the Portuguese and Danish fleets to augment it. The attempt of the Baltic Powers, Russia, Sweden, Denmark and Prussia to close the Baltic to British shipping led to the British attack on the Danish fleet outside Copenhagen. It was during this battle Nelson placed his telescope to his blind eye so as not to see Sir Hyde Parker's order to end the engagement. Our navy won that battle. But the Dane's have rebuilt their fleet."

She said, "So they are again a threat?"

"More so than before," he said. "I do not blame the Danish people, they are a heroic nation. But they are under the heel of a ruthless dictator. My assignment now is to find out where the Danish fleet is to gather in preparation of joining with the other vessels of Napoleon's navy. If we get that information properly in advance we can attack again and prevent the Danish Fleet from falling into Napoleon's hands."

"And if you are not successful?"

"The pressure against us will be almost unendurable," he said gravely. "We will either be forced to plead for a peace without honor, or be invaded."

"Then you cannot fail!" she exclaimed.

"Not if Europe is ever to know freedom again."

"How many of you, are there?"

He smiled wearily. "More than you'd imagine. I'm only one of a team. But we have great difficulty getting agents we can trust. It is a dangerous game."

"Are there any female agents?" she asked.

"Not in my division," he told her. "But there must be at least a few. Some of history's most successful spies have been women."

She looked across at him eagerly. "It is the sort of thing I would like to do. Take some action to help my country."

"You will be safer here with grandmother," he told her. "When spies are caught they are executed immediately."

"You go on taking that risk," she said, more admiring of him than she had ever been.

"It is my way of serving my country," he said quietly.

"Elizabeth is a fool!" she said angrily. "And I would like to tell her so!"

He stood up. "Perhaps we oughtn't to blame her. She sees me as a reckless gambler and unfaithful husband."

"But it isn't true!" she protested. "And if she loved you enough to marry you, she should believe in you whatever you do!"

His smile was sad. "I once thought love to be like that. It seems I was wrong. At least in my wife's case."

She now stood up. "What is to happen?"

"I'm going on with the work to which I have dedicated myself."

"I mean between you and Elizabeth?"

"We shall eventually separate. At least there are no children. We each will be able to live our own lives. Or perhaps before this cursed war ends I'll be captured and executed. In that case all will be solved. Her life will be her own once again."

"You mustn't die!" she said impulsively. Then she blushed.

"Thank you, Julia," the young man said in his quiet fashion. "I have always felt we had much in common. Now that you are here with Grandmother I know we shall become close friends."

"I hope so."

"And remember, not a word to Grandmother or anyone else of what I have revealed to you."

"You have my word," she promised.

This marked the beginning of a number of meetings between them. Whenever Gerald was in London he paid visits to his bedridden Grandmother and also took the opportunity of seeing Julia and talking with her. As he'd predicted, they became the best of friends. All the while she worried that something might happen to the young man.

She spent much of her time with his ailing Grandmother, Lady Giles. But there were moments of leisure when she was free to do as she wished. Lady Giles encouraged her to attend parties and any sort of exciting event so that news of it might be brought directly home to her.

"I know most scandal is less than half-true yet I enjoy believing it all," the old woman chuckled.

One of the activities which Julia enjoyed most was the occasional times when Beau Brummell took her for a ride in his carriage. They invariably went to Regent's Park and were invariably an attraction for those enjoying the green grass, the trees and the parade of aristocrats in their carriages and on their horses.

On a particular afternoon Beau was in good spirits. He had lately been despondent at times. His relations with the Prince were not as good as they had been and he worried about his financial position as a result. Yet he continued to dress well, be as arrogant as ever and behave as if he believed his good fortune would last forever. Only a few, like Julia, knew that behind this bold facade there was the beginning of a crumbling.

He sat in the carriage with her at his side, looking as regal as the Prince ought to have. His spotless fawn top hat, his imposing white cravat and fawn coat faultlessly cut made him a fine figure for common folk to admire. His hands rested easily on his silver-tipped walking stick. She was wearing a pale green bonnet with fairly wide shade, and a white dress with green trim.

Beau smiled at her, "You grow more beautiful, my dear. Living with Lady Giles has agreed with you."

"She is a fine old lady."

"Harridan!" he said with a laugh. "In her day she broke many men's hearts. Now I hear she is virtually a wreck."

"She has much spirit and is good company," Julia said. "She would like to entertain you and a few friends at a tea party in her room."

"Would she, indeed?"

Julia gave him a look of appeal. "You'd not begrudge an hour of your time to an old lady?"

He considered. "Not if you request it. And as you say, she could be amusing."

"I will tell her," Julia said happily. "And I have no doubt you will soon be receiving an invitation."

Beau nodded to a bearded man in a passing carriage. He told her, "That is one of my several bankers. I owe him less than most of the others so he is more friendly."

She gave him a worried glance. "Will you never be able to pay your bills?"

"Hopefully. I won 26,000 pounds the other night at the roulette table. And I lost all of it but two hundred pounds by morning."

She was shocked. "You had your chance and you lost it!"

"Another chance will come," he said airily and at the same time acknowledged the cheers of some common people standing by the lane's fence.

She said, "I have no liking for gambling."

"Then you cannot approve of young Sir Gerald Giles. He is a horse owner and gambler."

"He is different," she said. "I cannot but admire him."

Brummell looked amused. "What is the meaning of this banal hero-worship? It is not like you, Julia."

She blushed. "I see a good deal of him at the house. He comes often to see his grandmother. I think him a fine, clean-cut young man."

"Continue and I shall show jealousy," Beau warned her.

She smiled. "No need. I lost my heart to you long ago. Much good that it has done me."

"You are first in my heart," he told her. "Is that not satisfaction enough?"

"We cannot always go on like this."

"Why not?"

"Things change and so do people," she said. "We ought to seize the future while it is still ours."

Beau shook his head. "You will never understand."

"I feel you do not love me truly, That there is much pretence in what you say."

"How can you say that?" he asked her. "You know that I am only truly happy when I'm with you."

"You will not marry me."

"I cannot," he said. "And you know why."

The long silences that usually followed such discussions left her dispirited and full of doubts. She began to wonder if the elegant Beau cared as deeply as he professed or if his so-called "love" for her was superficial and so she would decorate his arm and his carriage. She could not help doubting him.

She informed the elderly Lady Giles that Beau had agreed to come to a tea party given by her. Lady Giles was much pleased. "I shall hold it the next time Gerald returns to London," she said.

Lord Alvaney's invitation to the ball at his home excited Julia. She was sure that the Prince would be there along with most of London's society figures. She and Lady Giles discussed what she would wear and the old lady had her personal seamstress come to live in while she sewed an elaborate crimson evening gown for Julia.

She was to be escorted by Beau and he was sending his carriage for her at seven. Old Lady Giles was tremendously interested in it all and insisted that Julia should come down to her room when she had dressed for the party.

Julia entered the bedroom and found Gerald standing by the bedside of his Grandmother, holding her hand. Confused, she apologized, "I did not mean to interrupt!"

"You are not interrupting," the old lady said at once. "Gerald remained because he wanted to see you. Isn't she lovely?" She asked her grandson this last.

Gerald was standing studying her with admiration in his eyes and on his bronzed face. He said, "I think she is the most beautiful woman in all England!"

"You see!" the old woman in bed said. "Come here, my dear. I have something for you. Something I wish you to wear this evening as a favor to me!"

She smiled and moved gracefully across to the other side of his grandmother's bed and gave him a knowing look. The old woman opened a velvet case which she held and took out a delicate diamond-studded tiara.

"My tiara," Lady Giles said, handling the sparkling silver and diamond creation in her wrinkled hands. "I have not worn it since my husband's death. I want you to wear it tonight."

"I couldn't!" she gasped. 'I'd be terrified of losing it!"

"Not at all," the old woman said. "It is my wish that you wear it."

"It is far too good for me to be seen with," Julia worried.

"No nonsense!" Lady Giles said and handed the tiara to her grandson, saying, "Put it on her head, Gerald. I wish to see it outlined against that soft, black hair!"

A smiling Gerald brought it to her and gently placed it on her head. He said, "You look like some lovely queen!"

"I shall feel like a Cinderella," she said, embarrassed.

Lady Giles chuckled. "In that case be sure and return before midnight when your carriage turns into a pumpkin. I wish to hear a complete account of what goes on and every scrap of gossip!"

"I'll do my best," she promised. "You are too good to me!" And she bent and kissed the wrinkled old cheek.

The old woman sighed. "It is you who are good for me! I need youth about to sustain me. I hoped that Gerald would have provided me great grandchildren by now. But he hasn't!"

Gerald had his turn to look embarrassed. He said, "Small children would only annoy you."

"Ridiculous!" the old woman said. "You were a small child once and a delightful one! Where is Elizabeth tonight? Is she not attending this fine party? And what about you?"

A wry look crossed his bronzed face. "Elizabeth thinks the London society group too frivolous for her. And I, as a dutiful husband, must remain at home with her."

Lady Giles looked indignant. "She is a prig and a fool ! You made a sorry mistake in marrying her!"

"Let us not mar Julia's evening with our personal problems," Gerald said. And to Julia, "I wager it is time for you to leave."

She said, "Yes. Beau's carriage will be at the door any moment."

"Be off with you!" Lady Giles said. "See her to the door, Gerald, then come back and talk to me!"

Sir Gerald saw her to the front door and then turned and surprised her by saying, "Grandmother is not fair! She tempts me beyond endurance! I vow she knows how I feel about you!"

She stared at him. "Feel about me?"

"I love you, Julia," he said in impassioned tone, "I have since our first meeting long ago!"

"Gerald!" She stared up at his troubled face.

"Forgive me! You are so beautiful tonight you made me confess it," he went on. "I did not intend to tell you. I hope it will not ruin our friendship!"

She shook her head. "No. But we must be sensible. You are married to Elizabeth, my friend."

"She hates you! Refuses to see you!" he reminded her. "Just as she hates me! Neither you nor I mean anything to her."

"It is a sorry situation," she agreed.

He took her by the arms and gazed earnestly into her eyes. "Sorrier still for me to be turning you over to another man!"

"I hadn't guessed," she said, but deep within her she knew that she had. That this moment had been building. She had slowly been falling in love with the good-looking bronzed man.

There was the sound of the carriage outside. Gerald took her in his arms and kissed her fiercely. Then he let her go with reluctance and in a low voice said, "We will discuss this later." And he saw her out to the waiting carriage. Beau was standing there, in black dress clothes, to help her inside.

Beau stared at her and exclaimed, "The tiara is the ultimate touch to your beauty, my dear!" And then he turned to Sir Gerald and with a friendly smile, observed, "You are back in London, dear boy! Alvaney would want you at the party if he knew."

Gerald said, "I fear that is impossible. I have only just returned and my wife is waiting for me at home."

"Ah, yes, the attractive Elizabeth," Beau said. "We have not seen her of late. You two must take life less seriously and join us once in a while."

Gerald nodded. "That would be pleasant. I trust you both have a wonderful evening."

Julia gave him a tender, lingering glance before she

let Beau help her into the carriage. He stood forlornly back as they drove off. Beau, at her side, gave her an amused glance.

"You draw gallants at every turn, my dear. I swear he looked quite unhappy at your leaving with me."

"His is not too happy a life," she said. "Nor has he too good a marriage."

"The same could be said of half the couples in London," Beau told her. "And the other half have reconciled to their condition. And you ask me why I refuse to marry! Marriage is the sure road to dissillusion, my dear!"

She stared ahead of her in the shadowed interior of the carriage and said quietly, "I think with the right people it might be a path to something quite different!"

He chuckled. "Not only are you a beauty, you are also a romantic. A dangerous combination for any male to deal with."

Lord Alvaney, looking more purple of countenance than ever, was at the door to greet them. He had adopted Beau's new fashion of dark evening dress and his jowels protruded over his white cravat as if stuffed by an enterprising taxidermist. He told them, "The music is under way. The Prince is in the blue room. Everyone in town is here!"

It was a slight exaggeration but the great reception hall and ivory-decorated ballroom was filled with people. The latest in gowns and evening dress was evident around them. The music provided a lively background to the animated conversation. It looked a likely place for Julia to pick up some gossip for Lady Giles.

"Shall we explore the ballroom first?" Beau asked.

"If you like," she said.

They were making their way through the various groups to the ballroom entrance when suddenly a figure appeared coming towards them, leaning on a crutch under his left arm. His left leg was bent and the foot off the ground. It was James Fitzroy in a gold-colored coat and blue breeches. He saw them and a look of hatred crossed his face which made her clasp Beau's arm tighter and fight a desire to tremble.

The crippled Fitzroy moved by them and Beau gave her a knowing look. He said, "His evil nature shows clearly in his face."

"He frightens me," she said, with a shudder.

"I doubt that he will bother you again," Beau said. "Let us dance!"

They danced for a little and then, since it was getting intolerably warm in the ballroom despite its high ceiling, she suggested they leave the floor.

"It is time we sought out the Prince," Beau said. And so they made their way towards the blue room, which was a short distance from the dancing. The doors to the Wedgewood Room were open and the moment they entered she noted the Prince, in dress military uniform of scarlet and gold, and standing with him in pale white satin was none other than Sir Orville Hewitt. The two seemed to be having an earnest chat.

"That bodes no good!" she whispered to Beau.

"He has been wheedling his way into the Prince's favor for some time," Brummell said. "I blame him for the Prince's occasional annoyance with me. But I still have the upper hand with Florizel."

"I hope so," she said.

Skiffy came and presented his compliments. "You look much more like a Queen than anything I have seen except on a playing card."

"And you have seen many of those queens," she replied with good humor.

"To my despair!" Skeffington replied. "The great trouble is they never grace my hand at the right time." And to Beau, he said, "The Prince has been asking for you."

Julia and Beau moved across to the Prince with Skiffy trailing after them. Others in the room seeing that Brummell had arrived and was joining the Prince, moved in to form a circle, eager to hear what might be said.

The Prince was more corpulent than when she'd last seen him. He regarded her with unashamed interest and said, "So, Beau has decided to create his own royalty! By Gad, I must say I approve."

She curtsied, "Thank you, sire."

Sir Orville spoke up, asking, "Where have you two been? We have been waiting for you." It was evident that he was making an attempt to show them as not properly respectful of the Prince.

Brummell smiled at him and airily said, "But my dear fellow, people who are late are invariably jollier than the people who have to wait for them!"

The Prince burst into laughter. "Jolly good, Beau. And I must say, true of tonight. It has been a dull occasion for me thus far."

Sir Orville crimsoned as he had been the Prince's sole companion as they entered. He told the Prince, "I hope my comments did not bore you, they were offered with the best intention."

The Prince blinked and said, "I fear I did not get the full gist of them."

Brummell said, "I sometimes wonder who does the most mischief. Enemies with bad intentions or friends with the best!"

The group around them, led by Lord Skeffington burst into approving laughter. Sir Orville apparently felt he could bear no more. He bowed soberly to the Prince and with a scowl for them withdrew.

As he marched out of the room the Prince said, "I wonder what is wrong with Hewitt? He took such sudden leave of us!"

Brummell smiled sweetly. "He is not a very bright fellow, sire. Our conversation was probably too difficult for him to understand. He has a feeling of inferiority which came of his discovering he was born in bed with a lady!"

The Prince guffawed. He pounded Brummell on the back. "Now, the evening is under way. Did you see old Lord Dudley, his wife, and her paramour as you came in?"

"I did, sire, "Beau said. "And if I may deign to speak coarsely before this lovely lady, I would suggest the paramour has adopted the commandments to hate thy neighbor and love thy neighbor's wife!"

This again delighted the Prince. And so the evening progressed. It was the duty of Beau to be court jester and keep the pudgy Prince amused. Julia, for her part, was content to stand silently by most of the time. She received many compliments about her tiara. And much of the time her thoughts were far away, with the man who had seen her to the carriage.

Sir Gerald's handsome bronzed face haunted her amid the pomp and glitter of the party. She could not but contrast his character and way of life with that of the people around her. And Beau and the Prince had to be included in those who led less meaningful lives. She began to think of herself. And the only credit she found on her side was her attendance on old Lady Giles. At least she was earning her keep in an honest manner.

Brummell turned to her and said, "I vow you did not hear my last and best quip! You seem miles away!"

She forced herself to smile and say, "Perhaps I'm becoming weary. The noise, heat and crowd!"

He looked around and said, "You are right. It is getting late and the pace is slacking."

"Also," she said, "I promised Lady Giles to be home before midnight."

"Then you shall be," Beau said. "I have promised the Prince to go to his place following the party. But you would not want to be there. It is strictly a male affair."

"Of course," she said.

They bade the Prince goodnight and then paid their respects to Lord Alvaney who had been forced to sit in a chair by the door to say goodnight to his guests. The old baronet complimented her on being a decoration to his party and they went out to their carriage.

Beau relaxed in the carriage and said, "I think I handled Sir Orville well enough."

"He is like a viper," she warned him. "As soon as his venom has renewed he will strike back again."

"I'm aware of that," Beau said. "That is why I must be at the Prince's place later. I have to work at keeping his favor."

"What if you tire of it, one day?"

"That will be the end for me," Beau said.

"You should build your life more sturdily than that," she told him.

His smile was sad. "Excellent advice. I fear it has come too late."

At the door he kissed her goodnight and confessed, "There are moments lately when I fear I may be losing you."

She smiled at him gently. "You will always have my love."

"But you?" he asked. "Will I always have you?"

She hesitated and then replied quietly, "Isn't that for you to decide?"

He nodded. "It always comes back to marriage, doesn't it?"

"I'm afraid so," she said.

He made no more comment but he did kiss her again, more tenderly than before. So that she went inside with an infinite feeling of sadness.

Mrs. Glenn, in her dressing gown and nightcap, came down the main stairway to greet her. "You did get back before midnight," she said. "Lady Giles will be pleased."

"I promised I would."

"And isn't she still sitting up awake, waiting for you," Mrs. Glenn said with Scotch despair. "Ah, well, it will do her no great harm! And tell her some grand gossip! Even if you have to make it up!"

Julia laughed. "I have been with the Prince and Mr. Brummell all evening, listening to their barbed wit. I have enough gossip to satisfy the worst gabbler!"

"What a wonderful thing youth is!" Old Lady Giles exclaimed as she came into the room. "You've been out for hours and you look as radiant as when you left!"

Julia smiled and came over to the old woman. "You ought to be asleep."

"Not a bit of it. I want to hear about it all!"

"Your tiara was a great success," she said, removing it and handing it to her. "I had many compliments about it."

Lady Giles fingered the sparkling piece of jewelry. "I'm sure it was good for it to be seen again. Now tell me what you saw and heard."

Julia sat by the side of the bed and said, "Well, Lady Dudley was there with her ancient husband on one arm and her young lover on the other!"

"The old crow!" Lady Giles exclaimed. "She was never a beauty at her best! If I were able to walk I'd be at the party and show her!"

"I'm certain you would," Julia laughed. And then she went on to tell her all the witty comments Brummell had offered to amuse the Prince.

Lady Giles listened with delight and when she'd finished, said, "Tomorrow you must tell me everything all over again. I have not enjoyed myself so in a long time."

Julia stood up. "I'll have Mrs. Glenn come in to see you comfortably asleep. Did Sir Gerald stay long?"

"He sat with me for a while," the old woman sighed. "That boy is not happy. He made a bad marriage." She gave her a warm glance. "Why couldn't he have chosen someone like you?"

Julia said a quick goodnight and hurried out of the room to cover her embarrassment. She sent Mrs. Glenn in to the old lady and went on to her own room upstairs. But she lay awake for a long while after going to bed. Her thoughts were less of the party than of

Beau Brummell and Sir Gerald Giles. She tried to compare the two in her mind but couldn't. She at last sleepily admitted to herself that she cared deeply for both of them. With this thought she fell asleep.

The next day she told Lady Giles that Beau and some of his friends would be prepared to join her for tea if she would only set the day. "I should be honored," the old woman said. "Let us make it Friday. I shall write the invitations in my own hand!"

Lady Giles was busy at this task when Sir Gerald called the next afternoon. He took Julia to the library and as soon as the door was closed behind them he kissed her again.

She looked up at him sadly and asked, "What is to become of us?"

"We have fallen in love."

"Admitting that," she said. "We are in an impossible situation. Elizabeth is bound to say I plotted to win you for myself. She already thinks me a creature of loose morals!"

"I will not let her spread such a lie," he said with indignation. "When the time comes to declare our love, all will know it was I who came to you."

"Gerald! We can only cause others unhappiness! Your Grandmother, who trusts me will lose her faith in me. Beau will consider me a mindless flirt!"

Gerald was in a tense mood. He said, "If there is any way for court or church to cancel my marriage I shall take advantage of it. But if this is not possible I offer you a fine house of your own and we shall live there as husband and wife, churched or not!"

"The scandal?"

"London is full of scandals. We would only be in the limelight for a little. Then we would settle down happily with each other. Will Brummell offer you as much?"

"He is not able to."

"Because he is dependent on the Prince's favor? Is that not so?"

"In a way," she said unhappily. "It is very complicated. He believes in what he is doing just as you believe in your way of life."

"I risk my life for England. For such as the Prince and Brummell."

"I know."

"I would not ask you to declare yourself for me if I did not think you loved me as truly as I love you. Or if it meant taking you from any more secure love. But Brummell will never offer you marriage while I will, if it is possible."

She gazed up at him, tears filling her eyes. "You are a good and generous person. And I have come to love you."

"So?"

"Let us wait just a little," she begged him. "Perhaps some miraculous event will solve some of our problems."

"I find myself impatient," he told her, his arms still around her.

"I know!"

"I cannot remain here long," he went on. "I shall soon be returning to Denmark."

"When?"

"A few days at most. Though I do not want anyone else to know. Not even Grandmother."

"I will not tell," she said.

His sad eyes searched hers. "You will give me your answer before I leave?"

"Yes."

"Darling, Julia!" He embraced her again.

Mrs. Glenn showed a wise expression on her thin, old face as she saw them come out of the library. She told Julia, "Lady Giles has finished her invitations. She wants you to address them and see them delivered."

"I will," she said. And to Gerald, "You must come up and see her. She thinks so much of you."

"I intended to see her," Gerald said with a smile.

They entered the old woman's room together and

her shrewd eyes fixed on them. She said, "What sort of conspiracy are you two planning?"

Gerald laughed and went over and kissed her. "Nothing, Grandmother. We were just discussing your party. If I'm in London, am I invited?"

"Of course you are," Lady Giles said. "I want you to be here. Julia is arranging everything."

"I shall try to be here," he said.

"You ought to," Lady Giles said with one of her wise smiles. "Beau Brummell is going to be the guest of honor!"

Julia knew she was blushing and she was beginning to believe that Lady Giles suspected more than she was saying. That the old woman knew Beau and Gerald were now rivals! And at the moment Julia wasn't herself sure which one would win her.

Chapter Eight

Julia found it incredible. Just when she thought herself faced with more problems than she could hope to deal with, a new one presented itself to her. It began on a foggy, wet morning when she was helping Mrs. Glenn prepare for the tea to be given by Lady Giles. They were deciding which of the maids they would use for the occasion when someone knocked on the front door.

Mrs. Glenn went to answer it and came back with a questioning look on her thin face, telling Julia, "It's a gentleman, Miss Crawford. He says he has some business with you."

"With me?"

"Yes."

"Did he give you his name?" Julia asked. They were standing together in the sewing room.

"Yes" the housekeeper said. "He's a Mr. Craft, a solicitor."

"A solicitor!" she said, astounded. "What could he want with me?"

"Perhaps it's a mistake. But he asked to speak with Miss Julia Crawford."

"It's all right," Julia said. "I'll see him. But I can't imagine what it may be about."

She went out to the living room where a fussy-looking, bald man in dark coat and gray trousers sat with a brief case on his lap. On hearing her approach he glanced up at her and she saw he wore old-fashioned square-rimmed spectacles and had an undistinguished face.

He rose quickly on seeing her and bowed. "Miss Crawford?"

"That is my name," she said carefully. "And you are Mr. Craft?"

"Mr. Thaddeus Craft," he said importantly as if that might make a great difference. He had the air of a small man trying to be impressive.

"What have you come to see me about, Mr. Craft?" she asked.

"A matter of prime concern, may I say," the small man assured her. "It will take a little time. Would you be good enough to sit down?"

"Very well," she said, still wondering what it might be about.

The little man managed a stiff smile. "Of course you have never heard of me before."

"No."

"Though I have made my reputation in the law," he went on, as he fumbled at opening the brief case. "But then a protected, young woman such as yourself would know little about the law."

Julia said, "Please continue, Mr. Craft."

He adjusted his glasses and studied a sheet of paper which he held before him. He explained, "I have made some notes for reference."

"About what?"

"The matter at hand," he said with true legal bafflement. It was evident that he meant to unravel his mission with the same slow progress as a spider weaving its web.

"I must confess I do not know what you are talking about," she said.

The little man studied her with surprise over the rims of the glasses perched on his button of a nose. He said, "Of course you don't. I haven't told you yet."

"I see," she said, resigned, her hands folded in her lap.

"You lived in Surrey?"

"Yes."

"As a ward of the Rev. Edward Weir?"

"Yes," she said. "Has anything happened to him?"

The little man lifted a hand to placate her. "No. He is quite well, enjoying good health considering his age."

"Thank goodness," she said. "For a moment I feared you had come to tell me that he was dead. I became very fond of him. He was like a father to me, or perhaps a grandfather."

The little man was studying her with interest. "Yes, of course. That is to be understood. Your late mother acted as his housekeeper for some years."

"Yes. We both lived at the parsonage. It is he whom I owe for my education."

"I would say he did a remarkable job of it," Mr. Craft complimented her. "You speak and act like a lady."

"Thank you."

He referred to the sheet of paper again. "You later lived with Sir Orville and Lady Jane Hewitt."

"Just before I came here," she said.

"Yes," he said, rather absently, as he studied the

paper. Then he looked at her with sharpness. "And your father?"

"Was an actor, sir," she said. "Not that he gave much time to it. Gambling interested him more. He deserted my mother when I was very young."

"Do you recall him at all?"

"No," she said, amazed at his line of questioning. "Why do you ask?"

The bald man fiddled with his spectacles. "So you neither saw him or talked with him?"

"I know nothing about him except what my mother told me," she said. "And considering what he had done I grew up hating his memory."

"Natural, I suppose," the little solicitor said.

"Of course he died years ago and lately I have come to feel differently about him," she confessed.

"Indeed?" Mr. Craft seemed interested.

"Yes. I have seen more of the world. I know what a hold gambling gets on some men. I can understand better how it happened to destroy him and make him neglect his family."

"Quite."

"Perhaps he wasn't a really bad person after all," she went on. "It was just that he did not fit in my mother's world. He could not make her understand and was not able to reform. I suppose in such circumstances it was best that he should vanish."

"There is much wisdom in what you say," the solicitor agreed.

She gazed at him in surprise. "But why should you be so interested?"

"Ah!" he said, with an air of mystery.

"Really, Mr. Craft!" she exclaimed with some impatience, "I cannot sit here all the day while you generalize. I must insist that you come to the point at once."

"Of course," he replied. "You said just now your father is dead."

"Yes."

The pale blue eyes behind the ancient spectacles beamed at her. "I say that he is alive."

"Alive?" she gasped.

"Yes," the little man said, obviously enjoying the drama of it all. "Not only is he alive, but he is prosperous and well, and living here in London."

Julia was shaken. She stared at the solicitor. "I'm sorry, but I have known from my childhood that my father is dead."

"You were told that to spare you," Mr. Craft said. "The Reverend Edward Weir will bear that out. He and your mother felt you would be less bitter if you felt your father had passed on."

She listened in a state of shock. Then she managed, "You are saying my father is alive and living in London at this moment?"

"More than that," the little man said. "You have met him."

"That is impossible!" she protested.

"Let me refresh your memory," he said. "You were a special guest at Witier's Gaming Club in the company of the President, Mr. George Bryan Brummell. You were introduced to your father at the roulette table. Of course he didn't realize who you were until later and you didn't recognize him."

She frowned and searched her mind and gradually it began to come back to her. A memory of a stern, tall, dark man! A professional gambler! Beau had introduced them and noted that they both bore the name of Crawford.

She looked at the little Mr. Craft again and in a taut voice, said, "John Crawford! He is the John Crawford who is my father?"

"You have it exactly," Mr. Craft said with satisfaction. "I did not wish to break it to you all at once. Quite a shock! Have known ladies to faint at this kind of revelation! Very awkward!"

"I shan't faint!" she said, rising and beginning to

pace back and forth. She found herself dealing with a confusion of feelings. She could barely sort them out, though gradually indignation and hurt seemed to take over.

"Your father sent me here," the solicitor said.

"Did he?" she asked coldly.

"Yes. He is most repentant for the way he has treated you and he wishes to make it up to you."

"Does he actually think that possible?"

"He hopes it will be. He is a most respectable businessman these days with vast real estate holdings. He owns the building in which the Witier Club is located and shares in its profits. He takes pride in having risen from the depths to his present position and he wishes you to benefit by it."

She was thoroughly enraged now. Tears of pain in her eyes, she demanded, "What a pity he couldn't have had this generous turn of heart before my poor mother died!"

Mr. Craft cleared his throat. "That is regrettable. But your father was the victim of a cruel lie. A lie perpetrated by a woman he felt he could trust. He sent her to Surrey to give you and your mother financial assistance from him in an anonymous manner, she returned with the word that your mother had married again and taken you along with her to Virginia, in the United States."

"How could he believe such a story?"

"I understand the woman was persuasive and he trusted her. She indicated your mother had married well and he decided not to pursue it since it could lead to bigamy charges for her. It was not until a year ago that he found this woman out in other perfidy and she boasted to him that she had lied to him about the circumstances of you and your mother. Needless to say he was much shattered. It was then he began the investigation which led me directly here today."

She heard the story with a continued mixture of feelings. She realized what the lawyer said might be true but she still blamed her father for his deserting her mother and herself in the first place and not coming honestly to them later with his attempts to undo the great wrong he had done them.

Julia said, "My father does not sound like a very honest person."

"On the contrary," Mr. Craft said, "Mr. Crawford now has an impeccable reputation. I look after his legal affairs and I can promise you he is a most just individual."

Bitterly, she said, "Tell him I congratulate him on his reforming!"

"I shall," he said, disregarding the sarcasm in her tone. He paused, then went on, "You will not be surprised to know that he wishes to see you again. He wants to know you better and he hopes you will forgive him."

She faced the lawyer with dignity. "That is unlikely, sir."

Mr. Craft looked sad. "Please do not make too rash a decision. Give yourself a little time to think on this. Your father is ready to set you up in a fine home, make you his sole heir, and generally make amends. He has already sent the old parson a good sum of money for his kindness to you."

"I'm grateful for that," she said. "Poor old dear Mr. Weir deserves something. But I have managed my own way this far. I need no help from my father now."

The little man sighed and closed his brief case. "Your father is not a stupid man. He realized you would be resentful. At least, at first. He hopes that later you may mellow somewhat toward him. He does not wish your answer now. You may reach him at his home at seventeen Bond Street or contact him through my office at ten Baker Street."

"I have no thought of contacting him," she replied.

Mr. Craft stood up. "Not now! Not until the shock has worn away. But he is your father. He does care for you. And it would be generous of you to forgive him."

She saw the little man out to the rainy street again and returned to join Mrs. Glenn in the living room. She was not sure if the meeting had really happened or if it had been some sort of weird dream. She collapsed into the nearest chair and stared at Mrs. Glenn blankly.

The Scotch woman offered her a kindly smile and asked, "Did you have a bit of a shock?"

"Yes."

"You look a mite pale," the woman observed. "Would a wee draft of brandy help you?"

She shook her head. "I'll be all right. It's just that I've heard something which has turned my world upside down!"

"As bad as that?"

"I'd say so," Julia said. And she quickly told the housekeeper why the solicitor had called on her and what her reaction had been.

Mrs. Glenn heard her out and said, "I can't say that I blame you. But at the same time have you a right to turn your back on your father and all that money!"

"I don't want him or the money!" she declared, tears in her eyes.

Mrs. Glenn sighed. "I understand. But as the lawyer advised, you should take your time about it. And you must tell the old woman. It will make her day! You know how she loves exciting gossip!"

"I don't want to even think about it!" Julia said.

"I'm afraid you'll have to do that now you know," the housekeeper said. "It will always be in your mind."

So a little later on Julia sat by the bedside of Lady Giles and recounted the amazing story for the old woman's benefit. Lady Giles reacted just as Mrs. Glenn had predicted. She was completely enthralled by the account.

The wrinkled face under the lace cap brightened and she said, "Do you realize what this means to you, my girl? You are a lady in your own right. Your father's legacy will make you financially independent."

"I do not want him or the money," she repeated

Lady Giles sighed. "That is sheer nonsense, dear child. You revile your poor father for not behaving properly toward you in the past and now that he wishes to make amends you revile him for that also!"

"I grew up feeling hatred for him!"

"Your poor mother would not have approved of that," the old woman suggested. "She must have once loved this man. Think of her happiness if she knew you two were reunited."

"Too late for her!" she said with a sob.

Lady Giles gave her a comforting tap on the arm. "I know how you feel. What a shock this has been. But I quite agree with that lawyer. You must think this over very carefully before making any decision."

"I can make my own way!"

"Of course you can," the old lady said. "But forget the money altogether. Consider what your duty is as a daughter?"

"I don't know," she confessed.

"Why not take it up with Mr. Brummell?" Lady Giles said. "You say he and your father are friends."

Lady Giles' reasonable advice prevailed. She had the old aristocrat's permission to use the carriage to call on Mr. Brummell and seek out his opinion on this startling news. Julia donned a cape with attached hood to guard against the drizzle and set out for Beau's house.

His man greeted her with the usual uneasiness. He said, "You have come at a bad time, miss. Mr. Brummell is having his bath."

"Will he be long?"

"Perhaps an hour," the servant said.

She told him, "I'm here on urgent business. I shall wait."

"If you insist, miss, I'll tell him you're here," the man said gloomily. "But he takes a good deal of time with his ablutions."

She sat down and picked up a copy of the latest "Tatler" which was on the table and began to read it. Among the items which she noted was one saying that

Sir Orville and Lady Hewitt were giving a party to honor the Prince. She knew how penny-pinching Sir Orville could be and realized he would only spend the enormous money a party for the Prince would entail if he felt he was getting more firmly established in the Royal circle. This could mean bad news for her and Beau.

She was deliberating on this when Beau came to join her. Handsome as ever in his rich gold and brown dressing gown, there was the scent of some pleasant spicy soap about him.

He kissed her and said, "Why this unexpected visit? Has Lady Giles changed her plan for the tea party?"

"No," she said with a smile. "This is a personal problem."

His smile in return was wry. He said, "Don't tell me you've deserted me and fallen in love with someone else?"

This was so close to the truth she blushed deeply. It brought Gerald back in her thoughts again. And that was still to be settled. But she said, "Nothing like that!"

"Then come sit with me and tell me about it quickly," he said. "I have yet to dress and I'm due to meet fat George."

She let him lead her to a settee and they seated themselves so they faced each other. She said, "Something quite unexpected happened today. Something of which you are a part."

"Go on," he said.

So she did. He listened in silence as she told him the incredible story. She could not tell by his expression what his reaction truly was.

He finally said, "So John Crawford is your father."

"So it would seem."

"You need not be ashamed of him."

"I have grown up despising his memory."

Beau frowned, "I think you are wrong. The story the lawyer told you explains why he didn't try to help you and your mother earlier. I know the woman he speaks of, who betrayed his trust, she was his mistress. She stole from him and ran off with a very common fellow. There's no question that she lied to your father. Telling him you were in Virginia. Now he wishes to make amends. I say, you should let him."

She hesitated tearfully. "You are his friend, Beau, he is a stranger to me! I can't help what I feel."

"I fully agree," Beau said, taking her hands in his. "I suggest you let me talk with your father."

"If you like."

"We are good friends," he went on. "And I will be able to present your point of view in the proper fashion."

"You mustn't tell him I forgive him!"

Beau smiled. "I won't go that far. But I think that some time in the future we should arrange a small dinner for the three of us. Then you may meet him under pleasant circumstances."

"I'm not certain yet."

"We will not rush it," he promised. "The situation has gone on so long there is no need for rush."

"I'm completely confused, Beau," she looked at him with forlorn eyes. "I'm still a hireling in Lady Giles' house. I wish I had real position. That I were your wife!"

Beau shook his head. "Then your position would surely be abominable! Think how detestable it is to be agreeable to someone day in and day out, year in and year out!"

"You always mock me when I ask about our future," she reproved him.

"Because I must, my little one," Beau said, rising. "Now I beg you go or I shall be late for the Prince."

"Always the Prince!" she said, standing up at the same time.

"Fat George is my lucky shilling," he laughed. "And let me tell you something. I have a half promise from him he'll attend Lady Giles' tea party. So do not say I refuse to put myself out on your behalf."

"Anything, but the one thing I want," she said quietly.

Brummell eyed her sadly. "I'm sorry," he said. "I swear it." He kissed her and saw her on her way.

When she arrived back at the home of Lady Giles she found Sir Gerald waiting for her in the living room. She undid her cloak and went in to him. He took her by the hands and drew her close to him and kissed her.

She whispered, "Be careful! The servants will see us and there'll be a scandal!"

"Let there be," he said. "My Grandmother is resting. She told me all about your long lost father turning up."

"I'm still in a daze."

"I can understand," the young man said. "I hope it will make no difference with us."

"Why should it?"

"You went to Beau Brummell for advice, my Grandmother said."

"Yes."

"What did he tell you?"

"To be discreet. To wait a little and he'd arrange a meeting with my father."

"Good advice," Gerald said with a shrug. Then he eyed her with wry amusement, "But I wish you had come to me for it rather than to him."

"I couldn't!" she protested. "Not go to Elizabeth's house!"

"My house as well," he said. "But I understand."

"Beau has long been my closest friend," she said.

The young man in brown said, "Would it not be more correct to say that you have been his protege?"

She gazed at him with eyes that were frank. "I have not been his mistress."

He looked uncomfortable. "If you say so. But you must know that most of London believes you are."

"I do not care what the gossips prattle!"

"I commend you for that," the bronzed young man said. " But you must also know that Brummell has had a string of women. He is a regular visitor at the house of

Harriete Wilson, along with the Prince. They have their choice of the most beautiful new girls."

Her cheeks burned and she turned away. "I think the Prince has much influence on him."

"There are those who say it is Brummell and his friends who make the Prince so profligate."

"He seems to come to it naturally."

"I agree," Gerald said. "Then there is the Duchess of York. The dog lover! Brummell boards his dog with her much of the time. And it is well known they have more than dogs in common. She is accepted as his mistress."

Unhappily, she turned and asked, "Why do you tell me these things?"

"Not to pain you!"

"Surely they must do that and you know it," she said. "In any case I have heard them all before."

Gerald looked at her bravely. "I repeat them because I'm madly jealous of you. And I want you to truly understand that Brummell will never marry you!"

"How can you be so sure?"

"Because I know him well and the group who are his friends. He is the best of them. But he will eventually bring himself to disgrace with his corruption and gambling. Only the Prince saves him from his creditors."

She stared at the troubled Sir Gerald. "And what have you to offer me, that is so much better?"

"My deep devotion! My unswerving faithfulness!"

"That sounds strange coming from the husband of my best friend."

"Elizabeth is no longer a friend of yours anymore than she is a wife to me," the young man declared. "And you well know it!"

"I'm sorry," she said. "But what is there for us?"

"The joy of being together."

"And the scandal!"

"I risk my life regularly for the King," he said with

some passion. "You are aware that spies are executed. When I leave on a mission I know that I may never return. I cannot live for the long future, I must seek what I want now, or risk losing it altogether."

"And you want me?"

"Yes," he drew her close to him again and she was aware of his pounding heart against her." And I believe I have earned the right to ask you to give yourself to me."

Her throat was tight with emotion. "I do care for you deeply, Gerald. But there is so much separating us. Your marriage to Elizabeth, my feeling that Brummell needs me, and my loyalty to your Grandmother."

He pressed his lips to hers and silenced her. Then he said softly, "Nothing as important as our love for each other."

"I must think about this," she said.

"There will be little time," he warned her.

She stared up into his handsome, bronzed face with some apprehension. "What do you mean by that?"

"I have orders to travel to Denmark," he said. "I shall be leaving no later than next week. The plan is to sail from Dover to Esjberg. There I shall contact a man known only to me as Lars who will give me the information the British Admiralty needs regarding the movement of the Danish navy."

"And then?"

"My orders are to move on to Germany where I will try to gain more information." He paused. Then he said, "You once told me you would be willing to serve your country as a spy."

"Yes, I did."

There was a stern look on his face. "Then I can offer it to you now. I need a trusted agent in Dover, and believe me they are hard to find, who will await the documents I send from Esjberb and see them safely delivered to the Admiralty offices in London."

"You are suggesting I be that agent?"

"Why not? The most anyone would suspect would be that you had become my mistress and were in Dover waiting for my return. It gives us the opportunity to become lovers and fellow spies at the one time!"

The offer both thrilled and excited her. She said, "You tempt me greatly!"

"Then agree!"

"But what of Beau? He will hate me forever!"

"Not if his supposed love for you is genuine. We can face him together and I'm sure he will continue to be your best friend."

"I wonder," she said with doubt. "And there is your Grandmother! She is so happy at the moment! The shock might make her ill!"

Sir Gerald smiled. "Believe me, my Grandmother has survived much worse things than us running off together. She will probably approve and thrive on it. Mrs. Glenn is capable of looking after her until you return."

"As your mistress I cannot well live here as your Grandmother's companion!" she reminded him.

He smiled. "We will manage that when we are faced with it. In the meanwhile I beg that you be ready to leave at short notice."

"Have you no idea of the exact day?"

"It depends a good deal on the Admiralty. I would say another week at most."

"At least that will give me some time to settle my affairs, and have some sort of wardrobe ready to take with me."

"You women!" he said with good humor. "Let me warn you that your wardrobe must be the simplest. Spies travel lightly."

Her eyes showed a rouguish twinkle in them. "Even when they are also lovers?"

"Even when they are lovers," he said, embracing her again.

Old Lady Giles had seen to it that her bedroom was literally filled with flowers. They were arranged every-where, great splashes of color to brighten the atmosphere. The old woman was propped up on pillows of red satin with a red satin throw covering her bed. She wore an orange dressing gown over her night dress and a maid had worked long and hard to fix up her hair attractively.

Now it was four o'clock and her guests were due to arrive. She smiled up at Julia from the crimson pillows and exclaimed, "What a treasure you are, my dear! I vow no one else would have been able to arrange this for me!"

Demure in gown of pale blue Julia returned the smile and said, "It is you who are the hostess. I could not have managed unless Mr. Brummell and the others wished to see you!"

The first guest to arrive was none other than Gerald, which seemed as it should be. He was wearing a smart brown jacket and came over to kiss his Grandmother and compliment her on the room.

"I vow it's the finest looking room in London," he said, gazing at the vases of flowers banked about everywhere.

Lady Giles gave Julia a fond glance and said, "Give this girl credit for it all!"

Next to be ushered in by Mrs. Glenn were Beau Brummell and Lord Alvaney. Beau was immaculate in a dark blue jacket and yellow trousers, while old Lord Alvaney was less splendid in black and gray. The handsome Brummell came to the old Lady's bedside, bowed and kissed the back of her hand.

He said, "Madam, my compliments. Your name is still magic in London's best circles."

The old woman looked pleased and said, "I'm sure I must be long forgotten but is is nice of you to suggest that a few still remember me."

"A few, my lady?" Brummell said with feigned amazement. "Is not the Prince coming to pay you his best this very afternoon?"

Lady Giles gasped. "The Prince!"

"His Royal Highness," Brummell said with a smile. "He should be here at any moment."

"It is too much!" Lady Giles exclaimed with delight. "We have the best champagne ready and every other treat you may desire."

Ancient Lord Alvaney paid his respects to the old woman, a broad smile on his purple, bloated face as he said, "You were always my favorite dance partner, ma'am!"

She tapped him playfully with her fan. "That is sheer nonsense. You danced with so many in your hey-day I'm sure you lost count!"

Gerald glanced across the bed to where Brummell and Julia were standing and told the dandy, "I'm most appreciative of your presence here today."

"My pleasure!" Brummell replied. "And how are the horses and the stables?"

"They keep me occupied," Gerald said with a smile. "In fact I expect to leave town on account of my interests next week."

"Best of luck to you," Brummell replied, not realizing the business Gerald meant. Or that she was to be part of it.

Julia felt a pang of guilt. She gazed from one handsome man to the other and was slightly embarrassed that they should both be here in this room. Gazing at the aristocratic Brummell for a long moment she knew that he held the key to her heart, but she also realized that all that Gerald had said was true. Marriage and a normal future with the dandy was most unlikely. She should consider herself fortunate to have someone as dashing as Gerald anxious to have her as his own. Even though he was married he had announced his willingness to set her up in her own home in London and live with her, whatever scandal it might cause!

She had not long to think about that for the Prince arrived, bumbling and overweight, with the thin Skeffy as his companion. The Prince kissed the hand of Lady Giles and murmured some low pleasantries and Lord Skeffington then simpered a few complimentary words to her.

Beau took charge and the party began. He was at his wittiest and after he had toasted the Prince, he offered a toast to Lady Giles, saying, "To my dear friend Lady Giles, every man wants a woman to help improve his character, to expand his morals and to help him behave in a saintly fashion, but even more he often needs a woman who can make temporarily make him forget all these things! Such a lovely and loving woman is our hostess!"

Lady Giles greeted the laughter which filled the room at this. It was the maddest of tea parties with these noble wits assembled at her bedside, a tribute to a woman who had played an important role in London Society for a half-century.

"Now fill my ears with social sewerage," Lady Giles commanded them.

Beau Brummell produced a snuff box and delicately touched a sniff to each nostril. Then, he said, "Lady Ann Foley, who according to Lord Glenverbie had a great many gentleman-friends, wrote to her husband after her latest lying-in, saying, 'Dear Richard, I give you joy. I have just made you the father of a beautiful boy! P.S. This is not a circular letter.' And I have this on the word of her best friend!"

"Excellent!" Lady Giles said. "I have heard other stories about Lady Anne!"

Old Lord Alvaney cleared his throat, "May I tell you about my friend the Duke of Argyll? He rang for his servant the other day, the servant came into the room and stood some time without the Duke's looking or speaking to him. The servant then asked if his Grace wished anything and the old man said, "Damme, am I obliged to tell you what I want?"

There was more laughter and another round of champagne and to Julia's dismay she saw that most of the other good things prepared for the tea were being neglected. It was turning into a merry occasion of wine drinking! Gerald made his way to her and when the others were occupied with entertaining his grandmother secretly took Julia's hand and squeezed it gently. She smiled up at him.

Then the Prince told Lady Giles, "I have heard that most of your friends are dead, my dear madam."

"True," she said sadly. "Most of them have entered into eternal rest."

The portly Prince winked at the old woman and said, "In that case, dear lady, I must insist you make a friend of my wife!"

Everyone guffawed at this, including Lady Giles. Skeffy was prancing about the room giving his imitation of a dancer suffering from the gout and the Prince was applauding him. The thin man did an excellent comic turn, wincing every time the supposed gouty member touched the floor.

When the merriment at this subsided the serious business of champagne drinking continued and Lady Giles told Beau Brummell, "I know you've captured the heart of dear Julia. But I hear you are also loved by half the women in London."

He gave her a courtly bow. "Because I'm such a villian, madam. Women love men for their vices rather than their virtues."

"So you are an exponent of free love?" the old lady said slyly.

"You could say that," Brummell replied.

She chuckled. "But I have always heard free love is ever the most expensive!"

"Ah, ha Brummell, she has you there!" the Prince chortled with glee. "It is good to have you put down once in a while."

The thin Lord Skeffington simpered, "Too much is made of love. I say you can always get someone to love you, even if you have to do it yourself!"

"Don't talk about yourself," Brummell told him. "We'll do that after you leave."

Gerald listened to it all with a small smile on his manly face. While he enjoyed the smart wit of the dandies it was not his game.

Beau Brummell challenged him, "You have stood quietly in the background saying little, Sir Gerald. Do you not approve of our talk?"

"Very much so," Gerald smiled. "It is simply that I do not have a talent for it."

Lord Alvaney asked, "Where is your wife, the lovely Elizabeth? I have not seen her lately."

Gerald sighed. "I fear she does not approve of most social life. She has adopted a career of helping the poor and less fortunate in our city."

"Gad! If she's interested in the less fortunate, I should look her up," the Prince blustered. "Since I'm the most unfortunate man in all London!"

Beau Brummell joined in the laughter and then told his friend, the Prince, "You are like a person afflicted with some itching ailment! Forever complaining! Yet it is well known that scratching oneself is one of nature's sweet pleasures, most satisfying!"

The jests continued until it was past six. Then Beau Brummell, seeing that Lady Giles looked fatigued, presented his compliments and said that he must leave. The Prince quickly took the cue and again kissed the hand of the old lady and departed first as was his right. Brummell, Alvaney and Skeffy followed. Lady Giles was left with Julia and Gerald at her bedside. She looked up at them with exhausted bliss and said, "For a little it was like the old days. I shall always remember this afternoon."

Julia said, "You have had much champagne. Now you must rest and have some food. I shall send Mrs. Glenn to you."

The old woman gazed up at her fondly. She said, "Don't think I wasn't watching you and this wicked boy, Gerald, out of the corner of my eye while the party was going on. What are you to do? Gerald, why did you marry that prig Elizabeth rather than this girl?"

Gerald crimsoned. "You're imagining things again," he told her. Then he kissed her and saw Julia out of the bedroom as quickly as he could manage it.

Chapter Nine

In the several days which followed all was fairly quiet at the gray stone mansion which Lady Giles ruled as mistress. The old woman was exhausted from her exciting company and only Mrs. Glenn and Julia were allowed to spend any time in her room. She was by no means ill but merely worn out from the preparations and the thrilling event of the party itself.

Julia found herself living in a state of tension. She was on the brink of making a decision which could change her entire life. The elderly Lady Giles clearly suspected there was a romance between Julia and her grandson but after the one reference made to it, she remained tight-lipped on the subject.

Torn between her genuine affection for Beau Brummell and her newly-discovered fondness for Sir Gerald Giles, it was a time of stress for Julia. There was also the feeling she was not living as useful a life as she might be, and Gerald had offered her an opportunity for adventure and accomplishment in becoming a spy and assisting him.

The business of discovering about her father also troubled her. A part of her wished to accept John Crawford, however unfair he had been to her and her mother. But the coldness towards him which she'd felt over the years had frozen her heart. She could not bring herself to embrace him. She had left the matter with Beau and felt that he would no doubt manage it wisely. For however badly he looked after his own affairs he took pleasure in helping others.

Then a servant arrived on an errand for Lady Jane Hewitt. The woman appeared at the door, according to Mrs. Glenn, and handed her a letter from her employer. Mrs. Glenn in turn gave the letter to Julia. She took it to her room and tore it open to find that there was a letter enclosed within the letter.

Inside the first envelope there was a slip of paper in Lady Jane's prim handwriting and a second envelope addressed to Julia in a hand which she recognized by it's flourish to be that of her tutor and former guardian Reverend Edward Weir.

The first note read: "My dear Julia: I trust that all is going well with you. From the little I'm able to gather from Sir Orville I hear you are much in favor with Mr. Brummell and the Prince. Heady company for a young woman like yourself. So I counsel you to be most cautious. I'm sure Lady Giles has made a good employer and I daily regret losing you. Your presence in our home was so delightful.

"I fear you have made a bad enemy in James Fitzroy. So you must try to avoid him at any cost. As a result of his duel with Mr. Brummell I understand he is now permanently crippled. My husband declares he has made threats against both you and Mr. Brummell. So be warned. Otherwise, this letter arrived a day ago from my dear brother. I'm sure it is of a personal nature and I'm sending it along at once, Yours affectionately, Jane Hewitt."

Julia had liked Lady Jane and was sure the warnings in her letter were well meant. But she was chiefly interested in the enclosed message from the old person who had been like a father to her.

Tearing the envelope open, she read, "My dear Julia, I'm addressing this to you in care of my sister although she has explained to me that you are no longer living with her. She neglected to mention your new address but I'm certain she will see that you get this.

"I'm deeply sorry that I exposed you to Sir Orville's vicious nature where women are concerned. I should have thought of this, but I could not see him attempting to vent his lust on a mere child like you. Which shows how naive I am about life and such men. However, my sister assures me you are now in a new post as a companion to a Lady Giles. I am most pleased and beg you not to have anything to do with the contemptible Sir Orville.

"On a happier note my arthritis is improved. And I'm now able to once again journey to several village churches and hold services. Some of these can afford no fee for a pastor, but I have been the beneficiary of a handsome annuity from a man in London who claims to be your father. His lawyer indicated that you two had met and I'm most happy about that.

"I understand that you cannot help but feel some sort of hatred towards this man who years ago deserted you and your mother. But if he is truly repentant and wishes to make amends it is your Christian duty to be charitable towards him. I need say no more on the matter, I'm sure. Now I come to what is surely sad news.

"I well remember that a few years ago you had a girlhood romance with John Lane. Shortly after, he went off to enlist in the army and hopefully make his fortune. I regret to say that his father has received a message from the Army that poor John was killed in action. It seems tragic and wrong that such a promising young life should be cut off. I think of the many lives sacrificed to the ambitions of that wicked man in France and nightly pray that we will one day soon defeat him with finality.

"Which brings me to the end of my letter. I'm an old man and my time cannot be long. If you should not hear from me again believe that I shall always watch over you in spirit. You have been like my own dear daughter. Fondly, Edward Weir."

Julia was seated in a chair by the window and as she put the letter down her eyes brimmed with tears. John Lane dead! And to her shame she had not thought about him at all lately. Life in the exciting social circles of London had taken all her attention. She had found a new, mature love in Beau Brummell and now this was being pushed aside by the rush of affection she felt for handsome Sir Gerald Giles.

Gerald, like John Lane, was risking his life for his country. Surely this was reason enough for her to give preference to the daring young man. By joining with him she could help avenge the loss of her first, young love, John Lane. She said a silent prayer for the repose of the boyish John's soul and rose from the chair more determined than ever to go off to Dover with Gerald.

The very next day Beau Brummell sent a terse message to her by his man. It read, "Expect you to attend dinner at my flat tonight. Your father and I will be the only others there. I have worked hard to arrange this and I depend on you to not let me down."

Julia went to the bedside of Lady Giles and told her of the message, saying, "I don't know what I shall do."

The old woman insisted, "You must go!"

"You think so?"

"Without question," the old lady lectured her. "You must find it in your heart to be forgiving."

"It will not be easy for me."

"Many things we face in life are not easy," Lady Giles said. "But this is the proper thing for you to do. And from all I have heard Mr. Crawford has become a very wealthy man. You may find yourself an heiress."

She tossed her head. "I do not care about the money."

"Perhaps not now," the old invalid told her. "But one day you may be old and helpless as I am and then you will know that money does have its place and can be most useful."

Lady Giles insisted on seeing what she wore for the evening. Julia decided on a subdued dark blue taffeta with little frills. The old lady fussed that it resembled a mourning dress but at last agreed it would do. And before she sent Julia off in a carriage, again gave her a lecture on how to approach her long lost father.

On Julia's arrival at Brummell's, it was he who greeted her at the door. He appraised her rather dull dress and said jokingly, "No fine feathers tonight!"

"I regard it as a sober occasion," she said in a small voice, inwardly quaking.

"Your father is waiting for us in the living room," Beau said. "You need have no fear of him. You've met him before."

"As John Crawford, London gambling house owner," she said. "Meeting him in this circumstance is bound to be difficult."

The immaculately dressed Beau took her gently by the arm and led her to the living room. There standing waiting with his back to the fireplace was the tall, dark man whom she had met before. He was dressed in muted fashion in gray and wore a white cravat like Brummell's. He still had the distinguished air of an actor about him and his rather gaunt face showed a deal of emotion. It touched her to see that he was as frightened as she.

Leaving Beau she took a step towards this stranger and made herself say, "Father!"

"Julia!" John Crawford said with emotion and embraced her.

"Well done!" Beau applauded with good humor. "Kean could manage no better. Now that you two have been restored to each other in dignity, we shall dine and discuss it all."

Julia was literally swept along by the arguments of her father and Brummell. She said, "It will take me a while to adjust to the idea of you, Father. And I insist on making my own way."

"There is no need!" John Crawford protested over the fine dinner of beef and good wines which Brummell had provided for them. "I'm a rich man. I have a mansion which you should grace."

"Not yet," she said stubbornly. "I think you were too

long in coming forward though I realize you had some excuse."

"That woman lied to me! Told me you had gone somewhere in America!" her father declared.

She shot back, "You should have sought out further facts for yourself. Then you would have caught her in her lies. But it seems the fate of my mother and myself was not of all that consequence to you!"

"Not so!" John Crawford protested unhappily. "I spent a great deal of time and money only to be hoodwinked by that wicked woman. I beseech you to believe me!"

"Listen to him," Beau chided her. "And do not attempt to sway us with the most important water power in the world, a woman's tears!"

She was forced to smile though she was truly on the edge of tears. She said, "You know my wit ill matches your own. Why take advantage of me?"

"Believe me, your father wishes to take no advantage of you," the elegant Beau said. "He wishes to treat you in a most handsome fashion and I say you should be grateful."

"I am," she said. "And in due time perhaps I can make myself accept whatever he wishes to offer. Just now I will try to make the first step by accepting him and his good intentions."

So it was agreed between them. John Crawford was jubilant and after they had left the table and were having wine in the living room, he told Beau, "I value what you have done for me, Brummell. I wish to repay you in some way."

Brummell smiled. "I want no pay. Julia is my dear love. I could not fail to try to help bring about this reconciliation."

"I must show my gratitude," John Crawford insisted. And turning to her, asked, "Don't you agree?"

She nodded. "Beau is too proud to want pay and yet it is well known that he has a gift for extravagant living. And may be in some debt."

"You do me an injustice, my dear." Brummell reproved her. "I'm most fearfully in debt! Always!"

Julia said, "And I know it will one day be your ruin."

"The Prince protects me," Beau said with one of his charming smiles.

John Crawford frowned. "That could change, my friend. You have many enemies here in London. Not the least of them Sir Orville Hewitt who is toadying for the Prince's favor."

"There is little he can do," Beau said with a shrug. "But if you wish to befriend me cancel my chits at White's. They have become a trial to me. And you are owner of the place."

"As good as done," her father said. "All your gambling debts at White's will be settled tomorrow."

Brummell looked pleased. "A generous gesture. I thank you. But I'm used to a kind of penury. There is something exalted about being tremendously in debt, while owing just a little appears to me to be demeaning."

As the evening wore on Julia became embarrassed. She wished her father to leave first and it appeared he had no intention of this. At last, in desperation, she told him, "Dear Father, I have some private things to discuss with Beau. So I wish you would take your leave now."

The man-about-town was like putty in the hands of his new found daughter. His gaunt face showed a thin smile and he said, "I see you not only have your mother's beauty but much of my spirit. Of course I shall leave."

They embraced again and Brummell saw him out. She stood by the fireplace gazing into the dying embers and wondering if she had betrayed her mother in thus far forgiving her errant father. She thought not. And she was inclined to agree with the Reverend Edward Weir that since his penitence was sincere it would not be Christian of her to turn her back on him.

Brummell came back into the softly lighted room and reached out to take her hands in his. His eyes met hers and he said. "You must not torment yourself. You have done the right thing."

"I hope so," she ventured.

"You have made him happy," Beau said. "And I can vouch that despite his success he has been a man haunted all these years. You can see the mark of it in his face. Now he has a chance to right the wrongs he did you."

Julia sighed. "I need a while before I can wholly be his daughter."

"He understands that and is willing to abide by it," he said. "You have made the first step and that is what is so important."

"Thanks to you," she said, close to him.

He kissed her gently. "Dear Julia!" And his arms still around her, he said, "I think I have fairly concealed it but this has been a sad evening for me."

"Sad? Why?"

His handsome face was solemn. "Come with me and you shall see," he said. And he quietly took her through a door leading to an ante room. There sat one of his footmen and on a cot, sprawled out on a crimson velvet pillow was a tiny white dog. The dog was emaciated and its hair straggly so that it showed patches of brown skin underneath.

Brummell approached the little animal who was panting and struggling for breath in a most touching fashion. The dandy knelt before the little dog and gently stroked it. The animal had been dull-eyed when they came in, but now it's small ears became erect and the eyes focussed on Brummell with what could only be termed great love.

"The poor dear! He's very ill, isn't he?" Julia said.

Beau looked up at her. "Yes. Very ill indeed. I fear poor Anon may not last the night. And in losing him I lose my closest and perhaps my best friend."

"Is there nothing to be done?" she asked.

Beau asked the lad who was on his feet now. "What did the doctor say?"

"There's small chance, sir," the lad said sadly, his eyes fixed on the little white dog.

Beau fondled the animal and it in turn weakly responded with a kiss of its thin, purplish tongue. Beau told Julia, "The Prince's own doctor has called on Anon tonight. That is how he is held in value. The Prince of all this realm sent his personal physician to attend to my little friend."

Julia was also on her knees before the little dog now. She touched him affectionately and said, "What ails him?"

"The disease which surely we are all heir to," Beau Brummell said. "Old age!" And he asked the lad, "Did the doctor give him any potions?"

The lad nodded. "Yes, sir. And he stayed by him and took his fever and the like. And he left some powders for you to give him during the night."

Beau was on his feet now. "Good lad," he said. "Stay with my little fellow. I shall return soon."

Julia paused to say, "Good night, Anon. I hope you are better tomorrow." And when they returned to the other room she asked Brummell, "Why didn't you mention this earlier?"

"It is not your problem."

"But you are badly troubled by this," she said with emotion. "You could have cancelled the dinner."

"No. It was important to you. And it was arranged."

"Do you think he will live?"

"My poor Anon? I hope so," the dandy sighed. "He has been with me in most of my good days. I feel when he goes I shall lose my luck with him."

"Nonsense!" she protested. "Perhaps the doctor's powders will cure him."

Beau smiled sadly. "I trust so. I can only say they do the Prince little good."

"And if the worst happens you can get another," she

said. "I hear your good friend the Dutchess of York is a dog fancier."

He studied her with weary eyes. "Still jealous?"

"I try not to be."

"There is no need."

She pressed close to him. "Then why do you push me away when I have gone only so far. Why do you keep this barrier between us?."

"For your good," he said, gazing down at her."

Unhappy tears flooded her eyes. "How can that be if it interferes with our love?."

"Our love must be a thing apart, otherwise like some frail flower it might soon wilt."

"I do not believe that," she protested with spirit. "There can be few frail flowers at Harriete Wilson's brothel and yet you find much pleasure there."

"Dear girl," he sighed, "surely you have at least learned the line between love and lust."

"I think they may be intertwined," she said. "And I beg you to let me be here to prove it tonight!"

"And scandalize poor old Lady Giles?"

"She'd applaud me for it!"

"Perhaps," he said with a small laugh. "Perhaps, she would. But I cannot permit it."

"Why?" she asked in desperation.

"Because my love for you is the one pure thing about me," he said. "And one day you will know it!"

"I want no pretty words! I want to be with you! As a woman with a man!"

He kissed her. "One day," he said quietly.

She pulled away from him. "You will lose me altogether!" she warned him.

The elegant Brummell stared at her in a kind of wonder. Then, he said, "No, that is not possible!"

"I mean it!" she insisted. "You know there are others who desire me!"

"Yes. I know."

"Suppose I go to one of them?"

He sighed. "As your father said, you have a good

deal of his spirit. I cannot predict what you will do. I only know my own feelings and what they are toward you.''

"You talk in riddles," she said unhappily. "We are quarreling and I do not wish it. I want to try to lessen your sadness. It seems I must be a poor consolation to you!''

"That is not true," he said firmly. "Do not ever think that. Now I will call your carriage.''

She left him feeling frustrated and sad that she had not been able to reach him. Even in this tragic moment he had fended her off. She could not understand him but she now felt more sure than ever her best move was to go away with Gerald.

Early the following morning Julia sent one of the maids to Brummell's house to inquire if the little dog had lived. She was haunted by the sight of the suffering creature on its crimson pillow and the obvious devotion offered him by his master. Some might think it neurotic on the dandy's part, but she well understood his feelings. She also had a great love for animals.

The maid returned in a doleful state to inform her, "I spoke to the footman and he said the dog died last night.''

"Thank you," Julia told the girl, and hurried up to Lady Giles' bedroom to explain what had happened.

The old lady was sympathetic. "Do go and give poor Brummell what comfort you can," she insisted.

Julia hastily donned cloak and bonnet and since it was daylight and the streets would be safe walked swiftly to Brummell's house.

The footman answered the door, looking crestfallen. "He's gone, miss," the man said. "Took the poor little dog with him to bury somewhere and he hasn't come back. He told me not to expect him.''

She was surprised, "He didn't say when he would return?''

The footman sighed. "When he gets in these moods, miss, there's no telling about it. He finds a place to drink and stays there. It will likely be a few days before we see him here again. He could be with the Prince or at that Wilson house. But I wouldn't advise your looking for him, miss."

"If he returns tell him I was here," she said, and left filled with distress for the man she loved but who apparently was not willing to give his full devotion to her.

As she walked back through the busy streets at a slower pace she debated trying to get in touch with her father. It was likely that John Crawford would be able to locate Beau and see that he came to no harm. She had about decided this when she reached the old mansion and found a pacing Gerald Giles waiting for her in the reception hall.

"I thought you would never get back," he said.

"I had no idea you might come here this morning," she told him. "Beau's dog died and I went to offer my sympathy. But he had gone off somewhere."

"No time to discuss that," Gerald said in a low voice. He led her into the library and behind closed doors, informed her, "I have had orders from the Foreign Office. I'm to take a stage to Dover at dusk. If you are to help me, you must be ready to accompany me."

She hesitated a moment. "I want to go. There is no reason for me to remain here. Beau doesn't seem to need me, he always turns to someone else when in trouble."

"I warned you he would."

Her eyes were troubled. "But Elizabeth will say I stole you from her! That I deliberately ran off with you! She'll know nothing of the spy business. Neither will your Grandmother."

"Grandmother will forgive you," he said. "And Elizabeth is bound to be unfair no matter what."

"What are the plans?" she asked

"We are to stay at the Gray Horse Inn at Dover. I will sail from there with the morning tide if the weather allows. There's the threat of a storm in the air."

"And I?"

"Will wait at the inn until either I or a messenger arrive with the plans of the Danish fleet strategy. Then you will bring them at once to a designated party at the Foreign Office whose name I will reveal to you later."

She was already thrilled by the idea of the expedition. "What clothing will I need?"

"Simple things. At least enough for a week or two. It will depend on how long it takes me to locate the information and get it back. But I need someone waiting in Dover who will be reliable. You are the one person I feel I can trust."

"You may be certain of that," she said. "I want to do my part in this struggle against that tyrant."

Gerald showed interest on his bronzed face. "I have never known you to sound so patriotic before."

"I have reason," she said. "A friend of mine was recently killed in battle over there."

"Many have died," the spy said grimly. "And so will many more."

"Not you!" she said, suddenly seized with fear as she went to nestle in his arms. "It mustn't happen to you."

He looked at her directly. "Let me make it perfectly clear we shall both be in danger. There are counter spies working here in England. No one involved is truly safe."

He left after giving her this warning and offering her a chance to back out of the plan. But she had committed herself and had no intention of giving up the idea now. Of course it meant she had to spend her energies on packing and getting ready to leave without attracting attention in the household. She no longer had time to contact her father about finding Brummell and could only hope this would work out all right.

She wrote a note to be given to Lady Giles after she'd left. The weather, as Gerald had predicted, turned nasty. It began to rain and blow hard. The wind was unusual for the time of year with near gale fury. And as the rain continued it began to come down in torrents.

When Gerald arrived for her in his carriage she was nearly drenched crossing to it from the door of the house. He put her bag in with them and told the driver to take them to the coaching inn.

"What a dreadful evening!" she exclaimed as the carriage rattled over the wet cobblestones.

He sat at her side in the dark, rocking carriage and said, "The opinion is that it will get worse. An old seaman, who is a close friend, predicted this yesterday."

"Will you sail from Dover as planned?"

He said, "I expect to be late but I dare not halt or give up the plan. We shall join the stage at the coaching inn."

It was the same at the coaching inn, torrents of rain filled the courtyard as drivers muffled in oilskins and a group of disgruntled stable workers moved about in the steadily blowing rain to try and keep the stages moving in and out.

The journey to Dover took many hours. And to make the ordeal worse at a point during the arduous trip through the rain, one of the huge carriage wheels became mired down in the muddy road. All the males in the coach were asked to go out and help get the wheel free of the mire. Gerald was foremost among the volunteers and returned muddied and bedraggled but with a triumphant smile on his manly face.

"At least we're under way again," he told her.

She looked at the other passengers and all seemed very weary. She said, "I shall be glad when we get there."

His smile was thin. "Has our profession already lost some of its glamor for you?"

"No!" she protested. "It is just that I was tired to begin with."

They arrived at the Gray Horse Inn before dawn. The wind and rain continued without abating in the least. It was evident that Gerald would not be able to embark on board the craft taking him to Denmark.

They registered at the inn as man and wife under the name of Mr. and Mrs. John Smith!

When they were alone in the upper room which had been reserved for them the young man took her hungrily in his arms and told her, "I'm glad the storm has continued. I did not want to leave tonight."

She smiled up at him sweetly. "Nor did I want you to!"

They were unpacking and she had more things to hang up in the closet since her stay in the room would be longer. Gerald had brought a vicious-looking revolver from his bag and now it lay on the dresser top as he rummaged through his valise. Above the howling of the storm there was a loud knock on their door.

"Porter, if you please," a voice called out.

At the other side of the room Gerald in his shirt sleeves glanced up irritably from his bag which he was repacking and told her, "Open the door to the fellow, Julia. Let us see what he wants."

She opened the door to be confronted by a tall man with a black patch over his left eye and carrying a tray in his hands. On the tray were two foam-topped glasses of fine brown ale.

He said, "Compliments of the landlord, my lady!"

She told him, "Put the tray down here on this table."

"Aye," the man said and limped over to the table which was close to where Gerald was standing with his back to him.

No sooner had the man put down the tray than he drew a dagger from inside his brown shirt and raised it to plunge its blade into Gerald's back.

A startled Julia saw the move in time to shout a warning, "Gerald!"

The young man whipped around and there was a second revolver in his hand. He shot point blank at the servant catching him in the arm. Blood spurted from the wound and the man stumbled out groaning and in a moment vanished down the stairway.

"Remain here!" Gerald ordered her and at the same

time swiftly picked up the other revolver from the dresser and vanished out the door in pursuit of his would-be murderer.

She sank down on the side of the bed only now realizing the close call Gerald had with death! Perhaps she would have been the next victim! But who was the murderous servant and what had been his motive?

Julia waited tensely, the candle on the dresser having its flame jostled by the wind, and the rain lashing against the tiny window panes. Then she heard footsteps coming back up the stairs and tremulously got to her feet.

It was an angry-looking, rain-drenched Gerald who came in and tossed the revolver on the dresser again. Then he closed and bolted the door. He told her, "I followed him out into the night but lost him!"

"Why did he do it?"

His smile was grim. "It was no servant. The innkeeper knew nothing of his errand. He devised the trick of bringing us ale to get in here."

"Who was he?"

"It took me a full minute to realize," Gerald said. "I remembered his face as I rushed after him down the stairs. I'm sure it was a French spy named Chemeray. The eye-patch threw me off and quite changed his appearance."

She gasped. "So this is the sort of counterspy intrigue of which you warned me?"

"Yes," he said, taking off his shirt to reveal his naked stalwart chest. "Are you afraid?"

"Not when I'm with you," she said softly, her eyes fixed on his.

He came close. "Chemeray will not bother us again. I gave him a nasty wound in the arm."

"What about his associates?"

"He works alone. A master of disguise and speaks perfect English. He is said to move about London like a native."

Julia was trembling slightly, knowing that familiar

hunger which she could so carefully restrain, or let flow as she wished to now. Without a word she began to unbutton her dress. She saw the adoring look on his face as she went on with her disrobing. Soon they were nude in the flickering light of the candle. And what she saw of him satisfied her.

His hands touched her soft nipples and his lips crushed hers. She felt the hardness of his manhood against her and her desire became almost unbearable.

"Now!" she whispered fiercely.

"My darling!" He gently lifted her and took her to the small bed. "You are more lovely than I'd hoped," he said as he bent over her.

"And you much more of a man! Quickly!" she implored him.

His thrust seemed the most rapturous moment she had ever known. And the love play between them quickened, and she moaned and arched her back and pleaded with him for more of the same brand of loving. And she knew that at last she had found perfection. A completeness she had never known before.

At the climax she cried out with urgency and then held him close and kissed him, saying, "No one but you!"

"I will never forget tonight," he said.

She murmured, "Nor shall I!"

They slept deeply and when they wakened the storm had ended and the sun was shining in through their window. They smiled at each other from their respective pillows. And she was in his arms for another fling of love making. When it was over they rose and went about their ablutions.

The landlord provided them with a hearty breakfast and Julia was amazed at her appetite. Later they strolled hand in hand to the docks where many ships were being loaded.

Gerald pointed to a three-masted schooner and told her, "That is the one I'll be taking."

"When?"

"My latest word is we leave this afternoon," he said.

He turned to face her as they stood together on the wharf. "Will you be afraid on your own?"

"I suppose so," she admitted.

"Stay close to the inn," he warned her. "Do not go out except during the day. Always keep your door bolted. It is highly unlikely you will be bothered until the papers which I'm going to Denmark for are delivered to you."

"What then?"

"You must take the first stage to London and deliver them to the name which will be on the packet. Do you understand?"

She studied him earnestly. "Will you bring the packet back?"

"That depends. There may be other work to finish."

"Please take no useless risks," she worried.

He smiled down at her. "But it is all a risk!"

"Be careful for my sake!" she pleaded.

"And my own," he said. "After last night we belong to each other. Nothing will keep us apart."

She nodded. "I feel exactly the same way. But I have a sense of foreboding. I'm afraid to see you leave."

"There is no choice for me," he said. "Let us go back to the inn and I'll load one of the revolvers and make you more familiar with it."

All too soon he kissed her goodbye and left. He insisted that she remain in her room and not accompany him to the wharf. He felt doing so might place her in needless danger. So she watched him march down the narrow, cobblestoned street leading to the nearby docks. And when he turned once to wave she felt her heart might break.

There was no doubt in her mind that Gerald was the man for her. And she only hoped she might help him in this most dangerous venture and hold him after he returned. She was sure Elizabeth would make things as difficult as possible, and she could not guess how her father or Beau Brummell would react to her running off with the handsome husband of her one-time friend.

The essential purpose of their elopement had to be

concealed since Gerald could not have it known he was a spy. If that happened his usefulness would be ended.

She was sure that Lady Giles would be on their side. She counted on this to help them. But all this was a long way off. For the moment the big problem was Gerald's accomplishing his mission with success. She worried that she was poorly equipped for her role in the adventure. The waiting was bound to be tedious and she would never feel safe.

Following his advice she did not leave the inn during the hours of darkness. But almost every day she went for a short stroll in the vicinity of the ancient hostelry. Three nights later when she went down to dinner the landlord confided, "A gentleman was here to see you today."

"Oh?" she said. "Did he give his name?"

"No," the old landlord said. "Just asked to speak with Mrs. Smith."

"I'm not expecting anyone. Perhaps he made some mistake. Smith is such a common name."

"Could be, miss," the landlord agreed as he placed her plate of cheese and bread on the table before her along with a pot of tea. "I told him you weren't in."

After the landlord left her she began to worry. Could it be that someone had followed them from London? Was their secret already out? Or, even worse, was it one of the French spies come to try and get information from her. She had little appetite for dinner and left most of her bread and cheese untouched on her plate.

Following a cup of strong tea she got up from the table and made her way to her room. Her heart was pounding as she mounted the dark stairway. A panic rising within her. Reaching the door of her room she flung it open only to find herself confronted by a tall smiling man with one arm in a sling and a gun pointed at her in his uninjured hand. Though he had done away with the black eye patch and the servant's rough clothing she recognized him at once as the super-spy Chemeray!

Chapter Ten

"Do come in quietly, Mrs. Smith," the master spy said with smiling charm.

Trembling, she obeyed him. He moved by her, keeping the gun pointed directly at her, and nudged the door closed. It was then she saw the room was in complete disarray. He had evidently gone through it thoroughly in an effort to find any papers of value which might be hidden there.

She managed to challenge him, "How dare you break in here?"

Chemeray showed amusement on his thin face. "Surely you do not have to ask me that, Mrs. Smith? Or should I say Miss Julia Crawford?"

Julia could not help but be impressed by the menace of the handsome Frenchman. She said, "And you, of course, are Chemeray?"

"So Giles informed you about me, it would seem," the man with the gun drawled. "I trust he confided other equally important information to you."

"You are wasting your time! He told me nothing! We came here as lovers!"

"I'm sure you did," Chemeray agreed. "But I have the idea you are also here to be employed in another role. Sir Gerald is as thorough as myself. Perhaps even my equal as a spy. Though I must admit my serious error in exposing myself to being shot."

"You had best go now and save yourself from other serious errors," she told him.

The Frenchman seemed to enjoy this. He relaxed a little and said, "You are an interesting young woman!"

"Unless you leave at once I shall scream for help!" she warned him.

"I think not," he said easily. "I could finish you with a single bullet and be safely away before anyone found out what happened."

"What do you want?"

"Information."

"What sort of information?"

"Anything that Sir Gerald Giles told you. Where he has gone? What his plans are? What role you are playing in all this?"

"I told you! I merely ran off with him!"

"Simply to bed here with him? You could have done that in London."

"We were less likely to be seen together here," she said.

He sighed. "You are lying, of course. It is very stupid of you!"

"As stupid as your ransacking my room!"

"Necessary."

"I think not!"

Chemeray said, "Make no mistake about it. You will be watched. Do not think you can get away with anything. You would do well to confide in me and give me your trust. I might at least save you further violence."

"From whom?" she asked. "You have no associates! Gerald told me that!"

"And a good deal more, I'm sure," Chemeray said. "Do not worry how I will manage things, just be assured that this is a game which you cannot win."

"Is that all you have to say?"

He smiled again in that same menacing way. "All for the moment. I shall leave you now. But first I must ask you to strip!"

Julia could not believe she heard him rightly. She stared at him, "What did you say?"

"Strip!" he repeated sharply. "Undress yourself! I wish to make sure a proper time elapses before you make any alarm. Nude you offer less danger."

Her cheeks flamed. "This is nonsense!"

"I think not," he said, his eyes meeting hers grimly. "You heard—"

"On my oath I'll let you escape," she promised. It did not matter now, he had done all he could. Made a ransacked mess of her room.

"I give you one moment to begin disrobing," the tone was grim and he took a step nearer her, the ugly muzzle of the gun's cold steel almost touching her. She saw that he meant what he said and it was pointless to argue further.

"You are a bully!" she maintained, her lovely face crimson as she went about unbuttoning her dress while the Frenchman watched with languid approval.

At last she let her last shred of clothing fall to the floor and stood before him naked. His pleasant, if somewhat hawk-like, face showed a smile. "Exquisite!" he said, studying her. "You are like the finest sculpture! I give Sir Gerald credit for his taste!"

Holding her hands to cover herself as best she could, she asked, "Are you satisfied?"

"Indeed not," Chemeray said. "My appetite is but whetted! How I regret I must give up the opportunity of knowing you better. But another time!"

"Cad!" she shot back at him angrily.

"Call me what you like," he replied. "I shall keep my word and leave now. But if you follow me or attempt to scream for help there is someone stationed in the hallway outside to take care of you."

"I do not believe it!"

His eyes danced with a strange, wild light in them. "You can be convinced by defying me and it will cost you your life!" He backed to the door. "Until our next meeting, dear lady." And in an instant he slipped through the door and shut it after him.

Humiliated and fearful, she stood there trembling

both from the cold and her fears. Slowly she picked up her things and began to dress. When she was fully dressed again she ran to the door and threw it open. She could see no sign of anyone in the dark hallway.

Racing down the stairway she ran frantically to the bar and accosted the brawny innkeeper, demanding, "Did you see him leave?"

The innkeeper paused in drawing a foaming beer from a keg to place the glass on the bar and ask, "See who leave?"

"That man! The Frenchman!"

He stared at her. "I saw no Frenchman, Ma'am. Only the good English gentleman who came here earlier and asked for you."

"His arm in a sling?"

"Aye," the innkeeper nodded. "He did have one arm in a sling, now that I remember."

"That was a French spy named Chemeray." she said with angry distress. "When I went to my room he was there! He had let himself in and turned the place upside down searching it!"

"I had no knowledge of that, ma'am."

"I think you should have kept a better watch out for me," she accused him. "Mr. Smith will be much annoyed when he comes back to pick me up."

The innkeeper looked worried. "I'm truly sorry, ma'am. I had no idea. He seemed a gentleman and spoke very well."

She said bitterly, "And so he has escaped."

"He left the inn," the man behind the bar said. "I can't say what happened to him after that!"

She said, "If you see him again you will know he is a Frenchman and is about some evil. See you raise an alarm!"

"You may depend on it, Mrs. Smith," the innkeeper said earnestly. "I trust you have come to no harm?"

She shrugged and turned to go back upstairs again. "No harm as yet," she said. It was pointless to tell him the whole story of being held naked at gunpoint by the rascally Chemeray.

Back in her room she went about putting things in order. She was filled with dismay at the turn events had taken. Gerald had warned her of danger and she had hardly believed him. Now she knew that it could be real. And if the valuable information arrived and she had it in her custody she might discover herself threatened by forces for whom she was no match.

She sat miserably on the side of her bed. Her lovely face a study in despair by the candle's flickering light. She had a great longing to be back in London with familiar faces, to hear the welcome voice of Beau Brummell, enjoy the security of being with him. She had only turned from the dandy because she felt his love for her was not genuine. Though each time he had insisted that it was.

What would Lady Giles say when she found her gone? And surely Elizabeth would raise a dreadful row when she learned that it was with Gerald she had fled to Dover! She had taken a dangerous step and it seemed there was to be no turning back. Certainly not before she helped Gerald complete the mission on which they had embarked.

She half expected that someone from London might come after them. That she would find herself facing Gerald's angry, young wife or even a saddened and reproachful Beau Brummell. But it seemed Gerald had left no clues and so no one came. The days went by and she was still close to being a prisoner in the ancient inn.

She made small forays to the docks and the few shops in the village, aware that she was an outsider and a source of curiosity to the natives. In the evenings she remained closeted in her room. She had several novels to read but soon finished them. After that she tried some embroidery but could not set her mind to it.

She had her meals down in the dining room of the inn and one rainy morning when she came down to breakfast she found seated at the long, plank table a massive, fat man. She was sure he must weigh at least three hundred pounds. His broad face was cherubic and good-natured as with so many fat men and he wore a black wig which was a little askew on his big head.

His clothing was shabby but colorful. His jacket a faded crimson and his trousers patched and gray. His cravat was food-pecked and dirty. But his manners were the best. On her entrance into the room he at once rose with great effort and bowed to her.

He said, "Mrs. Smith, I presume? May I introduce myself. I am your fellow lodger, Matthew Kemp, Esquire, proprietor of the Kemp Punch and Judy Show."

Julia thought she had never seen a more extraordinary fellow in her life. The massive, middle-aged man ambled over and pulled out her chair for her. She sat down and said, "Thank you. It is nice to have a breakfast companion on this miserable day."

Puffing slightly the big man returned to his own chair across the table from her and sank into it with a satisfied sigh. "A miserable day it is," he agreed. "And not at all suitable for my profession!"

"You say you operate a Punch and Judy show?"

"I do, indeed," the fat man said proudly. "One of the best in the land, if I may be so boastful! My Punch has character, with lines to amuse the adult as well as the youngster and my Judy is a true vixen, modeled off my wife, who deserted me a score of years ago for the tatooed man who worked beside us in a Museum of Wonders."

"I'm sorry," she said.

"Don't be," Matthew Kemp told her. "The solitary life agrees with me. I have gained at least three stone since the blessed day she ran off! I met the poor tatooed chap later and he was in a miserable state from drinking and trying to rid himself of her. Would you believe it? His tatoo marks were fading? He had the whole fall of the Roman Empire on his chest and back and they were fading out fast. 'What will I do for a living?' the poor chap wanted to know. I gave him a quid and wished him good luck and got away from him as fast as I could."

For the first time in days she actually laughed. She said, "That is a most outrageous story, Mr. Kemp, and I suspect you are making it up to cheer me on this wretched morning."

"If it serves to do that, I'm well pleased," the fat man said with a chuckle.

As breakfast was served she could not help but note his appetite was as large as his body. He accepted double helpings of all that was offered and then drenched the early morning feast down with tankards of ale rather than tea.

"Tea stains the teeth," he told her with a wink.

She smiled. "Do you plan to be here long, Mr. Kemp?"

"A week or two at least," he said. "I have a good variety of programs for my Punch and Judy. I usually become more popular as the days go by. You shall see for yourself. I shall set up in the courtyard here when the rain ends and present my first show."

"I'll look forward to it."

He gazed at her across the table and asked, "May I presume to enquire what a lady of quality like yourself is doing in this humble place? You are clearly from London society and at a loss here."

She felt uneasy under his sharp gaze and said lamely, "I'm waiting for a friend who will soon return from a sea voyage."

The massive man tapped the side of his wide nose significantly and said, "Have no fear! Matthew Kemp is a man of discretion!"

Surprised, she said, "I'm sure you are!"

He leaned forward and whispered hoarsely, "No doubt it is a gentleman whom you are awaiting. I hear there's a deal of smuggling going on despite the war. Could it be he's bringing you some precious perfume or elegant lace!"

She shook her head. "Nothing like that, I assure you!"

"Ah!" he said, knowingly. "It is a case of romance! I understand and I shall ask no more." At this he stood and striking a pose, with one hand on his chest, quoted with emotion, "Mysterious love, uncertain treasure, Hast thou more of pain or pleasure! Endless torments dwell about thee: Yet who would live, and live without thee!' I beg your leave, ma'am!" At this he bowed gravely and waddled out of the dining room.

Julia was of the opinion that he was one of the oddest people she had ever encountered. But at least he offered a diversion. And it was nice to have a friendly male, even a very fat one, around, should the elusive Chemeray decide to inflict himself on her again.

Later in the day she encountered the fat man again as he dozed by the fireplace in the main room of the inn. He opened his eyes as she approached and with a fat hand indicated the chair across from him. "Warm yourself by the fire, dear lady. I had the innkeeper build it for me just now."

Julia sat with a tiny shudder. "My room is cold and damp."

"Not like the fine rooms in London," the fat man said with another wink.

She asked, "Why do you always associate me with London?"

"Because you're so obviously a London lady," he replied. "What a place it is these days! A racy lot, I'm sure! They say that few can keep up with the Prince and his chums! Especially that dandy, Beau Brummell! I've heard tell he's as cold-hearted as he is well-dressed!"

"That's not true!" she burst out.

The massive man raised his eyebrows. "So you know him?"

Blushing furiously, she stammered, "I have heard

about him from sound sources. And I promise you he is a fine, warm-hearted man."

Matthew Kemp smiled slyly. "I accept your word and I ask no questions."

"Many people have wrong ideas about the Prince and his friends," she said. "Most of the stories told about them are greatly exaggerated."

"I believe it," the man across from her said. "I have spent much time in London town, that mighty mass of brick, smoke and shipping."

"It should be a good place for your show."

"It is," he agreed. "But then I get restless for the road and am off to some place like this. New worlds to conquer! Lo, the Punch and Judy man comes, Sound the trumpets, beat the drums!"

They sat by the blazing log fire for awhile and the fat man regaled her with stores of his adventures. He showed her his ability to change his voice from the hoarse cries of Punch to the strident falsetto of Judy. And he also let her see how he could make his voice seem to come from other parts of the room. This gift of throwing his voice, as he called it, had once saved him from being robbed.

He explained, "The coach was held up and we were all standing out there in the dark! This fellow in his long black cloak and black mask had a gun in each hand pointed at us. His henchman was emptying our pockets and taking the rings and lockets from the weeping women when I suddenly spoke with an oath and made it seem to come from directly behind him! 'Down with your weapons in the King's name' I shouted. And he was so caught by surprise he turned and as he did so the coachman threw himself on him and disarmed him. I was quite the hero of the occasion!"

Julia laughed. "So your talent comes in useful in many ways."

"I should have graced the stage," the fat man lamented. "What a Falstaff I should have made."

"It is not too late yet."

He shook his head. "I'm too old, dear lady. So I shall be content with my Punch and Judy. They have kept me fed and sheltered this many a year. And when the sun shines tomorrow you shall see us all at work."

And so she did. The next morning was warm with lots of sunshine. The fat man set up his stall with its little open stage at the top. He sat concealed on a stool and raised one hand with a Punch figure and the other with the Judy. He manipulated the two and provided their loud dialogues.

In a short time the faded blue structure with its gold painted top and small cut-out stage had a sizable audience. There was a peephole through which Matthew Kemp could watch his patrons and he changed the dialogue depending on whether he was catering to children or adults. He did the voices well and manipulated the figures in their quarrels! Their comic beating up of each other was a mainstay of each performance. And after he ended the program he appeared from around the back and passed a dish in which he collected whatever coins were offered. Sometimes the offering was small but he never seemed to lose his good humor.

"Mine is a calling like the church." he told her, after studying his nearly-empty dish one day. "I do it for love of the game and not for money."

"You are excellent," she said. "And you deserve to be paid well."

The massive man beamed happily at her. "Thank you, my dear. You are a true lady and your words have made me most delighted."

Julia began to wonder whether she'd ever hear from Gerald again. His expedition to the Danish shore must have come to grief, she worried. And what to do if no word came?

Then, one night as she lay awake in bed, sleepless because of her troubled thoughts, she heard a pebble bounce on one of the panes of her bedroom window. She sat up and another pebble bounced against the window. She was barely able to make out the figure of someone standing below.

She raised the lower sash and in a low voice asked, "Who is there?"

"A friend from Denmark," came the reply in a man's softly-pitched voice.

"What do you want?"

"A word with you. Giles has a package for you," the man said.

She hesitated, then told him, "All right. I'll be down in a moment." She hastily donned a cape and armed herself with the pistol which Gerald had left her, not yet convinced that the stranger in the darkness was a friend. It could be Chemeray again or some agent of his. Though Gerald had claimed the French spy always worked alone.

The inn was cloaked in midnight silence as she went down the dark stairs and then crossed to the entrance door and opened it. The stranger approached the doorway and she saw he was dressed roughly in a sailor's fashion and had a grizzled, gray beard.

He said, "Sir Gerald sent this to you." And he gave her a packet wrapped in oilskin. "You're to take it to London by the next coach."

"Where is Sir Gerald?" she she asked.

"Still over there."

"When does he plan to return?"

"Depends," the bearded sailor said.

"He is safe?"

"When I last saw him."

"Who are you?"

"A friend," the man said. "I must go now. My ship is out there waiting for me to return. We must be gone before dawn."

She glanced worriedly at the package. "To whom do I deliver this?"

"Charles Justice, the Foreign Office," the stranger said. "Remember the name."

"It is not a hard one to keep in mind," she said. "Give my warm regards to Sir Gerald when you see him."

"He said to do the same," the sailor replied. "He will

return when he can." And then the bearded man limped off into the night and was lost to her.

She closed and bolted the door and holding the packet close to her made her way upstairs. The packet was about seven inches long and three inches thick and was tightly bound in yellow oilskin. If Gerald had been successful, and it seemed he had, it should contain the plans of the Danish navy's movements. With this information the British fleet under Nelson could take aggressive action.

Julia was awed by the responsibility which was now hers. The very future of England might depend on her. She carefully hid the packet in one of her travelling bags and returned to bed, keeping the pistol beside her for the balance of the night. Needless to say she slept very little.

The next morning she asked the innkeeper when the next coach would leave for London. She explained, "I have an urgent need to return there at once."

The innkeeper explained stolidly, "It can't leave until it arrives, ma'am. And it won't arrive until about seven this evening. The return trip to London will depart shortly before midnight."

"Not until then?"

"The coachmen have to rest and the horses have to be changed," the innkeeper explained. "And there's always produce to load and maybe a few passengers as well."

"I will book passage on it, then, if it is the earliest," she said.

"I'll tell the coachmen when they arrive," he promised.

It wasn't until the afternoon that she realized the fat Matthew Kemp was no longer at the inn. She went to the innkeeper and mentioned this.

"Left shortly after dawn," the innkeeper said. "A wagon came for him and took him and his equipment on to the next town."

"Did he say where he was going?"

"No," the innkeeper shook his head.

She felt cheated. As if she's lost a valued friend just when she might most need him. She said, "Did he leave no message for me?"

"Nary a word," the innkeeper said. "I thought him a strange one, if I may venture to say so. Not that he didn't pay his bill and all."

"I found him interesting," she told the man with a hint of reproach in her tone.

She walked to the docks to see if there were any new arrivals but saw none among the many masted vessels gathered in and around the harbor. It appeared that the sailor had been truthful when he told her the ship he had arrived in was leaving before the dawn. No doubt by now on its way back to the enemy coast.

As she stolled she thought about London. She was to return alone. Gerald had hinted this might be the case but she had hoped until the last moment that he might return with the package himself. Now she must carry on the dangerous task and cope with whatever hostility awaited her. She wondered what Beau Brummell would say? She could not imagine his turning his back on her. Yet it might happen. There was always her father and his house, but she did not want to accept his bounty as yet. She would first return to Lady Giles after she'd delivered the package.

She packed carefully as evening drew near. More fearful of a return of Chemeray than ever. But so far he had not shown himself. Perhaps he had decided she was not all that important and had moved on to other things.

To add to her concern it began to rain in the late afternoon and by the time the coach from London arrived the coachmen were in a disgruntled mood. There was even talk of postponing the midnight trip back to the city. But two merchants arrived who were impatient to return and someone brought a bedraggled old woman who was being sent to live with her grandson.

The innkeeper came to Julia and asked, "Would you be good enough to watch out for the old woman? You'll be the only other female in the coach and it's sure to be a hard passage for her."

"I'll do what I can," she promised, rather glad of this distraction. Meanwhile, she kept the packet in a small handbag which she kept with her.

The woman seemed terribly old and weak. She sat in a black bonnet and long black dress in a corner near the fireplace. Her white hair showed beneath the bonnet in a wild confusion, partially hiding her mottled, wrinkled face. She wore steel-rimmed spectacles but seemed not able to see well even with them.

Julia approached her and said, "I'm to be your companion on the coach trip to London."

Querulously, the old woman said, "Are you the girl?"

"I think the innkeeper mentioned me to you."

"Yes," the old woman said in a whining voice. "He said you'd help me."

"I'll do my best," Julia promised.

The old woman hunched unhappily. "I can barely move. The rheumatism is in all my bones. The pain never leaves me. And now I'm being shipped away to London to look after my grandson's new baby. I'm not the equal of it!"

"The journey won't take too long," she said, trying to inject a cheerful note in the conversation.

"I might well die along the way," the old woman quavered.

"I'm sure you won't."

The old woman gazed up at her. "You'll see me safely there?"

"Of course," Julia promised, realizing this distraction was to be a mixed blessing.

As time to leave came near the coachmen complained, the merchants grew tipsy and drowsy with wine, and the old woman sat hunched bleakly like some unhappy, ancient bird come to nest. Julia helped the old lady out of her chair and with the assistance of the innkeeper managed to get her out to the carriage and safely installed in a corner seat.

When this was done the innkeeper grimly confided to Julia in a whisper, "I'd say that one isn't long for this world."

"She is very weak," Julia agreed.

She took her seat beside the old woman who was now dozing and the two merchants came stumbling up to sit opposite them. Their voices were blurred and by the time the stagecoach took off in the rainy darkness they were both snoring.

Julia was not obliged to carry on any conversation and so had plenty of time to think. The coach rolled on through the night in a turbulent fashion. She clutched the handbag with the parcel in it on her lap. She planned to take a carriage from the stagecoach yard to the house of Lady Giles. She would remain there for the night and then deliver the package to Charles Justice at the Foreign Office in the morning.

She felt sure the elderly Lady Giles would not be angry with her. And she knew she would be greatly relieved to be rid of the packet from Denmark. She would next visit Beau and try and explain her actions to him. Perhaps after that she would see her father. If Lady Giles was willing, she would continue to remain with her as a companion.

Rain lashed the windows of the stage and several times they were almost mired in mud. But at last they approached the outskirts of London. And within a short time they were in the courtyard of the inn where the stagecoach made its London headquarters. The two merchants came grumpily awake and climbed down from the carriage.

Julia turned her attention to the old woman and had great trouble awaking her. "You must wake up!" she cried. "We have arrived in London!"

"London?" the old woman said in surprise.

Julia patiently helped the bent old woman to her feet

and then got her somehow out of the coach and down to the ground. The coachmen had long since vanished and the big courtyard was almost deserted in the rain. Two lanterns hung from posts a distance away but they were of small help in showing the puddles they had to cross to get to the inn.

She struggled to keep the old lady on her feet and headed her in the direction of the inn's entrance. She cried loudly in the old woman's ear, "You really must try to help yourself!"

"What?" The old woman asked weakly.

"We are alone out here for the moment. I can't seem to manage your weight," Julia told her.

And then a most astonishing thing happened. The old woman suddenly straightened up and in a startling way appeared much taller than Julia. As if this was not enough a pistol appeared in the hand of the crone and it was directed straight at her.

"I don't believe it!" Julia gasped, confronted by this weird apparition in the stormy darkness.

"You had better," came in the familiar voice of the spy Chemeray. "And now Miss Crawford I will take your handbag if you please and the packet it contains!"

"No!" she drew back.

"If you want to die now is the time," Chemeray warned her. "I can shoot you and no one will hear!"

She considered this dismal prospect for a few seconds and was about to give him the handbag when from the shadows there appeared another figure. A shot blazed out and Chemeray, still grotesquely dressed as the old woman, dropped his pistol and clasped his hands to his stomach. Then with a groan he fell forward at her feet in a deep puddle.

"Quickly!" a crisp voice said in her ear. And she was roughly taken by the arm and hurried away from the spot where the fallen Chermeray lay.

In the confusion and rainy darkness she was barely aware of what was happening to her. All at once she was outside the courtyard and being shoved into a waiting carriage. Her companion nimbly followed her into the carriage and then it hurried on its way.

She stared across in the shadowed interior of the carriage and gasped, "Who are you? Where are you taking me?"

A chuckle came from the seat across from her and a familiar voice said, "You might at least thank me for saving your life!"

Julia gasped. "Matthew Kemp! But how do you happen to be in London?"

"Because you are here, my dear Miss Crawford," was his calm reply.

"You know who I am?"

"And why you were in Dover," the fat man said. "Also I'm well aware of what you have in that handbag!"

Still stunned, she said, "You are no ordinary Punch and Judy man!"

"That is true," the fat man replied. "I'm Matthew Kemp, formerly of the Bow Street Runners, London's police corps. Now a member of Her Majesty's Secret Service."

She stared at the massive figure of him as the coach rolled on over the cobblestoned streets. "Then you did not come to Dover by chance."

"Hardly! Did you think Sir Gerald would leave you there alone at the mercy of Chemeray?"

"I didn't guess!"

"You weren't supposed to!"

"Gerald warned me that Chemeray was a master of disguise. But I didn't once suspect he was the old woman."

Matthew Kemp said grimly, "I'd say his career ended a few minutes ago. I'm sure the shot was fatal."

"Horrible!"

"You think so? He would have finished you off in another minute."

"What a cruel business it is!" she exclaimed.

"That is what gives it interest," the fat man said rather cheerfully.

"Where are you taking me?"

"To meet Charles Justice at the Foreign Office."

"But it is nearly dawn!"

"There are occasions when the lights at Whitehall burn through the night. This happens to be one of them. Have you any idea of the importance of that package?"

"No. I only wonder they didn't deliver it to you directly rather than to an innocent like me."

"Part of a plan to deceive the enemy. And you must admit it has worked admirably."

The carriage came to a sudden halt in what seemed to be a dark alley. The fat man made his exit first and then helped her down. She then saw a doorway with a curved brick top. Above the door hung a lighted lantern in a rather ornate iron fixture. The fat man took her by the arm and helped her up several steps. Then he rapped on the door and they waited.

A man appeared and scrutinized them through the glass panels of the door. After which he unlocked the door and let them in.

Matthew Kemp asked, "Is Mr. Justice in his office?"

"Yes," the man nodded. "He is expecting you."

"Good!" the big man said. And he turned to her. "You must understand that you are to repeat none of the things which happen tonight to anyone."

"I understand," she said.

"We will go directly to Mr. Justice's office," the big man said and waddled along the broad corridor ahead of her.

They made several turns and she became confused in the maze of corridors. Lamps in fixtures along the walls gave off a soft yellow light. At last they came to an open door and Matthew Kemp stood aside for her to enter first.

Nervously she made her way inside and saw that it was a large office with one wall given over to stacks of files. There was a roundtop task at the other wall and a table and some chairs. The fat man directed her to sit in one of the chairs facing the rolltop desk.

Julia was acutely aware of the grim, brooding air of the place. Again the light was provided by lamps on the walls and these offered a murky, yellowish glow. She also realized how tired she was. The fat man stood by the open doorway as if anticipating the arrival of someone momentarily.

She closed her eyes in her weariness, still clutching the precious handbag on her lap. Then she heard Matthew Kemp say, "She is waiting, Mr. Justice," in a respectful voice.

She opened her eyes to see the legendary Charles Justice coming slowly towards her and in her utter astonishment was certain she would faint!

Chapter Eleven

The reason for her shock was that this Charles Justice was the same man she had come to accept as her father, John Crawford. As he crossed to greet her there was an expression of admiration on his thin actor's face.

"You are not dreaming," he told her. "I am called Charles Justice in this office."

On her feet, she gasped, "I don't understand."

Her father smiled bleakly. "Even owners of gambling houses are capable of patriotism. And also in a position to gain much useful information. That is how I have come to lately be leading a double life."

"I still can't believe it," Julia said.

Her father took her in his arms and gently kissed her on the forehead. "I have been terribly worried about your welfare. Only the fact that Matthew was acting as your guard allowed me to let you play decoy." He turned to smile warmly at the massive Kemp.

The fat man chuckled. "At that I only arrived in a nick of time. Chemeray almost had her!"

Her father said, "I trust you dealt with him?"

Matthew Kemp nodded. "I did that, sir. I vow he's dead this very moment."

John Crawford gave a relieved sigh. "One less to deal with." And he turned to her again. "You have done well, my dear. I'm proud of you."

She produced the oilskin package and gave it to him. "Did Gerald know you as Charles Justice?"

"Gerald knew all about me," her father said, as he went about opening the package.

"He never breathed it to me."

Her father smiled at her over his shoulder as he stood by the rolltop desk. "We are not encouraged to talk about identities in the department."

Julia found herself more confused than ever. She could not help but wonder if her father knew that she and Sir Gerald had become lovers and if he approved. The very thought of wanting his approval was strange to her since she had so lately been unwilling to recognize him. But now she knew having a father had become important to her and so had his opinion of her.

Her parent was skimming through the papers. He said, "Excellent! Everything we needed is here! We'll turn it over to the Naval Service at once."

She moved a step toward him. "What about Gerald?"

John Crawford frowned. "I wish I could tell you. I don't know. The last word we had of him was that he was seeking out a French agent in Calais."

Her eyes met her father's and in a low voice, she said, "You know what he means to me?"

"I understand," her father said gently. "I wish it had not happened. There is his wife. But you need have no doubts as to Gerald loving you. He is most sincere in that."

Tears filled her eyes. "I know."

Her father gave the package of papers to Matthew Kemp and instructed him, "Take these on to the navy people."

The fat man nodded. "Yes, sir."

"The carriage is waiting?"

"It is, just as you told me," Matthew Kemp said. And with a bow to her he left them.

Her father turned to her. "You're very weary! Time I took you home."

"Home?"

"My house is your home."

She hesitated. "I planned to go to Lady Giles."

"You may do so in the morning if you like," her father said. "It is much too late to rouse her household now."

Julia saw the wisdom of this and knew how near collapse she was. She was also seeing her father in a new way and could not help but be proud of him. Gradually the feeling of hatred built up over the years was beginning to evaporate as she came to truly know him.

He saw her to the carriage and after a short drive led her into a fine mansion in the best part of the city. An elderly butler let them in and her father then took her up to a spacious bedroom in which everything, including hot water in jars, and a tin bathtub, awaited her.

He said, "I can waken one of the maids to come assist you."

"No," she said "I can manage well on my own. And what I want most is sleep."

"I'll see you in the morning," he promised. Then he kissed her goodnight and went out and closed the door.

Wearily gazing about her at the magnificence of the pale blue and white decorated room she found it hard to believe that she was the mistress of it all. A long way from the simple country parsonage or her role of companion to old Lady Giles. Yet she knew she was not ready to assume this new role for a time. She wanted to return to the house of Lady Giles.

She filled the bathtub with water until the temperature was right then luxuriated in the warm bath. After which she donned the silken nightgown which her father had so thoughtfully provided and climbed into the huge bed. Almost as soon as her head touched the pillow she was asleep.

She came awake to a maid working about the room and saw that the jars of water, bathtub and towels had vanished and the room was in neat order.

The uniformed maid came to her bedside with a smile. "I'm Emily," she informed her. "I'm to look after you. I've taken the bath things away. And your breakfast is being brought up now."

"There is no need!" she protested.

The maid said, "Your father wishes you to breakfast in bed after your long journey."

She sighed in wonder. "My father is much too good to me!"

"I'm certain he enjoys it," the maid smiled.

A few minutes later a manservant arrived with an ample breakfast tray which was placed on the bed. Julia found herself hungry and went at the breakfast with energy.

She was having her tea when her father arrived and came to sit on the side of her bed. He smiled. "You look much more like yourself now. Last night you seemed like a pale wraith."

"I felt like one," she said with a small smile in return. "I'm not sure I believe any of this."

"It doesn't matter," he said. "The only thing I care about is that you are safe."

Her pretty face was shadowed. "If only we could say the same thing about Gerald."

"I hope he will be back in England before long."

"So do I."

Her father showed concern. "He is a fine man but I'm sorry you have lost your heart to him. He is a married man. And Elizabeth is a most difficult young woman."

"She has not been a wife to him for a long time."

"Few know that. And she would be the first to deny it."

"I expect we shall have to deal with her when the need arises," she said with a sigh. "Not matter what, Gerald and I will go on seeing each other. He has talked of buying another house and having me to look after it."

Her father shook his head. "I wouldn't advise that. Even in our Regency society there are limits of respectability. And though the situation might be accepted I would not like to see you expose yourself to it."

"I will do as Gerald wishes," she warned her parent.

Her father's actor's face showed resignation. He said, "And I'm certain Sir Gerald will do what he thinks best for you."

"You do like him?"

He nodded. "Of course."

"I'm worried about Beau," she admitted. "About what he will think. How he will feel. He was away from his house when I called to talk to him. Grieved by the loss of his little dog."

Her father eyed her in a kindly fashion. "I know," he said. "You must realize that Brummell is deeply in love with you?"

"I once felt him to be the only man for me," she said. "I might never have turned to Gerald had he shown any interest in me."

"Brummell could not be more interested in you."

"He refused to marry me."

"Because he fears such a marriage would only bring you unhappiness," her father said. "He is dedicated to a trying kind of life. He gives a great deal of his time to the Prince."

"Who will one day surely turn on him," she said with bitterness.

"He is not in the same favor, even now," her father agreed. "Sir Orville Hewitt and James Fitzroy have catered to His Royal Highness and done everything possible to try to discredit Brummell. So far they have only been partly successful."

"They hate him because of me. They are trying to ruin him because they know how much I care for him."

"That is possible," her father said. "But they have other reasons of their own. To have power with the Prince gives one a great deal of prestige."

She gazed at her father with troubled eyes. "Have you any idea how Beau has reacted to my running off with Sir Gerald?"

"I know exactly his feelings. I discussed it all with him only yesterday."

"You discussed it with him?" she asked in surprise.

"Who better to do it?" her father asked.

"What did he say?"

"At first he was deeply hurt, but then he came to see your side of it. He assured me it would make no difference in your friendship."

"He truly said that?"

"His very words."

"I do hope he meant it," she said, near tears. "I need his friendship more than ever."

"You have his love which is far more important," her father said gently.

"Thank you," she said, deeply grateful to the man she had once hated.

"There is one thing more," he told her. "You must not reveal to anyone that I am Charles Justice. Beau knows, but aside from yourself, he is the only one outside the service who is aware of my secret. Like Sir Gerald I have to play the role of a wastrel."

"Your secret is safe with me," she said.

He asked, "And what about your remaining here?"

"Later," she said. "Just now I wish to return to Lady Giles. If she will accept me back I want to continue as her companion. I feel she needs me."

"As you wish," her father said. "When you are ready I shall have a carriage waiting to take you to her place. But you must understand the old woman, like most others, knows nothing of the fact that you and Gerald were doing a service to your country as well as being lovers. To all these people you are doomed to simply be a selfish young woman who ran off with your friend's wife."

She smiled grimly. "Lady Giles may be elderly but she is broad-minded. Also she loves gossip, even when it has to concern her own family!"

Julia's prediction proved to be correct. Old Lady Giles received her like a long-lost daughter. Propped up in bed as usual the old woman reached out to take her in her arms.

"I prayed you'd have the good sense to come back to me," she exclaimed.

Julia smiled. "I thought you might hate me."

"For falling in love with Gerald! Of course not! I saw it happening! I'm not blind you know!"

"I'm sure we've caused a scandal!"

The old woman laughed. "A delicious one. And I'm right in the midst of it! And all the while I thought I'd become too old to be part of the town gossip!"

Julia asked, "And what about Elizabeth?"

"That mealy-mouthed creature!" the old woman said with indignation. "She is making the most of it after never being a proper wife to poor Gerald."

"I know."

"To cap it all, she has had the nerve to come here

every day," Lady Giles went on. "After neglecting me for years and saying everything evil she could about me."

"So she is trying to win you to her side."

"Apparently! But there is small chance of that," the old woman said. "I despise her. And she knows it but she keeps on coming here."

"It is awkward," Julia worried. "Do you want to keep me on here?"

"Of course I do!"

"It may cause more talk."

"As if I cared!" Lady Giles said. "I'm sure when Gerald returns he will find some way to deal with Elizabeth."

"I agree," she said.

Lady Giles demanded, "Have you any idea where he has gone?"

"He spoke of some racing event in Liverpool," Julia said, hating herself for having to lie.

The old woman groaned. "His love for horses is as great as his love for women. It's often the case in good men. We mustn't hold it against him. He will return soon and all will be well."

Thinking of the man they both loved so much still in the enemy country, Julia devoutly hoped the old woman would be right. She talked with Lady Giles for a while and spoke of spending the night in her father's house without telling her anything of her father's connection with the secret service.

Lady Giles approved, "I'm glad you've reconciled with him. I have felt from the first he is a good man."

Julia left the invalid and settled into her own room. She had barely finished this and gone downstairs to see Mrs. Glenn about some of the household arrangements when Elizabeth arrived.

The maid ushered her in and Julia had no time to retreat. Her former friend was wearing widow's black and a veil. On seeing Julia her attractive face turned into an angry mask.

Confronting Julia, she cried in a shrill voice, "So you have come back!"

"Yes," Julia replied quietly.

"You vixen!" Elizabeth screamed. "To think I once was a friend to you."

"I did not break the friendship," Julia reminded her.

This seemed to cause a mild hysteria in the other girl. She laughed wildly. "Listen to her! You run off with my husband and have the nerve to say that!"

"You know why Gerald and I ran off together," Julia told her in a low voice. "You turned your back on him long ago."

"Liar!" Elizabeth said angrily and drew back her hand and gave her a resounding smack across the face.

The stinging pain was severe enough to almost bring tears to Julia's eyes. But she fought against showing any reaction, saying quietly, "I expected that." And she turned away from her one-time friend.

"Did you?" Elizabeth said with sarcasm. And then she ran upstairs, clearly on her way to the invalid's room.

Mrs. Glenn had appeared in time to see what had taken place and there was an angry look on her dour face. She said, "It's a sad day when the likes of her is allowed to behave in that manner in this house!"

Now the sound of an angry exchange could be heard from above. Elizabeth and Lady Giles were clearly having some sort of violent argument.

Mrs. Glenn said grimly, "I'll put an end to that!" And she hurried up the stairs after Elizabeth.

Julia retreated to the rear hall behind the stairs. A few minutes later Elizabeth came rushing down and went out the front door slamming it shut after her.

Julia at once went up to Lady Giles' bedroom where Mrs. Glenn was attempting to placate the old woman. Julia said, "I'm truly sorry to have been the cause of such a scene."

"Don't blame yourself!" Lady Giles said with anger. "It was that silly baggage who came in here and raised the commotion. She'll not be here again. I've asked her never to enter my house!"

"Perhaps I should leave as well," Julia said.

"If you do it will be against my wishes," the old woman said sternly. "Now let us forget all about the incident."

Julia tried hard not to think about it but she found it hard to erase the ugly scene from her mind. She worried that it might be the start of a number of scenes of a like nature. Elizabeth had a place in society and a certain number of friends. She would be bound to use her influence to make things uncomfortable for her husband and the woman she blamed for stealing his affection.

She was in her own room pondering all this when Mrs. Glenn appeared with a gleam of pleasure in her eyes. The Scots woman said, "You have a visitor, miss. And a much more welcome one, if I may say so."

"Who?"

"Mr. Brummell."

Julia found herself nervous again. She asked, "Is Lady Giles resting?"

Mrs. Glenn nodded. "Yes. The poor old soul was exhausted after all that fuss. She's having a good sleep."

"Then I'll see Mr. Brummell in the study," she said. "Do show him in there. I'll be down shortly."

Mrs. Glenn went off to do her bidding and she quickly fixed her hair and added a touch of color to her cheeks. She was anxious to look her best for the man so close to her.

When she entered the study Beau had his back to her as he stared out the window. When he turned Julia was shocked by the change in him. He was dressed as elegantly as ever, in spotless white cravat, blue jacket and fawn trousers. But his face had a peaked, worn look. She was sure he was thinner.

"Beau!" she said emotionally and ran to him.

He took her in his arms and kissed her and held her close to him. Then he released her and with a tired smile, said, "You know we were worried about you."

"I'm all right," she said. "But you look ill!"

"Not really," he said. "A few problems. The Prince and I had a quarrel. However, it's patched up now. Barely! But at least we're on speaking terms."

"Sir Orville at work!" she said accusingly. "Not to mention Jimmy Fitzroy!"

"They haven't helped," Beau admitted. "But I have many others jealous of my influence with the Prince."

"At least it's all right again," she said.

"Yes."

"Have you another dog?"

He shook his head. "No. I doubt that any I found would replace Anon."

"You should try."

"He is buried at Oatlands," Beau said. "The Duchess of York has a dog cemetery there, you know."

"She also has many dogs. Surely she offered you one."

"She did and I refused," the dandy said. "I cannot forget poor faithful Anon so easily. Would that I had a few human friends as faithful."

"You have my friendship," she said gently. "You could have had me as a wife if you'd wished."

Beau gazed at her with infinite sadness. "I know."

She met his melancholy glance and asked softly, "Can you forgive my running off with Gerald?"

"You had no commitment to me. Why shouldn't I forgive you," he said.

"I hope you understand."

"You love Gerald?"

"Yes."

"And he truly loves you?"

"I'm sure of it."

"Then it is all right," Brummell said. "Except that you have to contend with Elizabeth."

Julia nodded. "She was here earlier. She hurled a good many epithets at me and slapped my face."

"It is the behavior I would expect from her."

"Lady Giles has refused her entrance to this house in the future."

"Good for Lady Giles," Beau said with approval. "I must try and arrange another party for her."

Julia managed a smile. "She appreciated the last one."

"You spent the night at your father's?"

"Yes," she said.

Beau gave her a searching look. "Now that you know more about him I'm sure you have different feelings towards him."

"I have," she said. "Thank you for helping me. I might have spoiled everything."

The elegantly clad Brummell sighed. "So all is well except for Gerald to return safely and somehow settle this business with Elizabeth."

"There is bound to be scandal," she said. "Perhaps we will never be able to marry."

"I will stand by you both," Beau assured her. "We must get you out in society."

"I'm not sure I'm ready for that."

"The sooner the better," he insisted. "When the gossips see you they will halt some of their slander. If you keep out of sight they will think their barbed tongues are destroying you and be all the worse."

She smiled ruefully. "Neither choice seems pleasant."

The handsome Brummell told her, "You have always taken my advice in the past. I beg that you take it now."

"Very well," she said. "I leave it to you."

"Excellent," Beau said. "I'm having a party for the Prince at my place tomorrow night. He likes your lovely face and it might help put him in a good humor if you are there."

"You're sure there will be no embarrassment to you?"

"None at all," he said. "All the guests will be your friends. Old Lord Alvaney and Skeffy and the rest."

"What about Sir Orville?"

"He is not on my guest list."

"I would say you are wise."

"I will send a carriage for you," Beau said. "And have one ready to bring you back here whenever you are weary."

She sighed. "I worried so that you would hate me."

He took her hand and kissed it and held it to him. "You shall always fill my heart with love not hatred."

He left a short while after and she saw him out with a feeling of concern. In some subtle way he had changed in the short time since she'd last seen him. Perhaps he had aged suddenly, although he was still handsome and carried himself with an air. There was definitely the signs of ill-health about him. It was distressing.

On Lady Giles' advice she chose to wear a pale green gown with white lace trim for the party. Her white gloves and fan carried out the color pattern. She had thought of refusing to attend the affair at the last minute and then thinking her refusal might upset Beau she determined to see it through, even though she might endure some unpleasantness.

The affair turned out better than she'd hoped. The Prince seemed genuinely pleased to see her again. His fat, florid face lit up with pleasure as she curtisied to him.

"Damme," he exclaimed, "You grow more lovely each time we meet. It is not fair!"

She accepted the compliment with a light laugh. "It is Your Majesty's admiration that helps me be at my best."

"Then I shall admire you most immensely and most continually," the Prince said.

Beau joined them and with a mocking smile said,

"My dear Julia let me warn you against the flattery of the Prince. Next to taking on a new mistress, his greatest pleasure is getting rid of the previous one."

The Prince protested, "That is not fair! I vow that Beau is dependent on his imagination for his facts."

Beau assumed an amazed look. "Am I to understand you are calling me a liar, Sire?"

"I vow you are damnably close to it, Beau!" The fat Prince sputtered.

Beau laughed. "After all what is a lie, Sire, but a truth in masquerade!"

The Prince laughed and she felt a difficult moment had been passed over. Yet she could tell the friendship between Beau and the Prince did not have the same solid basis as before. There was an edginess between them which bothered her.

Old Lord Alvaney was at his best. He slyly told her, "When I was very young I hit upon the idea of writing a play satirizing the human race, now that I'm old I feel more like writing an apology for us."

Skeffy, thin and effeminate as usual, told the old man, "You are too critical of yourself and others, Alvaney. Aside from being a politician your other qualities are to be admired."

The banter was liberally mixed with champagne and all seemed to be having a royal good time, especially His Highness, the Prince.

Julia was standing between Beau and His Highness, when he asked, "Why is Sir Orville Hewitt not here tonight?"

Beau said, "He is not here, sire, because he was not invited."

"I can't imagine why not," the fat Prince declared solemnly. "The Hewitts represent our best blood!"

Beau removed a pinch of snuff from his jewelled snuff box and touched it to his nostrils. Then languidly, he replied, "But Sire, surely you must realize that every so often the best blood winds up in mosquitos and fools."

The Prince blinked at him and then after a moment roared with laughter. "You are a caution, Beau. You care not how you insult me or my friends."

"I would never think of insulting you, Sire," Beau replied smoothly. "But for your friends I admire most those who think with their brains rather than their tongues."

Lord Alvaney burst into boisterous admiration of this comment and vowed, "What I say, Beau, is only fools hear all that they hear!"

"Come now," the Prince said. "We must be boring this young lady. Most of our talk is nonsense."

"There is no harm in talking nonsense, Sire," Beau said. "The important thing is to make it sound serious."

Julia laughed. "I say I have heard enough of sense and nonsense. I think it is time for me to leave."

All professed regrets at her decision and Beau went away to get her carriage. The Prince took her aside and asked, "What is all this gossip about you and young Giles?"

"Gossip, Sir?" she asked with innocence.

He winked and said, "Running away to Dover together and all that. I understand his wife is furious."

"It is tragic, Sire," she said. "We were once the best of friends."

"Indeed," the Prince observed. "But then it is always easier to love the husband of a friend than that of an enemy!" And he roared with enjoyment of his own joke.

Beau returned to say the carriage was ready and she said her goodnights. Then he saw her to the carriage. It was a dark night with no hint of a moon.

He said, "I ought to be personally escorting you home. But it is difficult for me to leave with the Prince still ready to drink for half the night."

"I understand," she said. "I shall be quite all right."

Beau kissed her. "You were the hit of the party."

"You saw to that by inviting no other females," she said. "Just one word of warning."

"What?"

"Do not be too saucy to the Prince."

"I shall treat him with the same respect as always," he said smiling.

"Which means very little respect," Julia replied. "I can sense that you might easily have another quarrel. There were moments tonight when he did not enjoy your humor."

"More's the pity for him," Beau said airily.

"I'm thinking of you," she insisted. "You need his patronage or you'd be ruined. You allowed your allegiance to him to come between us, don't casually throw it away."

"I'm sorry," he said contritely. "I shall be more careful."

They kissed again and then he closed the carriage door and waved to her as it started off. She sat back in the dark interior feeling thoroughly exhausted. The battle of wits which went on at Beau's parties could take a toll of one. Especially when she was worried about his angering the Prince.

She closed her eyes as the carriage rolled on. She was thinking about Gerald and wondering where he was when suddenly the carriage came to a rapid halt! She heard the driver shouting and other voices joining in. Then one of the carriage doors was thrown open and she saw an ugly face with a stubble of beard. Hairy hands reached in and grasped her.

"No!" she cried as she was pulled out of the carriage.

"Shut up!" A coarse male voice said and at the same time a hand closed about her mouth and she was grasped around the waist.

As she struggled she had a brief glance of someone watching her capture by the thugs. It was James Fitzroy, leaning on his cane, with a look of triumph on his face. Then whoever held her turned her around and hurled her into the back of a wagon.

"Let me go!" she screamed.

The only answer she received was a blow on the temple which sent her tumbling into a vast blackness.

Later, when she opened her eyes, her head was aching and she was in some sort of small, dark room.

She tried to sort out what had happened and found it all a blur in her mind. She had been on her way home in a carriage when it was held up by a group of thugs. The gang had been directed by James Fitzroy, she was sure of that, for she'd briefly glimpsed the crippled man. Then she'd been thrown into a wagon and struck so hard she'd lapsed into unconsciousness.

She tried to sit up and her head ached and reeled even more. So she lay back again on what seemed a very hard bed. She remained there almost motionless for a long while until her head improved. She knew that Fitzroy had planned and executed some sort of vengeance on her, but she had no idea what.

Now she managed to sit up and take more stock of her surroundings. She was on what appeared to be a bunk built into the wall and the room in which she was a captive was extremely small. And gradually she became aware of a regular motion which was not in her head but part of her surroundings.

The room was swaying gently! She could hear a sound like a rhythmic wash! And then she suddenly realized. She was on a ship of some sort. In a tiny cabin on some ship which was swaying gently with the movement of the waves. A prisoner on board some craft at sea! The thought struck terror in her!

She stood up and her head almost touched the timbers of the cabin's roof. Groping her way to the door she tried to open it and when she knew it was locked she began to pound on it and cry out for help. Her pounding served only to bruise her fists and her cries to make her hoarse. There was no light in the fetid cabin and she finally sank back on the bunk in exhaustion.

She was sobbing when she heard the key in the lock. Then the door was opened by the man with the ugly face and stubble of beard. In the light she could also see that he had yellowed teeth with gaps between them and was dressed in a merchant seaman's rough clothes.

He jeered, "Stop your yapping and come out! The skipper wants to talk with you!"

She hesitated. "Where am I?"

The seaman laughed coarsely. "On a good British ship outward bound!"

"How dare you take me prisoner!"

"You can talk to the Captain about that," the seaman said. "Now move and no more of your chatter!"

She decided to obey him. At least it would get her out of the dark, smelly cabin for a little. The sailor held her in a painfully tight grip of her upper left arm so that she winced.

"I won't try to escape," she told him.

He jeered. "Where would you go?"

"Then ease your hold on my arm!"

"Tender, I'd say! Too good for the likes of me!" He said with sarcasm. "Maybe you'll change your mind about that before this voyage is over!"

The sailor led her to a door which swung with the motion of the ship and shoving her roughly inside, said, "In there with you!"

She stumbled into the semi-darkness of a larger cabin and for a moment thought it empty. Then she saw a figure rise from a bunk in the corner and come towards her. As he came closer she saw that it was a stalwart man with a bronzed face and prematurely white hair. The odd thing about him were his eyes. They didn't seem to be fixed on her at all. He seemed to be staring directly ahead of him.

He asked, "Is this the prisoner, Hawkins?"

"Aye, sir," the sailor said.

"You can leave us now," the white-haired man said in a voice of stern authority.

"Right, Captain," the sailor said and shuffled off.

The white-haired Captain remained standing opposite her. In a cultivated voice, he said, "You are Miss Julia Crawford. Let me introduce myself I'm Captain James O'Hara."

"How dare you take me prisoner on your ship?" she demanded.

The eyes remained fixed in that odd, vacant way. He said, "I was paid well to take you as a passenger. Or if you prefer, as a prisoner."

"Did James Fitzroy pay you?"

"Yes," the youthful white-haired man said with a smile. "Let us get to know each other better. There is no reason why we should not be friends."

"I demand you take me back to shore at once!"

"I fear that is quite impossible," Captain James O'Hara said with patience.

"How dare you do this to me!" she said angrily.

"I dare do many things, Miss Crawford," the Captain said in his careful way. "I am a smuggler by profession. My crew and I take many risks. So accepting you as a prisoner is not unusual for us."

"I have influential friends in England," she warned him. "You will regret this."

"I doubt it," he said calmly. "And I do wish you'd sit down. Let me explain, by the way, I'm completely blind."

"Blind!"

"Yes," he said with a wry smile. "You may wonder how I manage command of a lawless crew and what use I am to them. It happens I have an excellent first mate with perfect vision and a loyal crew. I supply the brains for our expeditions. I plot the course we take and the goods we smuggle. So far I have had the best of luck! My only regret is that I cannot see your face. I'm told you're extremely beautiful!"

She stepped back from him. "You must be mad!"

"On the contrary," he said. "I'm the sanest of men. I'm anxious to befriend you."

"By making me your prisoner?"

"That is unfortunate," he agreed. "But aside from that I promise you protection from the crew. And I will make you as comfortable as possible until I deliver you to your destination."

With disgusted anger, she said, "You talk of me as if I were a bill of goods!"

"You are exactly that to me," the blind man replied.

"And what is my destination?"

"You are being sold to a brothel in Barcelona," the Captain answered most casually.

Chapter Twelve

The gray skies of England had been left far behind. The warmer days of the South Atlantic had been replaced by the almost unendurable, blazing sunshine of the Mediterranean. Julia stood by the rail of the nameless three-master schooner which had taken her so far from home and stared out across the endless turquoise water sparkling with the rays of the noonday sun.

Many things had happened since she'd first been taken prisoner by Captain James O'Hara. Strangely she had come to like the white-haired blind man. The courage he showed in his authority over the crew and his handsome presence could not help but impress. And yet she was at his mercy and destined for a frightening degradation.

Captain O'Hara had moved her from the small airless cubbyhole to a pleasant cabin which adjoined his own. In this way he had been able to give her personal protection yet he had requested no favors from her for himself. He was a strange enigma of a man with a code of honor which was strangely different and altogether his own.

By dint of care, washing and patching of her one

dress she managed to keep herself reasonably well-clothed. She had indulged in amateur dressmaking to cut the neckline of her gown lower and altogether remove the sleeves so as to make it a sensible outfit for this much warmer clime. Now she knew that the port of Barcelona was only a day or so away and the voyage was near its end. She dared not think beyond that.

She and the white-haired O'Hara had many long talks and she'd learned that he'd lost his eyesight during a battle with pirates, when a mast had splintered from the barrage of an enemy cannon. It had fallen and struck him a glancing blow on the head which had rendered him unconscious. Later, when he recovered his sight had begun to fade until he was now completely blind.

Julia kept close to her cabin and the area near that occupied by the Captain. She had learned to recognize his footsteps and could tell when he approached without even glancing in his direction. Just now she heard him coming slowly toward her.

He made his way to where she stood by the railing and said, "Miss Crawford?"

She stared at his rugged, bronzed face and said, "You amaze me. You seem to find me without any difficulty."

He smiled wryly. "No magic I'm afraid. I was standing on the bridge and heard you walk over to the rail from your cabin door. My hearing is more acute because of my blindness."

She said, "How long before we reach Barcelona?"

"Twenty-four hours should do it."

"Is there no way I can make you change your mind?" she pleaded. "No matter what Fitzroy paid you I will triple it if you take me back to England. My father is a wealthy man."

Captain O'Hara shook his head. "I have already told you that more than money is involved."

"A man like you, with your spirit, can't be afraid of James Fitzroy."

"I'm not," he said. "Not by any means. But I am beholden to the power that he and a group surrounding him holds over me. They provide me with the marketing for my smuggling. If Fitzroy had them shut me off, and he would, I would have a difficult time finding new outlets for the illegal goods I bring back."

"You could find other markets!"

"Perhaps," he said. "But I do not wish to try. Also, I made a bargain with Fitzroy. I will not break it. You will fetch me a small fortune in Barcelona. You are the most valuable bit of cargo for your weight I have ever carried."

Julia said, "You propose to sell me like some kind of slave?"

"Slavery is a rewarding business," he said. "Especially when the color of the slave's skin is white."

She clenched the railing and fought back tears. "I cannot think you so cruel!"

"You concern yourself too much," he said placatingly. "The house to which you will be sold is the finest in all Spain. It is patronized almost solely by the Spanish nobility."

"I will still be a prostitute!"

"And a prisoner," he agreed. "But your every comfort will be attended to. Donna Mario Bueno has great pride in her reputation as a madam!"

"I could cheat you by dropping over the side and drowning myself," she challenged him.

He shook his head. "But you will not. We cling to life. I considered suicide after my blindness came. But I decided to overcome it. Who can say that you will not overcome all this."

"I find that poor consolation," Julia said unhappily.

"I have come to have a certain fondness for you," the blind man said. "You are a delightful young woman. I'm told you are also a beauty. It is fortunate I have no eyes to see you with or I might be tempted to give in to your pleading."

"You are cold and hard because of your blindness,"

she said. "It has twisted you. That is why you can be so cruel to me!"

He shrugged and gazed out across the sparkling ocean with those eyes which saw nothing and said, "What you say may be true. But it will make no difference."

"I shall always be on your conscience," she warned him. "You'll never be able to forget what you've done to me!"

"I wonder," the white-haired man said. "I hope you are not right."

And that was as far as she was able to get with him. The following day they came within sight of land the blue, dark hills contrasting with the lush green, and giant olive trees made her aware that she was reaching the end of her sea journey. Then the city of Barcelona itself came in sight with its many, splendid white buildings and its harbor filled with the ships of every size.

Now she was kept a prisoner in her cabin again. The ship moved slowly into the harbor and anchored a short distance from the shore. She gazed out the porthole and the sight of many French flags among the ships was a grim reminder that Spain was under the heel of Napoleon. She was going to be left a captive in enemy territory.

She thought of Gerald and his expeditions behind the enemy lines as a spy and wondered whether he had returned to England and what he would think about her disappearance. She could not give up hope that her father would find out the truth about her vanishing and quickly use all his power and influence to save her. This single thought was what made her cling to life. The blind captain had been right in telling her that hope lingered long after one might expect.

Perhaps Gerald would personally lead the search for her. If he were able to link her capture to the craven James Fitzroy it would not take him long to make the dissolute young dandy admit to the truth. And then there was Beau who would be outraged and certainly would engage in every effort to find her. Beau with the Prince to aid him could surely do a great deal. And all of them working together would not see her long left to the degredation of a Spanish brothel!

Her thoughts were brought to an abrupt halt by the sound of her cabin door being unlocked and the blind Captain O'Hara entering.

He said, "I have no doubt you've been looking out at the harbor and city."

"Have you come to tell me you've changed your mind?" she asked.

"On the contrary," he replied. "I have come to say I will be taking you ashore this evening. For obvious reasons I will have to blindfold you, and see that you are gagged and bound. But I shall have it done so as not to make you too uncomfortable."

"Your consideration would be amusing under other circumstances," she said.

His bronzed face showed a grim smile. "It is customary to bundle up merchandise. And that is what you are to me."

"I realize that all too clearly," she said. "And I warn you that you may come to rue having any part in this."

"I shall always regret it," he said. "But you must believe that from my point of view I have no choice."

"You wish to think that!"

"Whatever you like," he said. "Once you have been delivered to Donna Maria you will be entirely in her hands. You will not have contact with me again. By the way, she speaks excellent English so you will have no problem there."

Julia crossed to him and took him by the arm. "You can still save me! I can't think of this as anything but a ridiculous nightmare!"

He carefully removed her hand from his arm and in a quiet voice, said, "I'm sorry, Miss Crawford. I shall return for you later in the evening. Life in Spain is paced in a different fashion. What we would call late night is the time of the evening meal here. But you will become accustomed to it."

Julia's spirits dipped to a low ebb as the sun sank and darkness spread over the city and harbor. She looked out at the distant lights and the lanterns hanging on the masts of nearby ships. She thought wildly of escape and suicide once more. But she knew she had left it too late. The only way she would leave the cabin was bound and gagged. Unable to move or cry out for help!

And that was the way it happened. An hour or so later Captain O'Hara came with two sailors, who none too gently tied her wrists and ankles securely, then placed a gag over her mouth and a blindfold over her eyes. She was carried out and placed in a small boat which was rowed ashore. She was then lifted from the boat and placed in a carriage. Captain O'Hara was with her all this time but said nothing.

After a short drive she was removed from the carriage and carried into a building. She was taken up a stairway and dumped down onto a wide, soft bed of some sort. There she was left, still bound and helpless. Her heart pounded with fear as she lay there in the silent room. She became aware of a smell of sweet perfume, like some sort of incense. It was not unpleasant but along with the heat and being bound made her feel as if she might faint.

Then a door opened and she was aware of others in the room. A woman and a man were speaking in Spanish in low voices. Someone came over to her and in a moment the bindings at her ankles and wrists were cut away. Then the blindfold was removed and she saw the stern face of a powerful black man as he went about cutting away the gag from her mouth.

For the first time she was aware of her surroundings. She was in a large ornate room, its walls decorated in complicated tile patterns, its arched windows having iron bars. The black man having finished with her stood back. He was massive and dressed in Moorish style.

"So a pretty English wren has come to grace my

birdcage," a low, mocking female voice said from behind her.

Julia was seated on the edge of the round bed and now she turned swiftly to see who the speaker was. She saw a slim, graceful woman of middle-age with jet black hair wearing a white silk gown and an orange and purple fringed shawl. The woman's face was faded but it was apparent she had once been a beauty. Most amazing of all she was calmly puffing on a fat, black cigar.

The woman said, "Don't stare at me as if I were a freak, my girl!"

Julia rose hesitantly. "You are Donna Maria Bueno?"

"At least you've got that right."

She hurried over to the woman, tears in her eyes. "You must listen to me, Donna Maria. I have been taken prisoner by enemies. My father is a wealthy Englishman, he will pay you anything you ask for my safe return."

The woman laughed in her soft fashion. "England is a long distance away. The French army and navy stands between us. I'm afraid your offer is not practical. I have paid a good price for you and so I must use you as best I can!"

Julia cried, "I will kill myself before I'll be a prostitute!"

The woman puffed on her cigar and her sharp black eyes fixed on Julia with some annoyance. "Captain O'Hara said you had spirit. He also said you had good sense! Prostitute is an ugly English word. We do not use it here!"

"This is a brothel!"

Donna Maria said, "This is a house of entertainment. I have a most splendid clientele. You should consider yourself fortunate and honored to be in such a house!"

Scornfully Julia said, "Honored! To sell my body!"

The older woman smiled grimly. "Courtesans come

in all levels. I assure you this is the highest of them. If you prefer to cause trouble I can have you drugged and shipped to the Arab brothels in Morocco. Between disease and the violence you'd live less than a year there. But they would repay my investment in you. So you have your choice."

Julia listened with increasing horror. She had heard tales from Captain O'Hara about the brothels of Morroco. The narrow streets of monkey cages in which unhappy drabs were bartered for a pittance and forced to offer their services in animal fashion with all around looking on. It was the lowest step in degradation!

In a taut voice, she said, "It seems I have no choice."

Donna Maria nodded approvingly. She moved about her studying her. "Despite that rag of a dress you are truly lovely. You will do well here. I must explain the rules of the house."

"My prison!" Julia retorted.

"But such a pleasant prison," Donna Maria said. "First, you will have your own apartment. We do not encourage any fraternizing among our young ladies. You will see only me, your clients, and the guards." She indicated the big black man who had been standing by impassively, "This is Oba. He will be your personal guard. He or one of the twelve we employ here will always be outside your door, to protect you as well as to make sure you don't escape. My young ladies leave this house only through some monetary agreement or by death."

"My father will come for me!" Julia said. "He will see this place destroyed."

Donna Maria puffed on her cigar. "I will take the chance. My house is government protected and my guards are fully armed. Oba is an expert with the dagger. You will have a maid to attend you when you wish. These girls are all mutes and I find this an asset in a discreet place such as this. Now let me explain your future here."

"Is that necessary?" Julia asked bitterly.

"It is, I assure you," the woman with the cigar said in her slightly accented English. "You will serve only one patron. He will bid for you. And until he wishes a change you are his alone. It is very much like being someone's mistress. Not at all vulgar. Tonight there will be an auction held for you. That is our way with all newcomers. Whoever bids the highest shall have you until he wearies of you. So it is to your advantage to please him well and so escape being returned to the auction block too often."

Julia said, "I refuse to stand before a group of men and be auctioned off like some animal!"

"You have no choice," Donna Maria said sharply. "You must think of me as a friend from now on. And I can be a good one if you do not disobey me!"

"And cheerfully degrade myself!" she said with anger.

"It need not be degrading," the woman said. "Think of yourself as a beautiful art item being auctioned to collectors of rare art. A maid will come to you shortly, bathe you in perfumed water, and give you a sheer white gown to replace that rag you're wearing. It will properly drape your beauty without hiding any of it, the bidders will be able to clearly see through it. That is the whole point!"

"And if I refuse?"

The woman shrugged. "Then we need waste no more time. Tomorrow I shall have you shipped to Morocco."

The woman then went out with the big black Oba at her heels. Julia watched after them for a moment and then began to pace about in despair. She went to the window with its stout iron bars and could see nothing but darkness. From far below she could hear the sound of native music. She was still in shock from all that had happened and all the strange woman had said to her.

But knowing the alternative she realized she must at least pretend to go along with the woman's wishes. When a small, black girl arrived shortly after with the diaphanous white gown which the Donna Maria had mentioned, she did not try to be difficult.

The mute girl had large sympathetic eyes and a gentle manner. She took Julia to an anteroom where there was a large ceramic bath in a corner. The girl filled it with warm perfumed water which the massive Oba brought to them in jugs. Then she silently helped Julia scrub herself in preparation for the auction.

After she had donned the simple white gown Julia gazed at herself in the large mirror of the dressing room. She was amazed at the change which it made in her. She looked completely enticing and even her hair, which had come to be filled with snarls during the voyage, had been expertly combed to silken elegance by the mute girl. She might have been ready to grace some wonderful party in London, except for the fact she wore nothing under the dress and even a casual scrutiny would allow anyone to see through it!

But this was not a time for prudery! She was playing a drawn out game to save her life. The maid vanished and the massive Oba spoke to her in gutteral tones, indicating she was to accompany him.

She followed him down a curving stairway to a large reception hall. In the middle of the hall was a circular stand draped in red velvet. Oba saw her onto the stand. Then he and another massive black man stood on either side of her holding candelabra so as to highlight her.

Her tension was so great she could barely breathe. She wondered what might happen next. When all at once the cigar-smoking madam appeared followed by a parade of a dozen well-dressed men of various ages. She let them make a semi-circle facing Julia on the crimson platform and then addressed them sharply in Spanish.

The men stared at Julia without embarrassment and made numerous comments among themselves. Then one young blood showed his appreciation by applauding her. The others joined in.

Looking pleased, Donna Maria told Julia in English,

"They consider you the most beautiful girl yet to decorate my house."

Julia found the compliment of small comfort. Now the bidding began in Spanish. It was fevered and the men were clearly excited! The prospect of winning her seemed to be making them bid recklessly and Donna Maria looked delighted.

One of the most frequent bidders was a tall, bald old man dressed in a fine brown velvet jacket. He had a short white beard and a courtly manner. It was easy to see that in his youth he might have been considered handsome. Now he was plainly very old.

The old man with the white beard called out some bid and the others gazed at him in astonishment. Donna Maria laughed happily and the other men shrugged, shook their heads and filed out of the room. The young man who had first applauded hesitated as he made his exit to take a last longing look at Julia.

Donna Maria came to her and said, "It has gone well. You have brought me a small fortune. You may go back to your room now. You will be the mistress of a nobleman, Duke de Parmesca. Consider yourself lucky, my girl!"

The old Duke stood back and gravely bowed to her as she passed him. Tears of humiliation were in her eyes as she followed Oba up the stairs. Back in her apartment she threw herself on the bed and sobbed.

She was still stretched out on the bed when she heard the door gently open and someone come in. The door closed and the newcomer was crossing over to her. She sat up to be confronted by the ancient Duke de Parmesca.

The white-bearded old man bowed gravely again. And in perfect English, he asked, "Why are you so sorrowful? Is it because I'm so old and ugly?"

"You speak English?" she said.

He nodded. "I have visited England often. Before this unhappy war."

She rose and confronting him, said, "You must be told that I'm not a prostitute. I was brought here against my will. Did Donna Maria explain all that to you?"

The old man looked embarrased. "She said you were gifted with an imagination. That you were a well known English lady, often the mistress of the famous, who preferred to think of herself as an innocent."

"She lied!" Julia said angrily. "I was sold to her by enemies. I have had only one lover in my life and he is the man I hope to marry!"

The courtly old man regarded her sorrowfully. "I find this both easy and difficult to believe."

"I'm telling you the truth!"

"But Donna Maria has sold you to me!"

"I'm only too aware of that," Julia said. "And I have the choice of giving you my body or being shipped to Morocco and worse degradation there!"

He looked alarmed. "That must not happen to you!"

Julia turned away. "Perhaps it would be better. Death would come soon and the agony would be quickly over."

The spare, old man came and touched a thin hand on her arm. "You must not despise me."

"I do not blame you," she said. "But if I'm forced to make love to you I cannot help but find it repulsive."

"You sadden me," he said.

There was something in his tone which made her turn to stare at him. She saw an infinite sadness and tenderness in his face. And she realized she was not dealing with some lust-maddened old roué but a man of character and great understanding.

"I did not mean I think you repulsive," she said. "I see you as a courtly, old man."

His face brightened. "That is most kind of you."

"It is the relationship which faces me which is so distasteful and which would be the same or worse were you anyone else."

"I understand," he said.

She sank to the edge of the bed in despair. "I cannot expect consideration from you. You have paid well for me."

"My dear child," the old man said awkwardly, "do not distress yourself. This situation is not as bad as you may think."

Julia looked up at him. "What do you mean?"

He hesitated for a moment, then said, "I shall make a confession to you. Tell you a secret that no one knows, not even my family or most intimate friends. I am incapable."

"Incapable?"

He nodded. "Impotent if you wish to use an ugly word."

Startled, she said, "Then why?"

"Why did I bid a small fortune for you?"

"Yes."

"Call it an old man's pride," he said. "I'm long a widower. My children have homes and lives of their own. I found myself wanting the comfort of a young woman's love."

"And you came to a place like this for it?"

"Where else?" he said with sorrow. "There is not all that much love available in the world. Desperate men sometimes seek it in a commercial setting."

"I do not call that kind of transaction love," she told him.

He sighed. "Perhaps, to be truthful, I had a faint hope that a warm, young body might revive some life in my own. But even as I gaze at you in that nightgown which exposes all your beauty I know it will never be possible."

"I see," she said dully. "So you will return to Donna Maria and get your money. I shall be on the block again."

"That needn't be," the old man said.

Again she stared at him. "What else?"

"I'm willing to continue our arrangement on a purely platonic basis," he told her. "I need youthful companionship and friendship. You can offer me these without compromising your character. The truth of our relationship shall be a secret from everyone, including Donna Maria."

Julia gasped. "You can't mean it!"

"I do," he said with a small smile on his ancient, white-bearded face. "And to merely observe the expression of relief on your lovely face now makes it certain my plan is worthwhile!"

She rose slowly, gazing at him in awe. "I knew you were a good man when I first saw you. I'm certain of it now. I cannot believe that a kind fate has placed me in your care."

"And in my care you shall remain," the old Duke said. "Perhaps later I shall be able to buy your freedom from Donna Maria and see you safely back to England."

"I shall live for that day."

"In the meantime I hope we may become true friends," he said.

"You have proven your friendship," she told him. "And I shall attempt to show you my feelings about you are genuine."

The old man took her gently in his arms and kissed her on the forehead, saying, "I feel I have a new, much beloved grandchild."

So began what was surely the strangest relationship Julia had known in all her young life. Her elderly lover kept his word in never making the ultimate claim of her. There were times, many of them, when she burned with desire, and wished that this gentle old man could satisfy her. But she knew it was beyond his physical ability to make love to her in the usual way.

Still, she was soon to learn that she had underestimated him. He induced moods of desire in himself and in her as well, by having her pose nude before him.

Often she remained naked all the time she was in his company.

Then one evening he had her stretch out naked on the wide bed and with a twinkle in his eyes, he said, "Tonight I shall show you a new variety of loving!"

She wondered what he meant and soon found out. He gently knelt and began kissing her on the mouth, the shoulders, the nipples and then his frantic lips moved lower to her pubic region and suddenly his kisses took on a new nature! As he caressed her soft secret parts she experienced a complete response. Soon she was having a full sexual experience. One filled with quite a different sort of ecstacy. She closed her eyes and thought of Gerald.

Her climax came and the old man slowly rose and said, "I have been unfair to you. We shall do this more often."

And they did. She came to know a new fondness for him and told him about her past and her struggle to decide between Beau and Gerald. He brought her flowers and talked of his dead wife.

Donna Maria visited Julia occasionally to ask about the Duke. She would sit with her cigar and stare at her. Her usual question was, "Is all going well?"

Julia knew she must be cautious in her replies. She said, "Yes. The Duke seems well satisfied."

"And you?"

"As content as any prisoner could be."

Donna Maria smiled grimly. "Prisoners are never content. At least you have not found it as degrading as you expected. Making an old man happy is a work worthy of a nun."

"I doubt that he would find the same solace in a nunnery," she said.

The older woman laughed heartily at this. "You English do have a sense of humor after all."

Julia said, "Have you thought of contacting my father?"

Donna Maria rose to leave. "Don't be tactless. I'm

quite content with things as they are. Just continue and you'll find yourself well treated."

Later, Julia repeated the conversation for the Duke. The old man sighed. "I have already talked to her of buying your freedom but she wouldn't hear it. I brought up the matter that I might not live all that long and she would do well to take her profit in a lump sum. But she isn't interested. I suppose she feels if something happens to me you'd bring a high price from someone else."

"But that would be different," she said. "I do not think I could go through with it."

"I have an idea she'll listen to reason one day." the old man said. "I have made her a good offer. After she gives it some more thought she may decide to accept it."

Julia kept her hopes high. She knew the old man badly wanted to help her and would continue to press Donna Maria until she consented to sell her. She also had the feeling that sooner or later she would hear from her father or Gerald. They would find out what had happened to her and come to her rescue. It was merely a matter of waiting. But as the months went by she began to feel more desolate.

Then one day Donna Maria came up to her room and seating herself as usual, lit one of her cigars. As she enjoyed the first puff on it, she said, "You may consider yourself lucky to be here, my girl."

"I can't imagine why," she replied.

"I'll tell you why," the older woman said. "Barcelona is stricken with plague. Most of Spain is reeling under it. People are dying in the streets in greater numbers every day."

"The Duke has not mentioned it."

Donna Maria cooled herself with her fan. "It must be because he wishes to spare you concern. But if it continues we may well have to close and leave Barcelona!"

This was as dismaying as the word about the

plague. If she were taken somewhere else as a prisoner she might lose the old Duke as her patron and her father or her other friends in England whom she hoped would come for her, would never be able to locate her. It was a dreadful complication on which she hadn't counted. And as soon as the Duke arrived that evening she questioned him.

The old man's thin face showed concern. He said, "I fear it is all too true. The plague is killing thousands. Spain is a death trap these days."

"Donna Maria told me about it," Julia worried. "She is talking about moving."

"In that case it may be for the best," the Duke said. "This might be our chance to persuade her to give you your freedom."

"Oh, yes!" Julia said. "Do talk to her about it again!"

Several days passed and the old man came to her apartment in the house as usual. She thought he looked especially haggard. He sat and sipped a glass of wine and told her, "I discussed your future with Donna Maria but she is in an obstinate mood. She has determined to stay out the plague and not leave the city."

"You are sure?"

"Yes. She says business has never been better. People wish to have a fling before they die. She will not even listen to an offer for your freedom."

Julia was kneeling on the carpet by the old man's chair. She implored him, "Then you must continue to protect me! Don't leave me!"

He gave her a kindly glance. "You are the most important thing to me in life. You need not worry."

"What if you get the plague?" she worried.

"I'm too old for it," he said, "just as I'm too old for almost everything else."

"You must take care of yourself," she begged him. "You do not look well."

He put aside his empty wine glass and taking her hands in his, confided, "I did not intend to bother you with this. But I have had the worst of news. My eldest son died this morning of the plague. His wife is also stricken as is one of his children."

"I'm so sorry!" she exclaimed.

"It is all right," he said, soothingly. "You cannot feel my grief since he was unknown to you. I do not expect nor wish to burden you with my sadness. But it has been a sore blow to me."

"You have other sons."

"And daughters," he agreed. "But he was my favorite. Still, I cannot expect to escape in this hell the plague has brought on us. I'm no better than anyone else. I only ask myself, where will it end?"

"Surely it must abate soon," she said.

"The chapel bells ring out as prayers are said for the living and the dead," the Duke said tragically. "Surely the Almighty will look down on our poor people with some healing sympathy."

It was a melancholy evening. And she sensed that he left her in as hopeless a mood as when he had arrived. She felt grief for him and new fears for herself. Not from the plague because thus far no one in the brothel had been infected. But of what might happen if the Duke should be struck down.

She did not have any visit from the Duke for several evenings. This worried her more than usual knowing about the plague. But she also thought he might have had to travel to another city for the burial of his son. Then one morning her guard, the massive black Oba collapsed as he brought a jug of water in to her.

The mute black girl who had been ready to help her with her bath gave Julia a terrified glance and then ran from the room. Julia found herself alone with the stricken giant. She bent down and discovered he was suffering from an intense fever and great beads of perspiration were draining down his round cheeks. His eyes had a yellowish cast and his breathing was difficult.

She was still kneeling by him, trying to get him to take a cooling drink of water when Donna Maria arrived with two of the other guards.

Donna Maria dragged her away from the man on the floor, crying, "Fool! Don't touch him! He has the plague!"

The two guards wrapped the fallen man in a wet sheet and carried him out. Donna Maria nervously lit one of her cigars and puffed on it.

Julia said, "He is the first here to suffer the plague!"

The older woman shook her head grimly. "No. He is the fourth. I have kept it silent. I do not wish the house to get a bad name. No one will visit us if it does."

"But you should warn people. Perhaps leave here," she said.

"There is no place to go, the whole country is suffering from this Black Death," Donna Maria said with anger. "We must wait it out."

"If anyone of us are still alive."

The older woman shrugged. "Thus far only two of my girls and one of the maids has been stricken. Oba is the first of the guards. Someone has brought the disease to us."

"We cannot expect to escape here in the midst of it," she said, alarmed.

"What about the Duke?" Donna Maria asked.

She stared at her. "What about him?"

"He has not shown himself here for the best part of a week," the older woman said. "That is most unusual."

"His son died of the plague. He may have had to go out of the city."

Donna Maria shook her head. "His family are all here in Barcelona."

"I do not know," Julia said unhappily.

The older woman looked at her sharply. "Perhaps he has been struck down."

"Oh, no!"

"Why not?"

"He said few of the older people were bothered with it!"

Donna Maria laughed scornfully. "What a lie! It is the old and the infants who perish first as in all such diseases. He told you that to set your mind at ease!"

Julia's eyes widened with horror. "What will happen to me if he dies?"

Donna Maria shrugged. "I shall auction you off again."

Chapter Thirteen

Even before Donna Maria returned a few hours later with the news that the Duke was dead of the plague Julia had felt it must be true. She was sure the old man had been ill on that last visit. She listened in dull shock as Donna Maria informed her that the old man's funeral had already been held.

"Makes no difference whether you be rich or poor, noble or peasant, they bury you right away these days," she said.

Julia paced back and forth. "I cannot think fate could be so cruel."

Donna Maria smiled at her sourly. "You had better accept it. The last bit of earth has been patted down on his grave. And now you must begin your career as a prostitute in true fashion!"

She turned on the older woman, startled, "What do you mean by that?"

The brothel madam's eyes narrowed. "Do you think

me a fool? Do you think I have no means of observing you or any of the others? There are secret viewing places in the walls of all the rooms. I know what is going on!"

"You spied on us?"

Donna Maria laughed harshly. "In your most intimate moments. And let me add they were not at all intimate enough to have satisfied most men."

Julia felt anger for both herself and the dead man who had treated her so kindly. "How dare you!"

"The Duke was a saint, wasn't he?" The older woman went on in mocking fashion. "But then at his age it was easy. The next time I shall see you get someone younger!"

"There will be no next time!" Julia cried.

Donna Maria smiled. "Think about it. There is still Morocco. But I'm sure you'll agree, despite the plague, you are better off here. I'll send the word out and hopefully we can manage an auction for tomorrow night."

With this warning of the things to come Donna Maria left. Julia again threw herself on her bed for a prolonged fit of sobbing. And when she recovered she determined to somehow destroy herself before the next night. She had abandoned hope of rescue from England. And she felt she would probably soon be struck down by the plague in any case. She needed only some object sharp enough to open her veins and drain out her life in the perfumed bath waters.

Donna Maria was careful about allowing any knives or objects that could be used as weapons to enter the apartments. But Julia had something she felt would serve. A golden pendant which had been one of the Duke's many gifts to her. It had a very sharp point at the bottom and she felt if she could hone it some way it would serve as a means of slitting her wrists.

She decided to wait until the next morning when her maid usually came to help her with her bath. As soon as the girl left her alone to soak in the water she would use the manufactured weapon to end her life.

The hours went by with grim slowness. The day and the evening which followed were unmercifully hot. She did not even have the energy to move about and ease her nervousness. There was no music from below and the great house seemed unusually silent. She wondered if word had spread that it had been struck by the plague and no one was visiting it.

Then she began thinking about England and the man she loved whom she would never see again. And her thoughts also included Beau, who loved her, but could not bring himself to marry her. How different things might have been if he had made her his wife. Surely she would not have ended in this dreadful predicament.

Was Gerald alive? She hoped so. And she fervently hoped that he would somehow free himself of Elizabeth and find himself some other woman who would truly love him. She worried about her father and what her vanishing might have meant to him. The parent whom she had at last come to so much respect might end his days a broken, old man. James Fitzroy had truly wreaked a terrible vengeance on her!

She stretched out on the bed and closed her eyes in an attempt to rest despite the sickening heat. All at once she was aware of someone slowly opening the door of her apartment. She sat up quickly, alarmed, and barely managed to prevent herself uttering a cry.

For there in the doorway, looking exactly as she had last seen him was the remarkable Matthew Kemp! The stout secret service agent touched a finger to his lips and bade her to join him.

Julia couldn't believe her eyes. It had to be some mad kind of nightmare! But the figure of Matthew Kemp was very real and he was now at her bedside. In a soft whisper, he said, "Fast! Your father is waiting for us in the corridor!"

"Matthew!" she whispered in near hysterical fashion.

"No time to falter!" The fat man told her and he led her to the door. After a cautious glance into the dark corridor he took her by the arm and they rushed down the stairway. There was no one in the reception hall and the entrance door was open. Matthew shoved her out into the open.

Her father was standing there in the shadows. As soon as he saw her he took her in his arms. "My dear, Julia!" he said hoarsely.

It was then she saw the prone bodies of two of the guards on the steps. There had been a silent, deadly duel out there and her father and Matthew had been the winners.

Matthew said, "Come along!"

"The carriage is waiting," her father said, his arm around her.

The carriage was just a block or so away from the house where she had been held captive. A man sat hunched on the driver's seat with a torch in a fixture burning beside him.

Her father saw her into the carriage and joined her. Matthew Kemp shouted, "To the docks, man!" And clambered in after them.

She sat close to her father in the open carriage as it was driven through the dark streets at a wild pace. She thought that he looked oddly white and ill but put it down to the flickering light of the torch's glare.

Matthew Kemp had also noticed and leaned forward to ask John Crawford, "Are you all right?"

Her father nodded. "Just a slight wound in my side. The second fellow managed to sink his dagger in me before you finished him."

The fat man was at once upset. "Open your jacket!" he ordered.

Julia saw to it that her father's jacket was opened and she saw the spreading stain of blood on his shirt at the same time as Matthew Kemp.

"It's a bad wound!" she cried.

"No!" her father said. "Only slight. The blood is deceiving. I feel little or no pain."

Kemp shouted something to the driver and the carriage rolled on even faster. Kemp produced a large white handkerchief and attempted to stanch the flow of blood with it. In this frantic state they arrived at the docks. As they transferred to a waiting small boat Julia saw that her father staggered rather than walked.

It seemed to take an eternity for the two sailormen at the oars to get them to the waiting ship. And by then Matthew Kemp had to almost carry her father up onto the deck.

"Ship's doctor!" Matthew Kemp called out at once.

Again there was a great deal of confusion as Julia followed her father and the friend who was supporting him to a cabin. There he was stretched out on a bunk. In a moment the side-whiskered, elderly ship's doctor joined them.

He saw the stain of blood on her father's shirt and setting down his bag, exclaimed, "What sort of deviltry have you been up to?"

"Attacked by thugs," Matthew Kemp said. "Dagger wound!"

The doctor was already exposing the wound. "I should say so," he spoke grimly. "Some water and a basin and bandages. This is not going to be a pleasant business."

Julia sank into a chair, her teeth chattering, shock and despair were taking a high toll from her. She watched as the doctor worked with skilled hands to clean and bandage the wound. He then gave her father some brandy and he seemed much better.

Julia went over and knelt by him. "Father!"

He offered her a wan smile and even managed to weakly take her hand. "I shall be all right. Just leave me to rest a little."

The bewhiskered doctor nodded solemnly. "Do as he says, Miss Crawford."

Julia allowed Matthew Kemp to escort her out onto the dark deck. She saw that the ship was already under sail and the lights of Barcelona were fading in the night.

"We're under way!" she cried.

The fat man nodded. "The sooner we leave that plague-ridden land the better. And it's not exactly safe to be sailing here in enemy waters."

"You found me!"

"Yes!"

"What about father?"

"I think he will be all right," Matthew said. But she worried there was doubt in his tone and the dark shadows of the night hid any betraying expression he might have.

"He must!" she said. "He must!"

"He is in good hands. Doctor McGraw is well qualified," the fat man assured her.

"How did you find me?"

"The trail began with Fitzroy," Matthew Kemp said in a stern voice.

"You guessed that he was behind it?"

"Not directly. But he drank too much one night and Beau Brummell happened to hear him boasting that he'd settled his score with you."

"So it was Beau who told you."

"He came to your father at once with what he'd heard. Your father and I had to question Mr. Fitzroy without being too gentle with him. Before we'd finished he told us what he had done and where you were."

"And then what?" Julia asked.

The stout Matthew Kemp hesitated before saying, "He was unfortunate enough to have a nasty encounter."

"What sort of encounter?"

"He was attacked by some thugs, robbed and his body thrown in the Thames. It was fortunate we'd questioned him earlier."

Julia was shocked. "So he was murdered!"

The fat man's tone was grim. "James Fitzroy was mixed up in a number of dubious schemes. He made a great many enemies along the way."

"I know," she agreed. "The man who brought me to Spain as a captive was smuggling goods for some group of which Fitzroy was the kingpin."

"Typical," Matthew Kemp said sternly. And then in a different tone, "Did you suffer much in your captivity?"

"I was fortunate," she said. "I had a protector in the

brothel. An old Duke who bought my services and asked nothing of me but my friendship.''

"Most unusual!''

"But he died of the plague about a week ago and I was to be put on the auction block again! You arrived just in time! How did you know where I was?''

"We had that from Fitzroy. And when we arrived in Barcelona and found it overtaken by the plague we quickly questionèd about Donna Maria's brothel. One of the carriage drivers warned us against going there, saying that it was full of plague. That Donna Maria had herself been stricken only that morning.''

"It could be,'' she said. "I didn't see her all day and that was unusual.''

"There's no doubt of her illness,'' the fat man said. "We did some further investigating and learned that all her guards except three had fled along with most of her girls. We were afraid that you might have been among those who ran off.''

"She kept me in ignorance of how badly the plague had infected the house. And she also kept me by myself, away from the rest of her girls.''

"Which turned out for the best,'' Matthew Kemp said. "Your father and I decided we could break our way into the house on our own. And we did. Unhappily he suffered that wound.''

"If only he recovers,'' she worried.

"He will have good care and it could not have been in a vital spot or he would have become unconscious,'' the fat man said.

"What about this ship?'' she asked.

"It is one used by our foreign service to drop off and pick up spies. Your father was given a leave of absence to look for you, my services and the use of this vessel. It had to look after some routine matters along the way so that held us up a little.''

Her mind at once moved to Gerald. She said, "Did Sir Gerald return safely from Denmark?''

"Yes,'' the stout man said.

"How is he?''

"You can discuss those things later, perhaps with your father if he is better in the morning. Just now I suggest you get some sleep. You have gone through a great ordeal."

"True," she said. And she indicated her nightgown. "I cannot make the voyage in this!"

"Your father thought of that," he said. "He has a full choice of your clothing in the cabin reserved for you. He would not believe that you were dead or that we would not find you."

"Dear father," she said warmly. "And you, Matthew! How often I have thought of you. And of Gerald and Beau as well."

"Beau was most anxious that we make the voyage in search of you."

"How does it go with him these days?"

"Badly!"

"Really?" She was at once upset.

"He has had a final quarrel with His Royal Highness, who is now the Prince Regent and has a new circle of friends, one of them Sir Orville Hewitt."

"My old enemy."

"Somehow Beau has managed to keep his facade and stave off his creditors. But it cannot last for long!"

"Surely my father will help him."

Kemp sighed. "I understand he has offered him help many times but Beau has refused it."

Matthew Kemp showed her to her cabin. By this time the vessel was well out at sea with the shore line of Spain no longer visible. In the cabin she found a trunk with a rich store of clothing, shoes, hats and everything she might need. Her father in his efficient way had thought of everything. She spread out the familiar dresses with a feeling of delight. It was the next best thing to being home in England again.

She prayed that her father's life might be spared. And she worried that she might be infected with the plague and bring it to the ship. The best hope was that her segregation from the others might have saved her.

But she had been exposed to the old Duke who had succumbed to the dread disease and to Donna Maria, who now lay dying of it.

Memory of the stern woman with her cigar smoking came back. What a weird character Donna Maria had been! And how strange to think of her dying in misery alone in that great house which had been her kingdom. She had reigned over it like a queen, with her guards and servants and the unfortunate girls who were her slaves. She had no doubt accumulated a fortune. All useless to her now!

A fresh nightgown and the clean sheets of the bunk relaxed her. But she was too stirred to be able to sleep immediately. She worried about the change of fortune which had come to Beau Brummell and about Gerald. Matthew Kemp had told her that Gerald had returned safely from the mission to Denmark but he'd said nothing else. No message, nothing! Could Gerald have decided she was dead and gone back to his wife?

With this troubling thought she fell asleep. When she wakened the sun of another day was streaming in through the porthole of her cabin. She quickly dressed and went on deck to be met by the massive Matthew Kemp.

He told her, "Your father is resting well. There is no reason to believe he will not recover."

She felt a great surge of relief. "When can I talk to him?"

"The doctor has given him a sedative," the stout man said. "I would not disturb him until he wakens of his own accord."

"How long will it take to return to England?"

"It depends much on the weather," Matthew Kemp replied. "And we are continually in peril from the French as long as we are in these waters."

She had breakfast and felt much better. Then she took a stroll on the deck and sought out Matthew Kemp again. She began to ask him the questions she would have asked of her father.

She said, "You told me last night that Gerald returned from his mission in Denmark. But you said no more."

The stout man eyed her with some uneasiness. "That is true," he admitted.

"Surely he was concerned about my disappearance?" she suggested.

"He was greatly concerned."

"And?"

Matthew Kemp was slow in replying. Then he said, "I think this would come better from your father."

"I do not wish to bother him in his present state," she argued.

The stout man looked unhappy. "It is difficult."

"Please! What are you trying to conceal from me?"

He stared down at the deck. "Sir Gerald was much upset by your kidnapping. He felt you would never return alive."

"So?"

"The service needed an agent for an especially difficult mission in France. Sir Gerald volunteered at once."

Julia said, "Is that all?"

The big man gave her a resigned look. "That was some months ago. He has not been heard of since."

She was shocked. "You think he may have been captured?"

"We fear it."

"And he would be executed at once as a spy?"

"That is the rule," Matthew said solemnly. He at once hurried on, "But that need not be so in this case."

She fought back her desire for tears. "But he should have returned by now?"

"He should have," the fat man said. "But many agents are missing for longer times and still turn up alive. There is the possibility of his being in prison."

She pressed a hand to her throat and turned away and walked speedily to the bow of the ship. There she let her tears come. Matthew Kemp had wanted to make it easier for her but she knew she must face the facts.

Thinking she was dead Gerald had undertaken a dangerous mission and almost surely lost his life.

Between the shock of this revelation and concern for her ailing father it was a bad day for her. She kept to herself, feeling little joy in her rescue. Gradually she came to understand that she was being selfish and she must think of her parent. In the coolness of the early evening when he had wakened she went and sat beside him.

He gazed up at her from his bunk with a fond look on his thin actor's face. He said, "We shall soon be back in England and it will be all right."

"Yes, Father," she said quietly.

He stared at her sadly. "You have talked with Matthew. You know about Gerald."

She nodded. "Yes."

"I'm truly sorry. But I have not given up hope. And you must not. I spoke with Gerald before he left and we discussed your vanishing. I refused to give up hope for you and I managed to convince him into thinking the same way. He did not leave in a spirit of despair, but looking forward to your survival."

"This really was what he thought?"

"Yes. So I believe he will fight to the utmost to preserve his life and return. Do not be surprised if when we get back to London he is there to greet you!"

"Oh, Father, you've given me new heart!" she exclaimed and bent down to kiss him.

John Crawford smiled wanly. "I simply wanted you to know all the facts."

"And I feel better for knowing them," she said.

Her father gave a deep sigh. "We have not battled our way all this far to accept defeat. We must fight on!"

"We shall," she said. "Just so long as you recover."

"The doctor says I'm out of danger," her father said. "But all of us are in grave peril until we clear these waters. There are few friendly craft about."

"I know," she agreed. "Matthew says that Beau and the Prince have had a final quarrel and it seems they will never be reconciled. Do you believe this also?"

"I fear it," he said.

"What happened?"

"Beau has strong pride," her father said. "And the Prince insisted on making him do his bidding. At some turn in events Beau rebelled. The Prince is not used to having anyone cross him."

"But they were the staunchest of friends."

"At times the best friends become the worst of enemies. He knew the Prince was most touchy on the subject of his weight and this led to a dreadful scene in St. James' Street. The Prince attempted to administer the *coup de grace* in public, using Beau's own weapon of the direct cut. They met on the street according to one version of the story, the Regent walking with a friend and Brummell walking with another dandy named Jack Lee. To make the cut as deadly as possible, the Prince stopped to converse with Lee, while looking straight at Brummell. After some conversation which Brummell bore patiently, the parties separated and moved on. Then Brummell said loudly enough for the Prince to hear, "Well, Jack, who is your fat friend?"

"Poor Beau!" Julia said. "He has always been too quick with a reply."

"A sharp tongue was the badge of merit of his set, of the Prince's set," her father said. "He should have found it in his heart to forgive Brummell."

"But he hasn't?"

"Not at the time I left London," her father said. "It seemed likely that Beau's creditors would come down on him and he would be ruined."

"Surely you can help him."

"I would willingly do so, but he has refused my aid," her father said. "He was much concerned about you. We can only hope that with your safe return he will listen sanely to my offers of help."

"Maybe I can convince him," she said.

"If anyone can," her father agreed.

She left him to rest and went back on deck. The portly Matthew Kemp was standing by the rail gazing out at the sea. He turned as she approached and offered her a smile on his broad face.

"Your father is much better, don't you think?"

"I do," she said. "I feel sure he will recover."

"The doctor says there is no question. Once we have run the gauntlet of the French navy there will be little to worry about."

"Will the war never end?"

"Napoleon cannot last much longer," Kemp said.

"You think he will be defeated?"

"He is defeated now. It only needs a deciding battle. England and her allies are strong again."

She gave him a meaningful look. "Then none of the sacrifices have been in vain?"

"I sincerely hope not, Miss," the secret service man said.

The days went by. When they were well north of Gibraltar an armed French frigate crossed their path. But instead of challenging them it sailed on causing much speculation on board.

Matthew Kemp predicted, "I swear the French must have been defeated. Wellington's troops must have met and conquered the returned Emperor."

Her father, who was now able to move about the ship on his own, agreed, "I think it likely. If so, England will be back to normal again."

For Julia's part she cared only if Gerald had returned. If the war had ended and his life with it, the victory would mean little to her. She kept hoping that her father would be proven right and the man she loved would return safely.

Much of her thought was also of Beau Brummell and how she might help him. She considered going to the Prince on her own and trying to convince him that Beau should have another chance. But she knew the prospects for this were not good. The one hope was that Beau would accept financial help from her father and thus maintain his position in London society. He could survive if his debtors didn't foreclose on him.

When Julia and her father arrived in London, all England was still in a glorious haze of victory. The tide that would turn against the stubborn and depraved Prince Regent had not yet begun. All that England could think about was that Napoleon had been finally defeated and was now on his way to exile in distant St. Helena.

Waterloo was considered the great victory. Though it was perhaps Nelson at Trafalgar who had saved the nation from being invaded by the finest army Napoleon had ever had. But after Waterloo it was Wellington's name that was lifted high, the bad tactics of the French and the obstinate courage of the Germans under Blucher being largely ignored. Standing on deck as their vessel docked Julia and her party could almost smell victory in the air.

Since their arrival had not been announced she could not expect anyone to be there to greet them. Matthew Kemp was the first ashore and by the time she and her father followed, the stout secret service man had a carriage waiting for them. It took them to John Crawford's fine mansion where Julia had agreed to remain as mistress of the house.

Her mind was filled with questions as to what had gone on since she'd been away from England. Most especially she was concerned about Sir Gerald and Beau Brummell. The traffic of the congested main streets was worse than ever, wagons and carriages fought for space. The gray skies and damp air was most welcome to her. The very smell of the great city was good!

When they arrived at her father's mansion she sent Matthew Kemp with a message to Beau Brummell asking that he dine with them that night. The stout man went off on her errand without complaint. Meanwhile she and her father were greeted warmly by the servants. She went upstairs to refresh herself and change into another dress.

A little later she joined her father downstairs in his

study and was surprised to find him in the company of a young man with dark brown sideburns and a pleasant face made distinctive by a high brow and shrewd brown eyes.

Her father introduced him, saying, "Julia, this my manager, Mr. Anthony Laver. I do not think you have met before."

"I think not," she said.

The personable Anthony Laver bowed. "My great pleasure, Miss Crawford." He was conservatively dressed in a dark gray jacket and trousers of the same color.

With some pride her father said, "Anthony has managed my affairs well during my term at the Foreign Office and in my absence finding you. I have rewarded him with a full partnership in my business."

"Which I in no way expected," the young man protested.

"The share is small enough, but you deserve to reap some benefits of the good work you've done," her father told him.

"Business has been excellent," Anthony Laver said. "Rentals have grown and the proceeds from White's has never been better."

Julia said eagerly, "I'm starved for some news of London, Mr. Laver. What has been happening?"

"Not a great deal," the young man said. "All our attention has been fixed on Waterloo and the great victory of Wellington."

She said, "Have you heard anything of Sir Gerald Giles returning?"

Anthony Laver said, "I'm afraid I do not know him."

Her father quickly interjected, "Anthony wouldn't have met Gerald. I shall be in touch with the Foreign Office and they will have the latest word."

"I hope so," she said.

"Lord Byron is creating a scandal," Anthony Laver told her with a wry smile. "But that is not new for him. The Prince is losing the popularity he had and I think he will be as disliked as his father. And Richard Sheridan, the playwright is dead."

Julia was shocked. "He was our best playwright. Both *The Rivals* and *The School for Scandal* are fine comedies."

The young man nodded. "He is a great loss. And of course there is Sir Orville Hewitt. He has been struck down."

Her attention was caught. "What has happened to him?"

"Apoplexy, I hear. A stroke so severe that he is neither able to move or speak. The physicians have given up on him. It is only a matter of time, they say."

Her father grimaced. "After all his efforts to win favor with the Prince Regent."

Anthony Laver said, "Many think the Prince Regent will end up the same way if he doesn't curb his excessive eating and drinking."

She said, "And Beau Brummell?"

The young man spread his hands. "The talk is that he has insulted most of his friends and refuses to deal with his debtors. He is bankrupt but won't admit it."

Her father said, "We must do something about that."

"I have sent Matthew Kemp with a message telling him I have arrived safely back in London and inviting him to dinner here," she said. "This might be an opportunity for us to talk to him."

"An excellent idea," her father agreed. "In the meanwhile I shall take a carriage to the Foreign Office and get the latest word there."

"Shall I go with you?" Julia asked.

"No," he said. "I think it better you remain here. I shall return with whatever word there is as soon as possible."

"Please do!" she begged him.

He kissed her and said, "In my absence I leave you in the company of Anthony."

After her father left she felt a trifle embarrassed in

the presence of the young man who, while important in her father's business, was still almost a stranger to her.

As they stood together in the living room of the great mansion, he said, "You must have gone through a great deal!"

"More than I care to remember," she said.

"You have emerged looking quite lovely despite your trials," he said with gallantry.

"Thank you," she said. "I do not recall ever having met you before."

"I saw you several times with your father," he told her. "But you would not have noticed me."

"You have worked for my father for a while?"

"Since my youth," he acknowledged. "Actually he has treated me like a son. I came here with nothing. He gave me my opportunity and has even insisted that I live here. He has been far too generous with me."

She smiled. "I'm certain he found deserving talent in you or he would not have taken such interest."

"My only wish is to live up to his expectations," the young man said.

Julia explained, "You know that I was only shortly reconciled with my father before my kidnapping."

Anthony Laver said, "He told me the story. And I can promise you he was like a madman when he heard of your having disappeared."

"The wonder is that he found me."

"As soon as Mr. Brummell told him of James Fitzroy's drunken gloating he went straight to that young man's house. I hear that he and Matthew Kemp beat the truth from him."

"And soon after Fitzroy was murdered?"

The young man with the pleasant face and long brown sideburns said, "In his case I cannot feel any pity."

"His was a sad waste of a life," she agreed.

"So now you will be living here with your father?"

"Yes."

"Perhaps my presence in the house will be awkward

for you two," the young man said. "I'd be quite willing to find quarters elsewhere."

"No need!" she protested. "My father has come to depend on you and I'm sure he'll wish you to remain."

"And you?"

She smiled. "I find you most agreeable."

Anthony Laver's young face glowed with pleasure. "That is most generous of you, Miss Crawford. I had hoped we might be friends if you returned."

"Then let us be," she said impulsively. "And let us dispense with formalities since you are like one of the family. Do call me Julia!"

"If you will call me Anthony!"

She laughed. "Then it is settled."

The pleasant exchange was interrupted by the arrival of Matthew Kemp. The stout man came into the living room with his tophat in his hand. He cleared his throat and glanced at Anthony Laver.

The young man was quick to take the cue, saying, "If you will excuse me, I have some letters to finish in the study." And he made a hasty departure from the room.

As soon as they were alone Julia went up to the fat man and asked, "What is the word?"

"Not good," he said.

"Did you talk with Beau?"

"No."

"Was he not at home? Did you leave a message?"

The broad face of the secret service agent showed a gloomy expression. He said, "He was at home. But he would not see me nor would his man let me leave a message. He has virtually barricaded himself in his house."

"That is ridiculous!"

"Not when his debtors are constantly threatening to jail him."

"It is as bad as that," she said with dismay.

"I gathered as much from the little his man said," Matthew Kemp said unhappily. "And I had a hard time getting even that much from him."

"Surely Beau would want to know that I have come back to London."

"I told the man that but he's new and thick-headed and your name seemed to mean nothing to him."

She turned away with a sign. "It seems I must try to approach him personally."

"I apologize for my failure," Matthew Kemp said.

She gave him a troubled smile. "No need after all you've done for me. I shouldn't have sent you I ought to have gone to his house myself."

Matthew Kemp said, "If you plan to do that I would lose no time, Miss."

She frowned. "Why do you say that?"

"There is a rumor that he is about to flee from London," the secret service man said.

Chapter Fourteen

The files of the Foreign Office seemed as difficult to penetrate as the thick London mists to which Julia had returned. John Crawford made a half-dozen visits to various associates before he could come up with any definite word concerning Sir Gerald Giles. And when he did get an answer it was not a happy one.

Four days had passed since Julia's return to London. And as her father entered the front door of the fine old mansion she knew at once from his manner the news was not good. He removed his top hat and came slowly toward her with a sober expression on his thin face.

Taking her by the arms, he said, "You must be brave, my dear."

"What did you learn?" she asked.

"The file turned up and was quite clear. Gerald was captured and imprisoned. The Foreign Office has marked *deceased* on his records."

"No!" she said, throwing herself on her father's chest with a sob.

"Mind you, this is merely an assumption. There is no clear record of anything beyond his imprisonment. But the information is based on the assumption he would have returned by now had he lived."

"And surely he would have," she said brokenly.

Her father held her close and sighed. "I fear I must agree. The Office sent this word to his next of kin weeks ago."

"How did poor old Lady Giles take it?" Julia wanted to know.

"By a great blessing the dear old woman died before the word reached her. A new Lady Giles has taken up residence there now."

Julia looked up at her father in surprise. "You mean?"

"Yes," he said. "Elizabeth has moved into the family mansion and is now the official Lady Giles. One would wish that were the end of it."

Sensing that something sinister was inferred, she asked, "What do you mean?"

"The story goes that the unhappy Elizabeth has taken a strong affection for the brandy bottle and a young footman in her employ. Her behavior with this young man has scandalized the other servants and her few remaining friends."

Julia gasped. "I can't believe it! Elizabeth always so self-righteous and straight-laced! It seems impossible!"

"Strong drink can bring out strange quirks in character," her father warned her. "It seems that Elizabeth's addiction to brandy was not until she received word of her husband's death and until the death of the dowager Lady Giles and her moving into the old woman's house."

"Surely she is to be pitied," Julia said.

"Her behavior can only lead to tragedy," her father agreed.

She said, "Now that Gerald is dead she must know he died as a spy. The charade of his racing interests has been revealed."

John Crawford agreed. "She surely knows the truth. That Sir Gerald was a hero rather than a mere playboy."

"Then I think it only fair that I explain that my being with him before his death was also part of his work. That it was more than a mere romantic tryst. I also acted briefly as an agent."

Her father frowned. "I do not see that it will make any difference in the way she views the matter."

Julia argued, "But it might. It is possible it may make her feel less hatred toward me."

"Or more if you reveal yourself as her late husband's aide as well as his lover."

"I can't see it that way," she said. "I know Elizabeth and I think I can make her understand."

"She has been most unfair with you in the past," her father warned.

"I can forget that. I must if I'm to try and help her. And from what you say she badly needs it."

Her father shrugged. "You must do as you please. I will not try to influence you in the matter. But it would seem to me you have a better friend whom you should try and help first."

She said, "Beau!"

"Yes."

"I have tried to see him," she said unhappily. "Matthew Kemp has attempted to get a message to him from me. He has been impossible to reach. He has a new footman who refuses admittance to anyone."

Her father's ascetic face showed worry. He said, "I fear he is thinking of something desperate. Perhaps taking his own life."

"It mustn't come to that!"

"He spoke of it to a friend the other day," her father said. "A former operator of one of the gaming tables."

"He often says things he doesn't mean," Julia said. But at the same time she was badly worried. "I must somehow get to him."

"Persistency, I'm sure it is the only answer."

"I shall go over there again this evening," she said. "And I shall continue until I do have the opportunity of talking with him."

She was coming downstairs in the dark cape which she had chosen to protect herself against the London fog when Anthony Laver suddenly appeared from the rear hall with a sheaf of papers in his hand.

He bowed. "You are going out in this fog, Miss Crawford?"

She halted at the bottom of the stairway. "Yes. I'm going to take the carriage over to Beau Brummell's place."

"You must take care," the young man said. "It is a bad night."

"I find the weather cruelly cold after my time in Spain," she agreed.

The young man's face shadowed. "I have heard the word about Sir Gerald. You have my sympathy."

"Thank you," she said. "It seems almost certain now that he is dead."

"I did not know him," Anthony said. "But I'm sure he must have been a fine man."

"He was," she said. "You are very kind to show such interest."

"I feel the troubles which affect you and your father must also be mine," the young man said with sincerity.

"It is good to have you here, Anthony," she said, pressing his hand in hers.

He saw her to the carriage and only when she was being driven across London in the murky night did she realize how much Anthony Laver was beginning to mean to her. He was quietly considerate and never intruded on her and her father. Yet he was always at hand when she needed advice or someone to merely converse with. Very quickly he had made himself a part of her life since her return to England.

She did not see him in a romantic light. He was more of a brother to her. And since she had been on her own so long having both a father and a kind of adopted brother meant a good deal to her. In the back of her mind she still clung to a small hope that Gerald might surprise them by eventually returning. Yet she knew that all the odds were against this.

So she felt that she must try and help his widow as a kind of penance. And she must also make a strong attempt to save Beau Brummell. With Gerald gone it seemed to her that Beau might finally consent to marry her.

Marriage with her would surely solve all his financial problems. Her father could take care of all the debts and not miss the money. And she was sure she could make Beau happy and offer him a new future. It was surely all to the good that his great friendship with the Prince Regent had come to an end. It could also mean the end of the wild dissipation which such an association had led to.

The carriage halted before the house in which Brummell lived. She went to the door and saw a soft light from behind the blinds at the front of the house. Taking heart she rapped on the door and waited.

The same, ugly footman who had greeted her before answered the door with an air of impatience. On seeing her he angrily declared, "You're not back again!"

"I am," she said firmly. "And this time I intend to see Mr. Brummell."

"He's not here!" the footman said, attempting to shut the door in her face.

She planted herself in the doorway so he could not do this without injury to her. She said, "Are you telling the truth?"

"I told you," the man said in a rage. "He's not here and that's that!"

"When do you expect him?"

"I never know," the footman said. "It's no use. I gave him your message and he doesn't want to see you. He don't want to see anyone."

"You swear that you gave him my name?"

"Yes!"

Julia asked incredulously, "And did he not react in any way? Say something of me?"

The grumpy footman rubbed his chin and recalled, "He seemed in a better mood for a moment. Said something like 'Thank heaven she is safely home.'"

"Then he does want to see me!" she insisted.

"No," the man replied. "His manner changed and he told me you were never to be allowed to enter."

"I see," she said, with a sigh of resignation. "Very well, then."

She left the door and went back to her carriage. The fog was still thick and the night cool but she told the driver to take her around the block and then take a position in the same street across from Brummell's house. There she could observe any comings and goings. With some luck she might catch him.

The driver gave her a blanket to tuck around her knees and he stomped back and forth on the pavement. She gave him permission to go to a nearby pub for an ale for which he was most grateful. In the meanwhile her vigil went on.

It was nearing midnight and she was chilled through. Traffic was almost non-existent and she decided her mission a failure. But just as she was about to open the trap at the front of the carriage and tell the driver to take her home a carriage drew up in the front of Brummell's house and he stepped out of it.

Julia raced across the cobble-stoned street and reached him before his footman could open the door for him. She pressed herself to him and cried, "Beau!"

Surprise was replaced by fondness and the handsome man in cape and top hat took her in his arms and kissed her. "My dear Julia!" he exclaimed in a tone of wonder. "As beautiful as ever!"

The ugly footman opened the door and saw them. He said, "I tried to send her on her way, Master. She wouldn't go!"

Brummell said, "No matter! It is all right!"

He escorted Julia into his living room and ordered the man to light a candelabra. He removed her cape gently and then his own flowing cape and top hat. Taking her hands in his he stood studying her.

"How often I have seen your lovely face in my mind," he said.

"And I have continually thought of you since our separation," she told him.

"So you escaped the worst of Fitzroy's villiany! Good! You are safely back in London and he is no longer alive!"

"Many have died. And in such a short time."

His eyes met hers. "You are thinking of Gerald. I know full well you gave yourself to him. And it was a choice which had my approval."

"Why did you refuse to see me?" she asked.

He released her hands and turned away from her. "I'm sorry. It had nothing to do with my deep affection for you."

"I wanted to believe that."

"And you may," Brummell said. "I have had a number of reverses. I've lost a great deal of money and many of my friends have fallen away from me."

"You have had a final quarrel with the Prince Regent?"

"That fat fool!" came the angry reply.

"Surely you could manage to tolerate him," she said.

"I should hate myself every day that I lived if I went to him pleading for his forgiveness. No, that is over."

"Perhaps it is for the best."

With a flash of his old wit, he turned to her again and with a bitter smile on his handsome face, said, "There are only two ways of getting on in the world. Either by one's own industry or by others' stupidity. I chose the latter, but I made the error of allowing the Prince Regent and his friends to know I considered them fools!''

Julia laughed. "Beau, you are incorrigibile."

"I found myself unable to say another complimentary word to our fat Prince and I made the mistake of not being wise enough to remain silent."

She studied his face and saw new wrinkle lines at the eyes, and deep-etched onces about his mouth. He was thinner and though well-dressed, he had the hint of shabbiness about him.

She said, "You have lost a deal of weight."

He shrugged. "That is my least important loss. You will note that all my fine paintings have gone."

She hadn't noticed but now she looked about the big room and saw the places on the walls where the paintings had once hung. And she further noticed that all the fine silver had vanished except for the single candelabra which provided light in the room.

She said, "You were forced to sell them."

"Let us say I found myself preferring champagne and food to their company."

Julia went close to him and slipped her hands around his neck. Looking up at his haggard face, she said softly, "I think it is time for complete honesty between us."

"It has always been that time for me," he said.

"Not truly," she reproved him. "You are trying to shut yourself off from friends and the world you know and love. If you do so, it will destroy you."

"I shall always remember you and that shall be my salvation." he said.

Her eyes met his. "You can do better than that. You can marry me. You know I have always loved you and turned to Gerald only when I'd given up hope."

"I wish we could marry," he said.

"We can! Father will settle your debts and you can be

as much a gentleman of London as ever. Mark my words, the Prince will beg your pardon in time."

He shook his head, "No, dear girl, I cannot allow you to do all that for me."

"I want to! Father wants to!"

"And I'm deeply grateful," he said. "You will never know how grateful. But I have a wicked pride. One which will not let me be a kept man!"

"What does it matter as long as we're together?" she demanded unhappily. "You could assist father in his many business enterprises. You were once the President of White's. You'd be ideal as the manager of that gaming house."

"Too easy," he said. And he drew her to him for another kiss.

Then he continued talking about the changes in London and served her some wine. He insist that she seat herself in a tall-backed chair and he stood before her.

At last, she said, "If you won't marry me and let my father help you, what is your plan?"

A faint smile showed on his thin, weary face. "I have always had good fortune at the roulette table. Do you know I lost twenty-six thousand pounds in one night's play."

"A fortune!"

"True. That is where most of my family money went. But I have also had exciting winning streaks. And I feel I'm on the brink of another in which I can win a pot large enough to pay off all my debts and start afresh."

"You will need a stake even for that."

"I have it," he assured her. "Proceeds from some of my paintings."

They talked a little longer and then he insisted that she return home. He saw her out and crossed the foggy street to see her into the carriage. She leaned out anxiously to ask, "You won't shut yourself away from me again?"

"No," he said.

"You must promise to see me when I call on you," she said.

"I promise."

"And have dinner with father and me when you are invited."

"I shall await your invitation," he said, his lips touching hers again.

He was standing in the foggy night waving at her as the driver took her home. She was in a troubled state but she had still a forlorn hope that she might be able to get Brummell to change his mind.

The sunshine and warmer weather returned the following day. She was out in the garden strolling alone when she saw her father come hurrying out of the house and down the gravel path to join her.

Still rather breathless, he said, "Anthony told me you were out here."

What is wrong?" she asked. "You look shaken."

He faced her grimly. "A lot of debtors will be feeling sorry for themselves tonight!"

A wave of dismay rushed through her. Her lovely eyes widened with apprehension and she exclaimed, "Do speak plainly, father!"

"I shall," he said.

"Beau is dead! He has taken his life!"

Her father shook his head. "Not as bad as that. But in a way his life has ended. He fled London in the middle of the night. He has taken passage to France!"

"If only he had listened to me!" she said, distressed.

"He was a proud and stubborn man," her father reminded her. "Never easy to reason with."

She faced her father anxiously. "You speak of him as if he were dead! He must be saved!"

John Crawford placed a hand around her protectively. "I promise you, my dear, that as soon as we know where he is, I and other of his friends will contact him. We will offer to pay his debts and have him return."

"You must not lose any time."

"I have sent Matthew Kemp to Calais, where Beau is rumored to have gone. If anyone can find him and deal with him, our fat Matthew is the man!"

She nodded approvingly. "That was the right move. I'm certain Matthew will locate him."

"We shall simply have to wait for a little," John Crawford said. "And you must not needlessly make yourself ill. It is bound to turn out all right."

It seemed to Julia that in this interval of waiting to hear about Beau Brummell she should make herself engage in the other gesture she had contemplated since learning of Gerald's death. She knew it would not be easy and might even end in futility, but she decided to go to Elizabeth and ask forgiveness. At the same time asking her one-time friend to once more join with her in friendship.

So late one afternoon she had the carriage halt at the familiar old mansion where she had served as companion to Lady Giles. Mounting its steps she thought of the fine party there which Beau had provided for the jolly old Lady Giles, even producing the Prince as a special attraction.

It seemed to her that even from the outside the gray stone house was more silent and brooding than in those good former times. She used the rapper and waited.

After a long wait the door was opened by Mrs. Glenn. The Scots woman looked thinner and slightly stooped. And she peered out at Julia for a full moment before recognition showed in her gaunt face.

"Miss Julia!" The Scots woman exclaimed.

"None other," she said with a smile.

The old woman came out a step and with a careful glance over her shoulder, turned to her and in a conspiratorial tone, said, "There's been talk that you were back in London safe and sound. All of us below stairs were delighted."

"I was very happy here," she said, feeling sad at the sight of the woman so aged.

"Aye," Mrs. Glenn said. "Those were good days for all of us. With the good Lady and Sir Gerald both still alive."

"We have had sad losses."

"That we have," Mrs. Glenn agreed. "I'm soon to return to Scotland to live with my brother."

"I'm glad I came by," she said. "I hope to speak with Lady Elizabeth Giles."

Horror crossed the old woman's face. "Not that one!"

Julia explained, " I know she hates me but I wish to explain some things and try to have her understand."

Mrs. Glenn took a nervous step back. "You oughtn't to have come here, Miss. And that's the truth!"

"Is it so bad?" she asked.

Before she could reply there came a shrill cry from the stairway. Julia knew it was the voice of Elizabeth even distorted by her anger. Mrs. Glenn fell back another step in consternation and the door was almost fully opened so that Julia stood revealed in the doorway.

"Slut!" Elizabeth screamed the word as she made her way unsteadily down the curving stairway dressed only in a sheer, white negligee. She had a half-empty brandy bottle in one hand and a glass in the other. Her once lovely hair was like a wasp's nest in its bedragglement. And her fine features were bloated conspicuously while her cheeks were a strange florid shade.

At this tragic sight Julia was flooded with sympathy for her former friend. Impulsively she took a step forward and stretching out a hand said, "I implore that you let me visit with you for a little."

"Visit with me?" the drunken Elizabeth said.

"I have much to tell you. I wish that we be friends again," she hurried on.

The drunken woman's mouth gaped open as she listened and descended the stairs at the same time. As she reached the bottom she cried out again, "How dare you come here? This is my house!"

"I know!"

"I do not want you to step inside my door," the angry Elizabeth went on in the same fit of drunken anger. And she lifted the glass and hurled it at her.

The glass shattered harmlessly on the tile floor by Julia. But she had seen enough to know Elizabeth was too drunk to reason with. She turned quickly and hurried out of the house.

"God bless you!" Mrs. Glenn called after her and shut the door.

Julie was still trembling as she returned to her carriage. She had heard the tales of Elizabeth's drunken and wanton behavior. Now she had seen some of it for herself. As the carriage started on its way to take her home she knew she would never make the journey again. That there was nothing to be said between her and Elizabeth.

On her return home she found Anthony Laver seated in the living room reading the evening newspaper. She went to him and asked, "Is my father at home?"

"No," the young man said. "He is dining at the Strand tonight. He will be home later. He is entertaining a business associate from Liverpool."

"I see," she said and turned to go upstairs.

He said, "Julia!"

She turned to him again. "Yes?"

His pleasant face showed concern. "I do not mean to trouble you but you seem rather unwell."

"I'm trembling!"

"I noticed," he said. He came to her and saw her to a chair. "You need a drink of good wine to warm you up." And he went to the sideboard and proceeded to pour her a glass.

She removed her bonnet and sighed. "I have had a most upsetting experience."

Anthony brought her the wine. "This is very good."

"Thank you," she said. She took it and sipped some of the rose-colored liquid and after a moment felt less upset.

"You're sure you're all right?" the young man continued to be worried.

She looked up at him. "Yes. I expected Father to be here. I needed to talk to him. It is strange how one comes to depend on those close to you."

The young man indicated the newspaper, "Is it by any chance that you are upset by the flight of Beau Brummell? There is mention of him in the paper."

"Really? What does it say?"

"That he has located in Calais. A reporter talked to him in his quarters there!"

She felt a great sensation of relief. "Then he is all right! I'm sure Matthew Kemp will find him and talk to him."

"The newspaper says little else but mentions that he left a host of creditors behind."

"I'm sure they're raising a fine clamor!"

"According to the newspaper the bailiff has taken over his premises and any posessions which were left. And I expect they were few."

"He had sold his valuables," she agreed. "I was not upset about Mr. Brummell. Though I have been waiting for word of him. What shocked me was the reception I had when I went to call on Lady Elizabeth Giles."

The young man's eyebrows raised. "You actually went to see her?"

"Yes. I hoped she would at least listen to me. I found her drunken and in what seemed a state of near madness."

"But her actions have been a source of gossip for months. She has that young footman in her bed. She dresses him better than Brummell. And a few nights ago he actually had the nerve to show up at White's for a few rounds at the gaming table. Men were laughing behind his back and calling him Sir Giles!"

Julia was further stunned. "So it is common gossip!"

"And common knowledge, I fear."

"How can she degrade herself so? And her husband's name as well."

Anthony Laver spread his hands. "It began when the

old woman died and she had no one to restrain her. From what I've heard the drink came first, then the footman, a sly fellow, who saw a chance to take advantage of her."

"Surely she has lawyers or a doctor who could step in!"

"From all that is said, she refuses any interference. Whenever she is approached she sobers enough to defend her right to behave as she pleases!"

"She has altered so in appearance," Julia sighed. "She no longer looks young."

"Spirits will do that in both a man and a woman," the young man said. "As with all good things it can most surely be abused."

"You are right," she said, rising. "My father tried to dissuade me from going there. Of course he was right. But I had it in my mind. Now it is over with and I shall try to forget it."

"You should, Julia," the young man said earnestly. "I ask you to forgive me if I suggest you have a tendency unusual in one of your youth, to live too much in the past. You must look to the future."

She smiled at him wanly. "That is sound advice, Anthony. I hope I have the good sense to take it."

His pleasant face crimsonded slightly as he went on, "I do not wish to presume. But I would like to help. May I take you out to dinner one night?"

She could not help but be surprised. And she said, "That is kind of you, Anthony. I should enjoy it."

"I will count on it," he said, happily.

Julia went upstairs grateful for the presence of the attractive young man and appreciative of his desire to help her. But she was anxious not to be unfair to him. Though Gerald was dead and a good portion of her heart dead with him, she still cared deeply for Beau Brummell and she was clinging to the hope that he might relent his stubborn stand. Forget his pride and marry her.

He loved her. He had made that clear and she did not

doubt it. But first one thing and then another had come between them. So she would continue, as Anthony had suggested, to live in the past until the business of Beau was settled. Meanwhile she would enjoy Anthony's company, as long as he did not become seriously interested in her. She worried that this might happen and she had no wish to hurt him. It presented a dilemma.

As it turned out she did not have to wait more than twenty-four hours longer for news of her beloved Beau. She was in her room when a maid came up to inform her that her father wished to see her. She went down and found him in his study and with him was the stout Matthew Kemp. The secret service man smiled and bowed to her.

"Good evening, Miss Crawford," the fat man said.

"Good evening," she said anxiously. "What is the word from Calais?"

Her father pulled a chair forward and said, "Sit down, my dear. This will take a little while."

"Did you talk with him?" she asked Matthew.

"Oh, I found him," Matthew said, his broad face showing pleasure. "He was in a rather shabby lodging house in Calais. It's not a large place so he wasn't hard to locate."

"How is he?"

"He seemed in a better mood than when I last saw him here," Matthew said. "I gave him the message your father had instructed me to and the money as well."

John Crawford interrupted at this point, to tell her, "I had Matthew visit Beau on the pretence he was sent to pay him a long-ago gambling debt owed him by Jack Lester."

"Did Beau take the money?"

"Yes," her father said. "As long as he felt it was not charity. You see Jack Lester does owe him a large sum and also about everyone else in London. But like Beau the poor old chap is unable to pay any of his debts. I made up a story that he had unexpectedly come into a small inheritance and wished to use some of it to pay Beau."

Matthew Kemp nodded. "Right glad was Mr. Brummell to get the money. Knowing that I had the acquaintance of Mr. Lester he never questioned that it might have come from your father or anyone else."

"Good!" she exclaimed. "That will see him through for a while."

"For quite some time," her father assured her. "As long as he doesn't get gambling again. And there are few chances for that in Calais."

Julia asked the fat man, "Tell me more about him."

Matthew rubbed his double chins. "Well, as I stated before, Miss, the lodgings are shabby but respectable enough. When I went in he was busy fixing some nice pieces of old furniture about the room. Apparently he had sent some things on ahead."

"Robbed the bailiff!" John Crawford laughed.

"Right, sir," the fat man said. "And he had an entire set of fine toilet of silver on a table. He bid me admire it and said it was a gift of the Duchess of York."

Julia nodded. "They have long been close friends."

"He's not alone," Matthew went on. "He has a bird for company. A green macaw that was perched on the back of a tattered silk chair with faded gilding. I vow the bird must be fresh off some vessel since it has a tongue full of oaths and impudence!"

"I'm glad," she said. "I hate to think of him alone amid a lot of foreigners."

The fat man said, "I think he's made a few friends among them already."

"Beau would," her father agreed. "He has a gift for friendship."

Julia felt her cheeks burn as she asked, "Did he mention my father or me?"

"Indeed he did," Matthew Kemp said heartily. "I was careful not to mention either of you since the main thing was to get him to take the money. And he wouldn't have touched it if he thought it was a gift from you."

"I understand," she said.

"But after we had a glass or two of wine we began to talk of many things," the fat man said. "And he questioned me about rescuing you in Spain. He wanted all the details and he seemed properly thrilled by the story."

"It was an exciting business," she agreed.

"He spoke of Mr. Crawford being one of his best friends. And then he mentioned you, miss."

"What did he say?"

"That you were as fair a lady as he had ever met and he wished you a wonderful future."

"Did he hint that he might be part of that future?"

Matthew frowned. "To be truthful, miss, he didn't. He seems to act like someone whose life is over. Very strange I found it. He talked of his London days and all. But always as if it were something he could never return to."

John Crawford said, "We will have to try and assure him there is still a life for him back here."

"Yes, sir," the fat man said.

"What are you doing now?" Julia asked him.

"I'm back with the Bow Street Runners," Matthew Kemp said genially. "I'm in a senior post, no longer one of the ordinary police."

"And so you should be," her father said with sincere admiration. "And I thank you for looking after this special task for me."

"I'm at your service whenever you need me," the faithful fat man said. "You can always reach me at the Bow Street Headquarters."

"It is good to know that London has it's own police force," Julia said. "A truly organized group."

"We're better organized and larger than we were when the war ended," Matthew said. "There's a deal of crime and violence in the city. It would surprise you."

Julia said, "And you see much of it."

"More than you'd wish," the massive Kemp said with

a deep sigh. "I've just come from Headquarters now
and heard a sad tale there."

"Really?" Julia said.

The fat man hesitated, "I'm sure if I speak of it here
and now, it'll not be repeated."

"You can rely on our discretion," her father assured
him.

"Chap brought in on charge of murder. He may
swing for it or not. At least he'll stand trial. Footman in
the employ of Lady Elizabeth Giles!"

"Elizabeth!" Julia gasped and jumped up.

"Steady!" her father said, taking her by the arm.

Matthew looked surprised. "Did I give you a start,
miss?"

"You did," she admitted. "We were once friends."

Chapter Fifteen

"I'm sorry, miss," the Bow Street runner said.

"It's all right," Julia told him as she recovered from
the first shock. "I would like to know the details."

The fat man shook his head dolefully. "Lust among
the upper classes, if I may speak so boldly, miss."

John Crawford said, "We have heard whispers of
some unfortunate happenings at Giles House."

"It will be shouted from the housetops now, sir," the
fat man said. "The penny papers will be on to it and
there'll be no end of it."

"What exactly happened?" she asked.

"Drunken brawl," Matthew told her grimly. "The
two of them was battling over money or the like. Lady
Giles ran from her bedroom to the landing of the

stairway. He came after her and struck her and she toppled down the full length of the stairs. The servants found her at the bottom as naked as the day she was brought into the world and with her neck broken!"

"Horrible!" Julia gasped.

"I would say so, miss," Matthew agreed. "The footman chap naked to the waist came down the stairs and started babbling and crying over her. He was still kneeling by her when the police came."

"A sordid business with a tragic ending," John Crawford said. "I thank you for telling us."

"Had no idea you knew the parties," Matthew said. "Well, you have the address of Mr. Brummel, sir."

"Yes, I have it on a slip here," her father said.

"Good," the fat man replied. "Well, I'll be getting along, sir. Goodnight, Miss,"

"Goodnight," she said in a small voice and sank into the chair again as her father saw the genial Matthew out.

She was still seated there, staring into space when her father returned. She glanced at him and said, "What a tragedy!"

Her father showed a grim look on his thin actor's face. "But Elizabeth was surely heading for such an ending. Drinking to excess and carrying on with that footman."

"I could never have predicted it. She was the most straight laced of any of my friends."

"Sometimes when they no longer repress themselves, like Elizabeth they go to wild excesses. I very often thank my Maker that I located you. Had I not found you I might have drifted back into a drunken, meaningless existence."

She took his hand as he stood by her. "Nonsense, father. You had reformed long before you began the search for me and mother."

"But it would have taken little to send me astray again," he assured her. "My main purpose in life is to take care of you. When you were kidnapped I almost broke. But I had Beau to encourage me. And Matthew to help me."

"I thank you for what you did for Beau," she said, looking up at him earnestly.

"It will help for a little while," her father said. "But I'm afraid this is going to be another tragic case."

"I pray not," she said. "You have his address. I shall write him."

Her father gave her a searching look. "You still want to marry him?"

"If he will have me."

"He is older and more world weary."

"I do not care," she protested.

"I'm afraid I do," her father replied. "I am fighting an uneven battle with age myself. It will be only a short time until I'm no longer with you."

"No, Father!"

"Be sensible! I'm no more immortal than any other man. A few years at most is all I can expect. And they shall be happy years I hope. But what about you?"

"I don't wish to think about such things."

"Better to think of them now than later," her father said firmly. "Who will there be to protect you?"

She smile ruefully. "I shall turn to Matthew!"

"Matthew Kemp!" her father chuckled. "He's older and much fatter than I am. I doubt he'll outlive me and if he did he'd be too old to be of any use to you."

"Then I shall learn to manage on my own!"

"I approve of that," John Crawford said. "And I think you may have the character for it. One must be strong."

"You have taught me to be strong," she said.

"I wonder," he observed wryly. "I often think of myself as the weakest of men. In my vanity I betrayed your mother. Bound her to a life of drudgery. What I have done for you repays only a small part of my debt."

She rose and kissed him on the cheek. "Dear, father! If mother were here at this moment she would receipt the full bill and toss it to you with a smile."

"You think so?"

"I know it. In her heart you were always there."

He eyed her with awe. "I do not deserve the love of anyone as good as you!"

"I'm not good at all, father," she protested. "I want to marry Beau and have you support both of us for the rest of our lives."

"I'll gladly do it if it will ensure your happiness."

"I know."

He paused a moment and then giving her a meaningful look, he asked, "What do you think of Anthony Laver?"

"I like him."

John Crawford sighed. "Do you? I have an idea you have barely noticed him. That he is like a wraith to you. Present but not part of your world."

She showed surprise. "I suppose I do take him a great deal for granted."

"Far too much so," her father said. "He is a most talented and deserving young man."

"I couldn't agree more."

"I depend on him a great deal."

"I know you do," she admitted.

"And yet I venture he is such a shadow creature to you that you know neither his favorite choice in music, or food or the daily newspaper? Not even the color of his eyes."

"They must be brown!" she said. "He has brown hair."

Her father laughed. "Wrong! They are green! I told you how little you know about him."

Julia said, "You're not being entirely fair. We very often talk. I have come to think of him as a sort of brother."

"He could be your brother. He is exactly your age."

"I know."

Her father's eyes met hers. "Or he could be your husband?"

"Father!"

"I'm quite serious. Here is this desirable young man whom I have helped and who is now one of the prinicpal managers of my affairs. He is a model of behavior, attractive in looks and I'm sure the mothers of many marriageable daughters in London would be delighted to have him show an interest in their progeny."

"Are you suggesting I marry Anthony?" Julia asked in disbelief.

"Not if the idea seems completely incongruous to you," her father said.

"But I'm barely over losing Gerald. And if I marry anyone it will be Beau. I have always loved him."

"Love or pity?" her father asked quietly.

"Please!" she begged. "Let me settle this myself."

"By all means," he said. "But I ask that you think of Anthony Laver and the kind of life companion he might make. I have no wish to influence you in any way. But I feel he is worthy of your interest."

That was the final word her father said on the matter. But it was only to be expected that Julia would find herself giving additional thought to it. While she wrote Beau Brummell at once and eagerly awaited an answer to her letter, she began to notice Anthony with slightly different eyes. He was likeable in a reserved way and she had the feeling that he was becoming much too fond of her.

It was difficult for her to prevent their friendship from growing rapidly since they were both living in the same house. She soon began talking to him on a more intimate basis and she had the impression that he was much more than a good man of business. He enjoyed music and the theatre and he prided himself on being a good dancer. It was a discussion of dancing which led to his inviting her to be his partner at the Duchess of Wiltshire's annual ball.

"It is a grand affair," he assured her. "The Prince Regent has attended every year so I think we may expect him this year."

She was going to refuse the invitation, but on hearing that the Prince Regent might be present, she decided instead to accept.

With a smile, she said, "I'm sure I should enjoy it."

Anthony was delighted. "You do me great honor."

With a twinkle in her eyes, she said, "It shall be my opportunity to test your dancing. To discover if you are as adept as you have claimed."

"I shall be a clumsy clout because of nervousness," he lamented.

She laughed. "I will accept no excuses."

Planning for the party gave her some needed excitement. She tried to avoid reading the newspapers. The footman who had thrown Elizabeth to her death was coming up for trial and the headlines were full of the sordid story. No letter had come from Beau Brummell and so she had written a second and a third plaintive note, begging him to answer her.

The night of the ball arrived and she presented herself to Anthony, radiant in a crimson gown and a tiara of diamonds given her by her father. Anthony resplendent in the black evening dress which Beau had made popular gazed at her with undisguised admiration.

"You will dazzle everyone present," was his belief.

"I'll be content if I get a word with the Prince Regent," she said.

Anthony promised, "If it can be arranged, I'll manage it."

"It shouldn't be too difficult," she said. "I have attended many small parties with him."

Anthony's pleasant, young face clouded a little. He said, "I presume parties given by Mr. Brummell."

"As a matter of fact, yes," she said lightly. "But you mustn't be jealous. That was long ago."

He looked happy again. "And tonight is ours!"

She let him lead her to their carriage feeling a little guilty. She was not being fair with the young man at her side. In fact, she was hoping to use him so she might meet the Prince Regent and plead for Beau Brummell. She had a feeling that if she could just once talk plainly to the fat Prince, he might find it in his heart to relent and take Beau as his friend again.

Perhaps Anthony guessed some of this, he was not at all stupid. But if so, he was trying not to show it. He gave the impression of being in the best of moods on their way to the ball and when they reached the scene of the exciting affair he was a model escort.

The dowager Duchess of Wiltshire received them most graciously and they strolled into the huge dining room just off the ballroom where liveried servants were serving drinks. Anthony got them some wine and spoke to several of the young bloods with amorous-looking creatures dressed in their best finery on their arms. Julia felt her own dress stood out and the diamond tiara was a help. They remained at the white clothed table long enough to sip a little of their wine. Then the orchestra began a waltz and a smiling Anthony led her out onto the shining ballroom floor. There beneath the glowing chandeliers, among the other elegantly-dressed couples, they swirled about in a most magical fashion. Anthony was as good a dancer as he'd promised and he seemed to actually lift her off the ground as they gracefully moved around the big room.

Julia felt utterly happy in this moment. When it was over she felt a sudden sadness. She applauded the orchestra and smiling up at the young man, told him, "That was all I had expected! You dance beautifully."

"I had to be at my best," he said with a bow. "I shall never again have a partner so lovely."

"That is nonsense!" she chided him.

"Dangerously close to the truth," he said.

Now the orchestra began a polka and they danced again. But it had not the magic of the waltz. Anthony danced just as well but she found her mind wandering. She was thinking of Gerald and how gallant he had looked in his dress uniform. And of Elizabeth, so lovely and young once, now cold in her grave as well. And mostly of Beau and why she had not heard from him.

The dance ended and her companion led her off the floor. She stood with a number of older ladies and gentlemen who were watching the activities from the side. Anthony had gone away on some mission and she was alone for a moment.

A small, dark-haired, middle-aged woman in a modest yellow gown came up to her and said, "Are you Julia Crawford?"

"Yes," Julia said, "Though I fear you have the advantage of me. I do not believe I've had the pleasure of meeting you."

The small, attractive woman smiled demurely. "You know me by name. We have a mutual friend."

"Oh?"

"I'm the Duchess of York," the woman said, and raised a hand. "Please no formalities. I've wanted to talk with you for a long while. To thank you for your kindness to Beau."

Julia said, "He was much dependent on you, ma'am."

"In a way," the Duchess of York said. "He loved the spaciousness of my house and grounds. And the dogs! How he loved the dogs! You know that Anon is buried at Oatlands?"

"Yes. That meant a great deal to him."

"I'm happy to know that," the Duchess said. "He often spoke to me about you. I think he would have liked to marry you."

"I would never have refused him," Julia said.

"I'm sure of that," the Duchess smiled. "But he is older and in great trouble now. I doubt that we shall see him in England again."

"I hope so," she said earnestly.

"The portents are not good," the Duchess said. "I wrote him and sent him money and he returned it."

Julia confessed, "I wrote and begged him to think of marriage with me. And he has not yet answered."

The Duchess gazed at her sadly. "Poor girl!" Then seeing Anthony coming back, she said, "I will go now."

Anthony came up to Julia with a look of surprise on his pleasant face. "I say, this is your night for royalty, that was the Duchess of York, wasn't it?"

"Yes," she said. "She came over to me while you were gone."

"Have you known her long?"

"Our first meeting. She came to speak to me about a mutual friend."

He looked wise. "The mutual friend again! Of course she meant Beau Brumnell! All London knows they were lovers and that she turned to him because her own marriage is such a disaster."

"I hadn't heard that."

"It is true," her companion said. "She is liked to the same degree that her husband is disliked. She is a great breeder of dogs. Her country estate boasts many breeds."

"I know," Julia said. "And what news have you for me?"

"The best," the young man said. "I have come directly from the Prince Regent. He will speak with you."

At once she was frightened. "Do you mean it?"

"I have gone to a great deal of trouble to arrange it," Anthony said. "Of course I mean it! I had to make my way through a host of people to get to him. But you will be flattered to know that as soon as I mentioned your name he remembered you."

"And agreed to see me?"

"Yes," Anthony said. "But I suggest we go to him at once. You know how impatient he can be! How subject to whims!"

"I learned that long ago," she said, still uneasy now that the prospect of facing the Prince was at hand.

"You seem suddenly afraid?"

"I am," she said.

"Don't be," the young man advised her. "You look lovely enough to please a prince. And he seemed truly desirous of seeing you."

"Very well," she said.

She allowed him to lead her across the ballroom, aware that many in the glittering assemblage had their eyes on her. Anthony took her to the far corner of the room opposite the orchestra where the Prince Regent stood surrounded by his usual group of sycophants. As they drew nearer and she had her first close look at him as he laughed and conversed with one of his courtiers she was shocked!

He had greatly increased in weight and his chins hung quivering and repulsive. Moreover his face had become like a great, angry purple mask. There was no hint of good looks left. The Prince Regent had become a shocking caricature of himself.

As she came up and curtsied, he beamed at her, "Miss Crawford! It had been some time."

"It has, Sire," she said. "A time of change."

"True," he said soberly. "But London is still the center of the world. All the world I care about at least."

"You make London interesting, Sire," she said politely.

Lord Skeffington as thin and mannered as ever, smiled at her and said, "You have never been more beautiful!"

"In an attempt at humor the Prince Regent said, "I declare it is a woman's duty to be beautiful, and far too many of them avoid their responsibility!"

A stout man on his right whom she did not know guffawed at this. And said, "You know that is why I separated from my wife! She was so blessed ugly! The only peace in a marriage is to be apart!"

The Prince Regent moved a step away from the man who went on repeating this and enjoying his own joke.

In a low voice he confided to her, "As you must be aware, we much miss the wit of Brummell these days."

"I agree, Sire," she said. "I miss him in every way. What a shame you and he could no longer be friends!"

The Prince Regent said, "I have long been willing to end the rift between us. But the harm appears to have been done. His creditors ruined him and his pride will not allow him to return."

She said, "But if you were to speak to him directly."

To her astonishment, he confided, "I have done that. I had reason to visit France. I passed through Calais and invited him to lunch with me. He refused because he said it was not the proper hour!"

"I'm stunned," she said in dismay.

"The poor fellow seems intent on destroying himself," the Prince Regent grumbled. "I suppose there is some of that in all of us. And his wish for self-destruction has gotten out of hand."

"I had come to you to plead for him," she confessed. "But I see it is useless."

"I have done my best," the Prince Regent said. "To let him know I was not angry with him I had Lord Palmerston appoint him as consul at Caen."

"Then he does have some sort of income."

"Not any longer," the Prince Regent said sadly. "He was in the post only a few months when he wrote Palmerston saying a consulate was not needed in the town. It made Palmerston angry and he abolished the office."

"I have written him many times," she said. "And he had not answered me."

"You are not alone," the Prince Regent said. "He has ignored my last message. And he returned money the Duchess of York sent him. Skeffy tried to help him and he insulted him. What can one do?"

"Nothing, I'm afraid," Julia said unhappily.

"You must forget him, my girl," the Prince Regent said. "It is the best thing you can do. Otherwise he will spoil your life along with his own. Enjoy the moment, and let the past fade into mere memory."

"I shall long remember him," she said wistfully. "I miss him greatly."

"And so do I," the Prince Regent agreed.

Others came to take his attention and she knew she had more than stayed her time talking to the man who soon must be King and even now acted for his mad father as Prince Regent.

Anthony escorted her away from the royal group and said, "You two seemed to find plenty to discuss."

"I had a fine conversation with him," she replied.

"Your tone is doleful," the young man said. "Did he say something to trouble you?"

"Not really," she said. "He was most kind. But I'm afraid he had no good news for me."

"Of Brummell?"

She nodded. "His experience has been much like my own. Beau has cut himself away from all of us."

"Perhaps he thinks it best?"

"How can it be?" she asked, near tears. "He was the brightest light in all London. His wit and style set patterns that are being followed here tonight!"

The young man looked troubled. "I did not mean to upset you. If you are not feeling well I will gladly see you home at once."

Julia looked at his stricken face and felt an inner reproach. She was not being fair with this very decent man whom she had used to help her get an audience with the Prince Regent. It was her duty to make the evening a pleasant one for him. She could at least do that!

So drawing a mask quickly over her feelings, she managed a smile for him and said, "I hear another waltz being played. You were so competent in the last one I must insist you take me on the floor at once!"

"With the greatest of pleasure," Anthony said, pleased.

So the night ended on a happier note. At least Julia

made it seem so for her companion's sake. And the masquerade served to somehow raise her own spirits. When they were shown to their carriage by a footman holding a torchlight, she was pleasantly exhausted.

Anthony sat close to her as the carriage rattled over the bumpy London streets. He said, "It was a fabulous evening. I shall never have a better one."

"Stuff!" she protested. "You will find yourself a pretty girl one day and be happy for all your life."

"If I'm to be happy life long with anyone it would have to be with you, Julia," he said quietly.

She stared at him in the shadowed carriage. "Anthony! You have never talked this way to me before! You have been like my trusted brother!"

"I do not like the brotherly role," he said. "I have fallen in love with you. I cannot help it."

"It is the aftermath of the wine and the music and the sight of so many lovely ladies. When the excitement ends you will not think of me so romantically."

"I shall always love you," he said in a tone so earnest she could not doubt him.

She touched his cheek. "Dear Anthony! I'm so fond of you! Do not spoil things between us!"

"Is there any hope for me?"

She turned away. "Please! I'm too confused tonight. I'm not ready for this sort of discussion."

The carriage halted before her father's house and he helped her down to the sidewalk. Then he saw her inside. As they stood in the empty but softly-lit reception hall he studied her with a great longing in his eyes.

"I want to always remember you exactly as you look tonight," he said.

She managed a small smile. "Anthony!" she said with gentleness.

He took her in his arms and their lips met so ardently that she was startled and almost frightened. She found herself responding to the passion of his embrace in a way she had never expected. Nor wanted! The moment between them was a long one. Then he released her and with a glance of confused amazement for him, she turned and ran up the stairs to her room.

Inside she found that she was trembling from the after-effects of the embrace. No matter what, Anthony had proved himself a manly lover capable of arousing her. And she was too fond of him personally. In the future she must take great care. She had first worried only about hurting him, now she began to wonder about herself.

Less than a week later a letter came from France. When her maid handed it to her she felt her heart in her throat. It was in Beau's handwriting! The long-awaited letter had come at last. She went to her own room to read it.

She nervously tore the envelope open and saw that the message was much shorter than she had hoped for. It began with:

> "My dearest Julia,
>
> I can no longer allow your anguished letters to go unanswered. So I have decided to write you and hopefully give you some peace of mind.
>
> "I'm not in any dreadful poverty nor am I suffering great loneliness. Indeed, after this simple pastoral life I would not return to London if I could. The continual acting required of one in my set became a bore to me. That may be why I deliberately set out to anger the Prince and in effect, be banished.
>
> "I miss you more than anything or anyone. Many times I have told you that I loved you. And I assure you that will always be true. The years rob us of the subjects of love, but the precious gift of memory remains. I shall always see you as you were when we last were together, young and lovely. And I hope you will not remember me with complete disdain.
>
> "I wish to be left alone. Do not attempt to

come to me. It would only make me unhappy.
And now I come to a part of my letter you may
find it hard to understand and still believe what I
have written above. I have found someone to
comfort me. She lacks your beauty and intelligence, but she has a beauty and kindness of her
own which supports me. Her name is Vicky. And
I hope that soon you shall be as happy with some
fine man as I am here in the company of my
Vicky.

Eternally yours,
Beau."

It took her a long time to recover from the letter. But
Beau had written wisely and kindly. And as she went
over it again and again she realized that he had shut her
from his life, just as he had closed the book on London.
She had no doubt that he still loved her. But it was a
love which offered no future to her. Now she understood why the Duchess had murmured, "Poor child."

She took comfort from the fact that he had found
someone. And she hoped that he would be happy with
his Vicky. In a sense he was as dead to her as Gerald.
She would remember them both. But the business of
living went on. She had to make her mind up about the
future.

One evening she sought out her father in his study.
She noticed that he had been coughing a good deal of
late and had become noticeably thinner. She went to
him where he sat at his desk and kissed him on the
cheek. Then she drew up a chair and began to talk with
him.

"You work far too hard for a man of your years,
Father," she reproached him.

He indicated a high sheaf of papers and said, "Things
to be done, my dear."

"Let Anthony do them!"

Her father sat back in his chair and it pained her to

see how his temples had hollowed with his loss of weight. He said, "Anthony works too hard as it is. The business has grown too much. This is a period of great expansion."

"Then sell the business," she begged him.

"I can't do that," her father said. "I wish to leave you a fortune."

She shook her head. "I have more than I shall ever want."

"The line!" he said seriously. "Your children and your grandchildren. I want them to know that John Crawford was a man of worth who left them an important inheritance."

"Bosh!" she said. "I'm not even married. So it is most unlikely you'll have this long line of descendants about whom you're so concerned."

"What are you going to do, Julia?" her father said, with great seriousness. "You cannot wait for Brummell all your life?"

"I'm gradually getting over that," she said.

"Good," her father said.

"You forget there was Gerald. And he has been gone only a half-dozen years."

John Crawford frowned. "You were lovers so briefly. Did he mean that much to you?"

"Apart from Beau, he is the only man I have ever truly loved," she said. "I would have married him if he'd been free."

"Elizabeth died too late."

"Don't say that," she protested. "But there was never a chance for Gerald and I. Yet we loved each other despite it."

"You can't mourn for him the rest of your life any more than you can wait stupidly for Brummell, who will never return."

She grimaced. "I have made a mess of my life it seems."

"You still have time."

"You think so?"

"Yes," her father said. And he leaned towards her and in a lower voice, "There is someone living under this roof who worships you and would make you the best of husbands."

She sighed. "I know. Anthony."

"Why not? He has position and wealth. He is like my own son."

"Perhaps that is the reason," she said. "I cannot turn my love on and off at will."

"Forgive me," her father said. "I won't mention it again."

"I like Anthony," she admitted. "But I'm not in the proper frame of mind to think about marriage as yet."

She little knew that evening that before the week had ended she would be faced with a turn of events which would swiftly change her way of thought. It was her father's personal manservant who came frantically pounding on the door of her bedroom early one morning.

She went to the door and opened it to ask, "What is it, Harvey?"

"Your father!" he exclaimed. "He has had some sort of attack. He cannot rise from his bed."

Julia recalled little that happened after that. It was a matter of mass confusion. A servant was hastily sent to fetch the family doctor while she and Harvey went up to the bedroom. Her father was unconscious and breathing heavily.

She'd only been at the bedside a moment when Anthony arrived. She got up from her knees and went to him. "Harvey found him like this!"

"I've been worried about him for weeks," the young man said. "I have seen him failing."

"He is unaware of anything. It must be his heart or perhaps a stroke."

Anthony frowned. "A stroke seems more likely. What are you doing for him?"

"Harvey is applying cold compresses to his brow," she said.

"That is probably all that can be done," Anthony said.

He remained with her until the doctor came. The doctor was a young man who had replaced the elderly practitioner who had taken care of her father until his own death. The young man had a short black beard and a sharp eye. He gave her father a thorough examination and then made his diagnosis.

"It is a stroke, as you thought," he said. "But I do not think it a massive one which will kill or totally incapacitate him. With good care and proper treatment he has a fair chance of recovery."

Julia found herself sobbing gratefully in Anthony's arms. And she felt that was the start of a new bond between them.

The doctor's optimistic verdict proved to be correct. But it was a long and painful business. John Crawford recovered his senses soon enough but for many months his left side was partly paralyzed. He remained an impatient invalid in his room for what seemed an endless time. At last with the help of a cane he was able to get about the house and even climb the stairs by taking a firm hold on the railing.

Summer had come again. And Julia was filled with a new vision of things. Her father had been restored to her but only as a shell of his former self. The young doctor had confided to her that within a period of time, perhaps a few months, or a few years at most, there would be more strokes. And one of these would surely kill him. So he had a definitely limited time.

She knew how much he wished to see her safely married before his death. And she knew of his wish for descendants to honor his name and share the wealth which he had acrrued. In all this time of trial Anthony Laver had been her mainstay. So her decision was easy.

One morning when she and her father were alone, she told him, "I'm going to tell Anthony I'll marry him."

Her father actually showed surprise and then some concern. He said, "You are doing it to please me!"

"Only partly," she said. "Though I know you do approve. But I think that perhaps it is time I turned my back on the past and looked to the future."

"The future is all important," her father told her.

Within a month she was wearing Anthony's engagement ring and they were making plans for a September wedding. The happy turn of events had been like a tonic to her father. He seemed in much better spirits if not in better health. And he engaged with them eagerly in plans for the wedding and their honeymoon.

"Scotland!" he said. "It is the ideal place for two people in love to be alone. I know some fine inns, any of which I'm sure you'd like."

Julia had to gently reprove him. "Anthony and I are quite capable of making our own honeymoon arrangements," she said.

Her father pretended crotchety annoyance and told her "Do what you like! You always have!"

One mid-August afternoon Anthony suggested they drive to the park and go for a row in one of the many pleasure boats rented out there. Julia enjoyed the prospect of the sun and fresh air in the park. So they went off for an hour or two leaving her father sitting reading the latest newspapers in the living room.

It was a Sunday and the park was crowded. But they found a boat and Anthony took great pleasure in rowing her out to the middle of the pond.

"What a lovely day!" she said, stretching her hands up to the sun. "What fortunate people we are, Anthony."

"I'm fortunate to have you," he said in his earnest way. "But I'm always afraid it won't happen. That we'll never marry!"

She stared at him with consternation. "What a gloomy person you can be! You must really get over it, Anthony."

He smiled at her as he rested on the oars. "Sorry. That was stupid of me!"

"I should say it was," she told him with a kind of fond indignation, "You very nearly spoiled my afternoon."

Chapter Sixteen

On their way back from the rowing expedition Julia said little. Somehow Anthony's comments had started a link of thoughts which ended in grave forebodings. She wondered if she were doing right in marrying a man she admired rather than loved. And she was frightened by his unexpected admission that he was also uneasy about their plans.

She tried to shake off the mood of gloom but had not managed to by the time they reached the house. Anthony had also said little or nothing, merely commenting on some of the scenes they passed on this Sunday afternoon. When they entered the house she saw that her father was still seated in the chair where she'd left him. But he was not alone!

Standing by him was a thin, distinguished-looking man wearing a black eye-patch. As she approached her father and his visitor with Anthony a few steps behind her, she had a shock. There was a startling resemblance between this older man and the young Sir Gerald Giles.

The man smiled and spoke, "Well, Julia!"

The instant he spoke she knew it was no question of resemblance. This was Gerald, much aged, back from the dead. She fainted at his feet.

When she came around the three men were gathered by her as she lay stretched out on the divan where they had carried her.

She stared up at this older, thinner, one-eyed version of the man who had been her lover and whispered, "It can't be."

"I'm sorry I upset you this way," Gerald apologized. His voice was the same despite the other changes in him.

Her father said, "I can tell you I was just as surprised as you, Julia. I could not believe my eyes when he came in and told me who he was."

Looking embarrassed, Anthony said, "You three will have much to talk about. I'll send the butler in to look after your refreshment needs." And with his usual discretion he retired from the room.

Later, with a glass of wine in her hand, Julia sat and listened to Gerald's remarkable story. He paced slowly back and forth between her and her father who had taken a chair opposite her.

Gerald said, "When I came back and found you had been kidnapped and shipped off somewhere I was in a state of despair."

"And I could think of only you," she said.

Gerald continued, "I was offered a dangerous assignment behind the French lines. I took it at once hoping I might be killed in service. As it turned out I was only badly wounded. Attempting to escape from the French police one night I was shot in the temple. That is how I received this scar and lost my right eye."

She gazed up at him and saw the livid scar which ran across his temple from the hair line to the corner of his right eye. She said, "But even though you were wounded, why did you remain away all these years?"

"I had damage beyond what the eye can see," Gerald said. "I was months recovering from the bullet wound. And when I was on my feet again I had no memory of who I was or where I had come from. I settled down to live in Paris. A kind of pointless existence."

"And no one had any idea who you were?" Her father asked.

"I encountered no one who had known Sir Gerald Giles. And thieves had stripped my unconscious body of anything which might have helped me identify myself."

Julia said, "So you became a lost person."

"Exactly," the man who had been her lover said. "Then one morning when I woke up I began remembering things in the past. Over a period of time the rest of my memory came flooding back. I knew who I was and that I must return here to the city and people I loved."

"Poor Gerald," she sympathized. "So many things have changed."

"My first discovery was that Elizabeth was dead," he said, staring grimly at the hardwood floor. "I'm still saddened by the method of her death. Despite our differences she deserved better than that."

"The fellow hanged," John Crawford said. "But that is an empty recompense."

"Grandmother had died," Gerald went on. "All London had changed and I now saw it with the vision of a battle-ravaged one-eyed man."

Julia's mind was in a whirl. She said with emotion, "I prayed for your return. But when I saw you I could not believe it."

"Have I changed so?" was his quiet question.

"No!" she said, rising and going to him. "It took me only a moment to know who you were. When you spoke there was no doubt left. It was just the shock!"

Gerald smiled faintly. "I understand. I have heard about poor Beau. It is a pity I did not run into him. But France is a large country and I understand he has remained in one of the coastal towns."

"Yes. No one hears from him," she said.

Gerald gave her a knowing look. "Your father told me. He also told me about your coming marriage. I like the appearance of your Anthony."

"Thank you," she said in a small voice. "We only recently came to a decision."

"You were quite right," Gerald said. "You could not be expected to go on living with ghosts in the past. I'm sorry my return is so inopportune for I'm surely one of those ghosts!"

"Please do not say that!" she protested.

From his chair, her ailing father said, "That is not the case at all. We are richer by another friend in your return. We can only be thankful for that."

"True," Julia said. She studied Gerald with troubled eyes. "Your color is not good. How is your health?"

"Not the best," Gerald admitted. "My doctor says that with the return of my memory my body will function more healthily. And with the passage of time I may expect to regain a fairly robust constitution. Aside from this scar and the fact I shall only have one eye, I should be back to something like my old self."

"You will manage well," her father spoke up. "I have been crippled by my stroke but I have learned to deal with it to a great extent."

Gerald offered another of his sad smiles. "The London I have returned to is like a city of strangers. I have few friends whom I can turn to."

"You have us," Julia said.

"That is why I came here so quickly," he said. "I could not wait to see you and your father. And you look as lovely as when I left you in Dover!"

"So long ago," she said.

John Crawford struggled to his feet and said, "You must forgive a sick, old man. It is time for my nap. But you must remain for dinner, Gerald. Do not think of leaving. You must get to know Anthony better and tell us more of what happened to you as we dine."

Her father hobbled away and Julia felt a flood of embarrassment at finding herself alone with Gerald. For a moment she hoped that Anthony would come back downstairs or that the butler would enter. Anything!

Gerald stood before her studying her sadly. "I fear my return has been ill-timed."

"No! No!" she protested, her emotions taking over. "I had never stopped thinking of you! I was thinking of you only today!"

"Julia, my love!" The slim, one-eyed man took her in his arms and it was like a home-coming. They remained in a close embrace for a little.

She whispered, "I dreamed so often something like this might happen. But I had given up hope that it would."

He released her. "I'm sorry. I no longer have a right to hold you in that fashion!"

"Gerald!"

"It's true," he cautioned her. "You are wearing the ring of another."

"My heart has always been yours!"

"There was Beau," he reminded her.

"I did love Beau," she admitted. "I came to you from him. But Beau is more dead than you at this moment."

"You planned to marry this Anthony."

"Because my father is old and ill. He wished it and I hesitated at facing the future alone."

"You do not love him?"

She shook her head. "No. I was worrying about the marriage only this afternoon. Afraid it might not work and we might both be badly hurt."

"I worry about that," Gerald said. "I had hoped to give the union my blessing."

"I have no choice now that you've returned," she said. "I must give him back my ring."

"I'm only a shell of a man," Gerald warned her. "I may never fully win back my health."

"At least I can be at your side to help you," she said and they embraced again.

She went upstairs in a state of total confusion. It had been the most eventful day of her life. She had known many experiences but none like this. She was elated and at the same time filled with sadness. She knew her happiness had been won at the cost of heartbreak for the manly Anthony.

She reached the landing and was on the way to her room when he appeared out of the shadows, his face pale and sober. Quietly, he said, "I was right, wasn't I?"

"What do you mean?" she asked.

"We will never wed. I had a strange feeling about it. I told you earlier. Life has been so good to me I could truly not expect to have the added gift of you!"

"Dear, Anthony!" she said with a sob and went to him.

He held her close to him. "It is not an occasion for tears but one of rejoicing. Lovers reunited!"

"I do not wish to hurt you!"

"I have been hurt before and will surely be again," the good-looking Anthony said. "Better that he show up now than the day after we were wed."

"I care for you so much," she sobbed. "I need you as my friend."

"You shall always have my friendship. And I will not desert your father in his business," Anthony Laver said. "But there is one thing."

"What?"

"I cannot go on living here and seeing your sweet face every day, knowing I have lost you. I must find another place to live."

"Father would miss you!"

"I will consult him daily on business," Anthony promised. "But it is too much to ask that I remain here. I shall slip out the back way shortly and go to a hotel. Later, when I have selected a flat I shall have my things sent to it."

"But Gerald is remaining for dinner especially to become better acquainted with you!"

"Later," Anthony told her. "I would prefer to be

alone this evening. But one evening soon we can meet and have dinner together. As your husband he will certainly be included in my circle of friends."

He kissed her gently and then vanished as quickly as he'd appeared. She went on to her own room and for a little cried for the man she'd cared for almost enough to marry. Then she had to refresh herself and put on her most becoming dress so that Gerald would see her at her best.

Her father was with Gerald when she came back down. And she knew by their manner that Anthony had spoken to her father, and he, in turn, had let Gerald know the changed state of affairs. Her ringless hand told it all.

The atmosphere at the dinner table was one of subdued happiness. Once during the meal, her father reached out and touching her arm said, "I'm saddened about Anthony. But I know you are doing what you must do. As long as there is a wedding I shall be satisfied."

She offered Gerald a small smile across the table. "I have yet to be asked."

Gerald's wan, handsome face revealed one of his charming smiles and he said, "I'm sure an offer will come. But I must warn you I've nothing much to offer. My estate affairs are in a bad mess. I seem to have little left but my title."

"There is yourself," she said.

"And that is sufficient," her father declared. "I need someone to take over my part in the business. Anthony will welcome you." He raised his wine glass. "I give you the union of our families!"

Julia had planned her wedding for September. As it turned out she and Gerald were married in mid-November. Her father was well enough to give her away and Anthony served Gerald as best man. A solid friendship had grown between them and they were working well together as business partners.

John Crawford had a gala reception at his mansion

following the church wedding. Much of social London was there. The Prince Regent had planned to be present but had a bout of the gout and could not make it. So Lord Skeffington served as toastmaster in his place.

The toasts were frequent and the food was of the finest quality, and there was more than enough of it. There was music and dancing and London seemed more like it had been when she'd first been exposed to its dazzling social scene.

The thin and mannered Lord Skeffington took her aside to say, "You know I shouldn't be here at all. I'm not a true advocate of marriage."

She laughed, still in her regal bridal gown. "But you should not discourage it in others."

"Perhaps not," Skeffington agreed. "It is true that married people always know their bedfellows while single men are never sure of theirs."

"You see!" she said. "I may win you over to becoming a benedick yet."

"I pray not!" he said with alarm. "I am too happily separated from my wife. And I find it convenient to be on my own. In my case when a beauty comes into the room my faithfulness goes out the window."

"You remind me of poor Alvaney, the Prince Regent and the fine parties."

Skeffington gave her a keen look. "I would hope that I most remind you of dear, lost Beau."

Tears filled her eyes even on this happiest of days. She said in a whisper, "Dear Beau most of all!"

"Alvaney is dead and suffers no more," Skeffington said. "Beau is in lonely exile."

"But there is someone," Julia said.

Skeffington's eyebrows lifted. "Are you sure?"

"He wrote me of her once. Then I stopped hoping."

"I have never heard of such a woman. He ignored my letters."

She sighed. "He told me her name. Vicky!"

"Vicky!" Skeffington said. "Sounds like an English

name. I'm glad for him." He raised his glass. "To the best of fellows, Beau Brummell!"

Just before the wedding party ended, Anthony took her on the floor for a waltz. He told her, "This is a day to remember."

"Yes," she said quietly. "I'm a most lucky woman."

Gerald took her to their bedchamber. And it was a renewal of that first night of love making in the tiny inn, all over again. But there was a difference now that they were wed, she knew this was but the beginning of a long life of such rapture. She felt relaxed and safe at last. All torment gone as the muscular body of her husband merged with her own softness. Their passion throbbed but it was with a gentle urgency and ended in such a moment of mutual ecstasy that she could no longer have any doubt. She had lost Beau but she had found the man who was truly right for her.

Two decades of happy married life followed. The Prince Regent became George the Fourth, and no more popular as a king than he had been as a Prince. Napoleon was long dead and the French threat a thing of memory.

London had grown at an amazing rate and the firm of John Crawford had enjoyed the profits of the expanding world trade. It was now one of the leading export firms in all England. Unhappily, John Crawford, was no longer alive to head it. He had died in 1822, a few years after the marriage of his daughter to Sir Gerald Giles.

But the firm was continued and enlarged under the direction of Anthony Laver and Sir Gerald Giles. It was a private joke between them that two titled lines ruled the family business. For in 1825 Anthony Laver had made a happy and socially desirable marriage with a distant cousin of Gerald's, Lady Caroline Brantree.

One of the night watchmen employed by the firm was an elderly, rheumatic former Bow Street Runner named Matthew Kemp who was regarded with great fondness by Julia Giles. It was well known that the old man could do no wrong as far as she and her husband were concerned.

Of course life had moved on for Julia as well. She weighed a pound extra for every year which had gone by. But Sir Gerald jokingly said that twenty pounds added only gave him more of her to adore.

And adore her he did. Their son, Gerald, was fifteen now and a student at Eton. Their other child, a little girl whom Julia insisted on naming Elizabeth was twelve and already a charming, miniature version of her mother. Sir Gerald's health had improved and he rarely missed a day at business.

Running a great mansion and taking care of her husband and her growing children left Julia little time for anything else. She and Sir Gerald preferred a quiet circle of friends to the larger social scene. They often dined with Anthony and his wife, and in turn they would come and dine with them. Thus far the Lavers had no children and it seemed most unlikely that they would. As Lady Caroline often joked, the Brantree women had not been prestigious breeders. She was an only child. But the two were completely happy and Lady Caroline dedicated much of her time to an orphanage in the East End of the city.

It was at a quiet dinner in the great mansion first owned by her father, and now the residence of Gerald and herself, that Julia learned some amazing news. By sheer accident Gerald had met Lord Skeffington on a busy London street, and the usually jolly fellow had looked so miserable, Gerald had insisted he join them for dinner.

So the three of them sat down to a candlit table loaded with fine food that evening, of which the choice dishes were partridge and excellent mutton.

Skeffington was bald now and had put on some weight. Mainly about the waist. Mid-way through the meal, he halted and asked Julia, "By George! I completely forgot to tell you I looked up Brummell!"

She put down her fork. "Beau!"

"Yes. Stupid of me! You were such good friends!"

Staring at him, she said, "Please go on!"

"Yes," Gerald said. "Do tell us about him."

Skeffington swallowed a mouthful of the good mutton and touched a napkin to his thin lips. "Dreadful!" he said. "Too bad altogether!"

"What about him?" Julia asked impatiently.

"I had reason to visit Calais," Skeffington went on. "First time in years. And I decided to look up Beau. It took a while. No one seemed to know anything about him. And then he'd moved around a lot. At last I found a lawyer who had acted as a go-between for him. Some friends in England had sent money to him through this man. The King among them."

"And did the lawyer take you to Beau?" Julia said.

Skeffington nodded. "Yes. He's living in a garret over a small restaurant. He's prematurely aged and his mind has failed him. He didn't recognize me at all!"

Her eyes brimmed with tears. "No!" she protested.

"I'm sorry but it is true," Skeffington said. "I talked with him and got nowhere. He is still a gentleman, most polite and all that, but the wit is gone. And he is no longer a fashion plate, I warn you. His clothing was both ragged and dirty."

"How shocking!" Gerald said with sadness.

"He has a little money left. The lawyer doles it out to him or it would all be gone. He still has no ability with money. He dines in the cafe below. And his almost constant companion is a dog of mixed breed called Stope. The dog belongs to the restaurant owner but he has attached himself to Beau and follows him about constantly."

"Beau always loved dogs," she said with emotion.

Skeffington smiled. "And still does even in his demented state. The dog is always at his feet at mealtimes. And if Brummell happens to be absent at the dinner hour, his canine friend places himself opposite his empty chair, his head peering from under the tablecloth, and his earnest eyes directed towards the door. No one can entice him away, not even with food scraps, the animal is completely dedicated to poor old Beau."

Gerald said, "And you say he no longer has pride in his appearance?"

"He was filthy when I saw him," Skeffington said. And turning to Julia he continued, "You mentioned a woman friend of his, long ago. A Vicky!"

"Yes," Julia said. "How well you remember the name."

"I'd actually forgotten it but I questioned the lawyer about her. Nice chap by the name of LaCroix. And he claims there never was a woman! Not at all! But for many years he had a pet dog and her name was Vicky! Must have been some sort of misunderstanding I should say."

Her throat tightened and she made herself seem casual in her acceptance of this explanation, though she felt her heart might burst with pain. "Truly a misunderstanding," she agreed.

Gerald glanced at her and she thought he knew something of what she was feeling. He quickly addressed himself to Skeffington, saying, "Are you sure he is in bad financial straits?"

"Without question," Skeffington said. "LaCroix is worried about what may happen to him."

"He need not worry," Gerald said quietly. "I shall see that he is provided for."

"Damn good of you!" Skeffington said. "I can't afford to help and the King isn't interested."

"Tell me more about the new house rules at your club," Gerald said, to change the subject.

"Blasted nuisance!" Skeffington said and deserted the subject of Beau Brummell to launch a tirade against his club.

When their guest had gone Julia and her husband faced each other with a meaningful look. Gerald took her in his arms and said, "I know what you heard about Beau had to be most painful to you."

She looked up into her husband's face. "I want to help him, Gerald. I want to see him."

Her husband frowned. "Are you sure? Skeffington says he has lost his mind. He will not likely recognize you."

"I do not care," she said firmly. "I never ask you to cater to mere whims. It is important that I see him."

"Then you shall," her husband promised. "I will clear things with Laver and we'll sail across to Calais next week. I want to see that lawyer LaCroix anyway and establish a fund for Beau."

Later in the middle of the night she wakened. Gerald was sleeping soundly at her side. It was then that full memory flooded back and she placed her face down in her pillow so she would not waken him with her weeping. Why should I feel this way about a man no longer part of my life, she asked herself as she sobbed. She could not answer, she only knew that her love for Beau had not ebbed.

Lawyer LaCroix was fat and friendly. An ex-mayor of Calais, the little man was known for his good heart and sunny disposition. On this late afternoon in June he smiled at Julia and her husband.

"What a wonderful expression of friendship you have shown with your generous donation for the benefit of my client, Brummell," he said.

"If more is needed let me know," Gerald said, as he sat soberly, top hat in hand.

The lawyer sighed. "It should be ample. He is not well." He touched a fingertip to his temple. "The mind has long gone and his body is now failing."

Julia had steeled herself for the occasion. She said, "You know we wish to see him."

"I doubt if he will know you," the lawyer warned her.

"That does not matter. I feel we should speak with him and give him the opportunity of knowing we have not deserted him," she said.

"An admirable sentiment," the portly Frenchman said. "Tarry at the inn for a little. Then go to the garret over the bakery about seven. You are sure to find him there then. He is most punctual about dining at the same time each evening no matter how sparse the fare. And you will likely find his sole companion, a mongrel dog, with him."

"What does he do the rest of the day?" Julia asked.

"Walks the beaches and the streets of the town. I fear some of the children throw rocks and jeer at him. But he does not seem to notice," the lawyer said.

"He was an eminent man in England at one time," Gerald observed.

The lawyer showed interest. "I have heard he was once actually a friend of your King!"

"That is quite true!" Julia said, rising.

"I am amazed," the little lawyer said. "But then there are still traces of it in his courtly bearing, his good manners. One can tell this man must have once been somebody."

Julia shook the lawyer's hand. "Thank you. We shall be taking the boat early in the morning. I do not expect we shall see you again."

"It has been a great pleasure, Madam," the little man replied, bowing.

"Keep in touch with me as to Brummell's condition," Gerald said as he bade the lawyer farewell.

"He is my client," LaCroix said with some pride. "You may depend on me to do my best for him."

Julia and her husband walked slowly along the narrow sidewalk which led to the inn. He said. "Are you sure you want to go ahead with this?"

She kept her head down. "Yes," she said in a low voice.

"It may be difficult."

"I think not," she said. "I will feel better for it."

It was a few minutes after seven when they approached the ancient wooden building with a bakery on the lower floor and rickety outside steps leading to an attic room above. They hesitated a moment and then Gerald led the way. They mounted the worn steps and halted before the old door with its cracked wooden panels.

Gerald rapped on the door. Julia stood there with her heart pounding furiously, promising herself she would control her emotions no matter what.

"Do come in," a voice weakly called.

She and Gerald exchanged a look. She said, "That is Beau!"

Her husband opened the door and they found themselves in a tiny room with a peaked roof. The chief articles of furniture seemed to be a cot in a corner, a wash basin in a stand, a sideboard and a table with a single candle lighted in a cheap candle holder and set in the middle of it. The table was wooden with no covering of any sort.

A few chairs were scattered about and at the head of the table stood an aged, ragged figure. Only his welcoming smile turned the wrinkled, copper face into a faint likeness of the features of the handsome Beau.

He continued to smile at them without any sign of true recognition, saying, "How pleasant to have visitors!"

Julia took a step forward. "Beau!"

The white eyebrows over the faded eyes lifted just a trifle. "Yes. I am Beau Brummell. You will have heard of me."

Gerald now moved forward to join her and said, "We have come all the way from England to be with you!"

"Did you hear that Stope?" The battered Beau said, turning and speaking to a mournful-looking mongrel who was seated beside him watching all that went on.

Julia said, "Don't you know us? Have we changed so much?"

The white-haired shell of Beau gazed at her with a

hint of sorrow. "All the world has changed, madam. Believe me, I know that well. I fear I do not know you and your good husband. But you are most welcome to dine with me."

Gerald said, "Surely you recognize my wife, Julia."

"I fear not but she seems a pleasant lady," Beau said in courtly fashion. "I have only wine and some crusts of bread but I insist you sup with me. Stope and I dine alone too often."

Again Julia and her husband exchanged looks. And she accepted the chair Beau set out for her at the other end of the table. He placed a chair for Gerald near her and took his place at the table head.

He smiled again and indicating several empty chairs at the table, said, "We must wait for our other guests to be seated."

Gerald sat there seeming stunned. The old man brought them glasses and poured some red wine in them with a trembling hand. Then he hesitated as if he'd heard a knock at the door and went over and opened it and bowed deeply.

Watching him, Julia could remember clearly his bowing in the same way to all the famous guests who had entered his flat. Her eyes blurred with tears as she watched the broken old man relive his moments of glory in his own demented mind.

He closed the door and came back to the table. Standing there in his ragged, dirty clothing, his cravat soiled and rumpled he rummaged in his pocket and produced a jewelled snuff box. He daintily took a pinch and touched it to his nose, then closed the box and replaced it in his pocket.

A smile creased the ancient face and with a bony hand he indicated, "The Duchess of Devonshire! Over there Lord Alvaney! And you must sit beside our honored lady guest, Richard! "And to her, he said, "I'm sure you know Richard Sheridan, the playwright?"

"Yes, of course!" she said joining in the game.

"The Prince Regent could not be here tonight," Beau continued as he stood there. "But I say let us drink his health! To the Prince!"

"To the Prince!" She and Gerald repeated and raised their glasses.

"There! What a jolly company!" Beau said with a laugh. "I'm so happy to have all of you here."

She watched him with her blurred vision and for a moment the flickering of the candle transformed him into the handsome, gallant she had known and loved. The illusion lasted for only a brief moment and then she saw the tattered madman he had become.

But there was to be more. With great dignity Gerald rose and with his glass high, said, "I will offer still another toast. To our host, Mr. Beau Brummell!"

"Beau Brummell!" Julia said with deep emotion and joined in the toast.

He gazed at them in awkward silence for a moment. Then he said, "This has not happened in a long while, ladies and gentlemen. I'm most truly flattered. I'm truly a rather unimportant person who happens to be blessed with a host of important friends. But let me say this, I do demand perfection of myself and of others. What I do, I try to do well."

"Hear! Hear!" Gerald said with what was genuine respect.

The old man Beau Brummell had become once again lifted his wine glass in a trembling hand. And this time the faded eyes fixed on her and his smile came slowly. And she was sure that he knew her. She waited tensely in that second for him to form her name on his dry lips. She felt herself ready to jump up and run to his arms.

But he did not say her name. Instead, he said, "To beauty and all that is good! For the good shall surely always retain beauty!"

She bowed her head as he and Gerald, and the unseen guests, joined in the toast to her. On the floor Stope hunched and sighed in his sleep. Beau Brummell sat down silently, paying no more attention to them.

After a little his chin dropped to his chest and he began to breathe heavily in sleep.

Gerald rose quietly and motioned to her. She joined him and they made their way to the door. The last glimpse she had of him was of his white head bent in slumber as he remained seated at the table. Perhaps lost in a dream of some long ago famous occasion.

They returned to England the next morning. And as a dutiful wife Julia made up her mind to erase any memory of Beau. She had a loving, faithful husband and she had no right to be unfaithful to him, even in her innermost thoughts.

But memory of Beau remained. Perhaps no longer as a lover but as one she delighted in knowing. One who had taught her much and made her stronger. She came to see that it was no more wrong to remember him with love than to remember her father. And she no longer avoided mention of him. When the occasion offered she spoke of him with pride and affection. And Gerald understood.

It was about a year later when she was in the sewing room with her little daughter, Elizabeth, that Gerald came in with a strange look on his still handsome face.

"I have just received a letter from Calais," he said.

Julia left her daughter seated with her sewing and went up to face her husband. "About Beau?"

"Yes," he said.

"He is dead?"

"Yes. I'm sorry," her husband said gently.

"I hope it was easy for him."

"I have a letter from LaCroix," Gerald said. "It appears that in his final days Beau became so weak and ill he could not look after himself."

"And?"

"The only place LaCroix could find for him was in a poorhouse run by some nuns in the town."

"Beau should have died better!" she protested. "You were sending money."

"It was not a question of money," her husband said

sadly. "It was a question of care. And the nuns were best qualified in LaCroix's opinion to give him tender care. Beau did not die as a pauper. LaCroix paid the nuns for their good services."

"He was not alone," she said. "Perhaps it was the best way."

"I'm sure of it," her husband said. "LaCroix is a good man. By the way, he enclosed an envelope within the letter. It contains some sort of message from Beau. Not addressed to you, of course. But it is something he wrote and put away among his things. LaCroix felt it appropriate to send it to us." He handed her a yellowed envelope.

"Thank you," she said, taking it.

Gerald gave her a wise look. "We'll talk more of this later. I shall be in my study."

"Yes," she said, knowing he felt it better not to talk too much about the matter before the young Elizabeth. But she was trembling because of the yellowed envelope in her hand.

Elizabeth was busily working at her sewing as Julia moved to the window. Julia's heart pounded as she opened the envelope and took out a folded sheet of soiled notepaper. On it was written:

> "The butterfly was a gentleman,
> Which nobody can refute.
> He left his lady-love at home,
> And roamed in a velvet suit.
>
> I would be a butterfly,
> Born in a bower,
> Christened in a tea-pot,
> And dead in an hour."

Julia bit her lip and gazed out the window with eyes blinded by her tears. She felt a tug on her dress.

Elizabeth was looking up at her in childish fashion, to say, "You're crying, Mama!"

"It is because of the death of a good friend."

"Beau?" the child asked.

"Yes."

"Who was he?"

She managed a smile and fondled the child's cornsilk hair, "A very famous gentleman, darling."

Elizabeth's childish face was puzzled. "Famous? But I have never heard of him!"

"You will one day," Julia said, the tears coming again as she stared out at the fallen leaves rustling across the grass. "I promise. One day you will."